Forbidden
Temptation

Thorgunn swung the door open and carried
Braetana to the wide fur-covered bench. But as he
laid her slender form atop the soft, supple bedskins,
his will weakened and his appetite for her grew.

He raised one hand to Braetana's face, stroking
a satiny strand of errant hair across her forehead.
As her full lips parted in pleasure, Thorgunn knew
that any hope of resisting her was now beyond
him. He lowered his open mouth to Braetana's,
brushing his warm lips ever so softly against hers.
Braetana's mouth parted further, her chest rising in
a gasp of pleasure. Soon his kiss grew in passion,
his lips pressing down hard, swelling her
excitement with every deepening exploration.

Thorgunn's powerful body now lay alongside
her. Braetana buried her hands in his thick curls,
pulling his mouth still harder against hers, uncaring
that she was barely able to breathe.

In one swift movement, he grabbed her tunic
and pulled it overhead—exposing her fully naked
body to his greedy gaze and the fire's dancing
light . . .

Love's Sweet Captive

Blaine Anderson

POPULAR LIBRARY

An Imprint of Warner Books, Inc.

A Warner Communications Company

POPULAR LIBRARY EDITION

Popular Library books are published by
Warner Books, Inc.
666 Fifth Avenue
New York, N.Y. 10103

W A Warner Communications Company

Printed in the United States of America

First Printing: March, 1989

10 9 8 7 6 5 4 3 2 1

To all those who dream and work during children's naps, after endless days at other jobs, and long past the limits of exhaustion, hold fast to the magic of hope.

I

Braetana stiffened as Edward's moist fingertips slipped beneath her flaxen hair, then traced an unmistakable invitation across the nape of her neck. Greedily, his hand advanced just under the top of her sendal kirtle, coming to rest on the velvety flesh of her back. Her spine suddenly shook with an involuntary shudder.

"Cold, my love?"

"No, it was only a passing draft." Braetana fiercely hoped her answer would deter any inclination her stepfather might have to warm her. She struggled against the depressing truth of the matter: his very touch filled her with loathing and despair.

"A toast," Edward proclaimed, rising from the feast-laden table and hoisting his heavy silver chalice above the merriment. "To my lovely betrothed—and to the soon-to-come day when we shall finally be wed."

A deafening chorus of voices rose up in salute from the thick smokiness of the cavernous hall. Uncharacteristically, Braetana too emptied her cup. She hoped the sweet-smelling mead would dull her senses against Ed-

-1-

ward's close proximity and that somehow she would be able to produce the expected smile.

Refilling his own vessel, Edward reseated himself, then leaned sideways. His breath intruded warmly on Braetana's ear as he pressed against her.

"You are exquisite tonight. Your promise to fill my marriage bed indeed honors me." Braetana sensed his effort to maintain appearances but knew him too well to believe him capable of decency.

"There is little honor in the bargain we've struck," she said, half under her breath. "All my suitors were refused by you. And you decided that I must become your wife in order to keep Glendonwyck. If she were still alive, my mother would weep to see the fate you've forced me to." She had not meant to fully display her hate for him, thinking Edward likely to be less abhorrent as a husband if he thought her willing. Yet his bold lies demanded her defensive honesty.

"Yes, my poor Eirlinn. I have missed her these seven years since the raid. Though the closeness my wardship of you has brought us recalls my fondest memories of her."

"I doubt you recall much of anything save her full purse and the revenues Glendonwyck brought," Braetana countered.

Edward leaned back slightly in feigned surprise. "How did I earn such enmity? Have I not protected you since the Norse pirates caused your mother's death? Is Glendonwyck not all the more secure for the walls I have built? Aethelred is pleased." His hand brushed an errant strand of white blond hair across Braetana's reddening cheek. Though her recoil parted them, the sensation of his unwelcome touch lingered.

"You have duped the king as you did my mother. Glendonwyck is critical in defending against coastal attacks. King Aethelred sees only that my birthright is safe from the Norsemen and doesn't suspect that it is prey to your greed."

Edward knew Braetana spoke the truth but insisted she participate in his well-crafted charade. "No one forces you to this match, my love. The choice is yours."

"There is no choice when any decision to refuse you will result in my exile."

"Then having made up your mind, I would suggest you appear more pleased with the result. I would not like my guests to think you unhappy with your decision." Edward reached beneath the linen-covered table and gripped Braetana's chemise just where it draped over her thigh. She promptly retracted her leg as far as was possible without fully losing her balance.

Freeing herself from her fiancé's leering smile, Braetana surveyed the crowded room, its great expanse filled with voices made loud from Edward's liberally offered mead. He needn't have worried about appearances; she much doubted the celebrants noticed her at all; their attention was turned more toward their own revelry than the purported reason for it.

A drunken jest from Edward's steward suddenly drew his gaze to the end of the long table. As he turned away from her, Braetana studied the creature she would soon call husband. Though his dark looks and muscular carriage were not physically repellent, the man behind them was. He was vile and mean, as full of avarice as he was of lust.

Still, their marriage was a concession she had willingly made in order to remain within Glendonwyck's high white limestone walls. No husband, not even one of her own choosing, could rival her bond to this proud bequest from Eirlinn. If she must marry Edward to have Glendonwyck, so be it. Somehow, she would find a way to make the bargain bearable.

The sound of Braetana's chair scooting back from the oak trestle table turned Edward's attention toward his betrothed.

"I am weary, Sire, and would retire to my room. I trust you can continue without me." Braetana sorely hoped she would not be forced to endure any more false celebration.

Edward's brooding eyes crept up the full height of Braetana's tall, slender form, then returned to linger on the swell of her firm breasts just visible beneath the brocaded kirtle.

"As you choose. It will not be long until our chamber will be a shared one."

The reminder of the intimacy she had promised to soon deliver set Braetana's stomach churning with sour misery. *How will I bear him,* she wondered silently. Then, nodding her head in farewell, she hurried past Edward's hounds to the stony base of the keep's spiral stairs.

Searching her thoughts for some much-needed peace, Braetana recalled the course that had led her to this unpleasant pact. Glendonwyck—that was what mattered. She had made her decision. Now there was no escape.

The heavy oak door to Braetana's darkened bedchamber crashed thunderously open, abruptly jolting her into sudden, confused consciousness. Instinctively she sat bolt upright, sweeping aside the luxurious folds of the thick damask bed curtain and twisting her upper torso slightly to face the now open portal. Quickly drawing both knees beneath her, Braetana braced her bare back against the cold timber of the keep's interior wall. With quick hands, she gathered the soft fur bed covers about her to shield herself against the early morning chill.

Her dark-lashed amethyst eyes, which were peacefully closed in sleep just moments before, now grew wide with alarm, then narrowed and hardened to scrutinize the towering form clothed in shadow just beyond the massive door frame. As she struggled to identify the frightening stranger, her heart and breath sounded the same ragged cadence, and, though Braetana thought herself mute with fear, some inner voice made sound.

"Who are you?"

The tall intruder offered no answer. Instead, he stepped slowly and deliberately from the black hallway into the dim shards of light still cast by last night's ebbing fire. Narrowing her gaze further, Braetana could at first discern little save the stranger's imposing height. As she became more fully awake, she gasped abruptly at the unthinkable vision before her—the man was a Norseman.

Braetana's breath quickened instantly at the horrifying apparition, and she stared wide-eyed at the distinctive conical iron helmet and ring-mail shirt, the latter partially obscured by a voluminous blood red cloak. The stone hearth's embers popped unexpectedly, producing a glint of light that caught the polished hilt of the Viking's sheathed blade.

The sight of the weapon drew forth from Braetana a

sharp memory of the last northern siege, one she had struggled for seven years to forget. As past and present fused into a single terrifying tableau, Braetana's eyes glazed with terror and fixed unmovingly on the ungodly specter looming before her.

A barely discernible smile etched slowly across the Norseman's face as his eyes took in Braetana's finely chiseled features and her bare alabaster shoulders. There, resting on her breast now heaving visibly with fear, hung the confirmation Thorgunn sought.

Although his burnished headpiece curved downward around the Viking's huge head, cupping his face and partially shielding it from Braetana's searching eyes, she did not miss the turning corners of the stranger's mouth. She shuddered involuntarily at the thought of what fate he would now impose. He was, after all, a barbarian by both birth and training. As the Northern heathens had done before in their all too frequent attacks on the Northumbrian coastline, he would now take what he wanted.

The memory of these marauders came clear in her mind, as painful as salted seawater over an open wound. The onslaught had been cruel and sudden, hastened by a flock of birds bearing deathly fire beneath their wings. Though Glendonwyck's wooden walls exploded with tinderbox speed, her defenders had waged a fierce, though futile, battle. Her mother Eirlinn had been but one of many Saxons felled that day by the Norse swords. Now Braetana wondered if her fate too would follow the same deadly course.

"Good morrow, madame. I suggest you dress warmly as we will be traveling a long, cold distance."

Such a response was not what Braetana had expected.

Her initial shock at the stranger's expertise with what was surely to him a foreign tongue soon gave way to the meaning of his well-spoken words. The point of his greeting pierced the confusion of her spinning mind like a sharp arrow—he meant to take her with him.

Braetana sensed that any display of the fear pulsing uncontrollably within her would add only to his force, undermining her already slim chance at escape. *He will not master me,* she thought, struggling to believe the silent declaration.

With confidence belying her inner trembling, Braetana pressed the palms of her hands against the yielding feather mattress and straightened her exposed back against the icy panels of the oak wall. Steadying herself, she forced in a long, deep breath.

"What do you want?" she exhaled.

"That is for later." Thorgunn's tone summarily dismissed her query. "Get dressed."

Braetana realized this was an order, not a request. Thorgunn reached purposefully downward toward the ornate wooden coffer atop which Braetana had laid her soft linen underdress. With one swift motion, he snatched the saffron-hued garment upward and out, hurling it with a loud snap directly into her lap.

Thorgunn's firm stance and stern voice made it clear he expected compliance, and Braetana was, in fact, ready to oblige. Then it occurred to her that, in her fear, she had made no attempt to summon help. Surely someone was near to aid her.

Though she suspected last night's celebration of her betrothal had resulted in everyone, especially Edward, bedded down in a mead-induced haze, someone must still hear her. Edward's chamber was adjacent to hers, and her lady-in-waiting Bronwyn occupied the tiny room on the other side of Braetana's. Surely this intruder and his men had not gone unnoticed past both the barbican gate house guard and the keep's watchman.

Braetana gathered her courage and yelled at a pitch she did not know she could attain: "Edward! Bronwyn! It is Braetana—I am held prisoner!"

Expecting the stranger to silence her, Braetana sat braced in anticipation. But instead of a speedy assault, her cry evoked only silence. Thorgunn stood like a huge wall between her and the door. Although she was considered tall, she could gauge from his height against the nearby crossbeam that he towered at least two heads above her. Any thought of forcing past him was pure folly. But if she were swift, she might well reach the shuttered window and shout again for help before he could intervene.

As if suddenly possessed, she abruptly swung her bare feet down over the pallet's edge onto the crushed camomile below. Like a panicked wildcat, Braetana scrambled free of the weighty bed covers and ran toward the tall stone arch she had so often leaned from in calmer times to survey the activity on the grassy bailey below.

In her flight toward the closed casement, Braetana clutched the crumpled lightweight gunna around her naked limbs as best she could. Her modesty, however, was subordinate to her need for help, a fact much evident from the scant protection the underdress provided. In her determination, Braetana was only vaguely aware of Thorgunn's strange disinterest in stopping her.

Within seconds of her explosive flight from the bed's warm cocoon, Braetana's palms slammed hard against the hinged wooden shutters. With dexterous speed, she quickly released the iron crossbar from its latch. Dropping the gunna, she flung the panels back, revealing the beginnings of a fiery dawn about to flood the horizon just beyond Glendonwyck's high bulwarks.

"Help me! There is a Norseman!" Her voice echoed into the cold early morning air that hung like a dark mantle over the bailey's eerie silence.

The long flaxen strands of her unbound hair cascaded forward, tumbling with abandon about her delicate face and bare shoulders. Her eyes frantically searched for someone to help, and Braetana leaned as far over the window's sill as could safely be mastered without pitching irrevocably out onto the keep's gate house two stories below.

Without even waiting to hear the desired response, she repeated her plea into the brisk early morning breeze. "Someone please help me!" Tendrils of hair swirled in an airy dance about her slender neck. Only a hopeless and terrifying stillness answered her desperate cry.

"Your kin cannot help you now." Thorgunn's deep voice broke through the stillness. His response was infused with a confidence that filled Braetana with unmitigated terror.

Suddenly aware of her nakedness, Braetana seized the dropped gunna, recovering it from where it lay at the window's base. Trying to protect herself from the Viking's impertinent stare, she clutched it dearly as she spun to face his somber words.

"Have you killed them all then?" She was unsure she could bear the answer that would follow.

"They are not harmed. Get dressed." When she did not move, he added, "Or I shall do it for you."

Whatever had become of Edward and the others, Braetana now understood they could not be counted on to help her combat this intruder. No one had answered her cries, and the stranger's unnerving calm bespoke no fear of capture. Glendonwyck's men were either dead or held silent at the sharp ends of the Viking swords.

"Shall I help you?" Thorgunn stepped closer to the open window where Braetana stood.

The closing of the distance between them made her quickly aware of the full extent of his commanding height. His size was greater than any man's Braetana had ever seen. Edward, in contrast, was shorter than her. This was not altogether surprising because, despite her seventeen years, Braetana was taller than any other woman at Glendonwyck. Yet neither she nor any of Edward's men-at-arms could rival this stranger's frightening size. The truth was unpleasant but all too clear: if this pagan warrior chose to overpower her, she would be little match against him.

"I need no help." Her abrupt response effectively halted his advancing progress toward her.

Thorgunn now faced her, his calm gray eyes locked like weapons on her own. As Braetana awaited his retreat so she could clothe herself, he made no further effort to move. The sudden shocking realization of his intentions made her mouth gape in astonishment. Shame and fury at once pulsed through her as she understood that he meant to watch her dress.

"Wait outside and I will ready myself for this abduction of yours." Her emphatic reply was filled with a mixture of anger and resignation.

Impatience flashed across Thorgunn's heretofore stony expression. "My lady, I can assure you that, while at this moment, I have little care for your modesty, I have even less for the presumed pleasures of your flesh. We do not have much time. Now make haste," he snapped, clearly annoyed.

Braetana felt the fury growing inside her redden her cheeks. "I suppose I should expect such base appetites from a godless pirate."

"I am unaccustomed to such impertinent refusals," Thorgunn countered. "And it is something far more valuable than a stubborn wench I hunger for." Then, even before Braetana's defiant expression could fully register this latest insult, the Viking effortlessly bridged the small distance remaining between them and snatched the soft yellow gunna from Braetana's clenched hands. Now she stood completely naked before him.

Thinking he had dressing her less than raping her in mind, Braetana whirled like a wild windstorm away from him, intending to bolt and seek cover in the nearby bed curtain. But before she could complete even one step in that direction, she felt Thorgunn's powerful arms encompass and tighten around her. Her own slender limbs were now pinned helplessly beneath the Viking's strong muscles, the confinement of his forced embrace an unmoving band encircling her bare arms and breasts.

Braetana had never been touched this way before. The sensation was oddly confusing, and her bewilderment quickly grew into humiliation and fear at what the Viking would do next. She tried to twist free of his hold, but each effort to loosen his lock on her seemed only to increase his incredible energy. It felt to her as if her captor actually drew strength from her resistance.

The broad expanse of his chest pressed hard against Braetana's naked back. Even through the thick mail that covered his upper torso, her skin registered the hammering thud of his heart against her. Held hopelessly tight, Braetana tossed her head wildly from side to side in protest.

Thorgunn could not help but notice the softness of her hair, but still mindful of the purpose at hand he knew there was no time to waste on the usual pleasures such a beautiful adversary could provide.

His men had bound Edward and the others while they slept, an easy task given the amount of mead drunk at the earlier celebration. But the hide ropes would not hold forever. Once freed, the Saxons would waste no time in seeking their mistress's whereabouts. Lowering his head over her ivory shoulder, he pressed his open mouth against her ear in an effort to steady her violent thrashing.

"Shhh . . . this will not help."

Although reason railed against it, Thorgunn's words seemed to halt Braetana's frenzied movement, tabling if not cooling the rage that had been spreading like wildfire within her. The heat of his mouth against her flushed cheek violated her notion of him. Somehow she had expected his flesh to be icily inhuman, not pulsing with the warmth of struggle, as was her own.

Close against the wisps of hair escaping his carved steel headpiece, Braetana's nostrils caught his rich sea scent. The ocean was a familiar pleasure, a special joy of hers ever since childhood, but her delight in the aroma faded quickly when she smelled it on this frightening stranger whose unrelenting embrace now imprisoned her.

With Braetana rendered at least temporarily still, Thorgunn released one hand, tightening the grip of the other to compensate. Bending his own knees against the backs of Braetana's, he lowered the two of them to the floor, recovering the gunna that now lay crumpled in a heap at her feet.

"Lift your arms," Thorgunn directed, once again straightening them both upright. His unwilling prisoner offered one last pitch of her head in protest, but that was all she was able to move. Exhausted and discouraged, Braetana now felt her anger surrender to resignation. Hot tears of misery welled up in her lavender-hued eyes, then spilled in growing rivulets down her high cheekbones.

"Please," she implored, addressing a captor she could now not even see, "do not do this. What do you want from me?"

Thorgunn felt damp pearls of tears fall like tiny raindrops on his encircling arms. Though he did not consider himself an easy mark for displays of feminine emotion, he found his grip inexplicably lessening in response.

"We must go," he announced to Braetana, who was now nearly oblivious to his words and failed to control the explosive sobs escaping her heaving chest. "I will place the dress over you. Will you lift your arms?" Thorgunn hoped he could avoid another all-out physical contest with his contentious prize.

Braetana nodded wordlessly in silent admission of defeat. With her assent, Thorgunn released his grip and raised the gunna over the crown of her head, threading the soft linen over her lifted arms.

Her hands once more blessedly free, Braetana

smoothed the dress's folds over her slim waist and coltish legs. Brushing a few loose strands of blond hair back from her face, she then turned toward Thorgunn.

A thousand thoughts competed in her mind. Most frightening was the dawning realization that she would be forced to abandon Glendonwyck, possibly forever. There was little sadness in leaving the promise of last night's unhappy betrothal, but she would lose the one thing she had compromised all to save: her home. Worse, she would be taken to a fate even her darkest nightmares could only begin to envision.

Braetana stood but a breath away from Thorgunn's chest. Her wide violet eyes were unblinking, growing larger and fuller of hot, stinging tears with each passing moment. Were her vision less clouded, she might have seen a flicker of understanding pass over Thorgunn's face, but a watery veil blocked out all save the searing pain bursting in her pounding heart.

Suddenly, Thorgunn reached toward her. Wordlessly, he closed one large bronze-colored hand about the amber and jet pendant that hung from the delicate gold chain around Braetana's slender neck.

"I will safekeep this for you." With a quick snap that made Braetana's neck burn, he broke the lavaliere free of its plaited rope.

Her fear, which had been rising with the apparent imminence of their departure, abated in a raging flash.

"Filthy thief!" she spat, her hands flying catlike at his face and clawing wildly in a futile attempt to recover the delicate piece. "You will not!" Her nails made bloody contact with Thorgunn's right cheek, which was conveniently exposed by the downward curve of his helmet.

The small circle of highly polished stones was all she

had left of her mother, the former ear clip's mate having been taken during the last fateful Viking raid. Since Eirlinn's death, Braetana had cherished and worn the jewel constantly.

Though moments earlier she had thought her strength spent, Braetana now discovered new reserves of fury. Unhampered by reason, she lunged uncontrollably at Thorgunn, struggling toward the hand that gripped her precious necklace. But even her unleashed anger was no match for the length of Thorgunn's arms. Grabbing Braetana just above the elbow, he effortlessly held her securely at bay in front of him.

"We must go." Thorgunn tucked the necklace into an upper pocket neatly concealed near the top of his chain-mail shirt.

Deftly, he caught one of Braetana's wrists. Her hand formed a fist that apparently meant to connect with his chin. Undeterred, Braetana continued her efforts to twist free of his grasp, reaching frantically with her other hand toward the pocket that now held the amulet.

"Have it as you will, my lady." With blinding speed, Thorgunn placed both hands on Braetana's shoulders and summarily spun her away from him. She felt his weight shift down and to the right as if he were recovering something dropped, then she flinched at the sharp sting of hemp binding her wrists tightly behind her. Before Braetana could mount any further protest, her mouth was filled with the unsavory taste of wool.

"I think this will make for a quiet, if not calm, journey," Thorgunn stated matter-of-factly as he tied off the coarse scarf around the back of her shaking blond head.

Helplessly bound, Braetana was sure she would explode from the flood tide of rage rising within her.

These murderers had taken her mother from her. Now they would take Glendonwyck as well.

To make matters worse, she was trussed and gagged as if she were a mere animal. A white-hot hatred burned from the amethyst depths of her sloe eyes. Even Thorgunn, intent on making haste to his waiting longship, felt himself momentarily caught in their heat.

He had not expected her cooperation, but the extent of her resistance and the ferocity of her struggle had taken him aback. Perhaps she truly is Magnus's, he considered silently. No matter, he thought, her fate would not be of his making.

Braetana snapped Thorgunn from his reflections with a skillfully administered swift kick to his shins. The blow earned her the satisfaction of an audible gasp of pain.

"Enough!" Thorgunn roared, now truly incensed for the first time. Reaching one hand down behind Braetana's hips and the other around her narrow back, the Viking easily swept his kicking charge up into his arms. With her muffled protests continuing, he strode with his furious package toward the bedchamber's door.

Despite her height and valiant attempts to regain the floor, Braetana weighed surprisingly little in Thorgunn's powerful hold. He had expected such a valuable prize —one that promised to bring him all he longed for—to be heavier.

Although imposing in size, Thorgunn moved with the speed of a much smaller man. No sooner had Braetana felt herself parted from the fragrant rushes beneath her feet than her frame shook with the swift pounding of her captor's steps down the keep's spiral stairs. Thorgunn's men, apparently posted both inside and out of the third-floor chambers, closed rank like a receding wave behind their leader.

As Thorgunn passed through the unmanned keep gate house, then into the open bailey that lay before it, images of high whitewashed walls and the soft green courtyard at their base blurred together. The effect on Braetana was a whirling collage of Glendonwyck's familiar sights. To the right were the barracks and stables where her favorite palfrey was kept, and next to that the smithy. Opposite the wide courtyard she could see the garden where she'd so often strolled among the fruit trees and grown heady with the warm smell of summer roses.

As the scenes of her childhood collided in a spinning farewell, Braetana struggled to remember every detail. If she could irrevocably etch all she saw in her mind, no fate, however dire or distant, could rob her of these treasures.

But the more she tried to see, the more her concentration unraveled, making her less and less able to focus with each passing moment. Though the bitter wool gag prevented words from escaping her lips, Braetana's tear-filled eyes cried out in an agonizing farewell to her beloved home.

Thorgunn's speed and power surpassed even Braetana's most fearful expectations. She felt it would be foolish to struggle against him. Her only movement was the swift turning of her head back toward the high tower walls within which she had lived until now.

A sudden command from Thorgunn, the words but not the tone unfamiliar, quickly interrupted Braetana's attention. As her eyes focused, she unexpectedly faced a huge and anxiously prancing cream-colored destrier.

The animal outsized and outweighed her dappled palfrey by at least twofold. If it weren't for the scarf around her head, Braetana's mouth surely would have dropped open at the contrast.

"I trust my lady can ride," Thorgunn half questioned. But before Braetana could answer, she felt herself pitched upward out of the Norseman's arms, landing squarely atop the broad back of the shifting stallion.

She had plopped atop the animal with legs splayed on either side. Though she had often ridden this way, she had never done so in so narrow a gunna as the one she now wore. The skirt was too tight. Its constraints forced her to bend her legs back awkwardly and tilted her upper body so far forward that, with her hands still bound, she nearly had to rest her head against the horse's thick chocolate-colored mane to stay seated.

Within seconds, Thorgunn mounted behind Braetana. Seeing the predicament of her twisted skirt, he reached with both hands down either side of her thighs. With a quick jerk, he hoisted the linen sufficiently up to right her unsteady position. The mount was moist beneath her, as if recently ridden, and his thick legs pranced to one side, then the other, in an anticipatory dance.

Without her hands for balance, Braetana began to worry she might tumble off. But suddenly Thorgunn closed his arms about her. With no warning, the Viking dug both heels into the warhorse's side, sending the three of them pitching forward in a frightening explosion of power and speed.

The destrier's long, muscular legs easily devoured the length of the bailey, sounding a deafening beat that kept time with the animal's loud, rhythmic breathing.

The gate house portcullis had been raised, striking

down the last barrier between Braetana's hopes and Thorgunn's intentions. Now free of the constraints of the castle walls, the horse seemed only to gain in speed, aided by the sharp downhill incline of the twisting road that curved its way toward the chalky beaches below Glendonwyck's sheer cliffs.

Thorgunn had not allowed Braetana much time to ponder the details of her fate. Still, even an eternity's worth would not have prepared her for the specter that rose up to greet her from the North Sea's churning shore. There, like death beckoning, loomed a striped red-sailed longship. Its prow was christened with a brilliant rearing golden dragon's head, and its shape was as full-bellied as if it had consumed all those aboard.

As Braetana struggled against hopelessness, Thorgunn inexplicably pulled his mount to an abrupt halt, speaking a few words in Norse to calm the hard-breathing animal. Braetana knew that, once aboard the longship, her fate was undone. Still, she could not understand Thorgunn's hesitation. Why did he wait? Was there some hope he had decided against taking her? She twisted her head uncomfortably back toward him, catching his eyes in a silent dialogue.

If she had been this close to him before, she had not until now been fully aware of the depths of his strength. For beyond any demands his body could make upon her, his eyes now commanded her as victor in a wordless conquest. So hard and unwavering was the burn of his look upon her, Braetana thought at first he must be staring straight through to some sight beyond.

Then, as suddenly as a change in wind, Thorgunn released her from their unbearable communion, his chameleon eyes softening so quickly they seemed to belong to another. Braetana's own lavender eyes registered her confusion, but Thorgunn offered no answers to her unspoken questions. Instead, his mouth eased into a bemused smile. Tossing his helmeted head backward, the Viking roared a deep laugh so loud Braetana was sure all of Glendonwyck heard. Then, while its sound still echoed, he dug his heels sharply into the destrier's flanks, speeding Braetana toward the ship and her frightening new destiny.

II

Braetana spilled unceremoniously out of Thorgunn's arms, landing with a loud painful thud on the slick pine decking of the drekar's stern. With his charge still gagged and bound at the wrists, Thorgunn strode unconcerned toward the prow of the single-masted ship, calling out commands as he passed the crew now quickly assembling on their sea chests.

Braetana was unsure of exactly how many men the great ship held, for the number seemed to grow each moment with the addition of the raiding party that had apparently followed them from Glendonwyck. She guessed there were at least twenty-five, not counting several crewmen arranging shrouds and forestays to secure the sail's towering mast.

As the Vikings assumed their rowing seats, they positioned themselves facing aft. The arrangement earned each a full view of an exhausted Braetana, who now slumped against the uncomfortable, exposed ribs of the curved oak gunwale.

Although the vessel was long, Braetana noted its draught was surprisingly shallow. Even from her seat on the deck, she could peer over the ship's edge to the foaming water below.

The drekar was partially beached, but a wooden gangplank had been laid to shore to expedite the loading of the crew and Thorgunn's huge destrier. Despite a crewman's attempts to calm him, the animal whinnied nervously as he stepped haltingly up the narrow board.

Just feet away from Braetana's position near the stern, three large Norsemen dressed similarly to Thorgunn leapt aboard, the last one releasing the gangplank from its hold in the sand and stowing it on two large gunwale hooks. As the rowing crew readied itself, each man in turn freed the hinge on his locked oar, suspending his wide, flat wooden blade in a two-handed grip above the churning surf below.

Seeing the necessary preparations for castoff completed, Thorgunn barked an order. In prompt response, three of the crewmen pushed the vessel seaward as fifteen oar sets sliced in practiced unison through the roiling surf. In time to a rhythm called by a muscular man near the prow, the oars rose and fell hypnotically.

Almost immediately, the drekar began to purchase great speed and distance from the shore. As the seascape before them flattened into a monotonous gray, Braetana noted with horror Glendonwyck's chalky cliffs receding behind the drekar's foamy wake.

Soon she could barely make out the small silhouettes of the mounted Saxons now assembled on the beach. At the vanguard of the group, she could see Edward's sorrel stallion, undoubtedly with her stepfather astride him. How like him, she thought, to arrive in time to witness her departure but too late to stop it—and at no risk to his precious skin.

Braetana reluctantly conceded that Edward might have made some effort to reach her. Yet she suspected that he could not help but be pleased with the outcome of this turn of events. Now he was undisputed master of Glendonwyck, and he would rule the fief without the burden of a headstrong wife.

It briefly crossed Braetana's mind that Edward might even have arranged this abduction. Perhaps he had struck some bargain with the Norse pirates. No, she concluded, even one as black-hearted as her stepfather was incapable of such treachery. Furthermore, his complicity was all the more unlikely, considering he had only last night parted with the dear price of their betrothal celebration.

The broad red-striped sail, the edges of which reached beyond the ship's width, had been partially reefed while the drekar was aground. Now it fully unfurled, issuing a loud snap as it burgeoned with a great gust of ocean wind. Braetana had not been aboard a vessel equipped with both sail and oars before, but she gathered from the slowing pace of the oars that wind was the faster means of propulsion.

By now her mouth and hands had both grown quite uncomfortable. Braetana worried that her tolerance for the pain would end before she was released—assuming Thorgunn intended to unbind her at all. She twisted herself up onto her knees into a more upright position, still leaning backward against the gunwale.

Suddenly Thorgunn appeared from the other side of the wind-filled sheet. He walked calmly and casually toward her, stopping briefly to address another man handling an oar-shaped rudder that swiveled from the longship's port side. The exchange was short; Thorgunn spoke and the man nodded, the two of them studying both the billowing sail and the cloudless sky above it.

Braetana's fear that Thorgunn would approach her rivaled her fear that he would not. Her words with him had been brief, but his enigmatic answers and the events of the morning made it clear he was not to be easily figured.

Braetana had always considered herself an astute predictor of character, her unpleasant arrangement with Edward having honed this skill. Given such talent, her current lack of sense regarding Thorgunn's intentions felt both dangerous and infuriating.

Turning his attention from the sail to Braetana, Thorgunn moved toward her, causing her heart to race as wildly as a trapped bird's. Surely he had not brought her this far to kill her, Braetana told herself, trying to ignore the gamut of other horrible possibilities that still remained.

Her captor looked down at the woman huddled before him. Her long blond hair had grown damp from the oars' flying mist and her form was suggestively outlined by the clinging contours of the moist yellow gunna. How small Braetana now seemed, so unlike the proud opponent he had faced earlier that day.

Thorgunn reached one hand beneath her chin and tilted her pale face upward. He sensed her withdraw from him, even though she did not offer any further physical resistance.

"You are cold?" Braetana nodded her head slowly in assent. "Turn." As Braetana rose and rotated away from him, Thorgunn deftly released first the fabric binding her mouth, then the hemp rope from her wrists.

Braetana's response began as gratitude but quickly

faded as she recalled how she had come to be bound in the first place. Recovering her earlier composure, Braetana turned a defiant face back to him while rubbing her aching wrists. It was as though in freeing her body he had inadvertently freed the anger he had only glimpsed before.

"You are too kind, my lord," she fired. "Surely not all of your prisoners can expect such thoughtful treatment."

"I would not know, since you are my very first."

"That is something I sincerely doubt." Braetana's choler was fully recovered and her eyes again radiated the hatred she felt for the Norseman standing before her.

Without warning, a sea swell broke hard against the clinkered hull, wetting Braetana's damp gunna even more. Already cold, she was now completely soaked, and the increased misery racked her with a violent shudder. Thorgunn noted her discomfort.

"There is a compartment the stern side of the mastfish. It is a hold tented for your use. Inside is a coffer of your clothes and some other comforts."

"You brought me gowns from Glendonwyck?" She narrowed her eyes in distrust.

"Did you think not to need them?" Thorgunn asked, smiling. "I can assure you, madam, that you are only to be the crew's cargo, not its sport."

No one had ever before spoken so impertinently to Braetana. Captive or not, she had little intention of enduring additional insults. Setting arms akimbo on her slender hips, she uttered an indignant "Humph" then marched forward in the direction Thorgunn had indicated.

She was not certain he told the truth. Still, any distance from this Norse ruffian was sure to improve her mood. And she was cold. Although it had been nearly two hours since this nightmare began, it was still early morning, and the easterly winds easily penetrated the thin linen underdress. At least she had been warmer when she was struggling.

The impressive size of the longship was now apparent to Braetana as she walked the length of its keel, threading her way down the narrow center aisle flanked on each side by closely seated oarsmen. She had passed eight or nine rows of Vikings when another heavy swell suddenly crashed over the vessel's prow, escalating its gentle rocking to a violent pitch.

Braetana struggled to stay upright, but the vessel's hard heel easily unfooted her equilibrium. Without warning, she toppled to one side, landing squarely in the lap of an unsuspecting but not displeased rower. The man looked younger than Thorgunn, perhaps closer to Braetana's seventeen years, and he smelled of salty sweat from his labors.

"Forgive me," Braetana began, mindless of the incongruity of her response. Suddenly the tow-headed sailor flashed her a toothy grin and, keeping one hand on the dipping oar, slapped the other rudely on Braetana's thinly covered backside. Nothing could have righted her more quickly. Without hesitation, she stormed resolutely toward the hold, ignoring the infuriating chorus of hoots and laughter echoing loudly behind her.

As Braetana raised her eyes, she saw, as Thorgunn had described, a wooden structure. Built up from the deck to a height slightly less than her own, the cubicle appeared to have three solid sides, with a top and fourth side tented over with a coarsely woven red tapestry. The vertical flap had been partially tacked back over itself, allowing Braetana a small view of the interior.

As she peered cautiously into the unlit compartment, her astonished eyes made out a familiar garment chest against the back wall.

As Braetana recognized it, she rushed forward, anxious to search its contents for drier attire. So great was her relief to discover anything familiar that she began to furiously work its closed latch without so much as glancing about the remainder of the small, tented room. Then a muffled human cry, just behind her, abruptly halted her efforts. Braetana gasped in fright as she turned to confront this latest surprise.

"Bronwyn!" The name burst forth from her lips as much in shock as in joy. Not trusting her eyes, Braetana scrambled forward to touch the hunched-over form, throwing both arms around the older woman and nearly crushing her in a torrent of strokes and sobs.

Braetana was so preoccupied that it was only with Bronwyn's second round of unintelligible protests that her mistress realized her lady-in-waiting had also been bound and gagged. She hurriedly loosened the thick fabric encircling the older woman's head and reached around her to unknot the hemp connecting her wrists.

Once free, Bronwyn eagerly returned Braetana's hug and clutched her close in relief. "My lady! Thank heaven you are safe! They have not harmed you?"

"No, no," Braetana assured her. "Not yet anyway. Bronwyn, it is so good to see you! I had thought myself alone in this terror."

Bronwyn noted Braetana was violently shivering beneath the damp gunna. "Lady, you are cold. I think there are garments from home within."

Bronwyn reached toward the wardrobe chest, then finished Braetana's freeing of the coffer's metal latch. Quickly, she pushed back the heavy lid, revealing a cache of her charge's clothes. Some of the dresses were regularly stored within, others apparently added in haste by the departing Norsemen.

After a hurried selection, Bronwyn exacted first a lavender twill gunna, then a light blue kirtle. Finally, she lifted out a sapphire-colored camlet cloak, its thick fabric lined with otter's fur and trimmed with fox on the mantle.

"Turn about," she instructed. Braetana, who knew Bronwyn would attend to little else until this task was finished, obediently complied. Hastily stripping off the wet gunna, she threaded her arms through the wonderfully dry garments. The ritual was familiar, for Bronwyn had dressed and cared for Braetana since infancy and with special love and attention since Eirlinn's death seven years ago. With agility belying her fifty years, Bronwyn dropped to her knees and began to again sort through the ornate coffer.

Braetana was incredulous. "Bronwyn, leave the coffer be. We must think to our escape." Bronwyn's busy fingers continued digging, oblivious to the plea. Just as Braetana reached down to interrupt her efforts, the older woman sat back on her knees, examining the sought-after cloak guard her efforts had produced.

"Good," she pronounced with satisfaction. Then, gathering her skirts about her, Bronwyn rose as she fastened the opposing sides of Braetana's blue camel hair cloak with the heavy gold-domed pin.

"Please." Braetana's voice now held more than an

edge of irritation. "This is not what matters. We must free ourselves from this prison."

Bronwyn stopped fumbling with the now clasped cloak pin and methodically smoothed the coarse woolen fabric out toward Braetana's arms. Her look told her mistress that she had already considered and dismissed the matter of escape. "Child, I fear there will be no freedom now."

"Nonsense!" snapped Braetana, astounded at Bronwyn's quick surrender. "We will not stay captives to these uncivilized barbarians! Now let us fashion a plan."

Bronwyn's eyes implored her impassioned charge to reason. "Think to our situation, lady. We are on a ship in unknown seas and outnumbered by at least thirty Norse warriors. We do not even know our destination."

"They said nothing to you as to where we go?" Braetana was hopeful that Bronwyn had managed to glean some useful information from their jailers.

"Nothing. I was caught while sleeping, made to dress, and delivered here as you found me. The one who took me spoke but few words of our tongue. And with you?"

"Much the same. The tall chieftain carried me here. He is odd, Bronwyn, full of contradictions and, I fear, quite unpredictable."

"Will they kill us then?" Bronwyn ventured apprehensively.

"I think not," she replied slowly. "Not soon anyway. I know not why they want us, but they have taken much trouble to bring us thus far. Are there spoils from Glendonwyck stowed aboard?"

"Not that I have seen," said Bronwyn, glancing about the small room. "Only my lady's wardrobe."

Braetana's eyes followed Bronwyn's review of the cubicle, then searched the woman's softly lined face. "Truly you are unharmed?"

"As much as can be, all things considered." Braetana could see Bronwyn was doing her best to produce a small smile.

"Wait here." Braetana moved toward the tented door.

"My lady!" Bronwyn's voice was filled with alarm. "Where are you going?"

"To get some answers."

Before Bronwyn could restrain her, Braetana burst out of the hold. Seeing no trace of Thorgunn, she ventured cautiously around the structure's perimeter until she faced the drekar's sunlit prow. Beyond the mast, rows of oarsmen, and a contraption that restrained Thorgunn's destrier, she saw what she was looking for.

There, towering like a pagan god over the open sea, stood Thorgunn. His polished silver helmet had now been removed to reveal a thick mass of tangled wheat-colored hair that spilled down the back of his neck, just brushing the top of his wide shoulders. He stood, intensely studying the course ahead.

Braetana edged past the sling that steadied Thorgunn's neighing mount, then passed four rows of oarsmen seated on either side of him. She stopped unnoticed several feet short of where Thorgunn stood. The longship rocked rhythmically to and fro, its strakes creaking with the sway of the waves' toss, and Braetana steadied herself with the forestay to maintain her balance.

"I would speak with you," she announced with what she hoped was authority.

Thorgunn at first turned only his head. Then, seeing who addressed him, he turned his entire body toward her, crossing his large arms across the gray mail coat that encircled his broad chest. "I see you are warmer now." The Viking raised one hand to his chin as he noted the addition of the thick sea blue cloak.

"It was very kind of you to abduct my clothes along with my person," Braetana snapped, irritated at his good humor.

"Ah, I see your spirit has also recovered from the dampness. Good. 'Twould be a long, dull voyage, I'm sure, were you more compliant." An impertinent smile crept across his face. Despite her fear of him, Braetana struggled against an overwhelming urge to slap it away.

Thorgunn watched her set, then release her jaw. With other more pressing tasks at hand, he had not, until now, really looked at her, so intent had he been on stowing her safely aboard. Now he beheld an exquisite woman, one not only physically beautiful but also capable of much poise, despite her awkward circumstances. Perhaps it was this proud bearing of hers that made her seem so striking, though her other attributes certainly helped.

Her flaxen hair spilled unchecked about the shoulders of her cape, its nearly white tendrils drifting slightly in the morning wind. Such a color was not uncommon in Thorgunn's homeland, but he remembered its remarkable texture and the soft feel of it on his forearms. The rising sun infused the color with still more radiance, creating a luminous crown atop her head that seemed to suggest she was more Valkyrie than mortal.

Beneath this halo, her dark-lashed eyes flashed in angry contrast, their color changing from moment to moment but now near an exquisite violet hue.

"It is ill mannered to stare so." Braetana's indictment

of him caused Thorgunn to temper his gaze. "Though lack of manners is the least of your many sins, I'm sure."

"My apologies, lady. I was admiring your stamina."

Braetana's wide eyes narrowed. "Yes. And I can do quite nicely without your admiration. How is it one so uncivilized speaks our tongue?"

"I had much time to learn in my youth. I was raised on the islands north of your coastline—amongst others who share your language, if not your spirit."

"I see," snapped Braetana curtly. "You learned to speak from Saxon captives."

Thorgunn clicked his tongue in disapproval and tilted Braetana's chin toward him. "Are you determined to think the worst of me? The Shetlands were an island trade base for many goods besides slaves. As I told you, you are indeed my first captive."

"Then you are a quick learner, my lord. As am I. Is it the Shetlands we make for then? The fulmars flying overhead travel north."

Thorgunn dropped his hand from Braetana's chin. "Very good. But we make for a place farther still. Where you shall be much more than a slave. And I no longer slave to anyone."

Thorgunn's evasion of her question sorely tried Braetana's already waning patience. As was her habit when annoyed, she set her jaw slightly forward and tapped one foot so rapidly it nearly made her frame shake.

Though her instincts told her she need not suffer this impertinent pagan, her more rational side knew she had few options. With great effort, she suppressed her growing indignation. Apparently she could demand little from her captor. Perhaps, she considered with difficulty, she would fare better with civility than rage.

Struggling to speak calmly, Braetana stopped tapping her foot as she again addressed Thorgunn. "Would it do you such harm to tell me why I have been taken?"

Thorgunn's mouth again turned upward in a suggestion of a smile.

Damn him, Braetana despaired silently, tensing both hands into fists and gathering wads of the heavy cloak into her grasp.

Thorgunn offered only the hint of an answer. "I doubt you would believe me, little bird," he replied cryptically.

"And why should I disbelieve you?" Braetana was slightly encouraged.

"Very well." Thorgunn wrapped his large hand around the carved edges of the drekar's gilded prow. "I am taking you home."

Braetana's features compressed in tangled bewilderment, then released into disbelieving annoyance. "I trust your games amuse you, since I find no humor in them."

"Nor do I. I tell you the truth."

"You tell me we are returning to Glendonwyck?"

"No, to a home you do not yet know. A moon's sail beyond the North Sea. Its name is Nordmannaland."

"Glendonwyck is the only home I know," snapped Braetana. She was growing more upset each moment at what Thorgunn obviously considered his sport with her.

"Now it is. But we can speak of this another time. My helmsman Lars motions for me to check our course and attend to the rudder."

As Thorgunn strode past Braetana toward the helmsman, she stood unmoving, her mouth slightly agape and her sentiments somewhere between bafflement and pique. Whatever the Viking meant with his enigmatic evasion of her questions, he had certainly shed no light on the reason for her abduction.

Braetana's thoughts returned to a plan of escape. Thorgunn had said they would sail to Nordmannaland. She had not heard the word before, although she guessed it to be the port of origin for this vessel and its hellish crew. Particulars on the Norse raiders were rare. Their contact with the Saxons was usually limited to activities that left little time for more normal social intercourse.

She struggled to remember anything Edward had said that might help her, but he had rarely spoken of the Viking attacks. His mind, she recalled angrily, was happier when focused on financial, not political, matters.

He had, however, rebuilt much of Glendonwyck's charred ruins after the 810 raid. It was an endeavor undertaken to ensure Aethelred's continued approval of his holding the castle. A huge cylindrical stone keep was constructed and a new outer limestone chemise added as protection against future assaults. Considering these changes, Braetana did not fail to appreciate the irony of this latest successful Viking assault, made without difficulty on Edward's improved fortress thanks to his unimproved debauchery.

Lost in planning her escape, Braetana's thoughts and feet drifted absentmindedly back toward the hold, then again forward. She paused when she reached the concave interior of the prow to steady herself against the hull's rocking with a nearby hemp forestay. As her eyes watched the slate-colored waters stretching before her,

Braetana strained to recall any mention Eirlinn had made of this place she now sailed to.

She fought back tears as her mother's soft voice echoed through her distant memory. "They are heathens," Eirlinn had warned her only child. "They took your father's life. And they will come again to bring us pain."

The word "father" rang like a muted bell in Braetana's mind. Eirlinn found the memory so painful she could barely bring herself to speak of Sir William. Because of this, Braetana knew little of him. Still, she now ached for the image she held in her heart—that of a strong protector who would shield her from the danger and loneliness she now faced.

Now she was completely in the hands of the cruel strangers who had deprived her of all she loved, and Braetana allowed a small sob to escape her lips as she wondered whether she had the will to survive this latest blow.

The self-pity was unfamiliar, almost frighteningly so. *I will find a way home,* she silently vowed, *whatever the cost.*

The call of her name from somewhere amidships turned her quickly about. "Lady Braetana." Bronwyn summoned her again as quietly as possible while still allowing Braetana to hear her. "There is food within. Please, come and eat."

Until that moment, Braetana had forgotten her hunger, but she had not eaten since the night before and was indeed pleased at the idea of a meal. She moved toward Bronwyn's call, briskly threading her way through the forward rows of oarsmen, then past Thorgunn's mount.

Seeing her mistress approach, Bronwyn reentered the chamber and busily filled two hardened bread trenchers with the salted fish and fresh apples a crewman had brought them. As Braetana entered the compartment, Bronwyn offered the younger woman a serving. Her eyes searched Braetana's face for answers to their desperate questions. "Have you learned where they take us?"

Braetana's eyes mirrored her unformed thoughts. "The Viking says a place called Nordmannaland." She reached forward and took the food from Bronwyn's outstretched hand.

The rations from Glendonwyck's stores were less appealing than Braetana might have hoped. The Norsemen had obviously made their selections in haste with an eye toward seaworthiness and portability. Still, hunger triumphed over preference, and, after a brief hesitation, Braetana greedily raised a small piece of the salted cod to her lips. She continued to eat until the entire trencher was scraped clean, unaware of her companion's pained expression.

"Nordmannaland," Bronwyn whispered, turning her face aside to hide her tears.

III

"Get your vile hands off me!" Braetana spun with whirlwind speed from the drekar's forwardmost seat, turning toward the rows of busy oarsmen behind. She fully expected to see Thorgunn's form towering over her, his outstretched arm guilty of the assault she'd just sensed on her own. No one was there.

With great embarrassment, Braetana realized that what she'd thought to be Thorgunn's caress was in fact only the gusting wind moving her own loose kirtle gently against her body. Most often, such suspicions were spent in the small hold while she struggled toward sleep. In fact, not once since the day she had been spirited aboard the drekar had she slept soundly.

Ever since the first searing burn of Thorgunn's hungry eyes settled upon her, she had known he wanted her. She now heard every noise, every creaking board as a potential prelude to her captor's unwelcomed entry into the hold. It seemed that each breeze convinced her he had finally come to lay his hands on her unwilling flesh.

Yet it was only the rocking of sea swells that cradled her, not his arms. And it was not the sound of his footsteps, but the wind jangling the mast pennant's metal streamers, that echoed through her fretful slumber. *No matter,* she thought, *if his lust has been stayed, it is surely only temporary.*

She was relieved that no one had seen or heard her startled reaction. Braetana sat down and again turned her face toward the silvery blanket of open sea that stretched before her.

"It would be a cold swim. I'd advise against it." Braetana would have recognized Thorgunn's sour attempt at humor, even had she not known his voice.

"Does such banter earn your affection with Viking women?"

Thorgunn's grin grew wider still. Issuing a quick, throaty laugh, he tipped his chin skyward and crossed his long, muscular arms over his chest.

"My lady needn't worry about rivals. I could be yours for the asking." It was a jest, yet he knew there was more than a little truth there.

Would his insolent teasing never end? It seemed to Braetana her captor actually delighted in irritating her.

"I would prefer a swim in the sea to your coarse company."

"We really needn't be adversaries. The drekar is far too confining to support a war."

Braetana certainly agreed with him on the second point. The huge ship had seemed to grow smaller as the sea-filled days wore on. At first she had chosen to remain cloistered within the tented hold. But the tight, dimly lit space soon turned stuffy, and, since this morning, she had decided to risk facing Thorgunn in exchange for feeling the snap of the crisp ocean air on her face.

Bronwyn had ignored Braetana's entreaty to join her. The older woman refused to leave the compartment, preferring the hidden if stifling security of its low oak walls to the exposure to countless sets of prying Viking eyes. At this moment, Braetana wished she too had remained concealed. At least Thorgunn did not talk to her as long as she hid in the hold.

Defiantly, she met Thorgunn's bemused stare and let go an exasperated sigh. Then she saw Lars bearing the morning meal. Thorgunn called the depressing fare *dagverror* in the morning and *natverror* in the evening. Braetana called both largely inedible, but at least the twice daily deliveries helped break the endless repetition of the days. The pilot passed Thorgunn a trencher of the ubiquitous salted cod, then filled an iron cup from a nearby bucket of beer. No sooner had Thorgunn taken possession than he extended the meal as an apparent gift toward Braetana.

"The sea seems to inspire your choler. Perhaps your appetite as well?"

Braetana detested the briny fish that was all she'd been offered since the grains and fruits stolen from Glendonwyck's pantry ran out. And she certainly had no intention of taking anything directly from Thorgunn's hands.

"I'd rather starve."

"You will if you can't stomach this."

Thorgunn set the food down next to her on the small wooden bench, accidentally brushing her skirt with his huge hand as he withdrew. Reflexively, she moved sideways, nearly landing herself in the drekar's narrow middle aisle in the process.

She knew her hunger would eventually overcome her

distaste for the dry fish, but Braetana would not allow Thorgunn the satisfaction of seeing her accede to his suggestion.

"I know this departs from what you are accustomed to. We shall change that soon."

She was tired of his damnably enigmatic replies! In the three days they'd been under sail, Braetana had yet to receive a straight answer from the Norseman.

"Why have you taken me?"

Thorgunn saw no reason to unsettle her further by discussing the motives for her abduction.

"Knowing would not change your fate."

Braetana's pique propelled her to a standing position, then set her foot tapping in quick, angry little beats. In the process of rising, she upended both the trencher of fish and the beer stationed next to it. Her clumsiness brought an infuriating smile to Thorgunn's lips.

Seeing how much her distress seemed to please him, it occurred to Braetana that a change in attitude might well serve her better.

"If you told the truth of your plans for me, it might change my feelings for you."

Thorgunn shook his head from side to side in amused astonishment. She was nothing if not determined.

"That is something I should not wish to bring about. The voyage so far has been quite entertaining. I will prepare you another trencher."

If he had been consistently cruel or continually solicitous Braetana could easily have read him. But the mixture of concern and insult in his attitude both surprised and confused her.

Such a paradoxical response had so far typified Braetana's dealings with Thorgunn. He had brutally kidnapped her from her home, but not without bringing along the amenities of her lady-in-waiting and a garment chest full of clothes. And now, though Thorgunn wanted to ensure that she was well fed, he seemed to take great pains to upset her.

Yet her vague appreciation for what kindnesses he showed stopped considerably short of real gratitude. What threat was she to him, after all? Her only option, apart from compliance with whatever new edict he chose to issue, was the voluntary swim he'd alluded to. That would most likely not only prove fruitless but also probably fatal.

With her efforts to get a straight answer from him thus far futile, Braetana tried to temporarily restrain her curiosity. Whatever destiny he intended for her, her energies at this moment were better trained on plans for her eventual escape.

After many reflective hours perched at the drekar's bow, Braetana sighed in exhaustion. All her resourcefulness failed in the face of her current predicament. Would she ever escape her captor's tight clutch? There was certainly nothing to be done while she was prisoner of this hellish ship.

Dejectedly, she settled her head heavily into her hands. Just then, a familiar cry overhead drew her attention. Guillemots! And puffins as well! Braetana could hardly believe her eyes—they were near land. Her hopes rose instantly, an expectation that was soon rewarded as she recognized what had to be the Northumbrian coastline rising in the distant west. Perhaps the

Viking had decided to find Edward and bargain for her release.

With the silhouette of the distant Saxon cliffs now growing in size, Thorgunn packed away the solarsteinn he'd used for navigation. At least for the time being the ship's course could be sailed surer and safer. Though he was a veteran sea rider, lengthy voyages across open sea were still hazardous and had often claimed the lives of better sailors than he. He had left the coastline as a safeguard against English pursuit, but now he could again afford the luxury of dead reckoning. With land once more in sight, Thorgunn breathed a sigh of relief.

"I imagine you'll be pleased to free yourself of me."

A surprised Thorgunn looked up to find Braetana facing him, arms akimbo and her angel's face wearing an inscrutable smile that unwittingly invited his pursuit.

"It is most likely. But not for some time yet."

"Not long, judging from the rocky cliffs off your ship's port gunwale. I must say, it would have been simpler to bargain with Edward at Glendonwyck. I think you have made much more trouble than you need."

"Who is Edward?"

Braetana thought it odd that he had not even learned the name of the man he was to do business with. "My betrothed, of course. The man who will pay your black ransom."

Thorgunn squinted in bafflement at Braetana, then chuckled lowly as a wave of understanding swept over his face.

"You think I'm returning you to that cold castle of yours?"

"Well, yes."

"Lady, I would hardly have taken such pains simply to afford you some ocean air. Why would I sail three days with a contentious shipmate, then take you back?"

Braetana struggled with her reasoning.

"I imagine you had a change of whatever passes for your heart. Edward would pay more than some slave trader—I trust you realized this. I doubt it was a matter of conscience."

"It is no matter at all. I fear your hopes differ sharply from my plans for you. We are far north of your Glendonwyck, following the coastline only to ensure our safe passage home. You will never see England again."

Braetana awoke at dawn to the sound of the crew packing away the hide bags in which they slept and positioning themselves atop their wooden sea chests for the long day's work. If there was wind, all twenty-eight slept the night; if not, a partial crew continued to row. During the day, everyone but Thorgunn and Lars worked the long oars, the flat paddles advancing the wind's work considerably.

As Braetana heard the familiar din of their efforts, she thought, as she had since her last conversation with Thorgunn, only of how much farther she was from Glendonwyck.

"Bronwyn, I could make use of your help."

"Certainly, lady. Which gunna and kirtle choose you today?" Bronwyn, though still rubbing the sleep from her eyes, rose quickly, ready to aid Braetana with her daily toilette.

"Not that. Help me find a way for us to lose this captor of ours."

Bronwyn wore a look of resignation. "Lady, we are at sea. And even once we dock—at this place Nordmannaland—we will be prisoners still. Our fate is no longer in our hands."

Braetana sensed Bronwyn's abandonment of any hope of rescue. Apparently, she could count on the older woman as little help in devising an escape plan. Braetana knew she alone must accept full responsibility for bringing about any improvement in their situation.

Absentmindedly, she fingered the folds on the rose twill kirtle that lay across the side of her garment chest. Next to it was a matching gunna, the latter edged with small sparkling amethysts on the sleeves and the low-cut bodice.

Braetana's violet eyes suddenly grew wide with excitement.

"Yes! As plain as the nose on my face!"

"Lady?" Bronwyn knew the look her charge wore and it usually boded trouble.

"I think he is somehow drawn to me. This interest of his—we will use the only weapon we have to undo his pagan plans. You would think, after Edward, that I would have come to such an understanding of the man more quickly since men are all alike."

She recalled how Edward too had tried to manipulate her fate, refusing all suitors of acceptable rank until she reached the embarrassing age of seventeen unmarried. Eventually, the matrimonial offers came no more, and the only option remaining to her was the shameful match with her stepfather.

Braetana often wondered if Edward had not counted

on their pairing even as her mother lived. His marriage to Eirlinn seemed an unhappy one, though her mother was not a woman to speak much of misfortune. Yet Braetana had seen the occasional dark bruises on Eirlinn's alabaster skin and knew they must surely have been the work of Edward's angry hands. What irony, she thought, that Edward's lusty scheme to marry her had come so close to fruition, only to be undone by another man's base desires. No matter, such unseemly needs would now serve her well.

At Braetana's direction, Bronwyn helped her with the gunna and kirtle, then began tying back Braetana's long flaxen hair with a bright blue silk ribbon.

"No, not today." Braetana shook her head free of Bronwyn's grasp, a soft cascade of blond hair falling loosely about her small shoulders.

"Lady, the wind will make a bird's nest of your head if we do not secure it." Bronwyn again raised the ribbon to complete her work. Braetana's hands quickly intervened.

"I shall wear the golden fillet instead."

"The betrothal gift from Edward? I thought you cared little for it."

"True enough. But Edward chose it, and he and this Viking of ours seem more the same every day. I think the piece may prove useful." Braetana laid the fillet on her crown of hair, then smoothed the gunna's soft fabric down over her slender waist. Refusing Bronwyn's offer of the fur-lined cloak, she made sure the kirtle hung loose, exposing as much of her figure as possible. She would be prey to the chilly north wind, but it was a concession worth suffering.

Bronwyn, who by now had abandoned all hope of

dissuading Braetana from her daring plan, sat disconsolately on her fur bed covers.

"Lady, the less said, the safer. He is a man easily provoked."

"I hope so," issued Braetana, as she pulled aside the hold's heavy tapestry and rounded its port wall.

IV

"Good morrow, Lady Braetana." Braetana found herself unexpectedly face-to-face with her Norse captor. Thorgunn stood in attendance on his destrier, who was still secured in a loose sling quite close to the Saxons' small chamber.

"You are early today. Is there an occasion?" Thorgunn's commanding gray eyes took in Braetana's free-flowing blond hair and the exquisite rose dress, now for the first time fully exposed for lack of the usual heavy cloak. Given her striking appearance, it occurred to him that perhaps something was afoot.

Braetana suppressed her embarrassment at his inspection. She reminded herself that this was, after all, the attention she sought.

She moved past both the horse and Thorgunn, then turned with calculated languor to face the Viking as she spoke softly.

"Indeed there is an occasion. I did not know you knew my name."

"I heard your lady call you." Thorgunn continued his vigorous brushing of the huge horse's cream-colored coat. "Though I need no name to know who you are."

Braetana bristled at his impudent familiarity. *How easily I could slap him right now,* she thought. Somehow she held her temper long enough to secure both hands in a tight grasp locked behind the lowermost button of the soft kirtle.

"I truly doubt you know much of anything about me." She spoke slowly and deliberately. It was apparent to Thorgunn that she spent a great effort to maintain her control.

"Loki and I are listening." Thorgunn gestured to his horse and smiled sardonically.

Braetana had not meant to educate her captor, but rather to garner what she could about his situation. She tried to dismiss the query.

"There is really very little of interest to tell. But I am eager to hear about you."

Thorgunn smiled again in response. They had already fought physically. Now it seemed they would spar on a different level. Unexpectedly, his warhorse issued a loud protesting whinny.

"Easy." Thorgunn stroked the animal, calming him. "The lady asks of us. Shall we tell her?"

Braetana's hands tightened their grip in anger until her knuckles turned white.

"I am Thorgunn. This is my stallion Loki. We ply our terrible trade abducting contentious Saxon wenches from their bedchambers." Thorgunn's jesting was in sharp counterpoint to a furious Braetana. She was little in the mood for such antics.

"I wouldn't doubt you do just that," she answered through clenched teeth.

Thorgunn noted that, even when cloaked in anger, her beauty was impressively radiant. The journey from

Trondbergen had been long and arduous. It was a delightful reprieve to have the return trip's monotony cut short with such a comely, if difficult, companion.

There was, however, no need to antagonize her further. "Forgive me, we are not as schooled in manners as Saxons. What do you wish to know?"

Braetana's hopes were buoyed with his seemingly changed approach.

"Who you truly are," she replied promptly.

"You know I am Thorgunn. Also Prince of Trondbergen. Son of Harald and brother to Konungr Haakon."

"Konungr?"

"You call it king. I am the older half brother to the king."

Although she had promised herself that nothing more this man could do would surprise her, Thorgunn's revelation about his parentage came unexpectedly. With his rough-hewn clothes and coarse manner, he did not seem royal, though Braetana quickly realized she had no idea what being royal entailed to Norsemen.

She had never even seen her own King Aethelred. Still, in his dress and manner, Thorgunn seemed altogether too common, too much about the business at hand to have any blue blood pulsing through his icy veins. If there were anything regal about this pirate, she observed begrudgingly, it was only in his damnably handsome face. It annoyed her to no end that she actually thought him handsome.

From the moment he had removed his silver headpiece, giving her a full view of his leonine, blond mane and strong, angular features, she knew it. Despite herself, she struggled and lost against the conclusion that he was the most attractive man she had ever seen, especially when compared to the short, beady-eyed Edward. And even more so than the would-be suitors her stepfather had dismissed.

Somehow it seemed right that one with so black a heart should wear a devil's looks as well. But whatever face he wore, she reminded herself she must not forget who Thorgunn was—a brigand and her captor.

"*You* are royal?" Her voice made no attempt to conceal her incredulity. Thorgunn nodded. "Then I gather piracy is a royal profession?"

Unruffled, Thorgunn dropped the brush from Loki's back and shifted his stance so as to fully face her.

"To some, yes. I will not deny I have captained raids on your coast. Our home is rocky and hard, so we often till the spoils of other lands to earn our livelihood. But there is also trading. It is a skill I learned as a youth on the Shetlands and one I have come to prefer in recent years."

"So now you trade in Saxons?" Braetana was close again to losing her hard-won control.

"Only one," answered Thorgunn, amused at Braetana's uncanny summary of the situation. "But fear not, little bird, you're hardly slated for the slave market."

"Why should I believe your lies?" snapped Braetana.

"Believe what you want. But I tell you the truth."

"You are godless. You know no truth."

"Ah, but in our land we have many gods."

"Then many truths?" volleyed Braetana, silently congratulating herself.

"My lady has a sharp wit. I trust in my company you will not let it grow dull?" Thorgunn asked mockingly.

"Only if it would please you for me to do so."

"Nothing about you, Lady Braetana, displeases me,"

Thorgunn said lowly, then checked himself. He had not intended to flatter her so. Such compliments would no doubt fuel her confidence and make her less tractable.

She already knew too much of his weakness for her. He vowed to bury it. Yet, despite his best efforts, his mind returned often to that first heated meeting.

The feel of her naked body in his arms had lingered long past their embrace. Her eyes, like amethysts set in alabaster, were branded in his memory as was her narrow, slightly upturned nose and the challenge of her petulant lips. Together, her many charms seemed to invite him ever closer to disobeying his good intentions. Despite his resolutions otherwise, he often found his gaze turned toward her whenever Braetana walked along the longship's prow.

She had felt the weight of his stare. Something of it recalled Edward's leering study of her. Yet Thorgunn did not have the same threatening element in his eyes.

Braetana tried to remain guarded, though she found herself growing more at ease daily with the Viking.

Thorgunn's present unsolicited praise provided the necessary spur to mount a resistance.

"I do not seek your approval, nor do I appreciate it." The audible bitterness in her voice took Thorgunn slightly aback.

"Consider it withdrawn," he assured her. "Do Saxons hold praise in such disdain?"

"Only when it comes so thinly disguised."

"What is it you think I have disguised?"

Thorgunn knew the answer and Braetana would invite no further embarrassment by explaining the obvious to him.

"You and Edward. You might as well be the same," she muttered, half to herself.

"Ah yes—Edward was to be your husband, was he not?"

Braetana looked away. "Yes, my stepfather. My betrothed. A thief."

"Small affection for a man you consented to marry. Though I must admit, he was not much concerned for your welfare. In fact, it was he who told us where to find you. That is odd for an intended—"

The revelation of Edward's duplicity, combined with Thorgunn's insults, sent Braetana into an explosion of anger.

"No!" she screamed. "I no longer find abuse all that odd. Edward took me in exchange for Glendonwyck, then you took even that. Such is the cruel way of men."

A high swell crashed hard against the drekar's starboard side, pitching the ship severely. Without warning, Thorgunn's destrier lost balance and stumbled sideways toward Braetana. Fortunately, Thorgunn sensed the animal's movement even before it began. He lunged forward, grabbing Braetana in both his arms and snatching her feet from certain injury beneath the horse's heavy hooves.

Until the ship returned to even keel, Thorgunn crushed Braetana against his wide chest, his powerful arms easily enveloping her tall but slender form. As he swept her to safety, she had instinctively thrust her own arms upward. They now framed Thorgunn's upper body, resting on either side of his broad, cloaked shoulders.

For a moment her head pressed sideways against him just below his chin, and she felt his warmth and heard the reassuring measure of his breath above her. At first

the feeling was one of simple security. But as he continued to hold her, an odd sensation grew inside her, a
vortex of swirling pleasure and excitement that made
her breath quicken and her head lighten.

She had never felt quite so unbalanced before.
Though she struggled to attribute the dizziness to the
roll of the ship, something told her this light-headedness
could not be corrected by a calmer sea.

Thorgunn was not unaware of a similar response on
his own part, his breath deepening and keeping close
time to Braetana's. The sudden stirring in his loins was
familiar to him, for he had sampled women's abundant
pleasures before. But his response to Braetana's voluptuous body betrayed his best intentions with uncharacteristic speed. Though he found her powerfully exciting,
this cargo was business. Any improper action could unsettle all he had worked for.

Abruptly releasing her from his embrace, Thorgunn
grabbed Braetana by the shoulders. Moving her slightly
back and away from him, he broke the seal their bodies
had made.

"Are you injured?" His serious tone attempted to
sanction the immodest embrace they had just shared.

It was a while before Braetana realized that, although
the ship now sailed smoothly, her arms still held fast to
Thorgunn's shoulders. She quickly retracted them, hoping that regaining her physical composure would bring
about a comparable state of mind.

"Yes. I mean . . . no. That was not necessary," she
stated tersely.

"Not unless you wish to walk on both feet again."

Braetana knew he was right but still felt a flush of
shame at the confusion his embrace had brought. Back-

ing out of Thorgunn's arms, she turned quickly to hide
her embarrassment and rushed, flustered, toward the
cargo chamber behind.

It was now nine days since they had last seen land.
During that time, the sea wind had grown insistently
colder with the heightened latitude, often filling the
heavy linen sail with frighteningly forceful gusts. This
seemed a welcome change, for it allowed the oarsmen
more rest than usual and completely eliminated the need
for the noisy night rowing.

But on the tenth night without a visible shoreline, as
Braetana finally succumbed to much-needed sleep, she
awoke with a start to what sounded like the full crew
hurriedly assembling on their sea chests. As the shuf-
fling outside shook her to full consciousness, a blinding
flash of light illuminated the hold's tented roof. Its brilliance was closely followed by a splitting crack of
thunder so loud that Braetana at first thought that the
hull had shattered.

Her initial response was confusion. But as she threw
off her sealskin coverlet and stood upright, the din's full
import became clear. Without warning, the ship heeled
hard to port, slamming Braetana against the same side
cargo wall and hurling Bronwyn half atop the lighter
woman. Braetana realized that a powerful spring storm
was upon them and that the crew rowed for stability, not
speed.

In her few short trips on Edward's small vessels, she
had never experienced truly foul weather. The idea that
they were now in for a serious gale sent a shiver down
her spine. She knew well the havoc North Sea storms
could wreak on land and could only imagine that the

experience at sea must far surpass the worst blow she had ever endured.

"Lady! What has happened? Are we aground?"

"There is a storm," Braetana answered, struggling to sound calm. "The oarsmen are rowing to steady us . . ."

Again the hold grew bright with an explosion of light and a deafening roar of thunder drowned out the end of Braetana's answer. Bronwyn's louder, more audible voice wasted no time in ascending to a high-pitched wail. "Lord in heaven! Save us from this fate. Mercy!"

"I think we have more need of safe harbor than mercy," Braetana answered breathlessly. Woefully unbalanced, she groped her way along the hold's starboard wall for as much stability as she could muster in reaching the door.

"I mean to go out and see what is to be done."

"Lady Braetana," pleaded Bronwyn, nearly hysterical, "you are no sailor. We must stay put."

Braetana was adamant. "I must see to our situation. Do not be frightened. I will return."

Braetana hurriedly donned the heavy camlet cloak, pulled back the door's thick fabric, and rushed headlong into the chaos outside. As she emerged onto the lurching deck, driving sheets of rain stung her eyes, momentarily blinding her from the surrounding confusion. Braetana squinted, leaving one hand in a tight grip on the hold's wall and raising the other to her brow as a shield against the gale force wind.

It was a frightening choice, for the vision that lay before her proved more fearful than sightlessness. Now she could not only feel but could also see the longship's uncontrolled pitching, its hull taking on great waves of saltwater with each successive undulation.

As each watery assault receded back into the anger of the churning sea, a legacy of salty rivulets hurried to follow suit. With practiced ease, each stream wound its way past sea chests and hemp rigging and joined with others to ring the still upright mast with a swirling skirt of white foam. The sea-soaked wind blew hard across the drekar's width with loud, deafening gusts. It seemed to come from every direction.

Braetana struggled to comprehend the surrounding chaos. Within her narrow range of vision, she could see several crewmen strapped with ropes to their seats, their oars cutting a mixture of sea and air as the longship's hull ascended and fell between swell and trough.

What remained of the huge sail was now ripped by the storm's rage into pitifully jagged strips. It hung half reefed from its uppermost beam, the fabric's destruction apparently hastened by its earlier efficiency in holding wind. In this turmoil, it was impossible to tell where Thorgunn stood. Yet some instinct in Braetana still sensed that he knew what to do and that she would be safe if only she could find him.

Despite the wildly pitching deck, she resolved to look aft. Still bracing herself with both palms pressed against the hold's low frame, Braetana took her first tentative step toward the ship's rear. Suddenly a familiar voice sounded a muffled yell from the prow.

"Braetana!" Thorgunn could not believe his eyes. Only madness could have propelled her from the safety of the cargo hold onto the watery furor of the drekar's open deck. It was a decision he knew she would soon regret.

Even he could barely manage his footing on the slippery planks. In fact, it was a position he would not have chosen to hold. But the forestay had snapped and the mast's upright position now hinged entirely on his ability to keep the rope taut.

If he could just maintain his place until Lars steered them in the direction of Einar's island, they had a chance of safe harbor. He knew the island was nearby, but he could not judge how long it would take to reach it. And now Braetana begged for greater disaster. He had to get to her, but to leave the forestay would ensure that the ship would capsize. There was no choice. Somehow, he had to make Braetana *choose* to go back inside.

"Return to the hold!" The surrounding blackness swallowed his voice and Braetana continued her dangerous progress, unaware.

Waiting until the vessel again pitched to port, she moved with difficulty around the structure's corner to its starboard side. She'd allowed the opposing rock of the deck to hurl her in temporary security against the wooden wall, but she knew she must round the hold and reach the mast beyond before the ship reeled back toward her.

Her precarious position was dangerously close to the starboard gunwale. Any further tilt in that direction would surely undo her already shaky footing and send her slipping over the shallow draft toward the chasm of roiling sea below.

As much as she could tell, the squall now seemed to blow from the darkness of the ship's bow. The wild wind had loosened her already wet and heavy woolen cloak from around her gunna, making it a burdensome weight. Her hair was completely soaked with mist and alternately stuck uncomfortably to her arms and snapped wildly behind her uncovered head.

Between the bristling cold and the ubiquitous wetness, Braetana had never been quite so miserable. Yet all thought of discomfort remained temporarily subdued both by fear and by the growing need to seek safe harbor under Thorgunn's aegis.

Working hard against the wind's insistent pull on her dragging cape, Braetana had just reached the mast as the pine deck began its expected shift sideways. Her field of vision had grown little with her progress forward. Though she knew better, she felt she was less on a ship at sea than prisoner in the angry eye of a furious, black hurricane.

Without warning, the huge crest currently cradling the drekar's keel withdrew. Its departure rendered the vessel momentarily airborne, then slammed it capriciously into a narrow hard-bottomed trough of sea.

The force of the impact made Braetana drop to her knees. Fortunately, she had already laced the fingers of both hands around the mast in a desperate bid to hold on. Were that not so, she would surely have been lifted in midair off the deck at some point in the vessel's precipitous descent.

She had been foolish to leave the hold; she knew that now, and knew as well that any attempt to improve her current position might well prove fatal. Wrapping both arms tightly around the juncture where the mast and mast-fish joined, Braetana pressed her drenched cheek sideways against the slick wooden piling and began to pray. Damn Thorgunn to hell—only God could help her now.

Her desperate prayer shattered with a deafening crack

overhead. As she turned her face skyward, Braetana was at first aware only of light. A beautiful blue brilliance suddenly silhouetted the mast and what remained of the sail against the midnight beyond. The flash seemed to bow in obeisance to the oak spire towering above her. Then, in horrific realization of the blow the light delivered, Braetana froze.

With a great crack, the peaked sailpost split, snapping off its height midway. There was no time to move, and nowhere to go had there been time. There were only the flooding ice blue light and Braetana's name called out from somewhere in the tempest's darkness.

An unlikely conspiracy of wind and wave dropped the beam directly atop her slender form, speedily releasing her mind from full consciousness and her arms from their grip on the mast's thick base. Like a child easily taken from its mother while sleeping, Braetana slipped without struggle toward the dangerous seduction of the ebony sea.

Her weight proved little match for the most recent swell. The cresting wave lifted her effortlessly onto a foamy bier, then swept her easily beyond the gunwale's submerged edge.

Until now, Thorgunn's instincts to reach Braetana had been held at bay by his need to make good the forestay. Now, the mast's angry handiwork had rendered his efforts useless, and he rushed toward the drekar's center in a last-ditch attempt to return Braetana to the hold's protection. But before his arms could reach her, those of the sea did. Braetana's face registered a distant, eerie calm, but horror suffused Thorgunn's as he helplessly watched his precious cargo borne into the churning sea.

Braetana's half-closed eyes caught the drekar receding from view. Yet, oddly, she felt no alarm at the separation. Perhaps it was only a rainy dream watched from Glendonwyck's high tower. Yes, that must be true, for she felt no distress, only peace and calm and an overwhelming need to sleep, if only for a little while. . . .

V

With great effort, Braetana turned her painfully bruised cheek away from the damp sand, rolling herself into the path of the sun's rays. The welcome heat gently lifted the mantle of seawater beads draped about her face and neck, slowly nudging her toward consciousness.

A guillemot called plaintively overhead, and Braetana opened her sleep-drugged eyes to a burst of blue and golden sky. She raised a sand-dusted hand to shield herself against the bright glare. As she lay motionless on the beach, just outside the reach of the retreating surf, Braetana struggled to recall the night's terrifying odyssey.

She remembered trying to reach Thorgunn and clinging to the mast, then she had felt a terrible blow. She had no memory of what followed, or of how she came to be on this beach.

As her eyes grew more accustomed to the bright spring light, Braetana raised her other arm overhead. With both hands, she began to smooth back strands of cold wet hair from her warming face. Suddenly the touch of her fingertips just above her right brow brought forth a sharp gasp of pain. Her hand withdrew quickly from the tenderness, then returned to assess the damage. There was a large red swelling above her eye. Braetana needed no mirror to appreciate the wound's severity. Now that she was fully conscious, it felt much as though she had been hit by—a mast. Of course! So this was what had sent her overboard.

As she tried to sit upright, the full extent of her injuries became clear. Her ribs ached from top to bottom, and she felt as though she had been beaten. Each breath filled her with dull throbbing pain, and it seemed that the more she awoke, the more she hurt.

Her shoes and cloak were gone, no doubt lost in her struggle with the sea. Fortunately, most of her gunna remained. The long linen skirt, however, bore a dramatic tear from left ankle to thigh, and a number of the amethysts that had formerly encircled the garment's skirt and sleeve hems had been lost.

Suddenly, she thought of Bronwyn. Braetana realized that her dear friend and caretaker, her mother since Eirlinn had gone, was now forever lost to her. A hot tide of tears surged upward within her, spilling with a sharp sting over the abrasions on her face. Braetana hoped she had survived, yet she knew better. The drekar had probably sunk. It was mastless and damaged from the storm. Still, a ship without sail could be rowed, provided some of its crew remained.

It was unreasonable to think herself the storm's only casualty. And yet there were thirty men at the start; if only a few survived, a partial crew could continue on their journey. But would there be any value now attached to an aging Saxon woman?

Although Braetana had not yet come to understand

her worth to the Norsemen, she knew Bronwyn's fate was clearly tied to her own. As Braetana sat dejectedly on the cold sand of an uncharted beach, she feared for her companion's fate.

"Do not be afraid," Braetana had told her beloved companion. "I will return." It had been a lie, though not an intentional one.

As if to flee the exploding pain that filled both her body and spirit, Braetana tried to stand upright on her bare feet. Then, with faltering but deliberate steps, she began to move slowly across the slate gray beach that stretched before her.

Images of Glendonwyck and Eirlinn and Bronwyn filled Braetana's mind. As if to escape them, she quickened her pace, and soon she was nearly running across the sand. Braetana's breath and the tight band around her chest rose together in a painful duet. Her stride easily outstripped the constraints of the long gunna. Without warning, the voluminous folds of fabric checked her movement in midair. Braetana pitched headfirst and facedown into the soft sand before her. The impact caused a renewed descent into self-pity.

"I would I had died!" she cried out loud for no one to hear. Her pain poured out of her eyes, her heart, her very soul. Finally, her strength, if not her agony, spent, Braetana's sobs subsided into the calm of exhaustion. Gradually, she realized that, though she might wish herself dead, she was not. And, if she intended to remain alive, she would do well to survey her new surroundings.

Standing upright, Braetana brushed the loose sand from her face and hair and rinsed the remaining grit from her chapped hands into the nearby shallow surf.

From the sun's movement overhead, she gauged it was now nearly an hour since she first awoke on the beach. She realized that she would have to start looking if she were to find suitable shelter before darkness fell.

Braetana directed her attention to the island that was now her new captor. Turning away from the unbroken seascape, she looked at the precipitous granite cliffs that loomed above her. Their play of shadow and light created a mysterious, dappled effect as they rose from the sand's end some distance inland.

Although the cliffs' height blocked most of the summit from view, Braetana could see that the lichen-splashed rocks were crowned by a pine plateau. The geography was repeated farther down the beachhead. There, thick conifer groves covered a more gentle hill and met the shoreline below. Amid these trees was the gateway to any further exploration of the island, and Braetana moved diagonally toward the closest copses. She noticed a nearly concealed footpath winding its way upward and inland.

The trail was well worn and so wide that animals could not have made it, a fact that led Braetana initially to the hope, then the fear, that she had washed ashore on a land already inhabited. She stopped suddenly as she realized this possibility.

Braetana did not know exactly where she was, or, indeed, where the ship was when she was last on board. But it had been days since she'd seen the Shetland coast. What she knew of the ship's subsequent course suggested she was now not only far from England, but also possibly quite close to Thorgunn's intended destination.

Wherever that was, it was enough to know Thorgunn's cronies might well be her new landlords. The unnerving thought suggested halting any further exploration. Still, her options on the beach looked bleak. The impending darkness would bring the cold, and, in her current state of fear and undress, Braetana was ill equipped to face either.

As lady of Glendonwyck, Braetana had little experience with such fierce physical adversity, and she certainly had none with surviving in a strange and hostile environment. But however pampered she had been before, Braetana knew she needed to find shelter, and she decided cautious investigation of the path was her only realistic choice.

As she wound her way upward, the roar of the surf receded and was replaced by the calm rustle of a cool wind moving through the heavy pine boughs framing the trail. The route quickly gained altitude, leading her up a serpentine ribbon of bends and switchbacks that accommodated the hillside's steepening terrain. The growth was so thick that Braetana could see little beyond what was immediately in front of her.

The climb was not one that would have normally winded her, but her painfully tender ribs protested each deepening breath. Finally, with great relief, she reached the trail's end and entered a grassy meadow rimmed with trees.

This was surely the plateau she had spied from below. But her current hard-won vantage afforded her a sight concealed before. At the meadow's far end, perched defiantly near the cliff's steep ocean-bound descent, stood a house. It was not like those Braetana had seen before, but nevertheless it was a large roofed structure obviously designed for habitation.

If she had missed the dwelling earlier, it was understandable, for the entire building appeared to be completely covered with thick, emerald turf. The structure gave the appearance of having simply grown straight up from the mossy grass below.

This was also true of the roof, which draped in an elegant curve over the long windowless walls. Broken only by the silhouette of a small chimney, it ended in a slightly upturned gable on each of the building's ends.

As she surveyed the odd configuration from the meadow's opposite end, Braetana's heart quickened with apprehension and excitement. The occupants could well be more of Thorgunn's kind. But as frightened as she was, she needed help and she would ask it of whomever was present.

Striding purposefully across the dense, ankle-high grass, she searched for some sign of life. The mysterious green house offered no encouragement. It stood lifeless and perfectly still, its silence issuing Braetana an unnerving invitation.

As she approached more closely, Braetana saw even more of its strange shape. On the rear end, facing inland, the sod roof dropped to a slightly lower level. The demarcation effectively partitioned the dwelling into one large and one small compartment, the latter roughly one-third the size of the former. Shadows from the turf gables had thus far concealed most of this section's wall. But now, standing only feet from the smaller of the two chambers, Braetana could see the outline of a mossy door mounted flush within the large verdant panel. Mustering what courage still remained within her, she reached one hesitant hand forward to the hemp loop that formed the door handle. With a deep, hopeful breath, Braetana pulled the weighty turf board toward her.

"Hello?" The smallness of her weakened voice was further diminished by the darkness. "Is someone here?"

Silence met her query and the lightless cavern stretching before her countered any inclination she had to step farther inside. A rounded stone rested to the right of the door frame. With her free hand and the aid of one bare foot, Braetana slowly pushed the heavy rock across the jamb, successfully propping the door open as far as its iron hinge would allow.

The visibility inside improved, though the rear portal and chimney overhead remained the primary light sources, save a few isolated fingers of sunlight seeping in from small cracks at the wall and roof junctures.

Now confident that the house remained at least temporarily unoccupied, Braetana took two tentative steps inside. The hard clay floor offered a chilly welcome against the soles of her bare feet, and the dank mustiness of unventilated sod and turf filled her nostrils. She was tempted to bolt back out into the fresh air. But as she forced herself to stay, the odor lessened, as did the darkness that had at first seemed to fill every nook and cranny of the huge structure.

She now saw more clearly in the dim light, well enough to discern what looked to be a small hinged window in the building's left wall. Braetana carefully stepped up from the sunken earthen trough that bisected the cabin's format, its edges framed on either side by parallel reed-strewn floor platforms.

From inside the house, Braetana could see that the turf exterior was braced on a frame of closely spaced birch trunks, each bound to the other with slender interwoven branches and hemp. Two poles were spaced more broadly apart, and between these was wedged a small rectangular window frame fashioned from similarly halved trunks.

Braetana's fingers worked the window's latch free from its hinge, then gave the panel a vigorous push. Though the wooden board resisted at first, she succeeded in opening it completely on her second try and was rewarded with a rush of bright light and fresh air.

What had looked from the outside like two separate chambers now appeared to be only one. The lowered roof on the structure's rear half, however, gave the feel of a smaller annex. Thick woolen curtains suspended from a wooden pole that spanned the ceiling's breadth where it dropped suggested that the areas were sometimes partitioned.

The sunken center strip in which Braetana had first stood ran the length of the longhouse. Numerous freestanding wooden beams framed it, each anchored in a stone setting, apparently to support the peaked roof. The clay trough broke midway for a slightly raised oblong hearth lined with small smooth stones. Its middle held a gray ashy residue, apparently from the last fire.

To Braetana's amazement, the more she saw of the building's contents, the more it presented a surprising picture of a well-provided, albeit primitive home. A huge black iron cauldron, dominated by an ornately twisted handle, rested at the base of a beam near the hearth. On nearby walls hung a full array of cooking utensils—a long-handled spiral grill for use as a gridiron, numerous soapstone bowls and ladles, and several rectangular wooden platters.

At the house's far end, a trestle-mounted table

perched on the raised side aisle. Long oak benches framed it on either side, along with bowl-shaped soapstone lamps mounted atop upright iron spikes.

Another bench, wider than those flanking the table, stood close beside her, covered by a luxuriously thick chestnut-colored bearskin. A lighter, unfamiliar pelt lay folded neatly near the other end. The temptation to wrap herself in the furs' soft warmth and escape the day's exhaustion was great, but Braetana knew there remained much to be attended to if she were to feel secure before nightfall.

The soapstone lamps still held oil from their last lighting, but judging from the dirty film floating on the liquid's top, they had gone some time without use.

In the far corner of the cabin, Braetana found small scrub kindling and larger birch logs. Neither would be much help to her, though, if she could not locate the tools and master the skill of building a fire.

A small bowl near the large hearth's edge held an adequate supply of both flint and steel, and Braetana had little difficulty in pressing the smaller twigs at the woodpile's edge into service as kindling. The actual making of the fire was another matter. Servants had performed such tasks at Glendonwyck. The most she had ever done as mistress was to stir a blaze already alight.

There was no one to help her now, she thought dejectedly, then began her unsure attack of flint on steel. Nearly an hour passed until Braetana hurled both tools across the width of the narrow room, her efforts dissolving into angry, frustrated tears.

It was not only getting darker, but also colder, a plight Braetana knew would worsen. As her frustration subsided, replaced by a discouraged persistence, she retrieved the necessary implements. Resuming her uncomfortably familiar cross-legged pose next to the fireplace's rim, she began again.

As she started to strike flint on steel, an unbidden image of Thorgunn rose in her mind. He thought her pampered, unable and unwilling to embrace hardship. Damn him—she knew he'd laugh if he could see the predicament she now struggled to overcome. As she worked unsuccessfully to suppress it, the deep timbre of his voice echoed through her mind.

"The rudder is hard to miss," he had told her, and she had winced, half in misery at the deep tear, half in anger to Thorgunn's witnessing of it.

"If this ship of yours could better handle the sea, I wouldn't have been thrown against its protruding handle. Now look, my skirt is torn because of your ill-designed vessel." The smile that brazenly appeared on his face and that always seemed to mock her every word now appeared vividly in her imagination.

"If memory serves, lady, you have many more dresses on board from which to choose. And those only a small part of your wardrobe from Glendonwyck. I think you have far to go before you match the heartiness of our Norse women. They should find any such dress, however imperfect, more than adequate."

"I would hardly seek to imitate the uncivilized stock you find appealing."

"You would do well to do so. Our trip will be long, possibly arduous. And once arrived, you may find a need to possess many skills you now consider beneath you."

Thorgunn had pushed Braetana's barely maintained control beyond the boundaries of her tolerance.

"How dare you insult me so! As if I had asked to be captive to your bullying ways and grim accommodations! In Northumbria I would have gowns and maids and something more palatable than your fishy fare. And a chamber slightly more commodious than the tiny hold you seem to think I should be grateful for. I have heard tales of your drekars before. I thought them larger than this little craft! I can only gather its small size reflects on your status as commander."

Unwittingly, Braetana had succeeded, with her indictment of his vessel and standing, in quickly wiping the smile from Thorgunn's tanned face.

"This 'little craft,' madam, is a Norse warship. Others are larger, but we required speed to elude your brethren, or so I thought. I had not counted on the Saxon stupidity."

Just thinking about his insulting insolence made Braetana's face grow red with fury and her hands tighten on the fire tools. It was galling enough that she'd been forced to suffer such impertinence from a heathen. But now, unable to manage the creation of even a small fire, she wondered if some of his alleged Saxon stupidity had rubbed off on her.

Biting her bottom lip, Braetana again faced her mind's eye image of the cocky Viking. The picture filled her with hot fury. Unthinkingly, she raised one arm overhead, delivering a frighteningly powerful attack of flint on steel.

To her shocked delight, the impact resulted in a spark. In a short time, Braetana managed to nurture the tiny light into a full-blown blaze.

Soon the longhouse was filled with warmth and light, its crackling heat bringing a delicious tingle to her nearly numb feet and hands. Standing before the fire, Braetana turned contentedly, warming herself on one side, then the other.

With the cold's bite now a mere memory in the glow of the ocher-tinted fire, Braetana began to fully explore the remainder of the house. With a small ember-tipped branch, she lit the oil in each of the nearby spike-mounted lamps. This addition improved the interior visibility dramatically and luckily so, because daylight had by now nearly disappeared.

Braetana closed the small shutter she had opened on entry, hoping to avoid any loss of the precious heat. With less ventilation, she worried at first that the room would grow smoky, but to her relief the chimney drew well enough to suction the fumes upward.

Her fears of freezing to death now allayed, Braetana turned her attention to her next need and grew intensely aware of her hunger. Nearly a day had passed since her last meal. She hoped that whoever had outfitted the seemingly well-stocked longhouse had left food stores as well.

There appeared to be no readily identifiable larder, but Braetana guessed that the small pine chest nestled against the tableside wall might yield something edible. Her assumption was only partly correct. From a few crumbs of vegetable matter resting sadly in the box's corners, it was apparent that it once held food, but unfortunately there was none there now.

Braetana sat dejectedly on the longhouse floor, her chin resting in her hands. Ever since her departure from Glendonwyck, this nightmarish odyssey had offered one challenge after another. If she did not drown, she would freeze; if she did not freeze, she would starve. Her gaze wandered aimlessly, settling on a small iron-belted wooden cask adjacent to the empty food coffer.

Rising to her knees, she poked one tentative finger into the container, parting the dusty film covering the bucket's contents. It appeared whoever owned the cabin had at least left her some stale beer. Though she had never grown fully accustomed to its bitter taste, Braetana filled a nearby horn cup and drank greedily.

If she were still ravenous, at least the beer made her somewhat less aware of it. Perhaps it would help her rest, but before she surrendered to her longed-for sleep, there remained the matter of a larger pine chest, ornately carved with intertwined bodies of strange two-headed animals. Braetana unlocked the metal clasp on the lid, then raised its heavy top to rest against the wall behind. Her lips parted in astonishment at its contents.

There, resting ominously near the box's bottom, were several pairs of belted pants, along with thigh-length woolen tunics and one two-pointed cloak. Tucked in the coffer's corner were two sets of goatskin slippers. The ensemble was horrifyingly familiar for it was nearly identical to that worn by Thorgunn on that first fateful day at Glendonwyck.

Braetana dropped the frightening garb back into the chest and slumped to the floor. Her worst expectations were true. If she were not where Thorgunn had planned to take her, she must be dangerously close. Whoever occupied this cabin dressed nearly the same as her former captor.

For a brief instant she had allowed herself the thought of freedom. Now it seemed her execution had been but stayed. How long until her refuge's lord returned and found a fugitive Saxon occupying his house? What clemency was there to be hoped for in the hands of another like Thorgunn?

Suddenly overcome by a need to suspend all thought, Braetana stumbled to the oak cask, took a final generous swig of the flat beer within, then collapsed between the bed's rich fur covers.

Yet her memories besieged her even in the intoxication of unconsciousness. In her dream, she was again aboard the drekar, but this time on calmer, kinder seas. The warm wind flirted playfully with her unbound hair, its dancing fingers twirling and teasing each strand into a zephyr-born curl.

She felt an extraordinary touch like nothing she had ever known before. It rested just barely upon the back of her neck, so light it must be the sea breeze and yet so unmistakably human it could not be.

Strangely unafraid, she answered its unspoken invitation and turned slowly, her long hair swirling gently all about her like a great flaxen cape. Suddenly there was no wind at all. It was Thorgunn's hands so lovingly upon her, their great masculine strength cupping either side of her face in a tender caress that held her with no force save her own wish to remain within them.

His fingers moved greedily across her features, tracing each curve of her face as if merely looking upon her would not satisfy him. The mastery of his touch made her weak and breathless.

His eyes, which had once seemed cold and withdrawn, now roamed adoringly across her own. Something familiar in them called to her, causing her to feel a yearning so strange and strong she thought herself surely bewitched.

Thorgunn did not speak; the force that drew them

ever nearer needed no words. He moved closer, and a small distant voice told her to flee. But she willed it away, wanting only more of the danger his dark eyes promised. As if he could understand her silent plea, Thorgunn brought her to him, his hands moving around the back of her head to tip her face slightly upward into the intense hunger of his stare. His fingers wound their way through the fine strands of her silky hair, and his sinewy arms encompassed her, surrounding her slender frame. He pulled her tighter, and together their flesh fused in a hot, seamless seal. In that portion of her mind that could still form thought, Braetana marveled that their bodies, though so different, could mold together in such perfect pleasure. Surely some destiny had forged their remarkable fit.

Although Thorgunn seemed not to move, he came closer still. Braetana closed her eyes, surrendering to the intoxicating warmth and weight of him against her. Unexpectedly, one of his hands left the back of her head, then descended in tortuous languor down the curve of her spine. As it wound its way around her slender waist, coming to rest just below the fullness of one breast, a gasp of shocked pleasure escaped Braetana's parted lips. What sorcery did his body know, to render her so helpless against his touch? For an endless time, his mouth lingered just a breath beyond her own. Her lips could feel its heat, and she wanted more.

As if he knew her thoughts, Thorgunn pressed his mouth upon hers, crushing her parted lips with no hint of restraint. His tongue soon probed deep within her, Braetana willingly allowing his delicious intrusion.

The feel of his mouth, his hands, his body everywhere upon her roused Braetana beyond any desire for self-restraint. Now she was not content to merely feel him against her; she wanted him somehow within, and she arched her back in a desperate effort to seek the satisfaction she sensed Thorgunn could help her find. As they struggled to fulfill the needs neither could now deny, Braetana moaned softly in profound pleasure.

Thorgunn understood. Effortlessly, he stripped away the gunna between them, quickly pulling her nakedness back hard against his partially exposed chest. His flesh seemed to blend into her own and Braetana's breath quickened in anticipation of the next plateau of pleasure she now trusted they would ascend. But as Thorgunn's searching hands reached to cup her full breasts, his fingertips brushing a sweet ache across each mound's peak, Braetana's passion-filled reverie halted abruptly. Her dream dissolved with a resounding crash that brought her quickly back to the longhouse and its accompanying predicament. Although unsure if she was awake or asleep, Braetana struggled to an upright position.

The heavy turf door flew open, revealing a huge, bedraggled form lying facedown across the longhouse threshold. With apparently great effort the stranger pressed both palms against the clay in an attempt to raise his head.

Braetana's mouth dropped open in shock. "You!" she charged angrily, not knowing what else to say. "Will you never cease these intrusions into my bedchamber?"

"My apologies, lady," the intruder began. But before he could complete whatever he intended to say, Thorgunn collapsed unconscious on the longhouse floor.

VI

Braetana's still sleepy mind was a kaleidoscopic jumble of the real and the imagined. The man who had filled her shameful dream and commanded her so powerfully as she willingly submitted to his burning touch now lay sprawled on her doorstep.

At first Braetana was unsure just how unconscious Thorgunn was. After several futile attempts to rouse him by name, however, she sat back in temporary relief. She was content for the moment that he was unlikely to launch any attack on her.

As the moments passed and he still made no effort to move, she began to wonder if he was alive. With this in mind, she cautiously approached him, and lowered one hand near his mouth for some evidence of breath.

To Braetana's relief, she felt his warm exhalation, then noticed he bled profusely from a wide diagonal gash across his left temple. The wound's edges swelled with the beginning signs of infection. It was clear that his recovery would require her prompt and skillful attention.

Now an unnerving idea crossed her mind. She could easily let him die by not taking care of him. Braetana shuddered involuntarily at the thought—she would be a murderess, no better than the barbaric marauders who had brought her to this miserable predicament. Still, this painful world was not of her making, and recent experience had well shown her that no one but she, and most especially not Thorgunn, could be trusted to serve as her protector.

Yet Braetana's need for her own survival argued strongly in favor of encouraging Thorgunn's. She had no food and little notion of how to secure any. Were she even to locate something appealing amid the island's thick growth, Braetana suspected she could not tell whether it was poisonous or edible. This was a problem that might well prove fatal. Thorgunn at least would not let her starve—providing he survived.

Having abandoned the prospect of hastening the Viking's death, Braetana became concerned she might not be able to prevent it. The wound was severe, and she had no medicine with which to treat it. But since the lesion was apparently incurred by the storm, the infection had not yet had time to spread extensively.

One thing was clear—she could not leave him lying in the doorway. His recovery required bed rest, and the open door was making the room uncomfortably cold. The preceding night had reduced the fire's roar to barely glowing embers, and the morning's frigid air was now in the process of rushing in and displacing the house's little remaining warmth.

Although Braetana had no idea if she would be able to move the large Viking at all, she knew she had to try. Fortunately, he had fallen unconscious with both arms outstretched toward her; if he had fallen atop them,

Braetana much doubted she could have pulled them from beneath him.

Positioning herself between Thorgunn and the bed, she bent from the waist and grabbed hold of both his wrists. Her hands barely encompassed the circumference of each, and, as she attempted to draw his body upright, Braetana succeeded in lifting only his arms. Despairingly, she soon realized the uselessness of any attempt to lift him.

If she could move Thorgunn at all, it would only be by dragging him. Thus she began the slow and difficult task of pulling a man nearly twice her weight the long haul between the cabin's doorway and the fur-covered bench.

With much effort, Braetana finally closed the distance, only to face the even more difficult task of shifting him from floor to bed. Had the assignment not proved so impossible, she might well have laughed to see herself. As soon as she managed to lift part of him onto the cot, he fell off again.

Though she would have been hard-pressed to explain how, Braetana eventually succeeded in landing him on the bed. By this point, she felt much in need of rest herself.

Other matters, however, required her more immediate attention. She stoked the waning hearth fire with birch from the corner pile and noted with concern that the wood supply was rapidly dwindling. It would soon disappear altogether if it was not replenished.

As self-appointed mistress of her makeshift household, Braetana considered the relative importance of the tasks essential to her well-being. Foremost in her mind was stopping her hunger.

It had been nearly two days since her last meal, and she was light-headed from the deprivation. Clearly, there was nothing in the longhouse. And however ill equipped she was for the confusing and dangerous prospect of finding some sustenance in the island's wilds, Braetana knew she must try. Though she doubted she could snare an animal, she hoped that she could find some edible plants.

Yet no sooner had she pushed the paneled door than the bite of the morning's cold issued an unhappy greeting. Its painful snap instantly drew her attention to her torn skirt and the leg that was almost completely exposed by its split fabric. The dress served well enough next to the fire, but it was no protection against the chill outdoors.

Reluctantly, Braetana returned to the wardrobe coffer and withdrew the trousers and tunic that had reminded her of her captivity. After all that had happened, dressing up as a Viking, and a Viking man at that, was about the last thing she wished. Still, it was better than freezing. With pragmatic resignation, she slipped out of the tattered gunna and into the Norse garb.

Covering her bare feet with the oversize goatskin slippers, it occurred to Braetana that her sleeping patient would certainly laugh at the sight of her appearance. With that thought in mind, she resolved to repair the gunna so as to make it wearable sometime before Thorgunn regained consciousness.

It appeared she could do so at her leisure. To Braetana's relief, Thorgunn had drifted, no doubt from combined exhaustion and shock, into a deep and sonorous sleep.

She had bound his head temporarily with linen strips,

having fashioned the dressing from a quick shredding of another tunic she had discovered in the wardrobe coffer. Although the injury still required cleaning and further treatment, she could do neither without water and herbs, both of which she hoped to find in her expedition outside.

Leaving to hunt for supplies, Braetana looked back from the doorway to the sleeping blond titan on the bed. His fierceness now seemed far away, replaced by a tranquil expression she sensed he seldom wore.

For the first time she was free to study him without his awareness. Braetana stared at Thorgunn's strong, chiseled features, strikingly set on his broad suntanned face and contrasting with his unruly mass of thick blond hair. The overall effect pleased her, all the more so for Thorgunn's departure from the shorter, darker men Braetana had been accustomed to seeing at Glendonwyck. She imagined his handsome face served him well in his homeland, earning whatever favors he sought from the local maids.

Somehow it seemed wrong to her that one so base should have such fine looks. Furthermore, in his calm sleep, he hardly projected the role of captor, but rather that of a hurt child in need of love and attention.

Braetana's brow suddenly knitted in disbelief. What was she thinking of? However appealing and helpless the Viking now seemed, Braetana knew he was not so. However unplanned, this malaise was but one more guise to sabotage her freedom. Slamming the turf door behind her, she stomped angrily into the meadow's morning light, telling herself that she would not care if he died after all.

The venture outside proved surprisingly productive.

On the meadow's left boundary, Braetana discovered a modest spring that spilled its bubbly overflow into the start of a small sea-bound brook. She had hoped for such a find, and, in her optimism, had brought with her the largest oak bucket the house afforded. Dipping her cupped hands into its icy effervescence, Braetana splashed her face, then drank her fill of the fresh, cold water. Soon the wooden container was filled to overflowing with as much spring water as it could hold. At least she wouldn't die of thirst.

In a nearby copse of trees, she found what looked to her like beetroot. Braetana had always had her meals prepared by someone else, and she had difficulty identifying vegetables in their uncooked state. What if the fare proved poisonous? She wondered if her past privileges might now cost her her life.

Yet so great was her hunger, the thought barely crossed her mind before she brushed the dirt from the uprooted plant and bit greedily into its earthy taste. If she didn't eat, she would surely die anyway. Having eaten as much as she could bear of the unwashed, uncooked plant, Braetana was relieved to find a pocket of what she was sure was cabbage. This, at least, would do for making a porridge.

Once she had gathered sufficient stores for cooking, Braetana turned her eye toward plants suitable for a poultice to heal Thorgunn's wound. Ironically, she was better at identifying these, having seen Bronwyn's medicine basket full of herbs.

Her gathering of supplies completed, Braetana returned the newfound provisions to the longhouse, then set out again, this time for firewood, which proved an easier task. The thick growths of nearby pine and birch had apparently been pruned by the preceding winter's storms, the trees surrendering their smaller branches to the force of the strong winds that roared in off the North Sea.

Picking her way through the scrubby debris at each trunk's base, Braetana was careful to choose only those branches narrow enough for her to break. She had not seen an ax for chopping thicker timber. In truth, she was not sure she could have wielded one, had she found it.

After several exhausting but fruitful trips to the house, Braetana sighed in satisfaction as she surveyed the substantial woodpile her labors had amassed. For a few days at least she would neither freeze nor starve. And, providing Thorgunn remained in his present weakened state, she had no immediate fear of assault.

When she reentered the longhouse, it became clear she needn't have worried about his recovering too quickly; the serene composure of his earlier sleep had decayed into a fitful delirium marked by burning fever and scored with a continual low moaning.

When she removed the brightly colored bandage from Thorgunn's head, she realized why his condition had changed. The wound had worsened considerably during her hours away. It now rose like a bright red beacon beneath his cap of blond hair. The infection had spread quickly, and Braetana wondered if it was her earlier underestimation of its importance that had brought the Viking to his current miserable state.

Yet how could she have been expected to know better? Though Bronwyn was quite skillful in herbal medicine and it was true that she often discussed her work with Braetana, as lady of Glendonwyck, it was not part of Braetana's duties to tend the sick. With matters of life and death well at stake, she now questioned the validity of her formerly held class distinctions.

This constant readjustment of her role in her ever-changing world was beginning to wear on Braetana. Though food gathering, fire building, and now the tending of sick kidnappers were practical chores she could apparently master, she wondered whether her emotions could continue to cope as easily.

At this moment she felt more irritation than pity for Thorgunn. If the untrustworthy lout had been more careful about staying on board, he would not be suffering so. Thanks to his clumsiness, she now had to face the prospect of an ugly wound that was beginning to fester and that would likely make her sick.

Still, the gash would not repair itself if Braetana ignored it. Thinking it best to get the unpleasant chore over with as soon as possible, she set about boiling water with which to make her poultice.

When the carefully chosen leaves and roots had been reduced to a pasty consistency, Braetana spread them atop a clean strip of cloth. Careful not to upend it, she laid the bandage within reach of her workplace near the bed. She dipped another rag into the steaming cauldron. When it had cooled sufficiently to touch, Braetana rang the excess water from the fabric and placed the damp cloth alongside the other dressing.

Now she faced the most horrible task—that of cauterizing the inflamed gash. When building the fire, Braetana had been careful to place an already hardened and slightly flat-tipped bough in the midst of the coals. Now she retrieved it, her eyes widening in dread at its white-hot tip. She could not imagine such an agony on her own flesh. Thorgunn, however, looked oblivious at best. Even if he were not wholly so, she considered he was deserving of the pain the searing would bring.

Steadying her right hand with the other, and taking in a deep breath, Braetana touched the smoldering bough to the swollen infection. As the outer edges framing the wound charred on contact, a sickening stench rose from Thorgunn's burning flesh.

Braetana struggled against nausea, thinking at any moment she would have to flee from the thick, smothering smell into the fresh air outside. Yet somehow she managed to stay put. Casting the branch back into the hot fire, she cleaned and bandaged the wound with the fresh linen, as much to contain the odor as to heal the injury.

Thorgunn acknowledged the bough's touch with only a low moan. He now seemed to have drifted farther from consciousness, for he lay silent and completely still atop the low fur bier.

It was three full days before the Viking awoke. In the interim, Braetana's time was easily spent with the myriad tasks of maintaining the household. She regularly changed the linen bandage, replacing each dried poultice with a new, moist one. When not tending Thorgunn, she spent her days searching for food and firewood.

Each task was handled more quickly now, and Braetana found, to her delight, that her newfound efficiency actually allowed her a few hours daily to herself. She indulged this welcome freedom with a stroll, each walk wonderfully purposeless except for a leisurely review of her increasingly familiar surroundings.

Despite the desperation of her circumstances, Braetana found herself almost enjoying the island. Its scenery was exquisite, the thick laden overgrowth and dense forest a pleasant change from the chalky starkness of Glendonwyck. And at least Thorgunn wasn't insulting her.

Although the prospect of imminent darkness meant she could not venture far from the longhouse, Braetana preferred to walk at dusk. The vista offered from the cliff's edge provided a spectacular view of glowing sea sunsets on the far horizon.

At first, she diligently searched the flat water for some sign of a ship. But she soon realized that, were she even to spot a vessel, she would have great difficulty in signaling it. More critically, its occupants would probably prove unfriendly.

Whatever had become of the drekar was not to be known. Braetana guessed that the gale had sent the ship to a watery grave. If not, it had likely been borne far beyond the reach of the island where she and the Viking were now unwilling prisoners.

With no passing ships promising rescue and no vessel of their own with which to leave, Braetana wondered apprehensively what future she could have here with her enigmatic kidnapper. Nothing acceptable came to mind. In fact, the notion of a lifetime spent in Thorgunn's coarse company seemed nothing less than grim. *I would rather be prisoner to a horde of them than sole companion to this one*, Braetana thought despondently, acutely aware of the threat Thorgunn posed to what remained of her honor.

She had never been alone with a man before, not even the leering Edward. Isolation with the Viking was a dangerous proposition at best. With only one shelter for the two of them, her chances of keeping Thorgunn at bay looked bleak.

Once he fully recovered, they would somehow have to find a way off the island. And Thorgunn would have to sleep elsewhere until that time.

Braetana's decision was well timed. When she returned to the longhouse at the third day's end, she found a fully conscious, newly strengthened, and completely upright Thorgunn. His color was less robust than usual and he appeared still somewhat shy of his former vigor.

Thanks to Braetana's constant ministrations, however, the infection's fever had passed. In fact, the Viking appeared almost as good as new, except for a freshly exposed scar where the wound had been. Braetana stopped suddenly as she stepped across the structure's sod doorway.

"I believe a thank you is in order." Thorgunn's large fingers massaged the raised welt on his left temple. "I would not guess a Saxon noblewoman to possess such curative powers."

"I've no need of your gratitude. It was in my best interest to keep you alive."

"I imagine so," Thorgunn replied. "And I see you have not only tended my wound, but dressed to lift my spirits as well." Thorgunn's eyes traveled Braetana's height, registering his amusement at the incongruity of such beauty clothed in a Viking warrior's attire. Then, seeing the outline of her long, coltish legs, visible even through the baggy woolen trousers, his thoughts turned more toward maintaining his self-control.

Damn! Braetana had hoped to relinquish her Norse garb before Thorgunn had the chance to make just such a snide remark.

"My gunna was torn in the storm. I needed something warm to wear here."

"Well, Einar would certainly smile to see his costume done such justice."

"And who is Einar?" Braetana's voice registered her alarm. Her fear that the longhouse's regular occupants were Vikings was confirmed.

"Our host in absentia. He usually tends the post only in summer."

"Then you know this place?"

"I know it well," said Thorgunn with a smile. "It serves us as a summer lookout for Frisian pirates sailing north to steal the spoils of our western trade. Einar is the post's watchman. He keeps vigil here during the height of the trading season. The rest of the year it is abandoned as you found it."

"We are then close to this Nordmannaland?" Braetana hoped that, if such were the case, at least it increased her chances of ending their imprisonment.

Thorgunn's lips curved upward in that maddening smile that made Braetana want so badly to slap him.

"My lady is ever the strategist, isn't she? We are two good wind days west, part of a long archipelago that hugs our coastline. Though I do not expect many ships by this early in the year. A month from now we will see the trade waters glistening with the golden prows of Norse longships. Until Einar arrives, we can consider ourselves his guests."

Braetana set her jaw and tapped her foot in an explosion of angry little beats. "As long as I am with you, I will consider myself only a prisoner."

"I see your spirit survived the swim. Your forehead, however, does appear a little worse for the wear." Braetana could see him appraise the fading but still sizable bruise above her right eye. Until Thorgunn's reminder, she had all but forgotten her own injury.

"If you're referring to this," she said, raising a hand to the purplish mark, "it's a present from your mast. That's how I came to this unfortunate lot here with you. I would to God you too had not washed overboard."

"I was not washed, madame. I came willingly."

"What?" Braetana's brow knitted in confusion. "Why ever would you. . . ." The query trailed off in mid-sentence with her disbelief at the obvious yet incredible answer.

Thorgunn nodded knowingly. "I confess it unlikely, considering that you have been more trouble than pleasure. But, as Odin is my witness, I actually did try to save you. I was working the forestay when lightning took the mast. I had thought you still safely in the hold. May I inquire as to what insanity sent you aboveboard?"

"The storm frightened me." Braetana chose the half lie as preferable to a confession that she was in fact looking for Thorgunn.

"Your error in judgment could well have cost us our lives. Had I not managed to hang on to you and the floating mast, it certainly would have."

"You caught me as I washed from the drekar?"

"After, to be precise. That tear in your precious gunna came from my efforts to pull you back on board. Unfortunately, the sea had other intentions. Seeing the mast floating beside you, I managed to strap the two of us briefly to it. Then, as it once more snapped in half, we again parted company. This prize on my head which you have mended so skillfully was a kiss from the keel as the ship passed over."

"And you knew we were near this island?"

"Yes. But in truth, I am surprised to find you still on this side of Valhalla."

Thorgunn's revelation left Braetana speechless. She knew from the growing heat that her cheeks had flushed bright red with embarrassment. Why had he risked his life to save her? Was it possible he harbored some humanity she had not heretofore thought him capable of? He could easily have let her drown—and yet he'd gone after her, incurring a serious head wound in the process.

She was glad that she had not let him die. Whatever kind of man he was, such a repayment would have been too much for her conscience to bear. Yet something inside her restrained what otherwise would have been an outpouring of gratitude. She still didn't know why he wanted her.

"You certainly took great trouble to save my life."

"Indeed. Perhaps it was a bad decision. From the day we met, you've hardly been easy company."

"Yes. And it is that most of all that makes me wonder what my value is to you. Surely this has all been too trying for the simple sale of a slave."

"As I told you, your destiny lies in no slave market."

"Then what? You must attribute me great power to think it so dangerous to arm me with the truth."

Thorgunn's brief inclination to sate Braetana's curiosity quickly fled as he recalled Magnus's request. The old man wanted to speak with her himself. And it would hardly serve Thorgunn to position himself in the middle of this dispute. His silence answered Braetana eloquently.

"I see. I am to know nothing still. Well, if you expect my thanks for ending up here with you, think better of it. If it had not been for your brutish abduction, I should still be safe at Glendonwyck," answered Braetana irascibly.

"With your loving Edward." Thorgunn found himself unable to resist the opportunity. Then, recalling that Braetana had just saved his life, he softened. "It seems for now we are housemates. Friends as well?"

Braetana's anger got a further boost with this affronting suggestion that they could be anything other than adversaries. "I do not plan to share the house with you." Her tone was unmistakably emphatic.

"You would sleep outdoors, lady? It is cold at night, but far be it from me to dictate your sleeping habits."

"Oh!" Braetana cried in exasperation, stamping her foot painfully hard against the ground. "You know what I mean. *I* will stay here—you will go elsewhere."

"And where exactly do you suggest I go?"

"You will find somewhere," said Braetana, her voice rising in pitch and volume and her patience waning.

Thorgunn answered calmly. "I already have a place, madam. I intend to stay exactly where I am. You are welcome to remain."

It was clear he was serious, but Braetana was speechless at the Viking's brazen nerve. Incensed and defeated, she turned and walked defiantly to the house's far end. There she dropped to the reed-strewn floor and sat, hugging her knees tightly to her chest. With as much indifference as possible, Braetana stared at the hearth's flickering golden flames.

Thorgunn was well acquainted with the cabin's contents. With Braetana's dismissal, he turned his attention to the pine wardrobe coffer and to improving his by now quite bedraggled appearance. As he had hoped, Einar's chest held one more suit of clothes, a fortunate piece of luck, given Thorgunn's current dishevelment.

His present garb had weathered the storm no better than Braetana's gunna; the tunic was badly torn around both neck and sleeves and what remained of the nubby material was thoroughly caked with an unattractive mixture of dried blood and mire. The trousers had not fared much better, for both legs were partially split and the front seam looked likely to follow suit at any moment.

All this had not gone unnoticed by Braetana. Had she been more favorably disposed to her unconscious charge, she might well have managed to change his clothes by herself. Given what she knew of the Viking, however, she was disinclined to face the inevitable questions that would follow if she had undressed him. She therefore had opted, at the expense of her own sense of smell, to allow Thorgunn the continued wear of the malodorous apparel.

Thorgunn pulled the fresh attire, a piece at a time, from the bottom of the deep wooden chest. His recollection of Einar had served; a quick perusal of the maroon wool trousers and matching scarlet tunic showed the man to be close to Thorgunn in size.

Although Braetana pretended to study the fire, the scene with Thorgunn lay nearly straight in front of her, and it was hard to miss. Before she had time to realize what was happening, she caught sight of Thorgunn's muscular body being stripped with cavalier abandon. In a flash he stood unabashedly naked before her and in no apparent hurry to rectify his undress.

Braetana was so shocked that she could find no words for her horror. For several seconds she sat frozen in disbelief, the violet eyes huge with incredulity, her full lips parted on the verge of unformed speech. Then, gathering her wits and her oversize trousers about her, she spun abruptly away, raising both hands to cover her burning face. Because she was not facing him, the gesture made no sense; nevertheless it felt right.

Thorgunn's first response was to laugh, but he reconsidered. He felt something akin to gratitude regarding her nursing of him.

With practiced efficiency, he donned the new garments, girdling the tailored long-sleeved top with a thick leather belt and finishing the pants with a pair of dark blue hose and goatskin shoes. The coffer also held a two-pointed cobalt blue woolen cloak and an ornate bronze-tipped baldric obviously designed for the sword Braetana had missed at the box's bottom.

Having completed his outfit, Thorgunn set about some work Braetana could only hear close behind her. She was still too distrustful of his state of dress to remove her hands from her eyes and turn about.

Thorgunn broke the silence. "There, I trust this arrangement will meet with your approval."

Braetana turned to find the house now partitioned, Thorgunn having separated the front half from the rear with a heavy pair of side-mounted curtains. Pulling the unfurled tapestries temporarily back toward the birch wall, he exposed a trestle table bench that he had positioned to serve as a bed in the newly created chamber. Extra furs, stored in another deep coffer in the house's rear, had been retrieved as covers for the makeshift bed.

Braetana was no less than stunned at the new arrangement. First Thorgunn had refused to leave the house. Then he had stripped himself shamelessly in front of her, leaving her with the full and terrifying expectation that her violent rape was at hand. Now, in its stead, the Norseman offered her a private bedroom.

"And which is mine?" she asked, still distrustful.

"This one." Thorgunn gestured toward the pallet where he had lain for the last three days. "You may sleep near the hearth." Then, unable to resist in indulging her all-too-transparent fears, he added, "If I am cold, I will need but to think of you."

Braetana sensed there was more than a little truth behind Thorgunn's jest. Her face again grew warm with a combination of irritation and embarrassment.

She chose to ignore the crude compliment. "A drawn curtain hardly secures my privacy."

Thorgunn smiled vexingly. "If I wished to ravage you, madam, a stone curtain would not prevent it. Rest easy, my lady." With that, Thorgunn disappeared into the newly partitioned chamber, snapping both curtain halves into a tight closure behind him.

An overwhelming fatigue crept through Braetana's bones, promising to free her from her thoughts. But even her great exhaustion was not sufficient to quell the confusion that spun through her mind. She labored to understand it, finally assuring herself that she had every reason to feel uncomfortable with a man who had first kidnapped her and who now imprisoned her with his coarse company in the middle of nowhere. Yet some part of Braetana, still without voice, sensed that perhaps it was not so much Thorgunn, but her own needs, that threatened her well-being. She came close to the knowledge, then dismissed the thinking as ridiculous. He had indicated he would not force himself on her. As long as that were true, she was safe. Braetana resolved to think no more on the matter. Still, she did not find sleep until much later that night.

There was similar restlessness on the other side of the curtain. Thorgunn's eyes did not close. Instead he looked at the beamed ceiling, questioning the unlikely arrangement the storm had brought them to. But for the gale, they would be nearly home by now, Braetana en route to meet her unknown father and Thorgunn ever closer to the silver Magnus had pledged in exchange for her.

Thanks to his brother Haakon's treachery, Thorgunn had gone too long without the position and wealth his birthright should have bestowed. Magnus's purse would buy him a manned ship from the Jutlanders, one that would successfully challenge Haakon's throne. But now, so close to having all he sought, he found himself facing a dangerous and most unexpected threat to his goals—Braetana herself.

When he had contracted to kidnap her for Magnus's reward, she had been only a business transaction. She was simply a half-Saxon cargo with which to vanquish the poverty and suffering his younger half brother had so skillfully caused. Braetana's beauty had come as a surprise; having envisioned her for so long only in terms of silver and ships, Thorgunn's first meeting with the flaxen-haired hellcat found him quite unprepared.

Not that he had been wholly deprived of the charms of the fairer sex thus far. In his trade travels and visits home, there was company enough, though women's affections for him often cooled with the revelation that his kingly brother had arranged for him to live in penury. Those to whom his poverty made no difference made little difference to Thorgunn. An ignoble marriage was what Haakon hoped for, knowing full well such a match would make Thorgunn unsuitable as challenger to the throne.

And so Thorgunn had lived a seafarer's life. He had enjoyed women aplenty, but without love, his heart as itinerant as his drekar crisscrossing the wide North Sea. Until Braetana—the likes of whom he had never before encountered.

Thorgunn found himself inexorably drawn to this wild-eyed wench. Though he restrained his body, he could not stop his mind from undressing and holding her close, even as she sat angrily across the room from him.

His mind drew an image of her long, snow-colored hair, as soft to the touch as pure silk. His thoughts lingered on her alabaster face with the blazing lilac eyes, and the full currant-colored lips, the lower one temptingly fuller than its mate, both unwittingly inviting an end to his precarious self-restraint.

As if he weren't already taxed enough, every move of her voluptuous body made him ache to hold her close. He longed to devour each sculptured curve of her small waist and full breasts, to feel the warm nakedness of her pressed hard against him, just as she had that first morning at Glendonwyck.

His demeanor had not betrayed him that day, but had Braetana faced him, he was sure his manhood would have, for he throbbed with the sweet pain of desire. Had he not been restrained by the importance of the goal at hand, he would surely have pressed her back onto the bed and taken her right there. And now, to be again so close to her, able to hear her breath just beyond the curtain's enclosure, made him want her all the more.

But this was madness. Were he to slake his thirst for

her all would be lost. The years of privation and degradation and Haakon's denial of Thorgunn's legitimate position would be for nothing unless Braetana were safely delivered.

Things had gone badly enough already. The lavaliere was lost, though he trusted Magnus would believe that Braetana once wore it. The current arrangement was also a problem, certainly less than proper. To sully her honor now would irreparably damage her value in Magnus's eyes. The old man might well withhold all payment, leaving Thorgunn with nothing to show for his long, dangerous journey save his own spent passion.

He could not have her, no matter what his needs. Thorgunn had felt this way before and knew that the feeling would pass. She was only a maid, and a half-Saxon one at that—hardly an asset in the Viking's eyes. Einar would arrive in a month's time and see them safely home. Once there, his ransom would buy better women.

Resolving to think no more on the matter, Thorgunn turned his face to the thick fur, closing his eyes in imitation of much-needed rest. At that moment, Braetana turned over, emitting a soft sigh as she snuggled deeper into the bearskins in an effort to find sleep. Thorgunn's eyes opened. He knew he would be awake for some time that night.

VII

"I suppose you would like me to pluck it too?" Thorgunn sighed, realizing his naivete in assuming his highborn charge would have much knowledge of kitchen work.

Braetana shrugged her shoulders imploringly. "Certainly you could manage the task more quickly than I. And if you are truly hungry . . ."

A look of exasperation swept across Thorgunn's face. "If my lady is as fond of the ptarmigan as she claims, it does not seem unreasonable that she would be willing to prepare it. You'll recall it was not you who was charged with taking the bow and killing the bird."

Braetana knew Thorgunn was well within his rights to expect her to pluck the still-warm hen. In fact, she would have made some effort to oblige, had she any idea how to proceed. But to admit to Thorgunn that she had only seen fowl in its cooked state would only make him more critical of her. Suddenly those attributes for which she had been revered in Northumbria—her ability to read, sing well, and win at chess—seemed useless. Now her worth hinged on her ability to pluck feathers from the flesh of a barely dead hen. At the moment, such worth did not seem overly high. She would not admit her ignorance—better to let him think her spoiled than incompetent.

"I was not required to perform such tasks at Glendon-wyck."

"I do not find that surprising. But neither have I been required to apprentice intractable maids in the arts of survival." Vexed, he set the bird on the trestle table and planted both hands fully on his hips.

Despite her lack of skill, Braetana still thought Thorgunn's request unreasonable. She had done her part. "I gather beetroot and cabbage every day. And I tend the fire. I would hardly call such contributions useless." She hated to argue with him, particularly since she usually lost. Yet bait like this demanded that she rise to her own defense.

Still holding the dead ptarmigan, Thorgunn wondered if perhaps he was being a bit too hard. Her new circumstances were no doubt dramatically different from all she had known. And her point was well taken about the vegetables and the fire.

"Very well," he agreed begrudgingly. "But this time only. The next bird is yours."

Braetana's relief at the reprieve was short lived, for observance of the task was only slightly less disgusting than the actual performance of it. The plucking was easy—it was the gutting she thought she could not bear, although, at Thorgunn's insistence she managed to do so the very next day.

Thank God, she thought, that at least her vegetables did not bleed.

That night, Braetana roasted the ptarmigan on an iron spit Thorgunn had rigged between two of the interior support beams. This process, which he called *steikja*, was a method similar to the cooking done at Glendonwyck. Though the preparation took several hours, it produced a rich and succulent meal.

The main course was served with the beetroot porridge that had become a dietary staple. And, thanks to Thorgunn's thorough knowledge of the island's vegetation, Braetana was now able to find both cabbages and an occasional onion to thicken the soup.

In keeping with the dagverror and natverror customs they had observed on the drekar, she served two meals daily; the evening meal always hot. Both were presented atop the trestle table on wooden platters.

To Braetana's delight, Thorgunn had shown her where the narrow path leading seaward branched sideways, exposing a nearly hidden thicket bursting with spring strawberries. It had been weeks since she'd enjoyed fresh fruit, and the discovery pleased her immensely. On her first visit alone to the grove she'd sat for some time, stuffing herself like a greedy child. She reveled in their taste, her nostrils full of the fruit's luscious sweet smell and her fingertips crimson from the sticky juice.

At the end of their first week together both of the cabin's residents limited their conversation to necessities. Nevertheless, they settled into a regular and comfortable routine. Thorgunn would hunt in the morning, returning with a ptarmigan and, if lucky, an occasional hare. The larder stocked, he then set out again to gather the night's firewood.

For her part, Braetana prepared both meals, filling the time in between with plant and fruit gathering. By late afternoon, when Thorgunn returned with wood, Braetana was usually seated near the hearth, cleaning the day's produce.

When the routine was broken Thorgunn initially thought little of it, assuming Braetana to have taken a longer, more leisurely route home. But as the fading light edged toward dusk, his concern grew. It was not only foolish, but also unlike her to delay so much so she would have to travel the steep, uneven path in the dark.

Correctly assuming that she had gone for strawberries, he found her halfway down the trail, sprawled across the narrow footpath and surrounded by a great spill of red fruit. Her almond-shaped eyes were glazed with tears and one berry-stained hand reached unsuccessfully toward a swollen ankle now turning a remarkable shade of blue. She had heard Thorgunn's loud approach through the bush. Not knowing it to be him, Braetana had thought herself likely to be some wild animal's dinner.

Seeing his tall frame towering above her, she spent her fear in a crescendo of sobs, their rising volume as much for relief at the sight of him as for the sharp pain from her injured foot.

Under normal circumstances, Braetana would have felt quite embarrassed at such a predicament. But the ankle now swelled and hurt badly, and she was unmindful of anything save the overwhelming pain and her need for sympathy.

"There was a root," she explained, half choking with tears and pointing to a large twisted growth rising from the trail several feet behind where she lay. "I was hurrying and I tripped. . . ." Her halting delivery trailed off as she once more began to cry.

The life of a seafaring trader had given Thorgunn

small opportunity to learn how to console distraught women. He stood silent and unsure of what he was expected to do next. She seemed so small and vulnerable now, so very unlike the tempting adversary he usually considered her to be.

He realized that he must somehow return Braetana to the house. It was clear they could not very well spend the night in this cold, unprotected place. Thorgunn inclined his head slightly, searching her contorted face with a sympathetic inquiry. "Do you think you can walk?" he asked, almost kindly.

Raising the back of one hand to wipe away the glistening tears clouding her reddened eyes, Braetana turned a childlike face to him. "I don't know," she half gasped, still struggling to control her ragged breathing. "It hurts too much to try."

"I will lift you to your feet." Before Braetana had time to consider otherwise, Thorgunn knelt beside her. Draping one of her arms across the beam of his wide shoulders, he reached in a tight grip around her slender waist.

"Ready up," he commanded, not waiting for her assent. Using the thrust of his shoulder beneath her armpit, he raised her quickly and easily to an upright stance. Braetana stood on her good foot, her right arm still slung across his muscular breadth, her other tensed awkwardly in midair.

Stilling her quivering lower lip, she braced herself for the pain to follow. Her voice filled with as much determination as she could gather.

"I will try my weight on it."

Leaning outward and shifting her stance to test the thickened ankle, Braetana realized she needn't have bothered. Even the slightest pressure filled her with waves of agony and caused her to hop back quickly onto the other foot. The loss of balance sent her equilibrium flying, and, with it, her body flat against Thorgunn's.

The unexpected embrace filled Braetana with so much embarrassment that she was at first unable to meet Thorgunn's eyes. She merely stood pressed tightly against him while staring straight ahead into his chest. Yet the shocking excitement of their closeness overrode her first instincts to free herself. Her hands opened flat at his shoulders, resting against his broad red tunic, but they made no effort to push away from him.

Twice before, once at Glendonwyck and again on the drekar, she had felt his hard muscles crush against her body. Each time, as now, his touch had filled her with a longing for something she had no words to describe.

This hunger he so easily swelled within her was terrifying in its force and need. Here was a man who, by every right, had earned her hate. Yet how could the enmity she felt for him make her so breathless and light-headed when they touched?

All the nights, first on the ship, then in the longhouse, when she had lain tensely awake, expecting every sound to be his approach, now faded from memory. At this moment, Braetana found her fear of him vanquished by an odd sense of safety and trust. Ironically, it was only when he held her that she knew he could not hurt her. It was a puzzle she couldn't explain in her current confusion.

Suddenly aware of the silence between them, Braetana looked into his eyes. She needed to get away from him in order to make sense of her thoughts. She was grateful when Thorgunn spoke first.

"The ankle's too swollen for you to walk, and we cannot stay here. I will carry you back to the house." With this edict, Thorgunn took Braetana's hand and once more curved her arm about his shoulders and neck. Easily, he reached under her back and thighs and effortlessly lifted her up into his supportive arms.

"Can you bear the pain?" He bent his head close enough toward hers so that Braetana could feel the heat of his mouth radiate onto her face. His breath smelled sweet and she breathed her own answer straight back into its honeyed warmth.

"Yes," she said softly, unmoving.

"Then hold tight around my neck," the Viking instructed. "I will try to walk evenly."

Following Thorgunn's directions, Braetana grabbed one hand with the other, encircling him with her slender arms. She was not sure the precaution was necessary. He supported her so firmly that she doubted she could have slipped free had she tried. Still, she held fast, out of fear and a disinclination to countermand him.

Thorgunn's thoughts also now returned to the first time he had held her thus. Though the mended gunna did not follow her curves as well as others he had seen her wear, he could still feel the flatness of her belly beneath its soft linen folds. The sensation filled him with a growing hunger. He hurried up the darkened path, as much to disguise his quickening breath as to end the agonizing temptation of her body in his arms.

Braetana, now as terrified of her own new sensations as she once was of Thorgunn, felt his fingers move imperceptibly across her stomach. It is because of the rocky path, she assured herself; he is not caressing me. At that instant, she wasn't sure which she preferred.

Neither spoke and the night's stillness was broken only by the rhythmic beat of Thorgunn's gait and his hard breathing.

Strangely, for her bruised and twisted ankle had fully commanded her thoughts just a short time ago, Braetana now forgot it completely. It was as if Thorgunn's hands upon her held some magic fire that healed. His touch seemed to pierce her very essence, soothing and igniting her at the same time. Surprisingly, the sight of the meadow with its turf-topped house brought less a feeling of relief than of strange disappointment. Now there would no longer be a reason for Thorgunn to hold her close to him.

The Viking's silent lament was similar. Unlike Braetana, however, Thorgunn well knew exactly what he longed for and exactly why he must not have it. Even wanting her as badly as he now did, he must resist indulging his needs.

Succumbing to his desire would mean risking all the past year's work, not to mention the restoration of his rightful position. The loss would be too great a cost for a taste of her; this was his resolution as he swung the door open and carried Braetana to the wide fur-covered bench. But as he gently laid her slender form atop the soft, supple bed skins, his will weakened and his appetite grew for the beauty who lay irresistibly before him.

The fire had waned to a warm ocher glow that showered Braetana's delicate features with a golden light. Her long, flaxen-colored hair, which of late had been gathered in a leather thong at the back of her neck, had been set free by the journey home. It now framed her exquisite face, spreading like silk across the cinnamon-colored fur and down over the bed's edge. Her rose gunna draped suggestively across her, the sides pulled downward by the fabric's weight. Each curve and contour that Thorgunn's arms had so recently possessed rose in a tantalizing silhouette.

He stared at her in confusion, his face filled with a look of disorder and hesitation Braetana had not seen before. It was as if he were asking permission for something. She was not sure what he begged for, but she sensed that, whatever his plea, she should refuse him.

She felt so close to danger. Perhaps it was because his fiery touch had made her feel consumed with desire for him. Perhaps it was because despite all she had ever been or believed in, she knew that, should he want her, she had no strength to resist, only a longing for total surrender.

Thorgunn raised one hand to her face, stroking a silky strand of errant hair across her forehead. Her skin was softer than he had imagined, like satin. The plea written in her half-closed eyes spoke clearly to Thorgunn, for he urgently wanted the same.

Braetana's breath caught in her throat at the gentleness of his touch. This was no accident, as his brush across her belly on the climb home might have been. This gesture was willful, deliberate, and wonderful. Wanting more, she turned her face into his hand, then again righted it, barely believing her wanton response.

Her body seemed less her own than some spellbound thing his sorcery could direct as he chose. He touched her face again. Unwillingly, her full lips parted in pleasure at the feel of his fingertips.

Thorgunn knew any hope of resisting her was now beyond him. Slowly, for he wished to savor this expensive passion, he lowered his open mouth to Braetana's.

Her breath was fast, part fear, part passion. Slowly, with torturous languor, he brushed his warm lips softly across hers.

Though Braetana's every fiber cried out for her to resist, her lips parted further in response. In a gasp of surprised pleasure, her chest rose suddenly at the moist play of his tongue on her ripe mouth. She had not dreamed her own flesh could feel such delicious sensations.

Soon his kiss grew in passion, his mouth now pressing down hard against her own. Braetana thought such fervor should hurt, but instead it only swelled her excitement with his deepening exploration of her.

She knew she should push him away and refuse his unholy assault, but she could not. Thorgunn's powerful body now lay alongside her, one hand cupping the smallness of her head close to his face. At Braetana's unspoken bidding, his other hand moved in a painfully slow ceremony across her arched body.

Though her mind still hosted a wild battle between her flesh's desires and her conscience, Braetana's hands seemed guided only by her need for Thorgunn. To his great delight, she buried her fingers in his wheat-hued mane, pulling him to her and pressing his mouth harder against her own. She was barely able to breathe for the force of him upon her, but she no longer cared.

In one swift movement, Thorgunn grabbed the gunna and pulled it overhead, exposing her fully naked body to his own greedy gaze and the fire's flirting light. Braetana had never been so shamelessly exposed before. Instinctively, she withdrew her hands from Thorgunn's thick hair, crossing them against her naked chest in fright and confusion.

He had not thought he could become more aroused, but the sight of her before him, partially shielding her breasts with her delicate hands, drove him to a new madness. Gently, he took each hand by its slender wrist, and, kissing each of her palms, he pressed Braetana's arms down on either side of her slim hips. Just moments ago, she had been mortified by his wanton removal of her gunna. Where was that indignation now? She needed it to battle him.

Thorgunn could think only of what a bewitching vixen she was. He needed her beyond any limit he had ever known. Foolish or not, there was now no quenching his thirst for her short of full possession. He felt himself grow hard in anticipation of her, his manhood all the more ready for the unsatisfied desires of the past several weeks.

Again Braetana's resolution to stop him failed against the agonizing sweet burn of his touch. Sensing this, Thorgunn's fingers etched a path across her skin. He slowly stroked her slender arms and shoulders. Then, as his fingertips came to rest on the ripeness of one tender breast, Braetana breathed a sharp gasp of pleasure.

Savoring the bewilderment in her wide violet eyes, Thorgunn raised one hand to his mouth, wetting one finger with his tongue. With lingering delight, he traced a torturous circle around her erect pink nipple. Just when Braetana thought she could bear no more, his hand greedily cupped the throbbing breast.

Wonderful, overlapping sensations flooded her sensibilities, each barely giving her time to comprehend its sweetness before it was supplanted by another. Braetana had never experienced anything so confusing and exciting. She could only think of the wild pitch of the drekar before she was helplessly borne away from it. She wondered if some great oceanic crest would now again take the feel of her feet from beneath her.

In an instant, Braetana felt Thorgunn shift his head down, the moist pull of his mouth gently teasing her breast's peak. A lightninglike chill wound its way down the length of her spine. This was the most exquisite surrender she could imagine.

Thorgunn's mouth continued its maddening possession of her warm flesh. His tongue brought each breast's rosy tip to a delicious ache, while his hands continued their brazen exploration, lingering lovingly on every inch of Braetana's tingling skin as he caressed her flat, firm belly, toward the treasure below. His fingers paused in the golden hair that crowned her taut thighs, swirling her soft blond curls into beautiful peaks.

Just as when she had become prisoner to the sea's unleashed passion, Braetana could hardly breathe. She gasped involuntarily at Thorgunn's every touch, yet she felt no alarm.

Unabashedly, he gently teased her, leaving her helpless to resist his daring fondling. As he slipped one flattened hand between her silky thighs, parting them slightly, Braetana, for the first time, actually cried out loud in pleasure. The sound surprised and embarrassed her. But no longer ignorant of where she most craved his searing touch, her hands made no move to stop him.

Gently at first, then with increasing force, Thorgunn's fingers entered her, slipping easily in and out of her welcoming wetness. Thorgunn heard her ragged breath.

Remembering her a maiden still, he knew the task was his to show her the path to even greater pleasure.

Freeing his hand from her, he paired it with his other on the velvet silkiness of her inner thighs, then gently pushed her legs ever so slightly apart.

With his withdrawal from her, Braetana's eyes flew wide open, pleading with him, catching Thorgunn's with a wish her voice could not yet speak. Sensing that her need matched his own, he suddenly swung from alongside and poised above her. His weight sealed them tightly together as his knees pressed her legs wider in preparation for his entry.

He ached to fill her, to take her fast and hard, but something inexplicable restrained him—not the greed that had checked his desires thus far, but something more akin to a gentler part of him that wished not to hurt her. Perhaps it was this that Braetana saw in his softened eyes as he rested, poised above her. Whatever lurked behind his hesitation, Braetana could bear it no more. However wrong what she was about to do, she wished nothing to stop it.

"Please," she breathed, her panting voice seeming to belong to someone else. Thorgunn both heard and saw the request in her passion-filled face.

He needed no further encouragement. Instantly his mouth crushed down upon her own. Then, with one sure stroke, he glided fully inside her, filling her soft chasm. Suddenly a dagger of unexplainably sharp pain shot through her, bringing an abrupt end to her arching movement beneath him. She speedily released her arms from around his back and pressed them against his bronze chest in an effort to free herself from their intimacy.

Thorgunn felt her jump and slowed his rhythm in response. He moved more gently in and out of her now, his hands lovingly stroking her head.

"Shhh . . ." he murmured, "it will pass."

Braetana opened her mouth to protest, but before she could speak she sensed he told the truth. The sharp sting between her legs almost immediately began to fade, and in a moment it was replaced by the wonderful fullness of Thorgunn inside her.

Braetana could not believe she was allowing such a shameful fate to befall her. But each time, just as she nearly marshaled the will to decry Thorgunn's brash violation, he again entered her, and she knew that she was unable to refuse him.

Soon his thrusts gained speed until each ended in a pounding gasp of pleasure, Thorgunn's repeated withdrawal bearable only for the thrilling reentry she knew would quickly follow. Braetana moaned out loud as he rode her. Thorgunn reached both hands around to cup her firm buttocks and pull her impossibly closer. It seemed he could penetrate no deeper, and yet they both struggled toward exactly that end. She had never known such oneness was possible, yet she felt they moved as a single person, that their bodies arching and releasing together in an explosive dance of passion was exactly what was meant to be.

With a deep animal growl, Thorgunn spilled himself into her, completing their union with several final convulsive thrusts. He collapsed atop her, the dampness of their labors sealing them together.

As her coherence returned, Braetana, for the first time since he had laid her down, felt a sudden hot flush of shame. She lay beneath him, her labored breathing slowing in horror at recognition of what had just happened.

She had offered up her maidenhood to a man to whom she was not only unwed, but who also was her captor. She had surrendered her honor to a heathen who had just satisfied his most base desires with her body.

Although his hardness had drained from him, Thorgunn remained inside Braetana. He still filled her with the humiliation of their unholy union.

"Get off!" she screamed. Braetana pressed her hands uselessly against him, struggling to free herself of his considerable weight.

Thorgunn lifted his head to look at her, once more suspending himself slightly above her.

"It is a little late for such a change of heart." His voice bespoke his amazement at the sudden storm that brewed beneath him. "But as you wish." He adopted a look somewhere between annoyance and bemusement. "Though it seemed but a moment ago that I was quite welcome."

"You were not!" countered Braetana. "Unless you consider your overpowering me to be willingness on my part." Braetana knew her accusation was a lie. Given the current circumstances, however, she could do no better. She would certainly not admit to having encouraged his seduction, though, incomprehensibly, it seemed as though that was exactly what had happened. She and her conscience would sort this out later. For now, preventing a second humiliating assault was the important matter at hand.

"Call it what you will, lady. But if our coupling was not to your liking, I assure you it will not happen again

. . . though you should know your opinion has not been shared by my other victims."

Braetana missed the jest. "Victims, yes," she muttered. "Exactly. I certainly was."

Thorgunn, who had his own problems regarding Braetana's willing surrender to him, had no inclination to parry further with his partner's twisted truth. Refastening his breeches, he retrieved his scarlet tunic from the floor and strode to his own makeshift chamber. As she turned her head away from him, Braetana could hear him bring the curtained partition to near closure before he fired a final volley.

"Rest easy," he offered, "your precious honor can suffer no more tonight."

Braetana responded with an angry bang of her good bare foot on the wooden pallet and an indignant "Humph!" then buried her burning face in the soft fur beneath her.

What had happened was so terrible, so deeply degrading, that she could hardly bear to think of it. At first she made a valiant but futile attempt to ease the entire incident from her mind. But the rich memory of their incredible union consistently vanquished all such efforts. Braetana sensed it would be a long time, if ever, before she could banish Thorgunn's touch from her thoughts.

Bravely, she struggled to reconcile the abhorrent act with the knowledge that she had allowed it. She had never in her life entertained thoughts of such familiarity with a man, certainly not with a man she didn't even like. What had overridden her upbringing and the ethics it had instilled in her?

In her heart, Braetana sensed that she had been lost

from his first indecent touch, indeed from the time he had carried her back up the winding trail. From that moment on, she knew well that only an unlikely act of self-restraint on Thorgunn's part could have prevented the disgraceful end to what her desire for him had begun.

If she were to be absolutely truthful with herself, she would have to admit she wanted him still. God, how could it be that some unfinished longing in her cried out to replay each illicit touch, each passionate kiss, each shameful thrust? How could she hate the man and still feel thus? Surely the mast had damaged her mind in order for her own body to betray her so. Had she been elsewhere besides a remote cabin on a lost North Sea island, Braetana might well have devoted more thought to the matrimonial ramifications of her deflowering. But now, with the threat to her integrity lying but feet away, she could only think that she must never allow herself to lose control this way again.

Somehow she must strengthen her will against the hazards of her own desires. She must remind herself, as often as need be, that he was heathen, her captor, and someone she could not trust.

With this resolution in mind, she closed her eyes, then parted her lips once more at the thought of his hungry mouth possessing her own.

Thorgunn, whom Braetana would have guessed now slept soundly, sat upright on the bench's edge, reflecting on his own unplanned actions. Yesterday he would have thought such a scenario catastrophic. Now, after the unfortunate fact of its occurrence, he struggled toward the hope that it was not so. Yet any cause for optimism seemed weak; Magnus certainly expected Braetana delivered in good condition. Thorgunn construed that to mean with honor unsullied.

Though the same act with other women might not make him the villain, Thorgunn knew that Magnus would consider his defilement of Braetana a clear breach of their bargain. Were the charge made, it would be difficult to defend, especially if Braetana chose to support it. The accusation would also be impossible to refute to the husband who would eventually claim her assumed virtue.

Usually cast as quite the opposite from a virgin-maker, Thorgunn had never before turned his talents to manufacturing innocence. Rubbing his brow with one hand, he realized he was inept to deal with this unusual task. If only he could undo the last few hours. A few moments of pleasure and now everything was lost between a wench's legs!

His passions had probably cost him his fortune. But there was an aspect to his behavior that he found even more disturbing. He had been unable to control himself. Though he had desired and taken women before, he had never yet suffered the complete loss of control the Saxon witch evoked. She had captivated him with those lilac eyes, cast a spell that made him burn fever hot at the touch of her and grow urgently hard with his need to possess her.

What a paradox this silky-haired enchantress was! He knew her to be untouched, for he had heard others cry with the pain of their first man. Yet what she had shown him was no virgin's ride; instead it was the wild mount of a woman well skilled in giving men pleasure. The arch of her back to meet him, the swell of her hips as they rose time after time to welcome his thrust—this was the madness that made him unable to stop, whatever the cost.

Thorgun wondered just how much his actions had cost him. If she were given to someone else in marriage, as Magnus no doubt would eventually arrange, his secret could not be kept. But were *he* her husband, he would have her silence and Magnus's fortune too! Perhaps he would not have to surrender all he had worked for.

The silver Magnus had offered him for returning Braetana was but a tiny fraction of his entire estate. They were holdings that, because Magnus's son Ingvar was killed last fall in battle, would now pass entirely to Braetana as his only surviving child.

The price for the trade, of course, would be his freedom. It was an exchange he had not thought to make so precipitously. Thorgunn as loving husband was not an image he had often entertained. He had always considered women greedy and duplicitous, full of tricks when they thought him moneyed and quick to leave when they discovered he was not. A wench was good for a ride when he was full of mead, but as a lifetime companion he had always thought himself better suited to Loki. Still, there was much to be gained here; and perhaps much more to be lost if he balked.

Magnus would think withholding the ransom insufficient redress for his daughter's shame. He might well expect Thorgunn's head in the bargain. An aging man who was no match for Thorgunn's twenty-six years, Magnus would choose a champion to seek his justice. Thorgunn's formidable battle skills would most likely see him prevail, but he was not eager to anger his brethren by killing another warrior in a challenge over a wench.

He tried to picture Braetana as wife. Of all those he had known, she would probably serve as well as any. She was beautiful to behold, her long flaxen hair and full ripe breasts as bedeviling as any. And he already knew she could arouse and satisfy him with unrivaled skill. Still, she could be contentious, and the spirit that had proven so entertaining in a cabin mate could become a nuisance in a lifelong companion.

She will learn, he thought. *The village women will teach her to feed me and bed me, then leave me to go about my business unhampered.* In time she would be a tolerable match, all the more so for the rich dower she would bring to their marriage bed.

Convincing Magnus of the merits of his plan might be difficult, however. Thorgunn's impoverishment did little to recommend him. Yet the elder had no need to make his daughter a money match, for he could provide for her lavishly enough himself. Perhaps the prospect of a royal son-in-law, however impecunious, would tempt the old jarl.

More than anything, though, the success of his plan hinged on Braetana. If Thorgunn could win her to his cause, Magnus was unlikely to wed his only daughter against her wishes. It all rested on Braetana's compliance. Judging from her current mood, such agreement might prove the greatest obstacle yet.

Thorgunn recalled their heated coupling of moments ago. She had shown him no resistance there. But though the lady's legs might have opened for him once, her subsequent behavior seemed to indicate they would not do so again. Given Braetana's denouncement of his charms, he was disinclined to discount her current convictions.

Einar would be here by month's end and Thorgunn had only until that time to turn Braetana's fury to love. He did not want for courting skills, but the time was brief and the task considerable. He knew he needed a well-defined plan, one that, when followed, would leave her not only willing but also begging to wed him.

He must court her, woo her without her knowledge until she ached to be with him and came to him willingly. The idea would seem hers; the battle spoils would be his for the taking.

Thorgunn considered how little she knew of her real situation and how that ignorance could damage his chances with her. In her current state, she thought him heathen, less than a Saxon; that attitude would not serve his interests.

He would do better to tell her the truth—that her real heritage rendered her more like him than not. Perhaps then she would return home willingly and, in doing so, find a new life in a distant place less frightening alongside a man she already knew. Yes, he would wait for the proper time, then bind her to him with both heritage and passion.

The matter of the silver would have to remain his secret with Magnus. Braetana would not give herself to him if she thought herself bought. How would she consider his suit if she thought he loved only her silver? Their respective finances must be concealed as much as possible until the wedding. By then, he would already have gained the wealth that his birthright commanded.

Thorgunn settled into the fur bed skins, content with his shrewdly crafted plan and confident he would succeed. Tomorrow, he thought, we shall begin. With that, he drifted into a distant, relaxed sleep, his dreams full of the night's earlier pleasures.

VIII

The hearth looked nearly as cold as Braetana felt. She was shivering, and an aching numbness filled her. To make matters worse, she was completely naked. It had not been her custom to sleep this way, but the tumultuous events of the preceding evening had not only prevented her from maintaining the fire, they had brought about her chilly state of undress as well.

In truth, she could not specifically remember the removal of the blue linen gunna. What she did recall, quite vividly, was Thorgunn's mouth, insistently and hungrily upon her own and his strong hands stroking and caressing her soft flesh with a skill she would not have guessed one so coarse could possess.

My God, she despaired, bringing both hands to her blushing face in embarrassment, *what have I done?* Braetana knew only that she must resolve to prevent any such future degradation. She shook her head as if to cast off any contrary inclination, then settled her eyes on the cold black coals.

Braetana felt an icy wave of discouragement wash over her. She realized that, for the first time since she had entered the cabin, she would have to repeat the difficult process of building a fire.

If she chose not to build the fire, Thorgunn most probably would. But the thought of any unnecessary reliance on the blackguard who had taken such shameful liberties with her filled Braetana with abhorrence. With tired determination, she resolved to rekindle the flames herself, even if the task proved as vexing as her first effort had.

Braetana forced herself to cast off the bearskin coverlet. She knew that delaying the work would not lessen her freezing distress, and she leaned over and recovered the blue gown from the floor alongside the bed, then stood to dress herself. Only then, as she applied weight to the swollen left ankle, did she recall how this whole disaster with Thorgunn had begun.

With an audible gasp of pain, Braetana tumbled backward onto the bed, both hands dropping the gunna and instinctively reaching to clutch her throbbing foot. The once slender ankle had now enlarged to nearly twice its normal size, its increased girth ringed by a bruised band ranging in color from deep plum to a most unattractive amber. The sprain was severe, as was the accompanying pain that now mounted with every effort she made to knead away its stiffness.

Clearly, the joint could bear no weight. This inconvenience would harshly curtail the independence to which she had grown accustomed. Still, she hoped to retain some mobility. After succeeding with much difficulty in dressing herself from a sitting position, she managed to pull a broom handle toward her that she thought might help support her.

The arrangement was less than ideal, but Braetana was pleased to find that, by shifting her weight from the injured foot to the broom's pine staff, she was able to move, albeit with an ungainly hopping motion. With this new means of ambulation, she struggled to make her way to the hearth where she began the tedious task of striking the flint on the cold stone.

Thorgunn had lain awake on his pallet for some time. He had thought to afford his companion the privacy she would now wish in light of the previous night's events. But the odd sound of the pole's jump on the sod floor, coupled with the familiar but unexpected ring of flint striking stone, piqued his curiosity. Unable to resist, he rose and separated the thick curtains for a view into the central chamber.

"Good morrow." Thorgunn was careful to impart the greeting with no more meaning than those of previous mornings. "The fire is dead?"

"Yes," Braetana replied with as much normalcy as she could muster, ignoring the obvious explanation for the cold hearth. "I am rekindling it now."

Thorgunn walked to the raised side aisle opposite Braetana's hearthside labors. She had not yet donned the goatskin slippers and the painfully bright ankle immediately drew his attention.

"I see your fall has left its mark." He gestured toward the swollen foot. Braetana made no answer, her eyes pointedly trained on her bungling efforts to produce a spark.

"I would willingly make the fire," Thorgunn offered, almost beseechingly.

"I can do it," Braetana snapped, not at all confident she could.

"I'm sure my lady can. It just appears your foot must be quite painful, and I thought perhaps this once you would do better to rest it in bed." Bed. The word fell like an ax between them, nearly shattering their strained efforts at civility.

If Braetana had been able to walk, she would have been hard-pressed not to run from the room at that moment.

"Please?" He extended his large hand for the tools. It struck Braetana that she had never heard Thorgunn use that word before. In fact, he had rarely asked her for anything, his talents lying more fully in his ability to command what he wanted. Yet, whether or not his offer of aid was sincere, it was sure to save her several miserably uncomfortable hours on the cold, sod floor.

"Very well," she conceded reluctantly, dropping the flint and stone alongside the hearth and conspicuously avoiding any physical contact with him.

"Thank you." She spat out the words, emphasizing her already transparent sentiments about the preceding night's tumultuous events.

Thorgunn's eyes registered what Braetana perceived as unexpected gratitude at her concession.

"Can you move unaided?"

"Yes." Her response reflected her terror that any delay would bring him springing forth to help her. "The broom works fine." She gestured toward it.

It was apparent the broom didn't work well at all, but Thorgunn allowed Braetana to struggle with it. He was relieved when she finally reached the pallet's edge.

Within moments he had successfully struck the fire, stoking it with abundant birch. Almost immediately, its heat began to fill the frigid room, chasing off the morning chill and improving Braetana's comfort dramatically.

Once the hearth blazed healthily, Thorgunn prepared dagverror, then soaked a linen strip in cold water and instructed Braetana to apply the dressing to her injured foot. At first the compress increased her discomfort. Then, as its chill worked through the swollen flesh, it gradually deadened the earlier throbbing. This, coupled with Thorgunn's suggestion that a little beer might aid the healing process, or at least make Braetana more oblivious to it, proved a therapeutic combination.

By the start of the next morning, Braetana felt again ready to try her weight on the tender joint. As she reached for the nearby broom, Thorgunn approached her and placed his hand on the stem.

"Wait, I have something better for you."

Braetana arched one eyebrow skeptically. She couldn't have been more surprised when the Viking produced another piece of pine, this one with an armrest mounted horizontally across the pole's top.

"You made this for me?" she asked incredulously.

"You are not much good to me in bed." Thorgunn was unable to resist a slight smile at his unintended play on words. "I mean to say, your chores will be easier if you can walk. I thought this would be an improvement over the broom."

Thorgunn placed the T-shaped support beneath Braetana's arm. As he backed away, she began to gingerly apply weight to the new device. To her delight, the movement she was able to achieve was significantly more effective and less painful than either the one-legged hopping or broom-assisted hobbling she had previously been reduced to. Perhaps she had underestimated his heathen ingenuity.

"I thought these might please you." Thorgunn extended a basket brimming with luscious vermilion fruit to Braetana.

"It is the fourth time in as many days you have gathered me strawberries. One would think you credited them with medicinal properties."

"They do seem to improve your mood."

Braetana was both baffled and somewhat uncomfortable with Thorgunn's newfound courtesy. Ever since their embarrassing intimacy, he had shown her a respect that hardly suited her image of him. Were such kindnesses mere concessions to her injured foot? Or was he perhaps feeling guilty for his unabashed assault on her?

"You needn't worry about my mood. It's unlikely to improve 'til I again see Glendonwyck." Thorgunn sensed her growing agitation. Gathering the berries had been an attempt to please her, and now, he'd inadvertently undone all he'd gained.

"I will leave the fruit here." Thorgunn set the basket atop the trestle table next to her. As was his new custom these last few difficult days, he was careful to avoid any physical contact. The effort did not go unnoticed by Braetana.

"I *am* fond of them. Thank you." As she reached for and plucked one of the ripe red berries, Braetana saw the quick withdrawal of Thorgunn's hand. She could not help but wonder what had engendered this change in his attitude.

He had certainly demonstrated no aversion to her that fateful night. Yet, ever since, he took great pains to avoid her touch. Thorgunn even allowed her to struggle with difficulty on the makeshift crutch, both of them knowing even a small amount of assistance from him would have eased her plight considerably.

Could it be that he had found something objectionable in their coupling? Braetana knew she now looked much the bedraggled shipwreck survivor—her mended dress still worn and snagged and her blond hair tied tightly at the nape of her neck, in concession to her daily tasks. Her already ungainly movement was made even less attractive by the appendage of the ridiculous pine crutch. She was hardly the prize gentler circumstances had once made her.

Suddenly, she snapped her head sideways, amazed at her own thinking. Whatever was the matter with her? Was she not thrilled that he no longer seemed likely to again assail her virtue? Was not this what she'd barely dared hope for?

"I trust it is not bitter." Thorgunn, having seen Braetana twist her neck, attributed the response to a rotten berry.

"What?" Braetana could barely answer, her mouth was so full of the juicy fruit.

"Is the berry bad?"

"No. It's fine. I was just thinking of the beetroot."

"Einar is likely to bring some improved fare."

"This Viking—Einar—he comes every year?" Braetana asked, relieved to change her thoughts' focus.

"Yes, the summer watch was a custom begun by my father Harald to curtail the Frisian piracy. Their trading at Hedeby earns them much silver, but only so long as they've wares to sell. In recent years, the less industrious among them have come to find boarding our goods-laden ships an easier choice than mounting their own sails. This outpost, though lightly manned, serves to deter their plundering."

Thorgunn was encouraged by Braetana's question for he saw her interest as a small but hopeful step toward learning and accepting the heritage they both shared.

It did not surprise him that the Saxon in her feared and hated his kin. The raids of the last twenty years, some by his own brethren, others by Frisians and Jutlanders, hardly earned them a congenial recommendation. Still, were he to succeed with his plan to win her, he needed her trust. He doubted she would offer it for anything less than the shocking truth he had to tell.

Braetana turned away from Thorgunn, her tense stance conveying her annoyance.

"Hedeby. Trondbergen. Nordmannaland. The words are as strange as the hellish fellows these places send forth. What could you want with a Saxon there?"

Thorgunn issued a quick, silent prayer to Odin that what he was about to say would earn him something other than her angry hand slapping his cheek.

"I want nothing with you. It is your father you have business with."

Braetana's brow furrowed for an instant, then released as she laid the crutch atop the table. Leaning back against it, she set both hands on her hips.

"I am truly ill disposed to listen to your riddles today."

"It is no riddle, lady. Though it may seem at first to defy your sensibilities."

"I asked why you had taken me. Do I understand I am now to receive the answer you have denied me ever since our miserable introduction?"

"Only if you wish to hear it." Thorgunn knew he must pace the delivery of what he had to tell her, letting it out only as quickly as Braetana could take it in.

"I think you should be seated."

"Please," sputtered Braetana, nearly exasperated by Thorgunn's reluctance. Then, seeing he had no intention of proceeding without her compliance, she gently lowered herself to the sod floor. Her violet eyes narrowed skeptically in a burning review of him.

"Well?"

Thorgunn could see her impatience would little bear any further delay.

"Your mother Eirlinn did not always live in England," he began, his efforts immediately bringing the response Thorgunn feared.

"How dare you speak of my mother!" exclaimed Braetana. "How do you even know her name?"

"Please, hear my tale. Then you can shout at me with your accusations." Thorgunn took her silence as agreement.

"Your mother once lived in Trondbergen. She was mistress to a man, a Viking jarl called Magnus. And you are their child—half-Viking, half-Saxon. When your mother left him, Magnus did not know where to seek her. But when he learned your whereabouts, he charged me with bringing you home."

Thorgunn paused, watching the full weight of the words come to bear on Braetana. The confusion that was apparent on her firelit face gave her a childlike look, as if she had suddenly lost her way in the woods and struggled to recall the path she had taken.

"My father was a Saxon lord," she protested slowly and deliberately, moving toward anger.

"Your mother's husband perhaps," Thorgunn corrected, "not your father." He could see that Braetana still did not believe him. "Magnus is your father. Whatever tale your mother spun to conceal her past I do not know. But I can tell you, as Odin is my witness, you are Magnus's daughter."

The story was too incredible to be true, even if it could serve to explain Thorgunn's abduction of her.

"England is large," Braetana reasoned out loud. "How could you know I was the one you sought."

"The pendant. Magnus holds its mate."

Until that moment, all thought of her mother's lost ear clip had been forgotten. Thorgunn's reminder brought Braetana's hand to her slender throat, her fingers touching the familiar spot where the jet and amber jewel had once lain.

"Where is it?" she demanded angrily.

Thorgunn sighed. "Lost in the storm, I fear. But no matter. Magnus will take me at my word." He had his doubts about this, but there was little point in confiding them to his already upset charge.

"Liar!" Braetana countered. "Had I worn a horsehair bracelet, you could have easily made that a gift from this Viking Magnus."

Thorgunn's expression registered his appreciation of her logic.

"Yes, true enough. And yet how would I know the necklace began as half of a pair?"

Braetana was dumbfounded. Had she told him this? She could not recall doing so, but . . . suddenly her thoughts jumped to the conclusion that must follow if Thorgunn did not lie.

"Then Magnus had her killed! How else would the other ear clip have returned to his possession?"

Braetana was beginning to believe Thorgunn's story, and hot, smarting tears filled the pools of her beautiful eyes, dampening her rosy cheeks.

"No." Thorgunn sensed his well-laid scheme turning sour. "It was not Magnus. The piece was taken by Frisians—they apparently missed its mate. The ear clip they stole was bartered at a trade market in Hedeby. When Magnus saw it, he recognized it and questioned them as to its source, for he had always hoped that Eirlinn still lived. Many years ago, when he learned that your mother had fled when she was with child, he had prayed that both she and her offspring could be returned to him. I traveled to Glendonwyck expecting to find both Eirlinn and her child. Once there, I learned from Edward that only you still survived."

Braetana considered Thorgunn's incredible story. "If this is true, then how came my mother to Nordmanna-land at all? Will you tell me she chose to leave England to become a heathen's wife?"

Thorgunn knew the answer but sensed it would little please Braetana. Eirlinn had been a pirate's captive, sold to Magnus at the Hedeby slave market. It was only later that she had willingly become his mistress, a fate that was directly responsible for her flight from Trond-bergen. Finding herself with child, Eirlinn had appar-ently left in fear for her unborn's safety. It was a legitimate concern in light of Magnus's wife Thyri's hatred toward her. To challenge Thyri's legitimate son's inheritance with another would surely have spelled doom for both Eirlinn and her baby. Thorgunn searched for an answer he could safely tell her.

"How did she get there?" Braetana angrily repeated the question.

"The Frisians trade many wares—silver, spices, wound Frank blades—and occasionally slaves."

"You say the Frisians kidnapped my mother?"

"Yes." Thorgunn was relieved that this much, at least, did not have to be laid at his village's feet.

"But this man Magnus—he bought her? He bought my mother?"

Thorgunn was beginning to wonder if his plan to make Braetana trust him had been an imprudent one. Once in Trondbergen, Braetana would eventually learn everything. Yet in his eagerness to educate her, he seemed to have stirred up her rage. Worse yet, Braetana misheard him—she thought her mother had been Magnus's wife. Thorgunn decided to let this point pass.

"Magnus treated your mother well," he offered.

"Truly?" Braetana's fury was almost palpable. "Then why did she flee him?"

"She feared for your future. And so it was said she bought passage to Jutland on a Frankish trade ship. How she returned to England from there I do not know."

Braetana would now need to ponder Thorgunn's selective truth. He would wait and hope that she would not only believe him but also forgive him the undesirable task of bearing such devastating news.

Eirlinn's abduction did not make for a very compassionate tale. In truth, he could not fault Braetana for her anger. Despite his best efforts to exonerate Magnus, the old jarl had bought Eirlinn, a piece of business sure to be ill thought of in Saxon eyes.

Thorgunn sat watching a pensive and silent Braetana sort through the debris of her mistaken heritage. It occured to him that perhaps he had gone about this badly. Perhaps his position could have been turned to better advantage had he dissociated himself from the actions of those she now had good reason to hate. Although he was Viking, he hoped Braetana could somehow come to see him as an ally against Magnus.

As her mother had already learned, Thorgunn knew Braetana could not contend against her father's wishes and win. Still, it could only help his cause to allow her to think she might prevail.

Thorgunn stoked the fading hearth, clearing his throat as he narrowed his gaze on Braetana's face. She sat close to him, yet her impassive eyes made her seem remote.

"I would I could help you," Thorgunn offered gently.

"I've had enough of your help." Braetana's voice was drained of emotion, her energy spent in her efforts to comprehend the upheaval Thorgunn's news had wrought.

"I do not even know that you tell the truth. And if I believe that you do, what could you offer me now?" She lifted her gaze from the fire into the beam of Thorgunn's unrelenting stare.

She was exquisite, even in her torment. The fire's glow lit her luminous lilac eyes, infusing them with the radiant light of fine opals. Thorgunn's blood raced with the memory of their coupling, bringing a familiar needy ache to his loins. Whatever reservations he had about wedding her, they were not shared by his body.

At that moment, he longed to go around the hearth and press her down, taking her greedily on the cool sod beneath them. But he knew such an indulgence would see the night's hard work easily undone. Though he was not altogether sure he could rise in his current excited state, he answered her question.

"Perhaps it would help simply to leave you to your thoughts. Good eve, lady." Despite his discomfort, Thorgunn stood and left the central chamber, partitioning himself off in the cooler end room. A reflective Braetana sat alone in the warm reflection of the dancing flames.

As she had often been of late, Braetana was surprised by Thorgunn's thoughtfulness. She appreciated the solitude. Had she ever imagined his answer to her insistent questions, she was not sure she'd have chosen to ask.

In many ways, her earlier ignorance proved easier than the task of sorting truth from lie in Thorgunn's incredible tale. It all seemed too strange. And if she were to give credence to his heretical description of her past, it meant her life thus far had been a fraud. She had believed a lifetime of lies from her mother, lies about the man she'd believed to be her father, secrets even about the very blood that pulsed through her veins.

Now that she thought about it, it *was* odd that Eirlinn always spoke so hesitantly of the man Braetana called father. She knew little of Sir William, save that he had died fighting off a Viking attack.

Was it possible her mother's silence bespoke a terrible lie? If so, Braetana needn't search far for Eirlinn's motive in keeping silence. A kidnap and rape by a Viking captor, as Braetana knew all too well, was a shocking degradation. It was not something any victim would willingly admit to.

Braetana looked down at her soft goatskin slippers. Had she any other foot coverings, she would have ripped them off, then cast the shoes into the roaring fire.

Right now, any further suggestion, however superficial, that she was indeed half-heathen, was too hurtful to bear.

She rose and walked to the pine wardrobe coffer, retrieving from its bottom the small metal mirror she used to style her hair. Slowly and deliberately, she raised the oval in front of her until her reflection stood level with her face. It was as if Braetana had never really seen herself before, for now she sensed she was no longer the same. She searched the strange image for some clue to a past that, though always present, had thus far remained hidden.

Raising her slender hand to touch her tearstained cheek, Braetana traced the finely chiseled geography of each curve and hollow. Her trembling fingers brushed a course over her eyes and nose, ending on her full, parted lips. A barely audible sigh escaped them as she continued to study her reflection.

How blond her hair now seemed in a stark contrast to Eirlinn's raven tresses. How strange she had not considered this before, thinking it only an oddity of heritage. But perhaps the real reason was a parentage she had never known.

No! Some anguished voice cried out deep within her, its only outward sound the crash of polished metal against the birch beamed wall. Thorgunn, who sat silently on the curtain's other side, hoped with all his heart it was only the mirror and not his future that Braetana had shattered.

IX

Two weeks after Braetana had first washed onto the island's shore and three days after Thorgunn had stunned her with the incredible revelation of her true parentage, Braetana was in turmoil, struggling hard against accepting what she did not want to believe. But each argument she mounted succumbed in the face of Thorgunn's quick responses.

Braetana was now sure she hadn't mentioned the pair of ear clips to him. Therefore he would have no way of knowing the jewel had an identical mate—unless his unlikely story were true. She decided to reserve final judgment until Magnus showed her the other amber and jet piece. Although she refused to believe that she could be half-Viking, the possibility still consumed her thoughts.

If Thorgunn told the truth, she wondered how many others knew. Could Bronwyn and even Edward have been privy to her mother's shameful past? Braetana did not know the exact length of Eirlinn's captivity, but surely even a short absence from Glendonwyck could not have gone easily unexplained. Because England was now far away and Bronwyn lay somewhere beneath the sea's gray waves, these were questions Braetana had little hope of answering.

Assuming Thorgunn's assurances of imminent rescue would come true, she would soon have only a frightening new future amid the strangers she had been raised to fear. Thorgunn said Magnus wanted her back; he had wanted her mother too, to the suffering Eirlinn's great disadvantage.

What hope did she have to expect better treatment at the hands of a man capable of purchasing her mother? Even if her blood were half-Norse, she doubted it would buy her any more freedom than Eirlinn enjoyed. Life had taught Braetana to expect the worst from men.

Thorgunn's behavior of late, however, had borne out few of her fears, for his attentions to her continued to be most courteous and gentlemanly. In fact, lately he seemed so respectful that his actions bordered on paternal.

Yet if his cool manner was now far from the fervor of their one night of intimacy, the memory of that passion was never far from her thoughts. Like the recurring pain in her ankle, it was ever-present, intruding without warning on her waking hours and unfailingly filling her dreams with the heat of his fiery touch.

To her great consternation, Braetana seemed devoid of morals while sleeping, for her nighttime visions of Thorgunn came more as delightful reveries than the nightmares they should have been. It was only upon waking that her mind was able to replace the delicious sensations of his hands on her body with the shame that was the more proper response to such actions.

Exactly one week from her injury in the berry copse, Braetana's ankle had healed considerably. Her renewed mobility brought on a corresponding optimism in her attitude, making her more like her old self and the pensive mood she adopted in the days following Thorgunn's revelation had transformed into an unexpected calm that Thorgunn found difficult to understand.

If asked, Braetana herself might not have been able to explain her changed disposition, for an honest review of her current circumstances hardly left her much about which to rejoice. Shipwrecked with a stranger who had already taken advantage of her, possibly fathered by a man she had every reason to detest, and bound for a home she did not wish to claim, Braetana faced a most uncertain future.

And yet, as complicated as her life promised to be, the present had been reduced to a welcome simplicity, especially when compared to the trauma of the weeks before. Braetana's routine of mundane tasks were now familiarly simple and her successful execution of them was comforting. To her relief, she found herself at peace and more resourceful than before her arrival on the remote North Sea island.

Beetroot and cabbage! Though Braetana remained grateful that the plentiful fare had allowed her to survive those first few solitary days on the island, she now wished sorely for the appearance of any other vegetable. Even onions were a rare find, despite Braetana's nearly constant search for them.

With Thorgunn's departure to hunt the day's ptarmigan, Braetana too had taken off across the meadow. To her delight, she discovered a previously undisclosed side trail. Perhaps this would present her with some new food possibilities. At the sight of some encouraging shoots, she leaned to pull out the mysterious plant, but instead found something quite inedible beneath it.

"Touch it not!" Thorgunn's voice warned from across the meadow's considerable breadth. Braetana looked up to see him running hard toward her. His face was suffused with anger, the intensity of which she had only seen once before at Glendonwyck when she had vigorously kicked his shins.

She stood up in fear. He looked as if he wanted to kill her.

"*Never* touch that! It must not see the light of day."

Braetana's mouth dropped open. "It is but a rock," she protested in bewilderment. "I thought the plant on top of it might serve for our supper."

"It is no simple rock." Thorgunn now looked somewhat less furious.

"It is a rune."

"Ruin?"

"Rune. I doubt there is a Saxon translation. They are carvings, often made in stone, sometimes wood. Odin sets their powers free."

"You truly believe this stone wields power?" Braetana stared at the smooth granite's face. *A typically backward pagan notion,* she thought.

"Underneath, on the belly you nearly turned toward sunlight, are runes, writings which hold great magic. From its placement, this one is surely a memorial to slain Vikings. Such runes are carved in darkness and kept from the sun. Their mysteries are only for the dead. You would have defiled it."

"You really think this rock holds some sorcery?" Braetana found the idea preposterous. She was precariously close to smiling. Thorgunn, however, looked so serious she held the urge in check.

"Most assuredly, lady, it does."

"It has worked some magic on your head for you to value it so. Even if it is some commemoration of dead Vikings, as you say it is, it is still only etching on rock."

"Hardly so. Runes are cut only by baying men."

"I would have thought only wolves bay. Vikings do so too?"

A look of exasperation flickered across Thorgunn's face. "Baying men are priests who understand the rune's powers. The strength lies always in the stone—only the baying men can reveal it. Even Odin himself did not create this force. He merely sent us word of it. Saxons have nothing of this sort?"

Braetana considered the question. "Well, I suppose there are relics. But Christians certainly don't worship rocks."

"I have heard some of your kind send their prayers to trees."

Braetana knew it to be true. The marsh people, those unschooled in the true faith, did consider nature a god of sorts. It was a heresy she had been raised to abhor.

"I would hardly call them my kind. They are heathens."

"Like Vikings," Thorgunn added. His intention was not to antagonize her, but to point out that Saxons, too, held beliefs that differed sharply from Braetana's. He could see her consider the point, then recover her philosophical footing.

"Anyone who does not follow the one true God is a blasphemer. Is it not true you worship many gods?" Although Braetana still wore a look of distaste, Thorgunn was encouraged by her curiosity.

"We have as many gods as are necessary for our daily tasks. Odin creates and sees all. He rules from Valhalla with its endless doors and commands the world from his throne Hlidskjalf. There is also my namesake Thor, who is god of the common man. And Ull, whose benevolence has helped my bow find its mark. These and many more are the race Aesir. The Vanir, the other kin, count Njord and Frey among them."

"And what does Frey do?" Strangely, Braetana now seemed genuinely interested in the Norse pantheon.

Thorgunn paused hesitantly. This was not a conversational turn he had intended to take. But she had asked.

"Frey is the god of pleasure."

"Such as dancing and sport?"

"It is a dance of sorts."

"What is it you mean?"

"Our god Frey governs the pleasure between men and women."

"Oh." Braetana felt her face grow warm and knew her sudden embarrassment would rapidly change its hue to crimson.

"Well . . . I . . ." Braetana detested herself when she ended up fumbling for words. "I did not mean to offend your foolish rune. I will put it back." Her slender hand reached for the stone, which her earlier handling had canted up slightly and now rested atop some thick grass.

"Please, do not." Thorgunn's hand swept down upon Braetana's, intending to stop its further movement. But as he caught her, his grip tight and powerful, his fears for the rune were replaced with the heat of their contact. He had forgotten the softness of her flesh. Though it was now only her hand he held, he recalled touching her in more secret places.

Braetana could easily have pulled away from him. Yet, as she gazed up from the stone, it seemed less his hand than his eyes that seized her. She knew this closeness should fill her with fear. Where was her modesty now?

"I am sorry," she sputtered, as much to herself as to Thorgunn.

"No, it is I who should apologize. I know my lady meant only to restore the stone properly. But it should be left. It is a very serious matter."

"Yes." Braetana rose and slowly moved forward through the high grass, pretending to look for other vegetables. Thorgunn was right. It was a very serious matter indeed.

The often unpredictable weather had now passed the cusp of the spring chill. As summer approached, a warm, honeyed breeze accompanied the change. Taking full advantage of the balmy weather, Thorgunn sat against the longhouse's exterior, leaning against its cool turf.

It was rare for him to sit so still. But if his body was motionless, his mind was not. Images of the beautiful Braetana made him smile with pleasure. Suddenly he realized the sun was too low; Braetana had left some time ago to gather berries and was now unusually late in returning.

Her tardiness filled Thorgunn with the dread that she had again injured herself. Speeding down the narrow path, he quickly reached the strawberry copse. But once he was there, he found only a basket full of the now abundant fruit—and no Braetana in sight. His heart raced, less from exertion than with concern for her whereabouts, and he considered the unpleasant possibilities of her fate.

The dense woods rose like a semicircular wall around the thicket, rendering it unlikely as a route into the trees. The only alternative was the trail winding seaward. Just a short stretch beyond the berry patch, the narrow course spilled onto an open expanse of bleached sand. Though Thorgunn could not imagine what Braetana would seek there, it seemed that it was indeed where she must have gone.

His concern growing with each twist of the trail that did not reveal Braetana, Thorgunn now ran at full speed down the footpath. As he passed the final curtain of trees and felt the slick grainy slide of sand beneath his goatskin boots, he came to an abrupt halt.

There, across a great breadth of beach, strolled Braetana, apparently lost in her own thoughts. Her arms were outstretched as if to catch the summery mantle of breeze draping around her.

As she walked slowly toward the distant cliffs marking the sand's far end, the playful wind danced in and out of her full gunna. Gusts of it alternately filled the skirt's billowing folds until it became a great cylinder swirling around her, then capriciously snapped it back against her, revealing her beautiful form as the dress's hem flew high enough to expose a tantalizing show of the slender legs beneath.

Suddenly Braetana's pace quickened. She abruptly turned toward the sea, skipping and hopping her way toward a small cluster of rocks. Their black silhouettes rose in sharp contrast against the ivory seafoam marking the afternoon tide's recent departure.

As Thorgunn watched her unnoticed, she picked a cautious course over the top of the jagged stones, finally coming to rest on a small rock table on the crag's seaward end.

Staring out toward the gray swells that rose and fell beyond, Braetana was framed on top by the brilliant cerulean blue of a cloudless sky and beneath by an equally smooth expanse of pearly sand. She looked to Thorgunn less like a woman than some Norse goddess in her ocean vigil, her tall frame proud and strong in its contrast to nature's expansive tableau.

Thorgunn called her name, only to have the sound of his voice lost in the crash of the surf and wind. As Braetana stood unmoving, her thoughts fixed on something he could only guess at, Thorgunn closed the gap between them. He advanced unheard, then mounted the far end of the rocky point from which she searched the horizon.

"Braetana," Thorgunn repeated his call, this time more than close enough for her to hear. Having thought herself alone, the sound startled her, and Braetana spun quickly about to face him. His voice echoed only her name, but the question in his dark gray eyes spoke more eloquently. She stared silently back at him. The agony in her own amethyst eyes was the only outward reflection of the battle between conscience and desire that raged within her. Thorgunn easily saw her struggle, for it reflected his own. Though he knew he could now feel much the victor, knowing she would be his, he felt more conquered than conquerer.

He stepped slowly, almost painfully, toward her.

As she held fast to the wet rock, the distance between her and the Viking gradually closed. With the tenderness of a mystic ritual, he raised his arms on either side of her, then slowly wrapped them about the narrow width of her taut back. His embrace filled her with both longing and panic. She felt an overwhelming weakness because of her struggle and knew she could no longer stand. With a relieved sigh, Braetana leaned into him. She was almost glad she had lost the strength to fight.

He had not known what he wished to say when he had called her a moment ago. Now he found himself speechless and only able to repeat her name again, this time in a hushed tone close to reverence.

It seemed forever since he had held her so, her full breasts straining against his wide chest, the cradle of her hips fitting so perfectly against his own. And yet the memory of her remained so deeply burned into him that he could not have forgotten its pleasure had years passed since their last embrace.

He made no effort to release her; instead he only freed one arm as his hand traced a loving outline around the edge of her perfectly oval face. Surprisingly, for he had recently been convinced she would resist any further advances, he found only willingness in her deep violet eyes.

Had Thorgunn been able to read her mind, his doubts about her response would have fled. Braetana, who only moments before had stood thinking of the man whose arms now encircled her, knew that any efforts to refuse him would be wasted. She had not come to the sea expecting his pursuit. And yet, in some corner of her heart, she understood that she had been preparing for just such a moment.

She still wanted to believe that she stayed so close only because he was capable of overpowering her. But she knew it was because her need for him overpowered all else within her.

Knowing now where his touch would lead, she craved the inevitable conclusion. The sweet ache growing deep in her belly increased her need for him with each moment that their bodies pressed against each other.

Her own hands now reached upward and wandered wantonly over the handsome ruggedness of his face. One lovingly brushed small wisps of honey-colored hair across his temple, the other pressed warm fingertips over his parting lips.

Thorgunn needed no further encouragement. With welcome abandon, he pressed his mouth down hard upon Braetana's open lips. Their breaths merged and his tongue was almost instantly inside her wet, warm mouth. Braetana let out a small moan in response and pressed even tighter against him, her breasts so close that Thorgunn could feel the erect nipples even through her dress's thick fabric.

Sensing her readiness, he backed slightly away and reached out silently, extending only his hand. It was a summons Braetana knew she had no power to refuse. Without breaking the erotic communion that their eyes now shared, she placed her slender hand in his, allowing him to lead her from the slippery rocks to the soft, dry beach several yards beyond.

It was not too late, she told herself. There was still time to break away. But Braetana's desires, more than for honor, were for the sweet passion she now knew Thorgunn could show her.

She would do as his gray eyes willed her. Slowly,

almost hypnotically, Braetana slipped the soft gunna down over her creamy shoulders. Laying the dress as a blanket beneath her, she turned back toward Thorgunn, breathlessly facing him in her complete and beautiful nakedness.

The full view of her quickened his already hard breathing even more. Bit by bit, his hungry eyes devoured her, moving with delicious languor from the full, velvety breasts and their erect pink peaks, down the smooth flat belly to the golden triangle below. She was indeed the most stunning woman Thorgunn had ever seen, her proud indomitable spirit contained in a body no man could be expected to resist.

When he could stand it no more, Thorgunn stepped slowly toward her, cupping the back of her head and bringing her mouth again toward his own. She tipped her head backward, making easy his intention. Ever so gently, he slipped the other hand between the silky thighs whose parting would reveal the treasure he sought.

He barely touched her. Yet the brush of his fingertips set off a wildly building crescendo that ran the full length of her arching spine.

Braetana cried out in a plea for Thorgunn to complete the fine torture his hands had begun. Knowing she was ready for him, he gently lowered her atop the sprawled tunic, his loins aching with need at the vision before him. Her arms stretched to bring him to her, and her beautiful coltish legs instinctively parted in anticipation of his entry.

Thorgunn quickly stripped off his own tunic and trousers, then straddled her, his manhood poised with desire. But though her need for him met his own for her,

Thorgunn would not take her yet. What he held in store for Braetana would exceed any expectations her mind could conjure.

She knew her will could no longer defend her virtue. Thorgunn's wild touch had made her a prisoner of her own flesh's desires. Now she lay beneath him, her breasts heaving visibly while her huge lavender eyes invited his every touch. She wanted him, so why did he hesitate?

The brush of his fingertips on her ripe breasts took all impatience from Braetana's mind as Thorgunn's hands played her like a fine instrument, each song more wildly wonderful than the preceding one. He would not rush such expensive passion. With deliberate leisure, Thorgunn lowered his wheat-colored head to her.

As Braetana arched her back to meet him, Thorgunn sucked one peak until it rose impossibly higher than before. With his hand he teased Braetana's other breast to the same ecstatic height, his expert touch all the while traveling a maddeningly slow circle around the base of each creamy mound.

Braetana now braced herself for the brief pain she knew would inevitably follow. As she stiffened, she began to spread her legs in anticipation, but found Thorgunn still held them close together with the straddling power of his own muscular thighs.

To her surprise, the Viking then began to move down, his tongue burning a slow path of pleasure toward her belly and beyond. As he reached the golden mound that marked the entrance to her warm, sweet chasm, Thorgunn spread apart the ivory thighs with his powerful hands.

Delightfully confused, Braetana lay motionless, every

inch of her wildly atingle with his explosive touch. Suddenly her closed eyes flew wide open at the sweet aching sensation between her legs. His searching lips were again upon her, his tongue taking the same wanton liberties it had with her mouth. When Braetana thought she could stand no more, he quickly entered her, bringing forth a grateful moan from her lips.

Braetana's pleasure climbed higher and higher, making her yearn for it to end and begin all over again. Her hips rose eagerly to meet each entry. Just as she thought she could bear no more, a blaze exploded within her. Wave after wave of searing pleasure washed through Braetana, and she felt as if her body was truly on fire. Yet she wanted nothing more than for its delicious burn to continue.

"Thorgunn," Braetana cried, as much in surprise as in fulfillment. Then, suddenly and delightfully sated, she collapsed beneath the warmth of his lips and hands. Knowing he had shown her an indescribable new magic, Thorgunn raised his head level with hers, suspending himself slightly above her face, and smiled.

"Yes, love, I know," he murmured, then buried his breath in the silken hair strewn about her. "And now you will take me there too."

Thorgunn knew she was already moist enough. With one hard, swift stroke, he filled her. Braetana gasped involuntarily, surprised that this time she felt none of the pain she had expected.

Slowly at first, then with rapidly accelerating speed, Thorgunn continued his strong, sure strokes. Each pounding impact filled Braetana with a blissful wholeness. Each withdrawal spawned her desperate need for his quick return.

"Yes," Braetana whispered breathlessly as Thorgunn's strong hands cupped her smooth, firm buttocks. In his tight grip on her, he brought her hips ever closer to him, allowing him to penetrate deeper with each thrust. Though only moments ago she had thought herself satisfied, she now hungered once more for him. Could it be that rapturous explosion could happen again?

As Thorgunn continued to drive himself into her, Braetana felt the beginning of a wondrous climb toward fulfillment. She arched writhing with need to meet each piercing entry of his full maleness.

Thorgunn sensed her building excitement. Knowing he would soon fill her with the wet warmth of his own desire, he drew his face back from the side of her head so as to see their joining reflected in the depths of the beautiful almond-shaped lilac eyes.

Braetana's half-closed gaze was transfused with her need for him. Her slightly open lips breathed a slight gasp with each of his thrusts, and she lifted her yielding hips off the gunna to embrace his final unrelenting entry. The movement pushed him beyond all control. With several quick, violent strokes and a low throaty growl, Thorgunn emptied himself completely inside her.

His final movements had again sent Braetana over the crest of her passions. Once more, she blew across a wild sea of pure pleasure.

Their feverish needs now met, Braetana and Thorgunn held each other motionlessly. Their bodies were still joined in the most intimate union, and their eyes locked in silent gratitude for the ecstasy they had shared.

I love him. The words formed without warning in Braetana's slowly clearing mind, and she found it all she could do not to speak them aloud. As incredible as it seemed, she now knew with certainty that she did indeed love this man. He had first taken possession of her body, then had done the same with her heart. She felt hopelessly and wonderfully enslaved.

She yearned to belong to him in a way beyond that most private one they had just shared, to trust him, to deliver her uncertain fate into his strong, willful hands. Braetana searched the satisfied gray eyes for some clue to his heart's disposition. Whatever was written there, it was beyond her interpretation.

She knew he wanted her body. And he had treated her with great kindness of late. But there had been no declaration of love, no indication, however slight, that she meant any more to him than a convenient vessel with which to relieve his desires.

Although she still knew relatively little of Thorgunn's own values, she had no reason to assume he viewed her willingness to lay with him as anything more than wanton whoring.

Thorgunn was a devastatingly attractive man; the kind of man she had often seen beautiful women jealously vie for. How many others had he lain with, satisfied himself with, only to cast them off afterward as he would a tired mount? As they were stranded here Braetana even lacked the assurance that she would have been his first choice as bedmate. Perhaps she had misunderstood convenience for commitment. A hundred humiliating doubts coursed through her mind, each discomforting in its own right, each made all the worse by her present naked position beneath him.

Thorgunn did not miss the look of confusion dawning

on Braetana's reddening face. He knew the expression well, for women wanted promises of love with their passion. It was a small price he had often and casually paid. Such vows were as easily forgotten as made, and Thorgunn was master at both. If he could make her love him, Magnus's gift of Braetana as bride would be easily had, as would the sweet fruits of his plan. Einar would be here within the week. There was little time left.

"Be mine."

Braetana's already radiant amethyst eyes seemed to glow even more at his words, though they still showed some bewilderment at the meaning behind them.

Thorgunn withdrew from her, then rolled alongside, lying on his back with his huge arms folded beneath him as a pillow. Although their bodies still touched in one long sensuous seam, he now appeared dissociated from her. His gaze wandered skyward and his voice again grew full and resonant, in contrast to the throaty sounds of passion breathlessly spoken only moments ago.

"As a child I dreamed of a Valkyrie who rode the night skies. She perched astride a winged white charger, a nimbus of flaxen hair awhirl about her. She was Odin's, her heart full of fire that burned through from her wild eyes, her face possessed of an unearthly beauty matched only by the strength of her spirit. Then it was only a boy's dream, a vision which lured me like a siren to an otherworldly ideal. As I grew, the goddess vanished, buried by women whose bodies and souls seemed base and earthbound in comparison. Until you."

Thorgunn rolled onto his side. He brought one hand to cup Braetana's chin and turned her face gently toward him. "It was no dream, Braetana. It was you, sent to me by Odin with a promise of our tomorrows together. Fate has now bound us. I did not know when we first met, though something strange and unsettling within me, something I fought to ignore, stirred even then. But I can no longer deny you. You have taken me beyond any desire I have ever known, beyond my need for anything else this wide world holds. Odin help me, I want you again even as I now speak."

Thorgunn tenderly lowered his mouth to hers, his kiss more gentle but no less full of the urgency he had communicated moments ago. With ease he remounted her and unsealed their mouths to press his warm breath tight against her soft ear.

"Say my name. Say it and say you want me."

Braetana could hardly believe the words she'd longed for. "Yes, I want you, Thorgunn. Please, again." She had never thought to hear herself speak so. Yet no more could she imagine keeping her heart's song silent.

Suddenly, he was once more within her, their bodies locked in the now familiar rhythms of love. This time Thorgunn moved more slowly than the last, showing a trembling Braetana still one more of his seemingly endless ways to please her.

With his easier pace, he whispered a stream of nothings to her, murmuring endearments softly in her ear. He often spoke her name accompanied by a smattering of Norse. Braetana could not understand his words, but she understood his tone. In response, she could only repeat his name, chanting it softly like an incantation each time he again entered her.

Though their lovemaking before had been a tempestuous storm, this time Braetana felt herself borne by a gentle breeze, a sail wind of pleasure moving her slowly but surely to a delicious destination. As their passion climaxed, Thorgunn gave her the one thing she most needed.

"I love you," he murmured. He had not meant to say it.

X

A cold shock of water lapped at Braetana's bare toes, shaking her from her pleasure-filled daydream back to the reality of the tide's return. With a small cry of alarm, she sat upright. Her sudden movements roused a sleeping Thorgunn, who also rose, though with less concern.

The descending sun heralded the high water's return, its foamy advances insistently reclaiming the temporary sandy bed it had allowed the two of them. Reaching for her gunna, Braetana ran uphill to dry beach, then began to hurriedly dress.

Thorgunn's speedy pursuit interrupted her efforts. Locking his arms around her still-naked body, his own nakedness pressing brazenly against her, Thorgunn roared with a deep, bemused laugh.

"I like you better as you are."

"Thorgunn, please!" Braetana complained, embarrassed not only at her nakedness but also at his overt reference to it. She could not deny her enjoyment of his embrace, but her modesty prevailed. "I am cold," she lied.

"I could ease that misery," Thorgunn answered tantalizingly, then grew more solemn. "I meant my words."

Braetana smiled, then lowered her eyes and turned her head so her cheek rested flat against the warm, soft hair of his chest. Thorgunn's reminder of his profession of love for her seemed somehow to sanction their present indecent embrace.

Still, she could not ignore the impropriety of her behavior. Though they had loved once before, their passion this time was tempered with no regret on her part, no resolution that such a moral transgression would not happen again. Despite the shame of their unwed coupling, Braetana knew she no longer had the power within her to resist his burning touch. She also knew that, as often as he wanted her, she wanted him even more.

He had said he loved her. From what she knew of him, she would be foolish—and disappointed—to hope for more. If he would only have her as his mistress, then, as disgraceful as the fate was, mistress she would be.

Thorgunn read the reasoning in Braetana's amethyst eyes. Now sure that she was ready to be his, he offered her a promise he hoped would seal their future.

"I want you as wife. We will ask Magnus when we return. I think he will approve. I'm sure he would if he knew how we now stand." Thorgunn released Braetana from his grasp, lifting her face in the cradle of his hands and softly kissing her forehead.

Braetana could hardly believe the words she'd heard. She had been willing to live unlawfully with Thorgunn, but instead he wanted her as wife! She had gained the man she loved and lost her shame all at once.

"Oh, Thorgunn!" she squealed joyfully, her arms flying about his neck as she raised her lips quickly to his. "Yes! It would give me such pride to be your wife."

How different she felt from the moment Edward had announced their unholy betrothal, how much more honest despite Thorgunn's somewhat premature intimacy with her. At least their sharing had been one of love, not the forced alliance Edward's manipulation of Glendonwyck had driven her to.

Less than a month ago, she had thought never to find any man she could love. Now, in the mad confusion that had since befallen her, she was slated to wed him. She stood on tiptoe to cover Thorgunn's tanned face with an impulsive explosion of exuberant kisses.

"Lady!" Thorgunn exclaimed in mock horror. "I fear you will ravish me again here on the sand!"

Braetana smiled shyly, embarrassed but not disinterested in the suggestion.

Thorgunn noted her playful look. "I think I have much to learn from your interesting Saxon ways. In the meantime, my more conventional appetite grows. The sun fades fast and I would have something besides your sweet kisses for dinner."

Braetana laughed liltingly, then offered Thorgunn his tunic and pants and resumed her own brief toilette. Once dressed, the two of them began their hand in hand climb back to the longhouse, stopping en route to retrieve the strawberries Braetana had left mid-path.

"Delicious fruit," Thorgunn cajoled. "I must send you out again tomorrow for such fare. Of course we have a long, chilly night until then."

As Thorgunn led her up the narrow footpath, Braetana smiled silently behind him. She too had thoughts of
the forthcoming night. She assumed Thorgunn would
now arrange their sleeping quarters to accommodate this
new development. It was a prospect she savored.

The ecstasy he had given her was more than she could
ever have dreamed. But now she anticipated with equal
joy the pleasure of sleeping next to him and the feeling
of his strong arms enveloping and protecting her.

As long as she could remember, she had never felt so
full of peace, never experienced such calm and trust at
the hands of another. How ironic that she had now come
to find this tranquillity in the embrace of a man who,
such a short time ago, had been her captor. Now she
was captive again, but this time willingly so.

Her longing for England, so strong it had actually
hurt in the first days following her abduction, had lessened of late. For though the uncharted course before
her still filled Braetana with fear, Thorgunn's presence
lessened her apprehension, and she instinctively felt he
would allow no harm to befall her.

Daylight fled just as the lovers returned to the longhouse. Before closing the heavy turf door, Braetana
noted that the stars seemed to glisten brighter than ever
before, as if they too had been touched by the glow of
her newfound happiness.

Both Braetana's and Thorgunn's hunger had been
fueled by their earlier lovemaking. Rapaciously, they
devoured the cooked ptarmigan he had caught that
morning, washing the gamey fowl down with ample
servings of the now nearly exhausted beer.

As Braetana stoked the fire, her nostrils full of its
sweet nutty smell, Thorgunn brought his pallet to the

central chamber. He laid it alongside Braetana's and turned the two bearskin coverlets sideways to form one large undercovering for the newly constructed bed. Despite the afternoon's intimacies and the ease with which Thorgunn had moved about her since their return to the cabin, Braetana found the sleeping rearrangement embarrassing. Turning away, she feigned tending the fire while Thorgunn finished the new plan.

"It will be warmer near the hearth." He sat down next to Braetana on the reed-strewn floor. "Though I am not entirely sure it is burning wood that will chase my chill away."

"Sir," protested Braetana teasingly, "you do make me blush with such unabashed comments."

"Words should embarrass you less than certain other matters."

Braetana clucked disapprovingly at his taunt, then raised her hand in mock attack. Like the hunter he was, Thorgunn swept one hand down, easily surrounding the slender wrist. Then, lowering his mouth as if to devour his quarry, he instead placed only a tender kiss on her palm, unfurling the delicate fingers onto his warm, gentle lips.

As Braetana watched in delight, Thorgunn's mouth charted a tantalizing slow path up the length of her arm, pausing as he reached the velvety base of her beautiful neck. The wetness of his tongue as it worked further toward her ear sent a palpable chill of pleasure up Braetana's spine. Feeling her body involuntarily convulse at his touch, Thorgunn growled softly. The Viking quickly offset her shiver with the heat of his breath against her ear, then whispered something in Norse. He followed with a suggestion she could not fail to understand.

Braetana answered with a soft, seductive laugh, then clasped both arms around his neck as Thorgunn carried her to the pleasures of the nearby pallet.

As the fire's crackling embers broke the silence of the morning chill, Braetana snuggled close against Thorgunn, breathing in the sweet smell of wood smoke that lay on his hair. Although she now felt more rested than she had in weeks, she woke often during the night, suddenly aware of the strong, masculine body that lay next to hers. Fighting the drowsiness that lured her back into sleep, she indulged her desire to lay awake, savoring the wonder of his closeness.

How small she felt against him, a sensation that would have left her fearful a few days ago, but that now filled her with trusting security. The more she knew him, the more he seemed the true Viking prince, for in both body and spirit Thorgunn seemed very much the master of all around him.

Braetana studied as much of the contours of his strong face as Thorgunn's half-turned position would allow. Suddenly, she was eye to eye with him as he rolled slowly toward her.

"Ah, my little partridge is awake early." Then, noticing the contemplative look of her lilac eyes, "You look as if you fly far away."

"Tell me of Haakon. How is it your younger brother, and not you, serves as king?" Thorgunn had been waiting for the question. He knew he must take care that his answer did not betray his penury. Eventually Braetana would know all the unpleasant particulars of his predicament, but if everything went as planned, by then she would be promised to him as wife.

"As a child, I was sent abroad by my father, as is our custom, to learn under the tutelage of a great Viking jarl. Ulf sought to teach me a trade other than piracy. Through my youth, I lived on the Shetlands, treated as my guardian's own son. During that time, my mother died and my father took a second wife, Ingrid, a jealous woman who soon after gave birth to Haakon. When my father fell ill, before he died he chose Haakon to succeed him as konungr. Our council, the loegretta, saw fit to honor his choice."

"It sounds an odd decision. In England, the firstborn is first to rule. Any other choice would be the gravest insult."

"This is not England." Then, hoping to deflect her curiosity, "I would not challenge Harald's judgment."

"You do not covet his crown?" Braetana seemed to disbelieve his acceptance.

"He'll covet you when he sees my Saxon bride," answered Thorgunn. He had again sidestepped her question and hoped to end the discussion before more dangerous matters came of it.

Thorgunn planted a suggestive kiss on the nape of Braetana's neck, halting her efforts to stoke the fire. She turned with a soft laugh to face him, tipping her head back as she pressed her cheek against his.

"You impede my housekeeping."

"My lady needn't worry about the fire—I've no need of further heat." The vibration of Thorgunn's deep resonant laugh tickled against her ear. "Though I must admit, you've become much the Viking maid with your newfound domestic skills."

"Do not." Braetana pushed away and turned her face

from him. Had he been able to see her eyes, he would have known they traveled to Glendonwyck.

A look of exasperation flashed across Thorgunn's face.

"You cannot still doubt what I have told you?"

"I know you believe it to be true. But I must meet this man Magnus before I can call him father." Although more and more Braetana subscribed to Thorgunn's tale of her mixed parentage, she still needed proof before she could fully abandon her allegiance to the Braetana she had always been.

It was all so exhausting. Was she Viking? Was she not? If she were, could she come to find decency in a heritage she had been trained to loathe and fear? And, most frightening of all, how much of Thorgunn's love for her hinged on his belief in the incredible tale?

"Would you love me less if I were all Saxon?"

"But you are not."

"If I were . . ."

Thorgunn had not considered this before. If Magnus were not father to Braetana, then Braetana was not heir to his silver. Thorgunn had therefore gained nothing from her abduction. Except Braetana herself.

Lately, he had come to view her as no small prize. In addition to the pleasures her flesh offered, he also took joy in her company. As hard as it was for him to admit, Thorgunn had come to value Braetana in ways beyond her full purse.

Still, lacking Magnus's wealth, she appealed to him more as mistress than wife. He had felt no need to marry before—his decision to do so now hung only on the silver he was to gain and the justice it would buy. No matter, he thought, dismissing the digression, she *is* Magnus's and we *will* marry.

"Thorgunn?" He could hear the alarm in her voice and guessed he had been slow to respond.

"Of course I would love you as much were you all Saxon. But I would understand less your willingness to see Trondbergen. What could you seek there if not your parentage?"

Braetana's mouth opened slightly in incredulity. "I would follow you, even into the arms of the fearful Vikings."

Thorgunn had not realized before now how much she really did love him. Soon he would have all he wanted.

"My brave love. Even were you not Norse, you should have earned the appellation by your courage. Now I, my lady, should earn us some supper." Plucking his bow from a nearby peg, Thorgunn disappeared out the longhouse door, only to reappear moments later.

"Are the ptarmigan walking to the hearth now?" Braetana jested.

"Einar is here. From the bluff I saw the red-striped sail of his drekar carving into the sand below. I had not expected to see him so soon. The warming weather has no doubt brought the trading season on early."

Braetana's face fell with shock and trepidation. She had known all along his arrival was both imminent and inevitable. Yet she had somehow hoped it would not come to pass. The last week with Thorgunn had given her all the fulfillment she had ever wanted from life. Having experienced such bliss, she could not imagine that any future, even one wedded to Thorgunn, could surpass the most wonderful present.

There would be problems in store, she thought. If

Magnus were her father, he could then control her fate. What if he refused her request to be Thorgunn's wife? Even if he didn't, there would be new customs and language to contend with. Why could she not just stay here with Thorgunn, unbothered by the constraints of their clashing cultures?

"And so we must go?" Braetana was already aware of the answer.

"If you are to be my wife."

"You are already husband to me in the most special way." Braetana spoke softly as Thorgunn gently cupped her sorrowful face in his hands.

"My little Saxon dove," he murmured. "I would make you wife in law as well as spirit." The Viking paused, sensing the acceptance growing in Braetana's eyes. "But if we would have that happen, no one must yet know of the closeness we've shared here. It would both shame you and anger Magnus."

"I must pretend that you are still my captor?" Braetana's look was one of disbelief.

Thorgunn assumed an almost parental tone toward her. "It would be safest. Just for a brief while. Though you need not pretend me your enemy. I doubt your father would consent to our union if he thought you disapproved."

"How long?" Braetana hoped for a shorter answer than any she knew Thorgunn was likely to give.

"Two days' sail back. I will ask Magnus as soon as possible. If he approves, there will be a proper betrothal, and then we can wed. Perhaps only a month."

"Having just found you, I must now live alone among strangers an entire month without you!" Hot tears filled Braetana's clouding amethyst eyes, then spilled precipitously down over her rose-tinged cheeks. Trying to imagine life without Thorgunn, she wrapped her slender arms in a band around his thick chest.

"Say you love me," she pleaded.

Thorgunn felt a strange compassion surge through him, one not unlike that he had experienced that first day at Glendonwyck as Braetana begged against her abduction.

"Shhh . . . Yes, of course I love you. We must only pretend for a while. Can you not be patient?" he asked, gently tipping her tear-glistened face up to him.

Braetana managed to check her tears, and sighed in resignation.

"Very well." She struggled to produce a smile. "One month only. One day more and I shall tell Magnus and the world how my virtue became undone."

"Good." Thorgunn, looking satisfied, kissed her quickly as a seal of their pact. "Now I suggest we set about some rearrangement here." He gestured toward the pallet. "Before Einar misunderstands our understanding."

In little time, Braetana and Thorgunn had restored the longhouse to its original plan, giving it all the appearance of a shelter reluctantly inhabited by two slightly inimical occupants.

They had barely finished when the crash of the opening door announced Einar's presence. There stood a man who was only slightly shorter but was apparently much older than Thorgunn. Dressed in his battle-ready apparel, he entered, sword drawn, followed by two similarly attired companions.

"Thorgunn!" Einar's eyes registered half-questioning astonishment. He had apparently expected the chimney's smoke more likely tended by foe than friend. "You live!"

"As you see." Thorgunn extended his arms and strode forward to greet and embrace his red-haired senior.

Einar's mouth still hung partially open as he took in the shocking vision before him. "When your drekar returned uncaptained, Haakon thought you dead."

"Nearly," explained Thorgunn, "but I rode the waves to safe harbor here instead. The ship and my men—they are not all lost?"

"Half survived. The rest now sit with Odin in Valhalla. What was left of your drekar combed the sea for you. But the gale had nearly cleaved the hull in two, and the vessel was forced to make good speed home to stay afloat. It was not considered that you could have survived the sea's toss and come here."

"I would not have chosen the course," Thorgunn answered.

Einar's eyes turned to the storm's other survivor. "This must be the charge of that shrewish Saxon nanny your drekar returned to us." He nodded toward Braetana. Maddeningly, she understood none of the two men's Norse exchange and she wore a look of guarded confusion.

"This is Lady Braetana, daughter of Jarl Magnus." Thorgunn gestured toward Braetana, who nodded slightly in acknowledgment of what she assumed to be her introduction.

Einar bowed deeply, then openly leered at the angel's vision before him. "So this is Magnus's issue? A pleasant cargo, no doubt?"

Thorgunn's stern stare brought Einar's dangerous course to a quick halt. "Well, no matter," the elder Viking replied. "I assume you wish to return with Sverri and Hoeskuld."

"When do they sail?"

"Tomorrow, if the weather holds," Einar answered. "Haakon will be very surprised to see you."

"No doubt," said Thorgunn with a laugh, silently thinking that surprise would be but the beginning.

Einar's ship had come heartily stocked. By afternoon's end, an entire summer's worth of generous food stores and other essential cargo had been hauled ashore and made its way to the longhouse.

The replenished larder provided nothing less than a feast that night. Einar had brought with him not only walnuts and dried plums, but also a good-size fresh lamb carcass which, with Thorgunn's help, Braetana roasted over the open spit.

The abundant new fare proved such a relief from the routine ptarmigan and beetroot that Braetana ate far beyond her hunger, nearly to the point of discomfort. In her enthusiasm for the fresh provisions, she had even tried something Thorgunn called lutefisk, a briny concoction of cod steeped in potash lye. But, though apparently a great favorite of her dinner companions, the soggy fish proved less palatable to Braetana. After only one bite, she hurriedly washed the abominable flavor from her mouth with ample amounts of fresh beer.

As before, much of the dinner conversation between Thorgunn and the other Vikings was in Norse, though Thorgunn occasionally directed some comments to Braetana in English. Naively, the language was a problem Braetana had not yet really considered, because Thorgunn was able to address her in her native tongue. But the isolation she felt in the midst of the four garrulous Vikings made clear the great distance between her and the new culture she had yet to encounter.

Thorgunn had assured her that there would be those in Trondbergen who could speak with her, Magnus in particular, because Norse nobility had the advantage of the trade contacts that provided the opportunity to learn. Still, Braetana would be mostly among strangers, people who couldn't speak enough English to become acquainted. She sighed dejectedly at the prospect of the enormous task that lay before her.

As the evening wore on, Braetana intently studied the house's new occupants, all of whom sat drinking jovially around the trestle table on the raised floor overlooking the hearth. Each of the three wore outfits similar to Thorgunn's thick wool tunic and knee-length trousers. Sverri and Hoeskuld, however, as befitting their lower social and military rank, wore coarser weaves than Einar's, and their baldrics lacked the fine ornamentation of their superiors'.

When the fire began to wane, Thorgunn set about further rearrangement of the sleeping quarters. He laid several thick fur skins on the floor to the far side of the curtained partition. These would serve as makeshift pallets for Einar and his men. Braetana was apparently to be allowed to remain in what yesterday had been their shared bed, a concession she guessed was of Thorgunn's, not Einar's, making. As the Norse crew layed in for their hard-earned rest, Thorgunn re-stoked the dwindling fire, then turned to address Braetana.

"Safe enough in your quarters?"

"I should ask you," Braetana replied. "I am not overly impressed with the deportment of your friends."

"They are sailors," Thorgunn said with a laugh.

168 / BLAINE ANDERSON

"They want only drink and a soft bearskin to end their long day. You forget your new rank in life. They would not dare touch you. Nor would I allow it, though the thought is much on my mind at this moment."

"Thorgunn." Braetana spoke his name softly, turning her head slightly away and blushing at the inference.

"I must go," Thorgunn announced, "though I have some good news for you to dream on. Bronwyn waits for you in Trondbergen."

"She is still alive?" Braetana was shocked, afraid the news was too wonderful to be true.

"Apparently your lady's affection for the hold served her well. Though Bronwyn must now think us dead."

"Oh, Thorgunn!" Braetana squealed joyfully, suddenly lunging toward the Viking with an imprudent urge to throw her arms about him.

Thorgunn stepped quickly back to prevent their near embrace. "Our pretense?"

"Yes," sighed Braetana. "Very well—but I shall not exercise such caution in my dreams."

"Nor I," said Thorgunn with a smile. "Sleep well."

With that, Thorgunn turned and made his way toward the far chamber, closing the curtain behind him. A brief exchange in Norse followed, the topic of which was apparently Braetana. The conversation then died down, along with the sounds of the exhausted men settling in for the night.

I must learn this strange tongue, Braetana resolved, now certain she would be quite disadvantaged until she did so. *But until then,* she thought, *I will have Bronwyn to speak with! Perhaps the future grows brighter still.*

XI

The weather held clear the next morning, making for an easy departure for the trip home to Trondbergen. Einar saw the party down the winding path, the men walking first, with Braetana a lonely straggler some distance behind. Already she found the charade with Thorgunn difficult. His sudden lack of attention to her was nearly unbearable, but Braetana calmed herself with assurances that his plan for their betrothal turned on the success of this feigned propriety.

As the assemblage reached the edge of the beach, Braetana got her first close-up look at what, from the palisades above, had seemed a modest drekar. In fact, it was much larger than her initial estimate, though still considerably smaller than Thorgunn's twenty-five-man vessel. Nevertheless, its full straked belly and red-striped sail recalled her first terrifying image of Thorgunn's own ship.

Braetana's pulse raced as the longship drew closer. It was an instinctive response to the horror she had experienced during her last boarding. She fought the fear, reviewing her change in fate since then. With her best logic, Braetana assured herself that the voyage to

Trondbergen would but speed her to her future as Thorgunn's wife, a destiny far from that which she had earlier faced as unwilling captive.

Though the ship was tethered to a beached log, the incoming tide still rendered it waterborne. No gangplank had been laid, reflecting the Vikings' indifference to a brief stroll through the surf. Knowing Braetana would not share this sentiment, Thorgunn lifted her into his arms, then boarded and carried her to a forward seat. Though this new pretext of formality had gone on but a day, Braetana had much missed the touch she had grown so quickly accustomed to. Now, as he held her, she rediscovered her need for Thorgunn with a sweet ache in her belly.

"I've missed you," she said as his huge arms wrapped intimately around her thighs and waist.

"The crew stands nearby." Thorgunn fired her a guarded look.

"Have you not missed me?" Braetana did not understand Thorgunn's terse reply.

"Yes, but it is untimely to discuss our passions now."

Braetana still could not fathom his reticence. "You said they spoke no English."

"Your eyes and tone address me in a language they do speak. Woman, I swear, you will undo us yet."

Braetana felt herself blush at Thorgunn's reference to her all-too-apparent affections for him.

"Very well. I shall play your victim awhile longer," she conceded, "but I make no promises of unending patience. The sail best catch good wind to bear us quickly to our nuptials."

Thorgunn smiled at Braetana's reply, then turned toward his Viking traveling companions. Along with

Thorgunn, Hoeskuld and Sverri issued Einar a brief good-bye, then heaved the anchor on board.

As Thorgunn mounted the helm, the two muscular men pushed the light vessel through the shallow, roiling surf, springing aboard at the last possible moment. The healthy wind quickly caught the unfurling sail. Soon the drekar glided easily toward the open sea, aided by the crew's swift oar work.

Braetana's tumultuous arrival on the island had not afforded her the perspective she now enjoyed. As the land's profile shrunk behind them, she turned to take in the tree-topped silhouette of her most recent home. It had only been a month since she first laid eyes on the remote setting. Strangely, she now found herself filled with an unexpected sadness at departing.

The emptiness was not unlike that she had experienced as Thorgunn and his huge destrier bore her swiftly away from the security of Glendonwyck's walls. It was odd that she had spent seventeen years there, yet in all that time had never felt the peace and comfort this secluded foreign place had afforded her.

As the promontory overlooking the beach receded below the horizon, Braetana turned her eyes seaward. She wondered if her undelivered fate could offer anything to surpass the bliss the drekar now parted her from.

She dreaded the ensuing time at sea. The voyage would find her cramped by the limited confines of the ship, afford her little privacy, and force her into a strange charade of formality with Thorgunn. Thank God he had said the journey would take only two days. Braetana tried to remember this, coupling it with the wonderful prospect of seeing Bronwyn, to make the sea trip more bearable.

Aided by good wind, the voyage lasted only a day and a half. The longship wound its way through a dotted coastal archipelago, the islands that marked their progress approximating Einar's in size. According to Thorgunn, all remained unmanned, as they were located closer to the coastline and therefore farther from the pirate routes the Frisians preferred.

The sail was smoother than Braetana's last, certainly than her very last memory on board. She sensed the ease of the current ride was due more to the islands' protection than any change in the still-unpredictable weather. Despite the peaceful voyage, Braetana found herself growing impatient. The monotony of unrelieved water came to annoy her, and it was with great anticipation that she rose the second day out to face a huge land mass looming in the distance.

Thorgunn, who had been manning the tiller when he too spotted the familiar shape on the horizon, correctly guessed the question in Braetana's searching eyes.

"Nordmannaland," he bellowed. "I think you will find it quite different from your Glendonwyck."

His assessment was correct. As the vessel drew closer, nothing about the land's heavily wooded coastline recalled the stony white cliffs of Braetana's former home. Even the pine and birch forests of Einar's island, which might have prepared her for the new terrain, now seemed dwarfed by the startling height of the coastal mountains.

Braetana could not imagine the possibility of an actual settlement in such dense timberland. It was only as the vessel drew alongside the forested coast that she realized Thorgunn meant not to dock at, but rather sail through, the peaks. A last-minute change in course revealed a startlingly narrow channel of water carved dramatically through the very spine of the rocky headlands.

The beautifully sharp contrast between the lapis blue rivulet of sea twisting snakelike through the ravine and the towering stone and evergreen spires rising above it nearly made Braetana breathless. She had never seen such power and calm united in nature before.

As the sleek-hulled ship wound its way through the narrow passageway, the only sound the rhythmical slice of the oars through its mirrorlike waters, Braetana continued her magical discovery. The highest lichen-covered cliffs were punctuated with a combination of fir and scrub overgrowth and often capped with a dusting of snow still left as a reminder of the past winter. Each bend revealed incredible new vistas as the fjord heights seemed only to grow taller. Glacier-fed waterfalls scored the dazzling views with the rustling roar of their cascades spilling down rocky facades.

Braetana could not deny that she felt some strange kinship with this rugged land, some sense of belonging that flowed from a mysterious place deep within her. The intensity of the sentiment startled her. She could not understand such instant affinity with a place she had not only never before seen, but that differed so in every possible way from all she was accustomed to.

Could it be that part of her that was Viking somehow knew these waters and mountains as home? Braetana sighed in confusion and dropped to a sitting position on the ship's forwardmost seat. As if to massage away her befuddlement, she leaned her head into her open hands. Suddenly, a presence behind her broke her reverie, and she spun quickly back to see Thorgunn towering above her.

"It is beautiful."

"Yes," Braetana answered softly. "Why do you leave it?"

"The fjords are a gift from Odin," Thorgunn responded. "But there is little farmland. And so we till the seas instead—for fish and trade and work that buys us what our rocky soil denies."

"Are we close to Trondbergen?"

"Two bends from here. Magnus will hardly be able to contain his joy at the sight of you."

Braetana's violet eyes suddenly pleaded with the gray gaze above her. "He frightens me. Though you have told me much, I truly know nothing of this man you call my sire."

Thorgunn was hard-pressed to present the aged jarl as a caring, loving father. Still, he struggled for words to allay Braetana's fears.

"He is old and ill. His wife and son are dead, and you are all that remains of his flesh. He will treat you kindly. As will I when he sends you from his house to mine."

The reminder that she would soon again enjoy her longed-for intimacy with Thorgunn lifted Braetana's dampening spirits. The thought made facing the prospect of an entirely new life somewhat more bearable.

"If he is my father, you say he will let me marry as I wish?"

"It is likely."

"But he may also gainsay me? This is Norse law, is it not?"

"As it is in England. It would serve our plans if you could show him some civility."

The notion of behaving kindly toward one she had little affection for recalled Braetana's hellish arrangement with Edward. The very thought made her shudder visibly.

"Need you my cloak?"

"I need only your love," she answered, her eyes smiling as she gazed at Thorgunn. "I am grown tired of these games I must play with men. But if Magnus is my father, I will find a way to some peace with him. I will do what is needed to ensure our future."

Thorgunn's hopes were buoyed by her commitment to try with Magnus, yet he was still somewhat unsettled by her doubts regarding her paternity. The ear clip, however, would prove his tale. But Braetana insisted on making Magnus's fatherhood a premise, not a fact. She was not yet prepared to think herself half-Viking. He hoped with all his heart the identity was one she could come to bear.

Without warning, the drekar rounded the last turn, bringing Trondbergen finally into view. Thorgunn held his post near Braetana, carefully standing far enough back so as to avoid touching her, but not so far that she could not turn to him for support, should panic overwhelm her.

Yet it was more awe than panic that coursed through Braetana as the drekar approached the fjord's narrow end. Now the steep granite walls that had thus far framed their passageway gave way to a gentle, green valley cupping the base of the channel. At first, Braetana could discern only a large wooden dock defiantly protruding into the deep blue waters. Behind it she soon saw an outline of a town.

"There are no walls?" Braetana was surprised that the encampment appeared undefended.

"The fjord is our bulwark. Those enemies foolish enough to sail in would find themselves trapped in their escape. You have not noticed the lookouts scouting us from the channel's cliffs?"

She had not realized they were being watched. The idea gave Braetana a feeling of uneasiness.

As their ship drew closer to the wooden dock's pilings, Braetana caught her first glimpse of Trondbergen proper. Houses in a variety of shapes and sizes were clustered together, most capped by one, and, in some cases, two smoke-spitting chimneys.

Some of the architecture echoed Einar's construction, with sloping gable-ended roofs dipping to the ground over turf walls. Other buildings were made completely of vertically planked wood or, more rarely, wood interspersed with wattle and daub.

Between the wooden dwellings, Braetana could now make out a bustling stream of pedestrians, some of whom were apparently moving toward the water to greet them. One man, dressed in what she now recognized as typical Norse trousers and tunic, hurried to the dock's end.

Apparently recognizing the drekar's prow, the greeter gave a wave and a shout, then disappeared into a nearby longhouse. By the time Sverri and Hoeskuld had guided the full-bellied hull safely within the calm harbor, the first man reemerged. This time, he brought a party of five more similarly dressed men. Thorgunn shouted an instruction in Norse to the group, which then scurried toward the ship's bow to aid in securing her.

As he prepared to disembark, Thorgunn turned to

Braetana. She stood with her slender arms wrapped about her, her eyes wide at the prospect of the strange new experience about to unfold before her. His own eyes countered her fear with the gentle assurance she had grown to depend on.

"Do not be frightened, little bird. Magnus will not harm you. And we will find Bronwyn."

Bronwyn. All through the voyage up the winding fjord, Braetana had been so preoccupied with her odd new fate that she had nearly forgotten the journey's end would bring a reunion with her cherished companion.

"Yes, please, quickly. My heart struggles against it, but I feel only fear for this strange place. I would you could hold me."

"I wish the same," Thorgunn replied, somewhat surprised with his response. Now, for the first time, he became acutely aware of how difficult their separation promised to be. It was only the sweet pleasures of her body he missed, he assured himself. That, coupled with his eagerness to right his misfortune, was what made her so damnably attractive.

Yet he could not deny that, whatever her draw, it would not be easily resisted for their time apart. But every gain had its price, and he considered his abstinence from her a small enough payment for all their eventual union would soon bring him.

"We must go," he pronounced, returning his thoughts to the task at hand. He offered his arm to steady Braetana as she stepped slowly over the low gunwale onto the dock's pine planking.

The walk up the gentle slope to the town's center went at a fast pace. Braetana was thankful it was not longer, for her breath quickened so in anticipation of meeting Magnus that she was sure she would have fainted had she been forced to travel much farther.

Once up the hill, she was afforded a full panorama of closely nestled longhouses and busy villagers. It was mid-afternoon and, judging by the number of people that crowded the narrow wooden streets, apparently the height of the day's activity.

Women of all ages, all attired in billowy chemises and sleeveless overdresses, scurried about carrying woven baskets brimming with the day's fresh fish and vegetables. Though Saxons also tended to be light-colored, never before had Braetana seen such a wealth of blond heads, each much like her own. The older women seemed to gather their hair in a knot at the nape, and both young and old alike wore festively colored ribbon headbands that Thorgunn had told her were called *hlao*.

A few of the women, as well as the lesser population of men vending wares and services, turned to stare as Braetana passed before them. But the midday crowd was large enough to make her presence largely unobserved. Those who did see the returning party ran toward Thorgunn, gripping his hand or even throwing their arms about him. The embraces were obviously intended to welcome back the sailor they had thought dead.

Thorgunn smiled at their greetings, usually speaking a few words in Norse. His replies were punctuated by his loud, hearty laugh. Braetana gathered he was amused at his friends' shock to find him still alive.

As Thorgunn wound his way through the bustling crowd, Braetana followed, bowing her head shyly in the hope that she could pass unnoticed. Although nothing about these strange people gave evidence of their reputed ferocity, their odd speech and manner overwhelmed her. She suddenly felt small and fearful, but to those she passed, her demeanor seemed neither.

Soon the loud noise of the crowd faded behind her. With its passing, Braetana lifted her eyes to find herself facing a larger but more remote and quiet path. This one was lined with bigger buildings than those nearer the dock. Thorgunn turned to face her, then gestured toward an imposing wooden structure whose gable overhung the lane's end.

"Magnus's house." The identification brought Braetana to an abrupt halt. Without hesitation, she instinctively reached for the corner of Thorgunn's wool tunic.

"I cannot," she pleaded breathlessly.

"You must," he answered firmly. "If we are to have each other."

In response to Thorgunn's dictum, Braetana reluctantly began to move forward, though she was so distracted she felt as though she were floating rather than walking.

The hard rap of Thorgunn's knuckles on the metal-plated wooden door snapped her attention back to reality. As the iron hinges creaked beneath the weight of the door's swing, Braetana stood frozen.

The door opened wide to reveal the longhouse's occupant, and Braetana's eyes struggled against the contrasting interior darkness to see the man who answered Thorgunn's call. He was much as Thorgunn had described him—slightly taller than she but less so than Thorgunn, his large head topped by a tousle of unruly blond hair streaked with ribbons of gray. A full beard and mustache covered his ruddy face, exposing only a pair of plump red cheeks and deep-set eyes.

Had Braetana not been so riveted by Magnus's face, she would have noticed the fineness of his dress, the elaborate embroidery edging the twill tunic and the precious multicolored stones inlaid on his silver brooch. But all that filled her mind and gaze was the old man's piercing eyes. He stared at his visitors in incredulity, training his eyes first on Thorgunn, then on his daughter. As she returned his look, Braetana saw in their blue depths a suggestion of lavender much like that her own eyes had long reflected.

"Min datter?" he asked, his low voice coated with the throaty hoarseness that bespoke his age. As he addressed Thorgunn, Magnus reached one large gnarled hand toward Braetana, barely brushing the side of her hot, flushed cheek before she jerked back in terror. If Thorgunn's hand had not caught her forearm, Braetana would have turned and run, though she knew not to where. But Thorgunn's grip both steadied and restrained her, forcing her to maintain the dead-on duel her eyes played out with Magnus. The shy reticence of the walk through town had disappeared, now replaced by a proud defiance she could not have anticipated any more than she could have repressed it.

Thorgunn nodded in agreement at the older man, then spoke to Braetana. "He asks if you are his daughter."

"Tell him to show me the ear clip," Braetana demanded defiantly.

"Praise Odin you are alive." Magnus spoke in unexpectedly clear English. Braetana had forgotten that Thorgunn had told her that the man knew her tongue. His apparent fluency calmed her fears somewhat, but did little to curb the fiery contempt she felt burning within her.

Magnus gestured toward the longhouse's interior. "Please, enter."

"I set no foot in the house of a stranger. Show me the stones," she repeated emphatically.

Realizing her intractability, Magnus disappeared into the darkness of the longhouse, then reappeared, extending a closed fist toward Braetana. It looked much as if he were going to strike her. He might as well have. Slowly, the gnarled fingers unfurled, revealing a painfully familiar arrangement of amber and jet set in gold. Braetana's breath caught in a gasp at the sight.

"A gift from me to your mother." Magnus's eyes lowered at the words, a hint of sorrow fleeting across his lined face. "Enter?" he again spoke, this time more as offer than command.

"I do not know you," Braetana spat venomously, unmoving from her stance in the longhouse's wide doorway. Thorgunn winced subtly at this unplanned resistance. He had thought her more committed to a better beginning.

"I know I am a stranger to you," answered Magnus, his uneven voice infused with kindness. "So we should begin what should have been done long past." This time, instead of repeating his invitation for Braetana to come in, he merely stepped aside, providing Braetana and Thorgunn an unobstructed path into the house's front room.

Though she still entertained a powerful desire to flee, something in Magnus's gesture worked strangely against that instinct. Without meaning to, Braetana found herself seated in a fur-lined chair alongside his hearth.

This longhouse differed radically from Einar's both in size and style. Though still dark, the interior was better lit because there were several wall openings instead of Einar's sole shuttered window. Each casement appeared covered with an opaque membrane which, though not allowing the occupant to see out, nevertheless admitted abundant light in.

Instead of one open room, as had been Einar's arrangement, Magnus's house consisted of four or five separate chambers, some lined up along the peaked roof's spine, and one or two extending sideways at right angles to the structure's main body. The sole curtain Thorgunn had used to partition their previous sleeping quarters now reappeared as several large tapestries, each much thicker and more ornately designed than the simple geometrical patterns of Einar's.

Both in spaciousness and in the fine detail of the rich furnishings within, the longhouse made clear that Braetana's father was a man of means. This was a fact she could not recall Thorgunn having mentioned. Such wealth, although unexpected in the household of a man she still considered little more than a heathen, did little to soften Braetana's heart. In fact, it had quite the opposite effect, making her even more angry that one so well positioned could mistreat a woman as good as her mother.

As the three of them sat tensely around an elaborate stone and clay hearth, Thorgunn spoke little. He thought it best to let Braetana's emotional maelstrom, however violent, run its course until spent. And if Magnus did not anticipate his daughter's enmity, he certainly was now aware of it. Even the unspoken words in her familiar violet eyes lashed out at him in fury and defiance.

"You have reason to hate me."

"And I do," Braetana allowed no hint of charity in her

hard-edged delivery. "Until this moment I had not thought to, but the mere sight of you makes me prefer death to my parentage. Is this where my mother was unwilling captive?" she asked accusingly, gesturing toward the large room. Magnus sighed audibly, now aware of the enormity of the task before him.

"It is true I bought her as a slave. But in time my heart became her captive."

"Truly? She was so loved she felt she had to flee you?"

Magnus knitted his weathered brow. "It is true she left. But I believe she did indeed hold love for me. Eir-. linn feared you would have no future in my house, that my son would inherit all and you would be threatened. It was only after she left that I learned from a maidservant she was with child."

"You have a son?" Braetana's mind spun wildly. She was confused. Why had Thorgunn failed to mention this?

"He is dead," Magnus answered lowly, sadness soaking his heavily lined face.

"Then my mother was not your only wife?"

Magnus cast a sudden puzzled look toward Thorgunn, then turned back to his daughter. "She was not my wife at all. Eirlinn was my mistress. When your mother lived here, my wife Thyri was yet alive. Though Thyri did not hold my heart as your mother did, Eirlinn feared her. And she feared your fate at Thyri's hands. But had I known that she carried you, I would never have let her go."

Braetana's lips parted at Magnus's revelation. "You were married to another?" In her shock, Braetana pressed herself against the arms of the large chair until she was fully upright.

"Yes," Magnus answered, futilely searching Braetana's face for a hint of understanding. "Yes, years before. Later, after Thyri and my son Ingvar died, I had relinquished all hope of pursuing Eirlinn. I sensed she had gone home to England, but I knew not where. And as a hated foreigner in a hostile land, how could I begin to look? How did I know she even lived? It was only the return of the ear clip through Frisian traders that gave me hope my beloved and my child might still survive."

Braetana continued to stand defiantly above the two seated Norsemen, her spine rod-straight in anger. "They did not tell you they killed her?" Braetana accused angrily.

A look of despair swept over Magnus's face as he lowered his head. "I feared they had. But seeing my concern for her, the Frisians denied it. I did not know with certainty—until now."

"The ear clip was returned to you seven years since." Braetana was hard-pressed to feel any sympathy for the old man seated dejectedly before her.

"Yes," Magnus softly conceded. "But time is no guarantor of wisdom. Then Ingvar still lived. Now he lies cold in foreign ground, fallen beneath the rage of an enemy's blade. It was with his death last winter that my thoughts returned to the child I knew must now be my heir. If you can forgive my foolishness, it will be a gift to an old, ailing Viking. But even if you cannot find that charity in your heart, all I have is still yours. Daughter?"

The implicit question was one Braetana felt she could not answer. It was enough that she was required to accept a whole new heritage, a legacy she had only held in complete disdain until a short month ago. Now this newfound father would ask her forgiveness for her own illegitimacy? It was a shame so terrible she had no idea how to even begin addressing it.

Thought after confusing thought tumbled through Braetana's swirling mind in an avalanche of anger and fear. More than anything, she wanted to free herself of this newfound burden. If only she could return to the simplicity of her previous fate, however unpalatable, at Glendonwyck. But then there would be no Thorgunn.

Even if she could flee, as Eirlinn had, she would lose her love in the bargain. Braetana suddenly realized that Thorgunn must have known her mother's situation all along.

"You . . ." She turned her confused gaze on him. "You did not tell me?"

Thorgunn had feared she would be angry at his concealment of her mother's true situation. Still, when he had first told her the extraordinary tale of her parentage, he had realized that her misconstruction of Eirlinn's role was better left uncorrected until she had grown more comfortable with the idea. Now he could see her cheeks flush hot and red at this additional betrayal.

"I told you Eirlinn was Magnus's mistress. But when you misunderstood, I thought it perhaps for the best. I knew it would only bring you pain."

He was right. Yes, she understood the reason for Thorgunn's silence. Unlike Magnus, whose coldhearted abuse had made her mother first a slave, then a fugitive, Thorgunn had thought only to spare her. It was an effort which, though laudable, now seemed almost laughable in the face of her overwhelming agony.

As she walked toward the chamber's far end, her fingertips pressing hard against the growing pain in her temples, Braetana heard the two men converse quietly in Norse. For once, she was glad she could not understand. Little about this new world seemed comprehensible, and the sorting out of this terrible new knowledge was hard enough without Magnus's intervention.

"I want to see Bronwyn," she demanded, suddenly spinning toward the two seated men. Their low talk halted abruptly as she spoke.

"Yes, of course," agreed Magnus. "She is nearby. I shall send for her."

Braetana stood, her back and palms resting on the edge of a large oak trestle table that provided her with much-needed support. Magnus delivered an apparent instruction in rapid-fire Norse to Thorgunn, who then rose and approached Braetana.

"I must go. Your father and I will speak soon. Will you be all right?"

The incredulity in Braetana's sloe eyes made an answer entirely unnecessary. It was all too clear that nothing about her current state even approached being all right.

"You are not leaving?" she asked in shocked disbelief.

Thorgunn could imagine the fright racing through her mind and knew he had little to offer her to stop its course. "I do not belong here now. Magnus and I will speak soon. In the meantime, Bronwyn will come. Please try—for us." Thorgunn spoke the last words softly, almost breathing them.

The reference to their eventual union made her ache to throw herself into the strong comfort of his loving arms. But even though her conciliation plans had been woefully undermined by her unexpected fury at Magnus, she had enough clarity of thought to know that any physical contact with Thorgunn would only worsen her current fate.

Thorgunn had not seen such a look on her face since their first day at Glendonwyck, and the compassion her pain stirred within him was nearly identical to that he had then experienced. He longed to reach out to her, to apply his embrace like a balm to her pain and confusion, to silence the forthcoming sobs. He ached to press his lips on her soft, yielding mouth. But there was business to be done first. Hard as it was, he would have to trust Braetana to her own instincts to survive this crisis.

What he *could* do was what Magnus had asked, to bring Bronwyn to comfort her. If he could not hold Braetana, at least Bronwyn could, hopefully calming her charge's thoughts.

"Soon," Thorgunn said as he left Magnus's long-house, leaving Braetana completely and unhappily alone with the last person she wished to share company with.

Magnus had easily read Braetana's confusion and anger. Recounting his past errors in handling women, he resolved not to compound either by forcing unnecessary conversation. Leading Braetana to the rear apartment that was to serve as her bedchamber, he quickly lit her small hearth. Once the fire blazed, he showed her the full wardrobe coffers he had prepared for her arrival.

"I had these prepared in the hope of your return. My seamstress could only guess your size. They will be made proper as you wish. Certainly, we will commission more—as you can see, there is a man's wardrobe as well. Though I cannot now envision you otherwise, I did not know when I sent Thorgunn if I had sired a son or a daughter."

Magnus was immensely pleased as he watched Braetana survey the Viking wardrobe. Only a few short weeks ago, he had thought to dispose of the clothing, his heart sinking with the news of his only child's and Thorgunn's untimely disaster at sea. Now Braetana would be able to wear the richly sewn selection of new chemises and overdresses.

Once she was satisfied her father intended to leave her alone, Braetana began a more in-depth perusal of the coffer's contents. It was clear that replacement of her current attire was much needed. The clothes Magnus had commissioned surprised her with their opulence, for the twill weave was quite fine and the embroidery edging each hem far more elaborate than any Braetana had observed on her brief trip through Trondbergen's main marketplace.

Though there was much to choose from, Braetana finally selected a mauve-toned chemise with a heavily pleated hem on both skirt and sleeves. Small aqua-colored stones she could not identify were sewn into a delicate leaf pattern around both.

From what she had seen of Viking women, she gathered the underdress required an accompanying apron, and Braetana chose a smooth sky blue linen piece as the chemise's complement. The straps on the apron, however, appeared to have no way of securing to the overdress's front, and the construction at first confused her. Then she recalled the women at the dock. Many wore domed brooches on their chests, and, sorting through a plentifully stocked pine jewelry box, Braetana found two silver clips and used them to attach both straps to the dress's front.

A beaded string of small rose quartz spheres completed the arrangement, hanging between the large round clasps and giving the appearance of a partial necklace. Sorting further through the jewel box, Braetana also chose teardrop-shaped quartz ear clips to match the brooches' beads. There was also a great selection of several wide-cuffed silver bracelets, and, though she had not worn such pieces before, Braetana chose one for each slender wrist.

Raising a small hand-held mirror in front of her, Braetana realized that, however she felt, she looked much the part of a Viking lady. Not only in her new wardrobe, but also in her fair porcelain skin and flaxen-hued hair, she much resembled the women she had seen en route from the drekar. With Magnus's confirmation of Thorgunn's story, everything inside her felt difficultt. The Viking clothes and adornments were but an outward reflection of the strange newness within her.

With a small ivory comb, Braetana began to slowly untangle her long, silvery strands of hair, methodically working each wind-wound knot to its strand's end. She prolonged the process, somehow hoping that her slow, hypnotic strokes could smooth away the unsolvable troubles that seemed to meet her everywhere she turned.

"Braetana." The call of Magnus's deep voice refocused her attention on the chamber in front of the closed tapestry. "Someone comes to see you."

Braetana set aside the comb and braced her back against the spine of a heavy oak chair in preparation for yet another of the shocks she had now come to expect as routine. But as the curtain parted, its opening revealed only the teary-eyed face of her much-loved Bronwyn.

"Lady!" The older woman rushed to embrace the adored child she had assumed lost at sea. "Oh, lady!"

Bronwyn buried her softly wrinkled face in Braetana's silky hair and clutched the younger woman tightly. For a moment, Braetana thought she would have to free herself from Bronwyn's grasp in order to breathe. Then, cupping both slender hands on either side of Bronwyn's cheeks, Braetana pulled slightly back with a careful look.

"Are you unharmed?" Bronwyn shook her head quickly.

"I am fine. Even well treated here. But I ached so, thinking I was alone. I was sure you were drowned."

Gesturing for Bronwyn to sit, Braetana unfolded the long, incredible story of her journey from the drekar to Einar's island and, finally, to her current situation. She recounted Thorgunn's tale of her past, augmenting it with what she had learned from Magnus. It was only as Braetana finished the saga that she realized Bronwyn's response was far from the shock she had expected to see in the soft green eyes. Braetana was puzzled.

"Is it not unbelievable?" she asked, leaning forward to place both hands on Bronwyn's well-padded knees.

"Not so as you might think, lady," she replied quietly. Braetana quickly understood the matter-of-fact response Bronwyn offered.

"You knew?" She was incredulous, unable to imagine how Bronwyn could possibly have knowledge of such an unlikely story.

Bronwyn lowered her head in shame at the secret she had kept so long. "I knew your mother many years before your birth. When she was your age, a Frisian raiding party came. There were many attacks in those days, and Glendonwyck did not yet have the protection of Edward's wall. She was taken, we thought killed. Two years later she miraculously returned to us, bearing an incredible tale of her life among the heathens.

"Your grandfather was delighted beyond belief to have her safe return and then he learned that she carried you. A husbandless daughter with child was a difficult fate for an ailing old man." Braetana's eyes narrowed as she understood the story's conclusion.

"So," Braetana continued, "he married her to Edward."

"Yes," Bronwyn answered. "Your grandfather and I alone knew the truth. He told everyone that your mother had escaped the raid and settled in East Anglia, married to a man soon thereafter killed. All knew of course that you were not Edward's; your mother was too far along when she returned to make that possible. But almost no one was aware of your real parentage. When Eirlinn's father and your mother died, only I knew the truth. And I was sworn never to burden you with the sadness of how you had come into this world."

Braetana could not believe the old woman's revelation. "How could you have kept this from me?"

"I did not think Magnus knew. But that morning, when Thorgunn came, I knew fate would bring you full circle. What will we do now?" Though twenty years Braetana's senior, Bronwyn's expression was now that of a beseeching child hoping for a magically simple answer to a complex situation.

Braetana turned away in silence, the truth of her situation suddenly much more final and real than ever before. She had thought perhaps she could come to accept her new parentage, make a sort of peace with her fate. But until now, until Bronwyn's confirmation of the incredible truth, the full import of her circumstances had not yet come to bear on her.

"Lady?" Bronwyn repeated. "What shall we do?"

Braetana touched one finger to her lips in thought, then sighed softly.

"Thorgunn will know."

XII

"A pleasant surprise, brother." Haakon's mouth twisted into a sardonic smile, his slight attempt at civility hardly concealing his distaste for Thorgunn. "I had heard from Niels you had been found, but dared not believe my good fortune."

"Disappointed?" Thorgunn's voice was a study in control.

Haakon held fast to the role of innocent. "I am afraid I fail to follow your logic."

"A brother lost at sea is little threat to your precious throne." Thorgunn strode toward Haakon. Defiantly, he seated himself in an impressively carved chair opposite Haakon's own on the raised wooden dais.

Haakon's face compressed into a familiar ugly sneer, which was scored with a cynical laugh. "Brother or no, an impoverished tradesman is no threat to my throne. As always, you flatter yourself. But that's just as well, for someone must."

Haakon shifted in the spacious fur-lined seat, tilting his head back in relaxed indifference. "And as much as I always enjoy your company, I must ask if there's a point to this unexpected visit?"

Thorgunn narrowed his eyes in scrutiny. "I thought only to assure you of my well-being, since I suspected you assumed otherwise. 'Tis all." Thorgunn rose, making his way toward the iron-plated door at the gabled end of the vast room. Placing one hand on the huge, curved iron handle, he turned back toward his brother. "We shall see more of each other now, I think."

"Truly?" Haakon feigned first ignorance, then sudden understanding. "Ah yes, Magnus's whelp is back as well. Did you not stand to gain some silver in that bargain?"

"Yes. Some silver—which I shall use to keep you close company."

Haakon had not considered that his ill-liked sibling would do anything else but return to the Shetland trade routes. Thus far, Thorgunn's visits to Trondbergen had been delightfully brief. The prospect of his half brother's more permanent residency displeased him greatly.

"You mean not to put back out to sea then?" Haakon was fearful he already knew the answer.

Thorgunn appeared to consider the issue, though his thoughts were already well set. "I am grown tired of the changing winds."

A hard edge returned to Haakon's face. "The winds may blow worse on land."

"Yes," said Thorgunn, smiling smugly at his nemesis. "But here at least I know from whence they come." Thorgunn opened the weighty door, temporarily flooding the smoke-filled chamber with daylight. The slam of the portal's weight against the longhouse's wooden frame was closely echoed by the sharp pound of Haakon's fist on the arm of his throne.

"A curse from Hel!" he said, then consigned his thoughts to silence.

The news of his brother's return had been bad enough. Now, Thorgunn's reward from Magnus proved an even more calamitous turn. At best, he would use the silver to buy his rightful residency. At worst, he could hire longships and warriors who might challenge Haakon's very throne.

Ever since their father Harald's untimely death, Haakon's mother Ingrid had made clear his half brother was best viewed with a cautious mixture of disaffection and mistrust. It was a sentiment supported in recent years by the sharp-tongued counsel of Haakon's wife, Gudrun.

So great was Ingrid's fear of Thorgunn's threat to the throne that she had repeatedly urged Haakon to banish his half brother completely. It was a suggestion Haakon would have taken, had he thought the jarls and fighting men of Trondbergen would have allowed it.

His right to rule depended on their goodwill. They had never trusted him as much as they did his sibling, and he knew his rights as konungr came only from Harald's annointing. To force Thorgunn out might well tax his nobles' faith in him beyond its means.

No, there was no room for mistreatment of his princely brother, however well it served his own purpose. But Thorgunn remained a burr under Haakon's saddle. Now he was one that promised to be a constant problem.

Suddenly the heavy tapestry separating the longhouse's great hall from a suite of private rooms snapped open, its parting revealing a richly robed and heavily bejeweled Gudrun. "I heard voices." She entered, pouring herself a chalice of mead from a nearby pitcher.

Gudrun's chemise and matching apron draped about her small form in closely matched shades of moss and light green. The color scheme was echoed by the amber beads and inlaid trefoil brooches that lay on the outfit's bodice.

Her dark ash blond hair, nearly a dullish brown, was gathered in a tight knot at her nape, and a silver hlao encircled her brow.

Around her neck hung a huge horse collar-shaped silver piece, its edges overlapping the domed side brooches. She looked and sounded much like an armored warrior as she moved toward her spouse.

Haakon dreaded the prospect of explaining the new predicament to his meddlesome bedmate. But he knew he must, were he to buy himself any peace.

"It is worse than I feared. Thorgunn not only lives, he means to stay."

"You allow this madness?" Gudrun fired him an accusing glance. "If we are to hold secure the throne, you must send him away," she announced summarily. "He is their favorite."

"I have little patience for your insults today." Haakon turned his gaze away from her. Gudrun often acted as if she, and not he, were konungr. It was a trait that he usually found extremely trying. Today, it was unbearable.

Had Ingrid not insisted on Gudrun's great political value to him as the daughter of one of Trondbergen's most esteemed families, Haakon would never have endured this quarrelsome match.

"What, exactly, do you propose I do?" he rebuked. "Will the jarls follow a konungr who exiles his own blood? I have already tried their patience by impoverishing him. That I was able to attribute to Father's preference for me. But I can hardly order him to leave without some explanation. He is not konungr, but, as you so generously put it, he is well liked."

"Which is exactly why he must go," Gudrun pronounced. "Who could say that, in daily comparison to you, the people would not prefer him?" Gudrun cocked her small head sideways, making Haakon for all the world wish to right it with a swift, hard slap.

"Such confidence from my beloved helpmate," he countered.

"I am more help to you than you know. And I tell you he must leave." Gudrun paused, filling a second cup with the sweet-smelling mead and offering it to the scowling Viking. "At any rate, he has no land and, thanks to the storm, no ship. He will find it difficult to earn the keep he wants as a trader here."

Haakon downed the drink quickly, then corrected Gudrun's misconception. "I believe he earns a great wealth delivering Magnus's precious package. He could buy drekars, crew—perhaps even some of his Jutlander mercenaries for an assault on Trondbergen. The jarls might even support such a daring claim, were he to mount it. And all this misery will be caused by Magnus's ill-conceived reward."

Gudrun furrowed her brow in disbelief, adding a most unattractive air to her dark-skinned face. "This is the doing of some half-Saxon brat?"

"At least you are only childless, not witless." The barb stung badly and Gudrun moved slowly away from him, her jaw set hard as she stifled a reply.

"I want only..." she began, but before she could

complete the thought, Haakon dismissed her with an angry slice of his hand through the smoky air.

"Be gone," he commanded brusquely. "My head aches enough without your company. I fear it will split wide open should you stay."

Gudrun knew better than to persist when Haakon wore such a black mood. Setting the cup on a nearby table hung with heavy gold brocaded fabric, she approached the same door from which she'd entered.

"I await your pleasure, my lord," she stated quietly. Pausing momentarily, she then left, yanking the curtain halves together in an angry seam behind her.

"Pleasure," grumbled Haakon to himself, although it would have concerned him little had Gudrun heard. "Little enough of that with this shrew." She had never been a great beauty, but Gudrun had seemed a tolerable match when Ingrid first chose her. What she lacked in appearance was more than made up by her family's silver hoards.

In truth, it was the power wielded by her father Jarl Halfdan that had most attracted him to her. When alive, his father-in-law had helped entrench and consolidate Haakon's own tenuous position as konungr. Now, two short years after his acquiescence to his mother's matrimonial choice, Halfdan was dead, and Haakon rued his hasty decision. No political value remained, only the legacy of an increasingly disagreeable wife.

How much silver had Thorgunn said? Haakon knew only that it was a great amount. Thorgunn had not named the weight, though Haakon's worst fears and his knowledge of Magnus's wealth suggested it was substantial.

He must find the old man and convince him to deter-mine grounds to withhold payment. At the very least, he must decide how much power Thorgunn could buy with the ransom.

The present day was nearly spent. Tomorrow would be soon enough to pay a visit to Magnus's longhouse. In the meantime, there was enough mead in the nearby pitcher. Refilling his heavy silver chalice, Haakon downed a full cup in an effort to numb his fears for his fate.

Since Braetana and Bronwyn had reunited, their time together was easily spent with the telling of lengthy explanations of the incredible happenings since their last meeting.

Braetana had shyly recounted her intimate relationship with her former captor and, although she'd anticipated a dramatic reaction from Bronwyn, she was surprised. Indeed, she received acceptance rather than chastisement.

Bronwyn smiled gently at her charge, raising one age-gnarled hand to stroke back an errant strand of Braetana's fine blond hair.

"So my child is to be married, then. . . ."

Braetana's own face reflected Bronwyn's soft smile. "God willing. Or rather Magnus willing. Thorgunn has promised to speak to him soon. I doubt I have done much to ease his way with my unbridled anger. Oh, Bronwyn, I don't know that I can ever make peace with this stranger I am told to call father."

Bronwyn searched for the words she hoped could lighten Braetana's heavy burden. "Truly his actions have not always been admirable. But from your tale, he tries to redress them. There may never be love in your heart for him, but perhaps you could learn to hold your hate at bay."

The task was a formidable one, an undertaking Braetana sensed impossible. Yet she knew Bronwyn was right. Little if anything could be gained from her continued enmity toward the aged Viking; much could come of their improved relations. As difficult as it would be, Magnus's daughter resolved to apply herself to making a relationship with him.

"Does the mutton suit you?"

"Yes, very well. I am fond of ptarmigan, but we suffered an overabundance of it on the island."

"I have not taken natverror in England. Is this very different?" Braetana sensed Magnus's great effort at conversation, but she wished he would let the matter be. Surely he did not care what she ate for supper in Northumbria. But she had promised Thorgunn to make a start.

"Mutton is common. As are beef and many meats and fruits you have here. Some of the spices differ. And there are some delicacies we do not possess. I had not tasted lutefisk until Einar's supplies came."

"I can have Cook make you some."

Braetana wondered what possessed her to mention the vile fish. Even an effort at simple conversation seemed difficult with Magnus.

"It is unnecessary. I would not want you to trouble yourself. Whatever you usually serve more than satisfies my preferences."

"It is a simple matter. It would give me pleasure. Tomorrow we shall have it."

"Very well." Braetana nearly choked on the mutton

just thinking about lutefisk's briny taste. Perhaps by tomorrow her stomach would do better.

"I trust your bed serves?"

"Yes, it is a great improvement over the bench I used on the island. Certainly better than the drekar."

A look of sorrow etched its way across Magnus's face. "The journey has caused you much hardship. I am saddened that my need to have you near me has cost you so. But to have my daughter here, in my own longhouse, is a joy I barely own words to describe. Is it too much to ask to be called Father?" He lowered his face as if to look up into Braetana's, searching for his hoped-for answer there.

Calling the cruel man who had bought her mother "Father" was the last inclination Braetana entertained. Still, Thorgunn would come tomorrow, and it would not do to infuriate one with much power over her fate.

"I will try—Father." The word came out hard. Both Braetana and Magnus knew it, and she reached for an excuse to end their embarrassment.

"I am tired from my travels. May I take my leave?"

"Of course." Magnus hoped a good night's rest would render her more tractable. The situation, at least, was not much likely to worsen.

Magnus's accommodations for Braetana were a great improvement over any arrangements she'd enjoyed since Glendonwyck. Instead of a bench fashioned into a makeshift pallet, Braetana now slept in a real bed, and its eiderdown mattress proved a great relief from the spartan accommodations on Einar's island. Nestled between the most luxurious bearskin she had ever felt and another unusual fur cover, Braetana spent the night drifting peacefully into the drugged weightiness of a dreamless sleep. Her belly was full and her body made warm by the blazing hearth Magnus's manservant, whom he called a *huskarlar*, carefully stoked before she retired.

Nearby, Bronwyn dozed on a similar cot. Though she had been spared much of Braetana's recent hardship, the old woman too slept a sleep much deeper and better than the fitful slumber of the preceding weeks. Her mind was now finally at ease with the knowledge that her beloved charge was not only well, but also close to her.

Thorgunn's accommodations were less sumptuous. His modest longhouse, unoccupied much of the year during his travels, consisted of but a few dark rooms. The longhouse's small, peaked roof nestled unobtrusively among a string of equally small domiciles on a roughly planked street. The location was some distance from both Haakon's and Magnus's more generous homes and bespoke his lesser status.

Unlike Braetana, Thorgunn lay with his eyes open, his mind a small craft blown unwillingly between the consciousness of sleep and his plans for tomorrow's meeting with Magnus.

In his brief discussion with the man, he had not hinted at tomorrow's intended topic. It was more prudent to allow Magnus the assumption that their conversation would address naught but the settlement of Braetana's retrieval fee. Despite the lost ear clip, Magnus apparently had no doubts about Braetana's true identity. Thorgunn eagerly hoped his plan to wed her would be as easily accepted.

Although painfully aware that his small wealth far from recommended him, Thorgunn prayed his royal lineage would hold some sway with the difficult jarl. And there was still Braetana, whose wishes Thorgunn sensed would not go unheeded by her father.

Her initially angry behavior toward Magnus had worried Thorgunn. But now he came to view it less as an alienating factor than an added incentive Magnus would have to grant his daughter's request. And, if Thorgunn could trust Braetana's eyes as he left Magnus's longhouse, she still wanted him. It was a sentiment his own loins echoed.

He struggled to dismiss his growing attachment to Braetana as mere lust. But ever since they left the idyll of Einar's island, his feelings toward her had grown into something beyond a need to gratify his baser desires.

Strangely, he now often found himself thinking of Braetana in other ways beyond that of having her beneath him. It was that angel's laugh—how it danced between a lilt and a throaty murmur and how she tossed that blond cascade of hair back like a great silken waterfall. Then there was her proud carriage, the way she defiantly stood in front of Magnus, unflinchingly facing a man many others more wisely feared.

Even longing for the feel of her velvet thighs spreading under him, Thorgunn now knew it was Braetana's spirit, as much as her body and fortune, that he needed to possess. This strange realization, the likes of which he had never before experienced, came to him as a feeling of surrender. It was a sentiment his hard-edged life and the values it spawned had given him scant opportunity to experience.

Even more surprisingly, Thorgunn found his attachment to Braetana less uncomfortable than he would have guessed. In fact, it felt more like a relief than an ambush. For the first time in his life, he was able to trust, completely and willingly, in the ability of another to not betray him.

Thoughts of Braetana's virtues played in his mind across a backdrop of her breathtaking beauty, possessing him again and again. In a futile attempt at sleep, Thorgunn tossed from one side of the bed to another.

Finally, conceding the inevitablity of wakefulness, Thorgunn rose, dressed himself in a heavy red woolen cape and left the small house in the hope that a midnight stroll might hasten his journey toward slumber.

The dark night air was brisk, although not uncomfortably so, and Thorgunn soon found himself following its slight wind toward the bathhouse perched on the grassy knoll just slightly away from the town's center. Tendrils of smoke curled skyward from the narrow chimney, beckoning him toward the cleansing heat inside.

Thinking some time within would aid him in sleep, Thorgunn stripped himself naked in the small anteroom and opened the door to the wood-paneled chamber inside. It was late, and, though the fire and small rocks surrounding it glowed hot from earlier stoking, the benches inside stood vacant. Thorgunn was relieved to find some much-needed privacy.

Dipping a long soapstone ladle into the oak water well, he threw the bowl's contents toward the gray hearthstones. The alchemy of the water and fire hissed hot, then rose in a burst of steam that suffused the small room with a moist cloud. Thorgunn added several more ladlefuls, then lowered himself slowly onto the long planked bench.

The tension of the past weeks escaped him at last. With a deep sigh, he rested his sinewy bare back against the penetrating heat of the creaking walls.

It had been a long journey to Northumbria and back, in more ways than he could have known at the voyage's onset. Where he had thought only to make his fortune, he had found a future as well, both joined in the sweet package of Braetana's soft and willing flesh.

Though they had only been three days parted, he ached for her, all the more for the knowledge that nearly a month would pass before the marriage ceremony could be arranged and their union finalized. It felt odd, to think of her in her absence. Women, once out of sight, were usually out of Thorgunn's mind.

Yet this half-English minx had the power to set his thoughts to her even while she was elsewhere. The new sensation was not unpleasant, and Thorgunn found himself more and more sure that this matrimonial arrangement would provide all his heart, as well as his purse, longed for.

The steam's heat had helped spend his need for her, and, after what seemed a long time, he rose and reentered the antechamber. Pouring the full buckets of water that stood nearby over himself, he washed the salty sweat from his flesh. As usual, the bath had left him feeling calm and languorous. Winding his way back toward his longhouse, Thorgunn's gait took on an uncharacteristic ease.

From the moon's height, he gauged it was nearly midnight, a guess confirmed by the still of the unlit streets that lay at the end of the path before him. Braetana was no doubt fast asleep within that darkness.

As his mind's eye painted its best memory of her exquisite features, Thorgunn stopped in his tracks. A slender silhouette approached from the trail below, it's form cloaked in shadow as it moved slowly toward him.

Unaware of his presence, the stranger lowered the woolen hood about her head and loosened the long mass of flaxen hair Thorgunn instantly recognized as Braetana's. Before he could speak, she lifted her head, meeting his stare first with surprise, then with joy at their unexpected encounter.

Though far apart, their bodies bridged the distance between them almost instantly. Mindless of any unobserved witness to their embrace, they met in a crushing press of passion, their arms encircling each other to bring them hard together in longed-for union.

Wordlessly, Thorgunn's mouth sought out the soft pleasure of Braetana's parted lips, his tongue entering her in a fiery explosion of unleashed love. Braetana needed no prompting to respond to his touch. She had thought to be long deprived of it. Now, miraculously, here it was in his hot, commanding mouth. She wanted it everywhere.

Thorgunn understood her need, and in one powerful move, he lifted her off the ground, his muscular arms supporting her as he carried their desire to a private nearby stand of fir. With one easy movement, Thorgunn knelt, then laid Braetana gently down atop the soft crackling bows on the small clearing's floor.

In their complete silence, each spoke all the other needed to hear. Thorgunn's powerful hands were eloquent in their brash exploration of Braetana's rose-tipped breasts, each greedy cup causing her back to arch in hungry need. She wished his touch to stay there forever. Then she prayed its fine torture to go on to her more secret places.

Her own fingertips slid beneath his cape and tunic and gently stroked the hard musculature beneath his bronze skin. His flesh was strong, unyielding. Its power seemed to radiate through her as her hands roamed across it.

Within moments, Thorgunn had relieved Braetana of both cloak and chemise. Having divested himself of his own tunic and pants, he spread himself atop her as a buffer against the evening chill. His mouth was now back on hers, their lips taking greedily of each other in unrelenting need.

Each knew this was only the beginning. In a moment, Thorgunn had nudged Braetana's soft thighs apart and rested poised above her, barely able to restrain himself from the entry he wanted so badly.

Her exquisite amethyst eyes locked on his own. She could not bear any more delay, but lacked the brazen words to ask for what she so desperately desired. Finally, she said all she could. It was enough.

"Thorgunn." Braetana made the name a plea, and he needed no further encouragement. With one sure hard stroke, he entered her, Braetana's warm moistness as welcoming as the rise of her hips toward him. Again and again he rode her, each penetration peaking in the union both so desperately needed.

Braetana moaned softly each time he withdrew, a wordless cry for his quick reentry. Time and time again he filled her, bringing her finally to the sharp edge of that explosion of pleasure she now knew would follow. As he slid in and out impossibly faster, Braetana felt herself climbing higher and higher, then blessedly slipped over the steep peak her senses had been ascending. He had set off within her a sudden cascade of pleasure. As Thorgunn's body found its own bliss inside her, he finished with one great thrust, burying his face in the sweet scent of Braetana's silken hair.

Until now, no words had passed between them, all that needed saying seemingly said with their bodies' sweet joining. But now Thorgunn grew aware of the danger their tryst might have entailed.

"Who knows you're gone?" he asked, rolling slightly to the side of her and lowering his voice to a serious tone.

"No one," she whispered, pausing to playfully kiss his cheek with her passion-bruised lips. "I could not sleep and slipped out for some air. I had not thought to find my stroll so invigorating."

Thorgunn issued a low, bemused laugh. Then he quickly rose, tossing Braetana's hastily discarded clothing back to her. "I have missed you," he said, smiling. "But however sweet, this was unwise. You must return quickly. And I should be more circumspect with my passions."

"I should hope not," Braetana teased. "Or I would come to think I had lost my appeal for you."

"Never. Only your virtue. Now back to your bed before we are both undone!"

Thorgunn planted a playful smack on Braetana's backside, then brought his hand back to caress the soft roundness of her buttocks. It was all he could do to resist taking her again, but reason prevailed. Against all instinct, he removed the offending hand and watched her poutingly obey his instruction to dress. With a quick kiss on the lips, he spun her to once again face the path, whispering softly in her ear as she turned.

"Tomorrow," he breathed, "I shall ask for you, and for that I shall need my rest. Now off!"

Thorgunn was about to provide a second backside slap when Braetana turned unexpectedly to him, pressing her warm lips against his own before he could protest further. Her kiss was long and passionate and yet gentle in a way that had not marked their most recent heated coupling.

Pulling back ever so slightly, she traced a soft path around his mouth with the wetness of her tongue, stopping only to breathe more than speak her good-bye.

"Tomorrow," she whispered, then turned away suddenly, scampering down the path and out of sight before Thorgunn had time to respond. In seconds she was gone, but the feel of her mouth on his own and the wonderful sense of his maleness inside her lingered on. He stood alone in the cool darkness, altogether preoccupied in a way he had never before known.

XIII

He's come to ask for me! Braetana suddenly connected Thorgunn's image with the guttural clacking of Norse spoken in the next room. Although she had been awake for some time, her excitement over Thorgunn's arrival had preempted her usual routine. It was now mid-morning, but she still wore only the light chemise she slept in.

Thorgunn's voice moved her to swift action, and she swung precipitously off the soft mattress and onto the oak planked floor. Eager to choose the most perfect outfit for this most special day, she scurried to the heavy wooden wardrobe coffer.

Braetana dressed hurriedly, intent on joining the conversation next door to add her own assent to Thorgunn's request for her. So great was her haste, she completely ignored the addition of the customary apron, wearing instead only a sky blue underdress whose form-fitting waist and low-cut embroidered neckline showed her slender figure off to fine advantage. With her long, nearly platinum hair unbound in a soft cascade around her shoulders, Braetana ran toward the main chamber's door, completely unaware she was still barefoot.

"It is an unheard of payment of silver!" Haakon looked much as if he had been struck by something heavy.

"She is my only child," Magnus added by way of explanation. The news etched Haakon's mouth into a disdainful snarl. He had never dreamed Thorgunn could command such a price, even for the return of so prized a possession. It was too great. With such wealth, he could buy drekars, mercenaries, perhaps even an assault on the throne. The jarls' support of him might fail if he were unable to defend against an attack by his Harald's firstborn.

"Have you thought to what end my brother might apply such a fortune?"

"It matters little," Magnus answered preemptively. "It matters to me only that my daughter is safely returned. My bargain with Thorgunn is one I choose to honor."

The curtain partitioning the rear chamber suddenly tore open, revealing a vision no amount of preparation would have allowed Haakon to anticipate. There stood Braetana, resplendent in the powder blue linen dress that clung suggestively to her bosom and slender hips. Her nearly waist-length blond hair gave much the appearance of an angel's mantle.

Haakon's review of her did not go unnoticed by Braetana. Though he was only one of several tall Vikings now facing her father, there was something especially disturbing about him that drew her immediate attention.

He released his clenched jaw at the sight of her. "Well worth the silver," he said, as much to himself as to Magnus. The words were Norse, but the appreciative leer creeping across his face needed no translation for Braetana's understanding.

Though she was accustomed to ignoring such rudeness, there was something particularly unsettling in the intense blue eyes that greedily stripped her of both dress and composure.

She had expected the voice to be Thorgunn's. Now, seeing instead a collection of Vikings, she suddenly grew aware of her inappropriately revealing apparel.

"I beg your leave," she spoke softly, lowering her eyes and turning to make her way back to the safety of Bronwyn and the bedchamber. She assumed her father was transacting some sort of business and would wish her gone. But no sooner had she taken her first step than Magnus's introduction brought her exit to an abrupt halt.

"Braetana, I present our king, Haakon."

Braetana froze at the sound of Magnus's words. Of course. The uneasy familiarity about the stranger now made sense. Expecting Thorgunn, it was instead his younger brother she found. Slowly and deliberately, she turned back to face the assemblage. But as she again caught sight of Thorgunn's darker-complected sibling, an unbidden shudder wound its way up the curve of her spine.

The facial features were reminiscent of Thorgunn, the broad curve of mouth, high brow, even the lay of the hair on his forehead. But there was something about the eyes. Though the shape was the same, some barely concealed malevolence swam deep within them.

Haakon's gaze burned through her, and it was only as a concession to Magnus that she suppressed a strong instinct to flee. Sensing her father would not allow her departure, Braetana remained the unwilling target of the Viking king's heated stare.

"So you are the fruit of my brother's labors. I see his voyage home was a pleasant one."

The compliment filled Braetana with discomfort, partly for its rude implication, but as much for the truth of its inference.

"Father," said Braetana in measured words, "I am unfamiliar with your customs—and with the proper greeting for a Viking king." The words were properly obeisant. Yet they were intended less for propriety than as a plea for Magnus to excuse her from her current awkwardness.

As she turned her eyes toward her father for instruction, Haakon answered before Magnus could. "Your presence is greeting enough, my lady. I trust you have not found your stay among foreigners too difficult thus far?"

"I am far from my home," Braetana replied cautiously, "but my father has done his utmost to see to my and my lady's needs. And your brother..." She halted mid-sentence, suddenly aware of the danger this imprudent conversational turn might lead her to.

"Yes, and my brother?" Haakon pounced on her words like a swift predator.

"Your brother—made my journey as comfortable as possible, considering the circumstances." Braetana felt blood rush to her face. She tilted her head down so that both Haakon and Magnus might miss the growing extent of her hot blush.

"You speak well of your escort—or should I say captor?"

"Haakon!" snapped Magnus angrily. "The circumstances of my daughter's return were unfortunate but unavoidable. What matters is that she may now assume her rightful role as my child."

"Yes, of course," Haakon conceded apologetically. And heir, he thought silently to himself. "My congratulations on your newfound family. Now, if you will pardon me, Lady Braetana, I must take my leave. I trust we shall see each other again soon."

"Yes, sire." Braetana hoped very much that would not be the case at all.

As Haakon and his retinue slammed the massive oak door behind them, Braetana felt the last few moments' tension drain from her body. The release was accompanied by an audible sigh. Though she still knew little of Haakon, just the few facts Thorgunn had told her, there was something about him she found distinctly disturbing. She pondered the stark difference between the two brothers, unaware of Magnus's stare.

"You are tired? It is still early in the day." It was a comment on her long sigh. "Perhaps I have underestimated the toll the trip has taken on you."

"No." Braetana then caught her intended explanation before it bought her more trouble. Haakon was, after all, king. Any intangible misgivings she might harbor toward him were nothing Magnus needed to share. No matter, anyway. How likely was she to cross his path once Thorgunn made her his bride?

"I mean, yes, perhaps I was taxed by the journey. Some fresh air might help. Am I free to walk about?" Though the morning had brought an improved mood toward her father, she still felt uneasy and awkward in his company. She hoped for some time to herself.

"You are my family now. Of course you may move about as you choose. A walk is a fine idea. The market is bustling this time of day. Perhaps Bronwyn can show you the stalls of wares. I'm sure my wardrobe preparations fell short of your accustomed dress. Your lady knows well the fabric vendors and seamstresses. And, if rumor serves, she can even strike a fair price in Norse. Though bargains are of little import to a lady of your station."

Magnus lifted the lid from an intricately decorated soapstone box atop a nearby trestle table. He withdrew a soft leather pouch of what sounded like coins, then pressed the small satchel into Braetana's hand.

"Please, see if our finery meets your taste." Braetana's mouth opened to protest, but Magnus closed her slender fingers around the silver before she could speak. "It would give me great pleasure. . . ."

Braetana lowered her eyes in accession. "Yes, of course. I shall ask Bronwyn." Braetana disappeared into the side bedchamber, thinking Magnus's suggestion would at least keep her mind from turning like a wild top over Thorgunn's imminent proposal. She would go as her father bade her. And, when she returned, he would greet her with the longed-for news that she would soon become Thorgunn's bride.

The last few days since she and Thorgunn had taken up their charade of unfamiliar propriety had been most painful. Her ache for his powerful arms about her and his hungry lips upon her own had only been made all the worse by the preceding night's delicious but hurried assignation.

Before Thorgunn, Braetana had known no other man. Now, having known him, she could not imagine how she had survived all the desolate years that preceded his fiery touch. Perhaps Magnus's suggestion would temporarily distract her from her longing.

At Braetana's bidding, Bronwyn dressed both herself and her charge, adding a saffron-hued overdress to the form-fitting blue chemise Braetana had appeared in earlier. With efficient instructions, she then guided her charge from Magnus's longhouse into the narrow winding street that led downhill to the pleasant chaos of the street vendors below.

Earlier, Braetana had only glanced at the cluster of jam-packed stalls on her frightening introduction to Trondbergen. Now she allowed herself a more leisurely perusal of their treasures. She was pleasantly surprised, both by the volume and by the quality of the merchandise that greeted her.

Such a display seemed unusual for a relatively small town. Bronwyn, however, with the advantage of an additional month as resident in the fjord's hamlet, explained Trondbergen's significance as a major western trade center.

Though small farms not far from town served the landed's needs, the village's main livelihood stemmed from its coastal trade, not only with other Norsemen, but also with friendly Frisians, Slavs, and Jutlanders. As seamen, the Trondbergen Vikings ventured wide, returning their treasure for trade in the open stalls lining the wide main street. On their journeys, they spread Trondbergen's trading reputation, a fact that accounted for the not infrequent appearance of other Viking longships winding their way through the deep-channeled fjord.

Magnus had been generous with his silver, the value of which became clear to Braetana as the cart borne by his huskarlar Knut grew full with her purchases. At Glendonwyck, Edward's tight purse often denied her the garments she should have owned. Now Braetana found much to please her among the fabric and designs the vendors offered.

From a seemingly unlimited selection of colors, for the Viking women reveled in bright dress, Braetana chose several pieces of expertly woven linen, her favorite a soft lavender. To be sewn as a complementing tunic, she purchased a radiant white silk, and finally, a spool of glistening gold thread with which to embroider the sleeves and hem.

The materials were exquisite—much more finely fashioned than Braetana would ever have guessed of what she recently considered a heathen culture. But even more surprising were the breathtaking wares of gold and silver, twisted and woven by Viking jewelry smiths into countless intricate patterns in brooches, rings, and serpentine-shaped arm bracelets.

If she had not known before that her father was a wealthy man, Braetana knew it now. The seemingly small purse of silver he had pressed into her palm indulged her heart's every desire, buying not only two domed silver brooches displaying a mysterious tangle of front-footed beasts, but also an equally lovely sterling arm band, its thick center a mass of silver and black waves lapping one upon the other.

The jewelry smith was apparently aware of Braetana's identity. He insisted on matching silver beaded ear clips and completed the ensemble with a twisted silver hlao band that encircled her blond head with a delicate acanthus leaf pattern. Altogether, the purchases were quite an embarrassment of riches.

Though Bronwyn vigorously protested, Braetana also insisted on adding to her maid's wardrobe coffers, purchasing fabric and commissioning several bright chemises and tunics for the older woman's rotund figure.

Finery in tow, Braetana, Bronwyn, and Knut threaded their way back through the thick crowd. Each was more than slightly aware of the hushed gossip that could be heard behind them as they passed.

As she drew closer to Magnus's longhouse, Braetana's thoughts of Thorgunn caused her pace to grow in speed. Soon, in a near dash across the hollow-sounding planks of the village street, she left both Bronwyn and the cart bearer breathless in their efforts to match her ever-quickening footsteps.

Thorgunn must have asked by now, she assured herself. She issued a silent prayer that Magnus would assent to her longed-for union and the happiness she knew it would bring.

Much the same hope occupied Thorgunn's thoughts as he faced Magnus's expressionless response to his request. The older man turned away from his daughter's imposing suitor, rounding the longhouse's main dining table. Slowly, he lowered his crooked but still proud form between two wooden pillars into the seat reserved for the house's lord.

"Your request is bold," Magnus stated matter-of-factly. Thorgunn's prayer for a future with Braetana now seemed less likely than his earlier optimism had led him to believe. He must play this carefully or he risked losing not only his fortune, but also quite possibly his life. Magnus must not learn that Thorgunn had deflowered his daughter.

"Yes, Jarl Magnus, bold enough to defend your daughter."

"Think you she needs defense?" Magnus appeared perplexed. He pressed both palms flat on the table's top, and suddenly rose with great effort.

Thorgunn sensed Magnus's irritation and hurried to explain. "I would hope not. She is, after all, daughter of Trondbergen's most powerful jarl, a man revered both as a great warrior and as a wise trader. And yet many will not forget your child is half-Saxon, daughter of a woman who, while a lady in her own land, was forced by circumstance to slavery here. Ours is not a culture of caste. But think you all can easily forget how many brothers, sons, and husbands have fallen on Saxon soil? With a marriage to the konungr's brother, Braetana would be safe, even if you were no longer here to protect her."

Magnus knew his ill health was easy to see, but was still irritated by the reference to his own mortality. He had not thought to marry Braetana off so quickly. Thus far, his thoughts had turned only to the proper legitimization of her as his heir and daughter.

Yet Thorgunn was right. What if he should die before he could see her safe with her birthright? Thorgunn was young and bullish and clearly a defender few men would choose to reckon with.

Magnus cocked his curly head sideways, lowering his eyes briefly in thought. Suddenly he lifted them again, training his stare on Thorgunn's motionless face. "And how do you plan to provide for her future? With the silver hoards of a disenfranchised prince, a man who initially sought my daughter only for the reward her return would bring?"

It was the question Thorgunn had dreaded but could not avoid. Age had not made Magnus any man's fool. All Thorgunn could do was to answer with the truth.

"As you well know, I own no great fortune. But I have earned my share of silver through trade. Enough to keep a wife. And if you still honor the business between us. . . ."

"Your finder's fee is a pittance compared to the fortune Braetana will one day possess. Surely your request has considered this," Magnus snapped suspiciously. He was less concerned with the disposition of his wealth than with Thorgunn's motives in seeking Braetana's hand.

"I consider the disposition of your estate entirely your business—and none of mine," Thorgunn answered calmly, hoping he'd handled this awkward matter as well as possible.

Magnus walked to a small wooden shelf mounted on the longhouse's back wall and poured himself a tall glass of ruby-colored wine. Without turning back to Thorgunn, he again addressed him. "The marriage of my only child is not a matter to decide quickly. I will think on it. Until then, take the silver from the soapstone box near the door. Should I favor your request, you can use it as your portion of Braetana's bride price."

"My debt to you, Jarl Magnus." Thorgunn had intended to forfeit the silver in the hope that such generosity would further recommend him as son-in-law. But, standing next to Magnus's money coffer, knowing he had the jarl's blessing to take it, some old and familiar need rose within him. What if his plan miscarried and Magnus refused? Then he would have nothing.

If Magnus agreed, all would eventually be his. But if

not, he had legitimately earned Braetana's ransom. Magnus heard the box's lid open and the jangle of coins, followed by the creaking of the longhouse front door.

Thorgunn thought it had gone well. He had never hoped for immediate agreement. Such an important decision was not one Magnus was likely to make in haste.

All things considered, he allowed himself every expectation fate would favor him. Then all he'd hoped for, worked for, deserved, all the power and position rightfully his but wrested from him by Haakon's jealous greed and fear—all would come about, and Braetana as well. Beautiful Braetana, still unaware of her great value as Magnus's daughter, frightened and confused by her newfound heritage, and willing to appoint Thorgunn as her protector.

How fortunate fate had come to him in such an irresistible package. He would wait two days. If, by then, Magnus had not answered, he would press his suit again to become Braetana's husband.

"Thorgunn?" Braetana's tone indicated it was not the first time she had spoken his name as he stood lost in thought. He was still within reach of Magnus's imposing front door. Thorgunn's eyes turned toward the radiant vision before him. Without his bidding, an odd yet pleasing feeling swelled in his chest, its outward markings the softening of his pursed lips into a gentle, welcoming smile. Braetana's eyes searched his broad, chiseled features for an answer to her unspoken question.

"He will decide soon. I should think he means to ask your thoughts on the matter."

Braetana's mouth burst into a beautiful smile, her lavender eyes echoing the sentiment as they danced with joy. "My father will say yes. I shall insist upon it! Then you and I shall be together as we were meant to be."

Without thinking, Braetana stood on tiptoe, throwing her arms about Thorgunn's broad shoulders and attempting to press her lips against his in expression of her wild joy. But before their mouths could touch, Thorgunn turned his head sideways, then took both her wrists in his large hands, pressing her back and away from him.

"Lady," Thorgunn said half laughingly, "you forget yourself. I have only just asked for you. Do not act for all the world to see as if our wedding would but legitimize the sin we have already committed. Your father believes I have been only your escort."

Braetana's mouth opened wide in shock at how easily she had forgotten herself in the broad light of day. Thorgunn was right of course. To now damage their chances together could be a costly mistake.

"Yes, of course." She swallowed breathlessly as she turned to search for witnesses. She was relieved that the cart bearer had already taken her wares around back. Only Bronwyn had seen her unleashed passion.

"Yes, sire, I must go in now and speak with my father. I have much to tell him of my preferences." With that, Braetana scurried inside, leaving a smiling Thorgunn behind in the bright Norwegian midday sun.

"Father! I would speak with you!" Magnus turned to face the daughter he could scarcely believe was his. How could he consider relinquishing her?

Though he sensed Braetana's still-distant mood, her demeanor toward him had softened somewhat from the anger of their first meeting. Magnus much hoped the bond between them would continue to grow into that of real parent and child. His expression bespoke a man who carried much on his mind.

"You look for all the world as if you already know that of which I would speak to you. Thorgunn. . . ."

"Yes, I wish it!" Braetana interrupted, uncharacteristically rushed in her insistence on speaking. "I wish to be his wife." Her enthusiasm caught the old Viking off guard.

"I must say your ardor gives me pause. I had not thought you to so quickly accept your new heritage, much less marry into it."

Braetana was suddenly aware of the need to temper her plea with logic, lest Magnus fully understand her need for Thorgunn. "Father, it is only through a quirk of fate that I was not yet married in England. I am of more than the Saxon age to be wife, certainly several years past that by Norse standards. Thorgunn has seen me safely through a difficult journey. He has earned my trust. I beg you to let him have yours."

Braetana gripped her hands tightly in front of herself. Anticipating Magnus's answer, her finely etched brows arched together in an unposed question.

His daughter's impassioned plea sent a look of tenderness across Magnus's yielding face. "I understand your wishes, my child. And I do not seek to counter them. But there is much to weigh here. Having lived so long without you, you must understand my reluctance to send you so soon from under my roof." Then, seeing Braetana's anxiousness for the answer he had not yet offered, he said, "I will give you my decision tomorrow. Surely one brief night of not knowing will prove bearable."

Braetana stretched out her hands, palms up, toward

her father in protest. "But . . ." She stopped herself mid-sentence, sensing that, despite Magnus's avowed love for her, there still were limits to her privileges. Better to hold her tongue for now. It was nearing natverror and the next day's sunrise would no doubt bring her the answer she desperately hoped for.

"Very well," she answered quietly. "I shall hear your decision tomorrow. I know it will follow my heart."

As Braetana left the main hall, disappearing into her chamber to help Bronwyn in sorting the new purchases, Magnus smiled. In all the ways that mattered, she was Eirlinn's child. Her tall, proud carriage, her lilting ribbon of a laugh, and especially her deep violet eyes all evoked long-buried images of the woman who had owned his heart.

His match with Thyri had been a loveless one. It was an unpleasant business arranged by their families and generally without joy, save the now dead son she had given him. Together Ingvar and Eirlinn had provided the hope that Thyri had managed to drain from his life. And now, with his son fallen in battle and Eirlinn taken by her own fears back across the North Sea, Braetana was the only treasure he had left.

Magnus considered her a great gift from the gods. It was for this reason that, unlike most fathers, who would easily accede to any sort of a royal match, Magnus felt the debt of his lifelong neglect of Braetana. Such responsibility prevented him from making any ill thought-out and hasty disposition of her fate.

The proposal from Thorgunn had come as a surprise, though with each passing hour Magnus grew better able to understand how their mutual attraction had occurred.

Thorgunn had apparently treated her well, inviting

more than her simple admiration in the process. And he was a handsome young man, much sought after by the local maids and as close to the throne as possible save becoming konungr himself.

It was true enough that Thorgunn's impoverishment did not wholly recommend him as son-in-law. Yet the size of his silver chest would bear little importance should he wed a woman as wealthy as Braetana would eventually be. And it was precisely this which worried Magnus. To see Braetana was to understand how easily a man could love her. Yet, as her father, he had also to ask whether Thorgunn loved his daughter, or whether he loved all she stood to inherit. Braetana seemed blinded by her affection for her former captor, and she had apparently not yet considered the import of her wealth. All the more need, then, for Magnus to think seriously on the matter.

The issue churned through the old man's thoughts throughout natverror, and Magnus barely spoke enough to inquire if Braetana was pleased with the roast elk and boiled potatoes. Though often prone to the luxury of more than one cup of wine with the evening meal, Magnus uncharacteristically abstained this evening. Braetana, half guessing that his behavior was due to the decision at hand, did not press him with questions on the matter. She ate little, her stomach still wildly aflutter with eager anticipation for her father's decision regarding her matrimonial fate.

He had promised an answer on the morrow. But, despite Bronwyn's urgings for patience, Braetana felt barely able to control the wild mix of anxiety and excitement coursing through her veins. Even Bronwyn's insistence upon occupying her with wardrobe preparation and the nightly ritual combing of Braetana's long blond hair did little to calm her. Her father *would* make the decision she hoped for—if she let herself believe anything else, it might curse her chances.

Repeating this belief over and over to herself, Braetana indulged in a cup of wine to allay her fear. Even so, it was hours after Bronwyn fell asleep that her charge found herself able to follow suit, and her final sweet descent into sleep was all the more wonderful for the long wait that had preceded it.

Braetana drifted far from the evening's fears to a haze-filled room where only she and Thorgunn stood, facing each other in the eye of a pool of swirling warmth that spun like water all around them. His large, strong hands reached out slowly toward her, cupping her delicate face on either side. Then, with deliberate intent, he pulled her languorously toward him, stopping only when their mouths were but a breath apart.

In exquisite torture, Thorgunn's lips moved gently across her own, his warm moist tongue daring to enter her mouth, then quickly withdrawing. His teasing left her hungry for more.

Suddenly, he was fully and forcefully against her, their mouths and bodies pressed tightly together in a fusion of white-hot passion. Had their union not been a dream, surely Braetana's ecstasy would have been defined in specific pleasures, in the touch of his eager, exploring hands on the tips of her full breasts, in the exciting feel of his weight upon her, his manhood ready for entry into her moist center.

But instead, the reverie washed like a great wave over the smaller ones her experience had known before, leaving her with the distinct sense that Thorgunn had not so much entered her body as her soul. In some unearthly way they could never again be quite separate, but were instead bound inextricably together in life and whatever would follow it.

Braetana's only wish was that their union would never end. So occupied was she with this wish that the knock at the door must have gone on for some time before its rapping sound intruded on her dream.

"Shh . . ." a deep-timbered whisper spoke into her ear. "It is nothing, my love. . . ." Thorgunn's voice trailed off into the dark oblivion to which Braetana had by now happily and completely succumbed.

XIV

"Where is my head?" In her efforts to don the rose-hued silk underdress, Braetana had managed to completely tangle the neck and sleeves. She looked less in need of Bronwyn's advice than of her quick ministrations.

"Lady, however did you manage to twist the dress so? I think you hurry too fast to serve your purpose."

"My purpose is to finish dressing so that Father can tell me that today I am betrothed to Thorgunn. I must look very special. Now please help me with this maddening chemise!"

Bronwyn could see that Braetana had no intention of resting until she had finished her preparations and found Magnus.

"I hope this day brings the fate you depend on."

"Father will not counter my wishes, but you shall if you do not share my high hopes," she added playfully. "Now, please, the aqua overdress. And the new silver brooch and hlao. Yes, today I shall dress for my part as a Norse bride!"

With speed previously unwitnessed by her maid, Braetana donned both the overdress and its latch brooches, then added the new silver ear clips and neck-lace. Braetana completed the ensemble with the hlao. A large imported mirror, purchased by Magnus from Frankish traders, reflected a radiant vision in soft blue and pink. Her slender figure was shown off to fine advantage beneath the tailored sea blue apron, and her long cascade of flaxen hair tumbled like a waterfall from beneath the richly designed silver band.

"Will I do?"

"Neither Magnus nor Thorgunn will have seen a sight as lovely as you, my child."

The compliment filled Braetana with much-needed confidence. Quickly throwing her arms about Bronwyn, she planted an enthusiastic kiss on the Saxon's cheek.

"Then let us not wait, for my destiny does not!" Braetana let forth a peal of girlish laughter, then hurriedly pulled the thick curtain aside. She almost ran into the main long hall where Magnus stood with his back toward her.

The rapid patter of Braetana's deerskin slippers on the wood-planked floor caught Magnus's ear and he turned slowly to face her. She was an unearthly vision in swirls of rose and blue fabric, her breathtaking beauty never before as finely displayed as it was now by the elegant clothing of a Norse noblewoman.

Braetana arched her blond brows in question. Receiving no response, she posed her urgent query in words. "My marriage—you have decided?"

Magnus's eyes locked on his daughter's. With slow, carefully taken steps, he approached her, stopping only when they were but an arm's length apart. Deliberately, he placed his huge wrinkled hands on each of her narrow shoulders, then spoke. "Yes. You shall wed. . . ."

Braetana gasped sharply with glee. Knocking Magnus's arms aside, she threw her own about his neck in an explosive display of gratitude.

"Oh, Father, thank you! My fondest wish is to be Thorgunn's wife!" In an outpouring that surprised even Braetana, she pressed her soft cheek against the graying mass of Magnus's curls, kissing his neck and laughing all at once.

Suddenly Magnus grabbed both her wrists in his hands, pushing her away from their embrace. Again facing her, his faded blue eyes looked intently on her own. It was only then that Braetana became aware of the odd fact that her father was not smiling.

"You will wed Haakon." Magnus waited, knowing the news would come as a shock. He thought it best to let the decision's import take hold before he offered any further explanation.

Braetana's lips parted in confusion and the deep amethyst eyes narrowed as if in order to better see what Magnus was trying to say.

"Haakon? He is already married!"

"It is permissible for a Viking to dissolve an ill-fated match. Haakon will soon free himself of Gudrun, and then you shall be drottning—his queen. It is an enviable fate."

Braetana's thoughts whirled in confusion.

"I do not understand!" A sharp snap downward of her slender arms freed her from Magnus's grasp. "It was Thorgunn who asked for me—surely you are mistaken."

"No," Magnus answered calmly. "But I understand your confusion. Thorgunn did come, yes. And in truth I was considering his proposal. Until later last night when

Haakon appeared at my door with a more desirable offer, one that no father who cared for his child could refuse."

"You dare to speak to me of conscience!" Braetana spat. "You know I love Thorgunn! What misguided act of conscience would deny me the husband I love, substituting instead a man I do not even know?" Hot tears of anger welled in Braetana's eyes and now spilled unchecked down her cheeks.

Magnus had expected some initial displeasure from Braetana regarding his decision. But if he had anticipated a small storm, his daughter now offered instead a full-blown gale.

Magnus paused, considering how best to deal with Braetana's apparently uncontrollable fury. Such resistance on a child's part would typically be met with harsh punishment. But there was nothing typical about Braetana's life thus far, and Magnus realized that certain allowances must be made.

It was clear that he had underestimated her attachment to Thorgunn. This in and of itself disturbed him. The man had befriended her on the frightening journey home, and it was not uncommon for captives to grow fond of their captors—Eirlinn had certainly shown him that. Still, he had thought his daughter would find the choice between an impecunious Norse prince and a wealthy king an easy one.

She was failing to fully appreciate the circumstances of Thorgunn's position. Perhaps if he could not improve her opinion of Haakon, he could correct her views on Thorgunn.

Magnus reached out, laying his hands on either side of Braetana's head and forcing her to face him.

"Unhand me!" She hurled her words at him like weapons, struggling to free herself from his touch.

"No," Magnus countered firmly, tightening his grip on her. "Not until you listen to my words. And *hear* me. I know my decision is not as you planned. But it is in your best interests, even if you cannot trust in that now. Let me, daughter, at least make clear what does not serve your interests. This preference of yours for Thorgunn—I think you do not appreciate all the qualities of the man whose bed you seek."

"I know enough!" snapped Braetana, not waiting for any further explanation. "I know he has treated me with kindness and concern and love, which I have experienced little enough of in my life. What else is important?" Tears now rolled liberally down her cheeks, making Magnus's task more difficult with each passing moment.

"Think you it is truly your love alone he seeks?" Magnus's eyes and voice softened. He had hoped to avoid confiding his fears to Braetana, but her resistance now left him little choice.

"My child, you are a very wealthy woman. My fortune, which will soon be your legacy, is one of the greatest in Trondbergen. Thorgunn is disinherited, and he has long incurred Haakon's ill will. In his current poverty, he cannot stay here—unless he finds a way to right his situation. Do you think he'd have brought you home had there not been a great amount of silver promised for your return?"

Braetana's brows arched in confusion, and Magnus could see that he needed to try harder to make her understand.

"You are a beautiful woman. Any decent man would

want you as his bride. But Thorgunn is a man whose stock in trade has always been greed. You think he loves you? It is your silver he loves—you must see that."

"That is a lie!" Braetana cried angrily, backing away from Magnus's reach as if physically struck by the insult. "Is it so hard for you to believe that someone could love me for myself?" Braetana's hands flew to her face, covering her eyes as her fragile composure dissolved.

"No, my daughter," Magnus offered gently, placing one hand on top of Braetana's shaking shoulder. "It is easy to believe that any man could love you, but Thorgunn is not that man. Before Haakon asked for your hand, I might have agreed. Whatever his motives, at least Thorgunn would have protected you. But now, there is no question."

Magnus had offered his daughter all the understanding and solace he had within him. Now it was time to proceed with the arrangements. Braetana would simply have to find her own peace with his decision.

"Haakon will handle the matter with Gudrun, although we need not rush, since you must first be legitimized as my heir. We can wait until tomorrow before we begin our plans for that. If all goes well, you shall be queen in less than two moons. That is how it shall come to pass."

The silence that followed Magnus's pronouncement jarred Braetana from her misery to the reality of her father's dictum. He would not negotiate this—well enough, neither would she. If she could not be Thorgunn's wife, then she would be no one's. She would not allow him to force her into an unconscionable union with Haakon.

"Fine." She spoke calmly, her crying finished and her voice controlled. "I will not wed Thorgunn, but neither will I marry Haakon. Unless Norse custom also allows you to speak my vows for me at the altar."

As Magnus stood facing Braetana, he saw much of himself in her stubborn independence. It was a resemblance that little pleased him at this moment.

"I can make you queen even without your consent," he followed. "But I trust that as you think on the matter you will choose to speak for yourself—and for reason."

Magnus sent a final somber stare in his daughter's direction, then turned and proceeded toward the door, stopping only to advise her of his immediate plans. "Arrangements must be made with Haakon. I shall return by midday."

"Better not at all," Braetana mumbled furiously. But it was too late for Magnus to hear her response. Her comment was met only with the slam of the longhouse door.

As Braetana looked upward, she crashed her clenched fist down painfully hard atop the oak trestle table. "What am I to do now?"

The thought of living without Thorgunn brought a sharp pain to her chest. Just moments ago, when she'd misunderstood Magnus's decision, she had thrown her arms about him in great joy, her heart bursting with the thought of becoming Thorgunn's bride. Now, alone in the huge, dark longhouse, she thought of how empty life would be were she forced to face it without Thorgunn's love.

They had promised themselves to each other, made plans, made love. Now the past paled before the thought of a future without any real meaning. A miserable and familiar feeling of despair, much the same as had dominated her when she had thought herself destined for Edward's marriage bed, reentered her heart.

Her mind dwelled on her problem. Perhaps she did not need Magnus's consent to marry. Thorgunn had apparently lived outside the canons of Norse law before— why not now?

Yes, she concluded, they could flee, perhaps back to Einar's island, to someplace free of Magnus's and Haakon's power. Unless. . . .

Braetana's plans of escape ground to an abrupt halt as she recalled her father's arguments. He had said Thorgunn was no more than a mercenary, a man whose lust for wealth had led him to pursue her. Magnus had claimed that Thorgunn's values were measured by silver, not by his heart. Could such terrible accusations be true?

Her father had paid Thorgunn to retrieve her. When Magnus first mentioned it, it did not seem all that odd. Yet it was strange Thorgunn had not told her.

She dismissed it as a simple oversight, and yet, if she could believe Magnus, she stood to inherit a tremendous fortune. Thorgunn had spoken little of his own situation, but she knew that his relationship with his half brother was strained at best, hardly one that would suggest much generosity on Haakon's part.

Could it be that he only pursued her for her silver? Could she have been so stupid as to have mistaken his greed for love? Did Magnus, knowing Thorgunn longer and better, tell the truth? She had been betrothed for money once before in the match with Edward. Had it nearly happened again?

Each time the thought went through her mind, Braetana shook her head as if to dismiss it, only to have it return again moments later.

Braetana examined and reexamined Thorgunn's behavior, hoping to find some definitive action that could prove or disprove Magnus's damning claim.

But she knew she would not find her answer in logic. This was a decision to be made clearly and simply in her heart, a part of Braetana which, at the moment, was no better than a chorus of contradicting voices. She struggled to end her doubts.

No, he had said he loved her; what more proof of his motives could she ask for? Were she impoverished, he would have behaved no differently from the way he already had.

The problem was not with Thorgunn, but with Magnus. Her father had made it clear that he would allow no such marriage to happen. Worse yet, she was now to be promised to Haakon, a man about whom she knew nothing except that his very gaze made her flesh shudder with fear and loathing.

She had spoken brave words of refusal to Magnus's stern edict. In truth, Braetana did not know what ends he might resort to in order to see his plan through. All this was made so much worse by her captivity in a pagan land an ocean away from her home. At least with Edward she would have had Glendonwyck. What would she have here as Haakon's queen? Surely only more suffering and misery. Having temporarily escaped such a fate, she was now sure she could not bear it again.

Braetana released a long sigh. Her anger and fear had drained her. No longer able to support herself, her body collapsed exhausted atop the smooth oak planks beneath her.

The creaking sway of the ponderous door caused her eyes to open suddenly. Though the sun from outside flooded the dark central chamber and her eyes narrowed with the explosion of light, she could still tell that the silhouette towering over her was Thorgunn. She had seen him thus once before, that first day at Glendon-wyck when he had come to steal her away.

What does he come for now? She asked herself, afraid of the answer.

"Braetana." Her name was spoken gently, as if the word were a plea. "I have seen Magnus. We will find a way."

The sight of him banished all doubt from her mind. There was love in his eyes. This was all a terrible mis-understanding. She raised her arms up to him and he lifted her effortlessly into his tight embrace.

"He plans to wed me to your brother." Braetana had thought her tears spent, but now they came again, un-controllably.

"I know. But it will not come to pass."

Thorgunn placed both hands on either side of Brae-tana's shoulders, which rose and fell with every ragged breath she took.

"My darling, I had hoped this would go easier. But even if Haakon frees himself of Gudrun, it will be some time before all can be put in order for your nuptials. Your father will not force you once he sees the pain his decision has wrought."

"He has seen it and it matters not. I will go anywhere

you want. Back to Einar's, to the mountains. I need no home beyond that of your arms. We cannot stay here."

My God, she means to leave! The thought dealt Thorgunn an unexpected blow. He had barely had time to consider the problem of Magnus's refusal. It had not yet occurred to him that Braetana would choose flight over her planned fate. On reflection, he could understand why. Still, he had to make her see the wisdom of remaining. If she fled Magnus, there would be no dower. The old jarl might even demand the return of her retrieval fee.

"Surely you do not mean to leave a father you have just found?"

Braetana was stunned by Thorgunn's response. He, better than anyone, knew how she felt about Magnus.

"He is no better than a stranger to me. And even if I had feelings for him, I would still lose him gladly in order to be with you. We must go!"

"We cannot."

"I do not understand your meaning," Braetana said.

"Even on the fastest drekar, they would catch our wake. Magnus and Haakon would not let you escape. They would turn the seas bottom up to find you. You forget the lengths to which your father has already gone."

"Surely I could have no safer guide than you. Unless . . ." Slowly, painfully, Braetana began to understand what he was really saying. It was not that they couldn't flee—it was that Thorgunn wouldn't. Suddenly her heart felt as though a spear had pierced it. Magnus was right—Thorgunn was only interested in her wealth. She removed her hands from his chest and with measured, methodical steps, backed away.

Thorgunn realized that he had been foolish to think that his plan could survive without Braetana's discovery. Now he had betrayed his intentions with his reluctance to leave. If he had loved her as she believed he did, he would have offered to take her away without hesitation. A sudden ache grew deep inside him.

"You took silver for my return."

Perhaps, he thought, *I can still stop her fears.* "It was not a dishonorable bargain. I did not know you when Magnus and I contracted."

"But you took it." Braetana wore a strange smile. Thorgunn had never seen her look so odd before.

"Why does this distress you so? The silver will ease our plight once married."

"It was only the silver you wanted, not me. Everything you said was a lie." Braetana shook her head up and down in quick, angry little nods.

But a moment ago, Thorgunn had still hoped he could salvage his plan. Now, seeing the frightening distance growing in Braetana's eyes, a new need overwhelmed him. Why had he not understood it before? It was so strange, he could hardly speak its name, and yet he knew. It was not the silver, it was Braetana he wanted. He had to make her understand.

"Braetana . . ."

"Do not speak my name! Father warned me that you hunted fortune, not love, but I could not believe him until now."

"It *was* true. . . ."

"It is true. Offer me no insults by lying more."

"No, I offer no more lies. I want you only to listen." He could see salty tears escaping Braetana's tightly closed eyes and knew she could no longer see him.

"I owe you the truth. At first you were a cargo, a means to right my penury, and, on Einar's island, it is sadly true that I devised a plan to make you my wife. Haakon had wronged me and made me hungry for the justice Magnus's fortune would buy. It is true as well that his silver would allow me to marshal a force against Haakon. But it would be a hollow victory were I to lose you in the bargain. There is no honor in the schemes I have spun. But, as Odin is my witness, I now renounce all my plans if you will have me. We will go as you wish, far from here, anywhere your heart chooses. I need no crown or silver to fill me up. I need only you."

Thorgunn sensed she would not tolerate his touch, and he wisely stood where he was, allowing Braetana to turn toward him in her own time. The look of betrayal on her face pierced his heart.

Throughout Thorgunn's plea, Braetana had bitten down hard on her lower lip, half to contain her fury and half to control her sobs. Now, bracing herself against the table behind her, she allowed both her pain and her fury to escape.

"Liar! Why should I believe you now? Even if you tell the truth, as you so convincingly plead you do, what other choice do you have? If I leave with you, how do I know that, once married, you will not return me to Magnus? However I came back to him, he would be unlikely to deny me his support. Then you would have lost nothing."

Fear, an emotion quite foreign to Thorgunn, began to

rise in him as he saw the growing indifference in Braetana's eyes.

"Damn the silver! It is you I want—I know that now!
Why else would I offer to take you away from here?
Were it only Magnus's fortune, would I be fool enough
to ask you to leave it behind? We can go, start anew,
bury this deceit behind us. Truly, I have caused you
much pain, but do not bring more upon us by throwing
our love away."

Thorgunn reached out to stroke Braetana's wet and
reddened face. But before he could come close, she
reeled back and slapped his hand clear of her, delivering
the blow with a startling amount of force.

"I am no one's fool. Do you think I could live with
you knowing this? How could I let you hold me and
make love to me without feeling the suspicion that your
thoughts were winding their way back to your precious
birthright? I wish never to see you again!" Braetana
spoke once more, giving each word great weight.
"Never again. Leave me. Now."

Thorgunn stood stunned, his characteristic composure
nearly undone and his face a mixture of confusion and
grief. He knew that he alone had done this, with his
greed and blindness. His duplicity had caused a lasting
damage he did not know how to repair.

Thorgunn was given to neither self-doubt nor self-
criticism, but as he stood face-to-face with Braetana, he
felt both. For the first time in his life, he didn't know
what to do next.

Braetana, sensing his reluctance to move, repeated
herself. "Leave me," she said, then turned her back to
him and waited.

Thorgunn knew he had no choice. Perhaps Braetana would reconsider his plea later, but for now, he had no other words with which to further his cause. He walked slowly to the door and pulled its heavy iron handle toward him.

"I do love you," he said quietly and calmly. Braetana felt a great swell rise in her chest. Involuntarily, it escaped her lips in a loud sob, its sound drowning out the clink of money dropping into Magnus's coffer.

XV

"Odin will curse you!" Thorgunn's deep-timbred voice roared with audible loathing.

Haakon turned indifferently to face him. "Some wine, brother? In celebration of my betrothal, of course."

Standing before his dark-haired sibling, Thorgunn thought about how the differences in their appearances mirrored the deeper distinctions between them. He hardly thought of Haakon as his blood at all.

How easily he could kill him. One swift blow of his sword could take the smile from Haakon's face, and wrest Braetana from his lecherous grasp. His hand already upon the weapon's gilded handle, Thorgunn gripped it hard in an effort to control his own rising fury.

"It is not enough that you steal my birthright—now you take my betrothed."

Haakon gave a quick throaty laugh. "Yes. And how I shall enjoy that ripe body of hers."

The insult pushed Thorgunn to the limits of his self-control, and without warning, he rushed Haakon. His shorter and less athletic sibling could scarcely comprehend the attack before Thorgunn's right fist connected with Haakon's insolently posed chin, knocking the smaller man off his feet. Before Haakon hit the floor, Thorgunn's other hand caught him by the collar of his tunic.

"How pained Father would be to see you now." Thorgunn could feel Haakon trembling slightly and the palpable fear pleased him.

"You shall join him in Valhalla if you do not take those filthy hands of yours off my neck," Haakon sputtered.

"Gladly." Thorgunn smiled, but his eyes flashed with volcanic unpredictability. As he complied with Haakon's request, his brother fell painfully onto the hard planking of the wooden floor.

"She will not have you." As Thorgunn made the assertion, he issued a silent prayer to Odin that it was true, but allowed no trace of his own doubts in his tone toward Haakon.

Haakon arched one brow contemplatively. "Perhaps she may not choose me. But she will still be my wife. And in time, your sweet beloved will come to know my half brother as I do, as a scheming thief who seeks to steal my throne."

"Magnus will not pledge her against her wishes." Thorgunn slammed his fist down so hard on a nearby table that pieces of fresh fruit and a half-full wine chalice flew off with the impact.

Haakon winced at the sound of the crash, and struggled to calm himself before Thorgunn sensed his growing fear.

"Magnus has the right to give her away as he chooses. She is pledged to me, and will be mine within two moons' time."

"After the ceremony to legitimize her as Magnus's heir, of course," breathed Thorgunn. "You would not want her without her silver." Contempt burned like a fire in his eyes as he squinted at Haakon.

"Nor would you," Haakon answered acidly.

The provocation proved too much. Thorgunn swung one huge muscular arm sideways, nearly clearing the dish-laden table of its contents, all of which crashed and scattered in disarray around Haakon's feet.

"I love her. That is something a man like you can little comprehend."

"Well," Haakon clucked, "it seems I have truly undone you here. I had hoped only to injure your pride, and now it appears I shall have your heart thrown in with the bargain. Perhaps you should serve as witness when we wed."

"There will be no wedding." Thorgunn spoke through clenched teeth.

"I promise you, brother, there will. And you shall be there to see it—unless you would care to have your beloved meet with an untimely accident after the ceremony."

Thorgunn sensed Haakon was only baiting him, but could he afford to ignore such a dangerous threat?

"You would not harm her?" he asked, disbelieving.

"No, of course not, providing I have your full cooperation . . ."

Thorgunn would not dignify Haakon's horrible suggestion with a response. He stood, silently facing him, with a look that all too clearly communicated its intent.

"Over the years," he finally spoke, his voice low yet impassioned, "you have tried to heap dishonor upon me. I admit I have suffered and hated you for it, but now I see that the greatest dishonor is yours alone, for you've mocked our father's fairness and truth, and sullied every ideal he championed.

"Now, seeing you for the pitiable excuse of a man you are, I hate myself for sharing even half of the blood that runs in your veins. Step carefully, my brother, for this disgraceful scheme of yours to marry Braetana may shake your throne so much that you cannot hold it." Before Haakon could reply, Thorgunn marched through the longhouse's front door, leaving his brother alone to consider the import of the harshly spoken words.

Thorgunn's presence unsettled the Viking king, that much was true. Although Haakon held the throne, he was uneasy where his half brother was concerned. There was more to be feared from a hungry man than a sated one, and Haakon wondered if the deprivation he had caused him had inadvertently made Thorgunn even more of a threat.

Haakon told himself that Thorgunn would not dare harm him, for assault on a Viking king was treason and punishable by death. Even Thorgunn would not be hot-headed enough to undertake such foolishness.

Had Braetana been formally betrothed to Thorgunn, there might have been grounds for a combat challenge, one that Haakon suspected he was not likely to win. But the jarls would permit no challenge over an unsanctified promise.

Then there was the matter of the little Saxon herself. Magnus had barely mentioned his daughter's angry reaction to the proposed union, but Haakon knew that she vehemently opposed it. It was possible she still argued for the match with Thorgunn, but Magnus apparently considered her desires to be unimportant.

Should the worst be true, should Braetana insist on

Thorgunn and refuse Haakon, Magnus could still marry her to whomever he chose, even against her wishes. It would not be an arrangement that would enhance his royal image, to have a bride dragged to the altar, but for the silver gained, he could stand a little scratching and biting. The thought almost appealed to him, and the vision of her valiantly resisting, then finally being forced to submit, brought a smile to his lips.

Yes, Haakon thought to himself, in many ways this could prove an interesting match.

Haakon considered his spouse, his wife's image bringing a quick frown to his face. What an unseemly matter this would be. Though divorce was lawful, Gudrun was no ordinary Viking wife. She had been made drottning, and it was a position she was not likely to relinquish easily.

The unpleasant deed would not be so simple were there a child involved, but Gudrun had thus far failed to conceive. It was a fact that often made Haakon wonder if she would ever give him the heir he needed.

A son would ensure that Haakon's rule could pass smoothly to his own blood, and not to Thorgunn. Haakon must have a male heir, and Gudrun offered little promise of that.

Braetana, on the other hand . . . Haakon's pulse quickened as he considered her full breasts and amethyst eyes. How he would love to trace the contours of her inviting body with his eager hands. And how much sweeter the pleasure would be with the knowledge that Thorgunn would agonize over his every aggression on her.

"My lord?" The address shook Haakon from his lustful reverie. Gudrun stood before him, and the angry tone of her voice made it clear that he had failed to respond to an earlier inquiry.

"I did not hear you enter."

"No," she replied calmly, her sea green eyes unwavering as they trained like weapons on Haakon's own. "You seemed lost in thought."

Haakon sensed that she somehow already knew of his plan for disposing of her. But, like a child hoping to postpone punishment, he thought perhaps he could evade her inquiry.

"Matters you need not concern yourself with." He smiled as he reached his hand toward her face.

Gudrun suddenly drew one arm back, then forcefully slapped Haakon's hand in the opposite direction.

"You think it does not concern me that I am to be replaced as queen?" She spat the question, every muscle of her small frame tensed with the fury burning inside her.

Haakon let go a long, tired breath. "You have spoken to Magnus then?"

"I have heard the gossip in the market, and I've seen that ill-bred whelp's sire leave your chamber," she fired.

Haakon could see Gudrun's rage growing, and he struggled to quickly end their unpleasant exchange.

"I am sorry you heard it elsewhere, but however you found out it does not alter my plans. Better than anyone, you should know that I have little choice in this. If I do not marry this Saxon, Thorgunn will have her, and all the silver she brings. To empower him so cannot be allowed, and what's more, I need an heir." Gudrun was furious at Haakon's indictment of her womanhood, and her tongue soon found the weapons she sought.

"How interesting that you lay our barrenness on me. Perhaps were you more of a man . . ."

Haakon's fist clenched, then rose threateningly near Gudrun's defiant face.

"Yes, strike me. You can manage that. But if you think I am so easily replaced, think better of it. You are konungr. But I have those who support me as well. Many will not smile on your choice of a Saxon whore as bedmate."

"At least *she* will serve me in bed." Seeing that his words had delivered the blow his fist intended, Haakon lowered his arm to his side.

"I am in your debt, my lord. Until your cruel insults, I had thought to find myself at a loss without my title. Now I have a reason to continue: I will make hating you my cause. I will be gone by sundown, but my wrath is yours to keep." Gudrun spun away so quickly that the train of her apron made a snapping sound as she disappeared into the private chamber behind Haakon's throne.

The confrontation had been even worse than Haakon had imagined. Thankfully, the final obstacle standing between him and Thorgunn's destruction was now struck down. Tomorrow the Norse nobles would hear the required declaration of divorce, and soon he would have Braetana in his bed.

No doubt Magnus had reached home and advised his daughter of the final wedding arrangements, including the natverror the intended bride and groom would share this evening in Haakon's longhouse. At Haakon's urging that a meal might calm her fears, the old man had agreed to send Braetana alone.

In truth, Haakon thought those fears well founded, for

he had little interest in Braetana, save her fortune and her unwilling flesh. Yet Magnus still would expect some token effort at gaining her trust. At the very least, it might make the wedding less eventful if he could convince her to walk willingly to the altar.

"I will not marry him!" Braetana screamed emphatically. "You promised to honor my wishes. If that is true, you will not force me to this fate." Braetana looked at her father imploringly.

Magnus collapsed with great exhaustion into his huge oak chair, a deep sigh marking the difficulty of the day's events. He had thought the matter settled, and now Braetana seemed ready to do combat once more.

"Daughter," he answered, leaning his blond gray curls back against a knife-carved design of warriors carrying spears, "I do care what your heart wants, but now it overrules reason. Even though I had not been able to guide you as you became the beautiful woman you now are, my experience in this life still entitles me to advise you on matters I understand better than you do. And though you may not now believe me, this marriage is one such matter. It is for the best."

Braetana stood speechless, her chest heaving with anger.

Magnus had hoped this would all go better than it now went, and he struggled to understand her response. "Surely it is not this misplaced affection you have for Thorgunn that inspires your refusal . . ."

"No!" snapped Braetana curtly. "Not that. I would no longer have him as husband!

"I do not want him," Braetana continued. "But neither do I want Haakon. Why do you force me?"

"You must trust my choice." Magnus was close to losing patience with his daughter's insolence. "Now enough of this pointless discussion. I have arranged for you to share the evening meal with Haakon, and I expect you to look your best. Dress yourself as befitting a Viking queen."

This latest revelation of dinner made Braetana even more angry, but before she could organize her protest, Magnus dismissed her. "Now off to your chamber to prepare. This fathering of you frankly wears on me." Magnus waved Braetana off with a swoosh of his arm, the gesture making clear his unwillingness to continue the conversation.

Discouraged and defeated, Braetana accepted Bronwyn's outstretched hand and retreated to the security of her chamber to rethink her ever-worsening fate.

"He means to do it," she said quietly, casting her eyes in a sideways glance at Bronwyn. "He is going to marry me to that awful man. Oh, Bronwyn, this is a nightmare and I cannot seem to awaken. I don't know which is greater, the pain of knowing Thorgunn betrayed me or the fate of being condemned as wife to his brother."

Bronwyn saw a wave of fear sweep over the younger woman's face as she spoke of Haakon.

"Can he truly be so terrible?" The marriage seemed inevitable, and Bronwyn hoped to bring Braetana to a more pragmatic view of it.

"I know mostly what Thorgunn has told me, that Haakon is greedy and cruel." Braetana stopped, remembering that these were traits she now knew Thorgunn possessed as well. "I know that he has cast off another woman for me. It frightens me to think of a man who finds his women so easily interchangeable. I met this

Haakon only once. His voice said little, but his eyes spoke of . . ." Her voice trailed off in unpleasant memory.

"Bronwyn, it was that hungry look Edward had for me that made my flesh crawl. What am I to do?" Flinging her arms about Bronwyn in a desperate embrace, Braetana nearly toppled her.

"There, there." Bronwyn stroked her soft mane of hair lovingly. "Perhaps you are wrong," she said hopefully. "In any event, there's naught to do now but make the best of this." Braetana held Bronwyn tightly for a few moments. Suddenly, Braetana pulled quickly back, staring Bronwyn squarely in the face with a look her companion knew to mean that some scheme was hatching.

"The best thing we can do now is make our way back to Northumbria," Braetana announced determinedly. "We will simply have to leave."

Although Bronwyn knew Braetana had something hazardous in mind, she would not have guessed a plan so bold as this.

"Lady, tell me this is but a jest. Surely you cannot expect an escape to succeed?"

"I can hardly consider staying, given what that now entails."

"I doubt I can row those heavy oars."

The ridiculous image brought a slight smile to Braetana's face. "No, dear Bronwyn, but the Vikings can. Thorgunn has told me that traders come to Trondbergen to barter their wares. Surely they come with crews— and with greed. This, coupled with a goodly amount of silver, should secure us the passage we need. The summer trading season is now upon us, and these dour nuptials they have planned for me will not come to pass for two moons yet. Surely, in that time, we can persuade some hungry soul to take us home."

Bronwyn still could not accept the incredible notion. "Is it possible they would sail to England?"

Braetana had just now worked the logic through. "Probably not with anything less than assault in mind, but perhaps we can get to Hedeby. From there, we can surely find a way to secure passage to Glendonwyck."

"Lady, it is all too perilous to come about."

"Nonsense!" Braetana snapped. "It has succeeded before. My mother, after all, did it. Am I not her child? And my father has stocked my jewel box with more than enough fare for the journey."

A loud rap on the wall near the curtain to Braetana's chamber drew her sudden attention. A young Viking woman, her English minimal but her gestures clear, indicated that Braetana was to bathe in a side room.

Braetana suddenly remembered the dinner with Haakon. Her bath was no doubt part of Magnus's preparations in packaging her for delivery there.

"I will not go," Braetana announced to Bronwyn. But before her confidante could answer, Magnus did.

"It is not your choice." He stood in the doorway to her chamber, looking annoyed and intractable. "Ragnhild will aid you. Now about the business at hand!" With that edict, Magnus snapped the thick curtain closed, leaving a befuddled-looking maidservant alone with the two openmouthed Saxons.

"I will not marry him." Braetana knew her declaration could hardly prevent it, but she still needed the comfort of speaking the words.

"Very well, lady, but supping with him does seem inevitable."

Braetana knew that Bronwyn was right. Magnus looked genuinely likely to drag her there if she resisted. At any rate, it was only supper, hardly the wedding. Braetana had learned to concede small skirmishes in order to save her strength for the great battles.

With a tired sigh, she followed Ragnhild toward the steaming tub the maid had prepared for her. If the intended purpose of the soak distressed her, at least the process did not. She relaxed into the hot water as the young woman poured bucket after bucket of it on top of her.

After a long soak, Braetana dried herself, then conceded the evening's inevitability with her choice of a bright red garnet-encrusted chemise with matching jewels. Finally, she enlisted Bronwyn's help in fixing her long flaxen hair into a partial twist atop her crown, the remaining hair allowed to spill freely down from beneath a delicate silver hlao.

Haakon, too, had dressed himself in finery, selecting an amber velvet tunic embroidered at both neck and sleeves with a leafy pattern of polished onyx stones. Atop the tunic rested a thick gold choker, its center a tangle of snapping, biting horses' heads. It was an unsettling theme echoed as the necklace twisted around his neck into a mass of other unearthly beasts. Like Braetana, he also wore a hlao, but his was crafted of pure gold, its front a thick braid that flattened for closure in the back by a black silk ribbon.

As he finished, the Viking reviewed himself in the huge, imported mirror hung from the back wall of his chamber. He thought smugly to himself that she was lucky, this Saxon wench, to have a man of his imposing physical stature. Before Gudrun, he'd enjoyed considerable success with the local maids, his dark, haunting appearance adding even more to his attractiveness as konungr. Those had been rich days, with women aplenty and no need to choose for more than one night. His marriage to Braetana would again relegate such pleasures to the past—perhaps.

Despite his frugality, Haakon had spared no expense in the preparation of the meal. His cook, with Haakon's explicit instructions, had prepared an elaborate display of stuffed quail, roast elk, and a cornucopia of strawberries, apples, and fresh greens. Haakon had even ordered a large pitcher of his finest imported wine and had just moved to fill his chalice with a generous serving when he heard the sharp rap on the dining hall's front door.

"Enter," he commanded, taking a hearty swig from the cup before the visitors appeared.

Magnus's manservant Knut presented himself first, then announced the presence of Haakon's long-awaited guest.

"Konungr," he said, bowing his head slightly in greeting, "I bring you Jarl Magnus's daughter, Lady Braetana." Knut stepped back, revealing a heavenly vision. Braetana's current appearance exceeded even Haakon's best memory of her. She looked less mortal than divine, her trim yet full figure resplendent in closely fitted yards of crimson silk. The absence of the customary loose-fitting apron showed her trim figure off to almost immodest advantage.

Her hair, as when Haakon had first seen her, cascaded downward, a few silky strands clinging suggestively to the swell of her rising breasts. As a mate to the silver hlao, Braetana wore an opal and silver necklace, whose five large oval stones seemed to radiate light onto the creamy contours of her face. To see her standing there, even more beautiful than at their first meeting, made Haakon's loins ache with longing.

"You may go." Haakon's command caused the servant's prompt departure, but not without a final unspoken plea from Braetana. Her look begged him to stay. But it was to no avail. The slamming of the longhouse door left her completely and frighteningly alone with Haakon.

"Sit?" He gestured toward a thickly cushioned chair opposite what was obviously his own place at the long cloth-covered table. Silently, Braetana moved toward it, stopping as it became clear that Haakon intended to pull the chair back so he could seat her.

As she lowered herself, lifting slightly so that he could move the seat closer to the table, Braetana felt Haakon's hands brush against her back as they gripped the chair's arms. She moved forward quickly in an unsuccessful effort to elude his touch.

"Little Saxon, do I frighten you so?" Haakon's voice was a mixture of mockery and concern.

"You think me so easily undone?" Braetana replied calmly. "I am hardly so."

This was the tone Haakon had been expecting. "Tell me then, what you are."

"I am tired of men's efforts to alter my fate," Braetana answered emotionlessly, taking his gaze on squarely as he moved around to the end of the table and seated himself opposite her.

"Ah, you no doubt speak of Thorgunn and your father. They are well meaning, but clumsy. I believe I could handle you better."

"You will have no such chance, have I any say."

"Truly?" Haakon was surprised that she was bold enough to resist him so openly. "Surely you know our wedding will come to pass."

"I know that the thought horrifies me." Braetana hoped that, if Haakon saw her distaste for him, he would withdraw his proposal, but she achieved quite the opposite effect.

Without asking, Haakon poured a second cup of wine, then placed it directly in front of Braetana. Hoping the liquid's wiles would somehow distance her from his crude company, she raised the chalice to her full lips and took a generous drink. An annoying smile crept across Haakon's face. "Are you not worried I'll take advantage if you lose full command of your wits?" he asked.

"Sire," Braetana offered tartly, "my wits are better dulled against this effrontery of yours. And unless I am quite mistaken, I believe you have already taken all the advantage you need."

Here was the attitude he'd planned on. Yet Haakon had not expected such acuity. "Little minx! You are not only lovely to behold, but bright as well. I can understand Thorgunn's affection for you."

"Do not speak to me of him!" Braetana exploded, rising suddenly from her seat. In the process, she accidentally upended the nearly full wineglass, and the red liquid seeped toward Haakon.

"Very well," Haakon responded, noting how very much the matter touched her. "Once wed, we need never even think of him—after, of course, he witnesses our joining."

"You persist in believing that we will marry, though I have told you otherwise. Though my father is now misguided, trust me that he will come to respect my wishes in this matter. But even should he persist in his unconscionable plan, why would you wish Thorgunn there? It is not my understanding that you two hold great affection for each other."

Haakon laughed. "It is wasted breath for us to argue on the matter of our marriage. It *will* come to pass. And Thorgunn, I think, will come to witness it. He might even find some odd pleasure there—as might you, judging from your apparent distaste for him."

Braetana did not miss Haakon's close scrutiny. She realized that, whatever her current feelings for Thorgunn, and even she wasn't sure what those were, they were a topic best avoided with his brother.

"I enjoy nothing about this new fate of mine. So do not speak to me of pleasure."

"Tsk, tsk," Haakon half whispered. "Such a shame. For pleasure is something I could give you much of, should you allow it." Breatana now cast her eyes down to an untouched plate of fruit in an effort to conceal from Haakon any truth they might hold. Still, she caught him rising from his chair, circling the table, and stopping all too closely behind her.

Almost imperceptibly at first, then more definitely, Braetana felt Haakon reach one hand beneath the back of her hair, his fingers tracing a suggestive course along the side of her neck. His touch made her shudder visibly, a response that brought forth a low, coarse chortle from Haakon.

"You can learn to like this, little Saxon. Many have."

Braetana guessed he certainly spoke the truth on that count. It was all she could do not to turn and apply the heavy silver cup she now held in her hand to the jut of his impertinent chin.

Just as she was considering the point, Haakon lifted her from the chair by her shoulders and spun her quickly to him. Panic swelled within her, and her fear was in no way calmed by the familiar glint of desire she caught in the back of his dark eyes.

Suddenly, like a predator, his lips were upon her own. He pressed down painfully hard, intruding with his tongue as she struggled to twist her own mouth free of his.

Her response might have been quicker and more effective, had she not been momentarily stunned by the violence of his advance. No touch of Thorgunn's had ever been anything like this. For one brief moment, Braetana almost forgot the agonizing events of the previous day, and prayed to God that somehow she would open her eyes to find herself in the arms of Haakon's brother instead.

"Saxon whore!" The words were in Norse but quickly drew both Haakon's and Braetana's attention. Gudrun rushed wildly toward their embrace, wedging herself like a lever between the two of them. Furiously prying Haakon and Braetana apart, Gudrun's nails drew blood from Braetana's slender neck.

"I'll teach you to sell your wares where they're not needed, you round-heeled half-breed!" she screamed.

Before Haakon could intervene, Gudrun pushed him aside and landed Braetana squarely on her back amid the table's bounty. Her hard fall sent pieces of meat, fruit, and large splashes of red wine in all directions.

Like a wild alley cat, Gudrun scrambled atop Braetana, grabbing huge fistfuls of her long blond hair in an attempt to pound her head against the tabletop. Haakon jumped forward to dispatch the aggressor. But, as he began, he realized that Braetana was doing well in fending for herself. She was taller than Gudrun and quickly threw the stockier woman off.

Except for the encounter with Thorgunn, Braetana had never before been in an actual fight. And yet, with considerable skill, she dropped to her knees and straddled the spitting Gudrun, brandishing the silver wine goblet as a weapon above the other woman's head. There was no contest now; Braetana had clearly won, though she was not entirely sure just what she had accomplished. As she continued her dominance over her panting, fire-eyed opponent, she realized who the woman must be.

"Well done, ladies, if I may call you that!" cheered Haakon, clapping his hands loudly in mock applause. "I'm quite flattered, and impressed—Lady Braetana, your talents continue to amaze me."

Haakon's approval of Braetana's triumph served to loosen her hold on Gudrun. With as much dignity as the strange circumstances would allow, she released her victim and rose, stepping quickly back and away as the other woman scrambled to her feet.

"I told you to leave," Haakon commanded Gudrun

angrily. His amused tone of moments ago had completely vanished.

Gudrun's eyes narrowed, giving her all the appearance of an incensed cat ready to strike. "I wanted to see the whore. Quite large, is she not?"

Braetana bristled at the insult, spoken in English for her benefit. Though she was svelte, her height had always embarrassed her, and Gudrun's verbal attack made Braetana shake with anger. She struggled against the urge to rekindle the fight.

"If the decision were mine, you would be welcome to him." Braetana's words lifted Gudrun's brows in amazement.

"She speaks?" Gudrun laughed mockingly. "Well, my Saxon lady, let us hope you can do much more than that, for our king is a man more of action than words. Sleep carefully."

Haakon was ready to oust Gudrun from the dining hall when she preempted him by going on her own. In a moment, both her witch's laugh and the sound of her footsteps echoed down the path outside.

"Well," exhaled Haakon, "I had hoped this evening would have run a somewhat different course. But, given our little interruption, I think you have had enough for now. I shall arrange to have Knut see you back to Magnus's."

"I can walk alone," Braetana answered, hoping to organize her escape plan en route.

"Yes, I'm quite afraid of that," Haakon reconsidered. "I will get Knut. Good evening for now, my love. Perhaps next time we meet, we will satisfy our other appetites as well."

Braetana turned so as not to face Haakon's leer, averting her eyes even from Knut as he saw her the short walk back to Magnus's. But as she slept that night, tucked in snugly amid the thick fur bed covers, the voices in her head would not be silent, and the images in her mind's eye showed her a terrifying future.

XVI

Braetana hoped with all her heart that she looked like a Viking. She had taken great pains to duplicate their curious dress, even going so far as to wear one of the billowy overdresses she had come to consider unwieldy and awkward.

Normally, she would be loath to be thought a pagan. Now, however, she wished for just that. It was the sole sure way she could hope to board the waiting longship unobserved.

"Hurry, Bronwyn, or we shall arrive at the dock in time to wish farewell to our Frisian hosts!"

"I am trying, lady. It is the skirt's train that impedes me, and the great weight of jewelry you've forced me to wear. I would not have guessed four bracelets to be so heavy."

Braetana pulled her companion close to her in an effort to hush her complaints, as much as speed her progress.

"Shhh . . . I know it is cumbersome, but it is also the only way to buy our freedom since I hadn't access to the hack-silver father keeps locked away. The Frisian Captain Vagn assures me this will serve, but it will be of little use if we call attention to ourselves with our strange speech. Now be still."

Though the Norwegian dawn saw nearly all of Trond-bergen's residents fast asleep within their longhouses, Braetana still bowed her head as though she expected a passerby to recognize her. Her odd posture, combined with the draping fur-lined cape hood covering her face, almost prevented her from seeing where she was going. Still, she scurried as surefootedly as though she knew the placement of every stone. She and Bronwyn had waited patiently for this chance to execute their daring plan, and they could not afford to fail.

"We must go faster. Look ahead, the last of the furs are loaded for trade and the Frisians are readying to cast off for Friesland. Vagn was easily bought, but I doubt he intends to risk discovery. If anyone sees us, we are undone. For heaven's sake, Bronwyn, just pick up the train!"

Braetana turned back momentarily and saw that the older woman's skirt had caught on a crag. As Braetana reached to free it, her backside collided with great impact with what was surely a boulder.

"You make much haste somewhere. Is something wrong?"

Braetana could hardly believe her eyes. Of all people to run into now, the worst had to be Thorgunn.

"All that is wrong is that you seem to be impeding my progress. I would pass, if you would not mind moving."

"Since fate has brought us together, I would speak with you." In his recent solitary voyage to Einar's island and back, Thorgunn had thought of nothing but Brae-tana and the passion they had shared there. He had sailed back looking for a way to exorcise her from his heart, and he had returned surer than ever that he could never forget her.

Perhaps she had softened toward him. Here at least was the chance to plead his cause again. Thorgunn hoped desperately that she was willing to listen.

"You have said all I should ever want to hear. I've no need of more duplicity and betrayal."

Thorgunn's heart sank. Nothing had changed.

"Little dove, I . . ."

"Do not!" Braetana spat angrily. "I have had enough of your lies already! I have no need to hear more."

In fact, Braetana too had suffered during the past two weeks. Although she had sworn to herself she was glad Thorgunn no longer courted her forgiveness, her heart was heavy at the news of his departure. Why, if he truly wanted her, had he gone? Apparently he had abandoned her, because no one who loved her would have surrendered so easily. What was this ruse he now attempted?

"I asked you to let me pass."

Thorgunn was ready to comply when he noticed her strange appearance. "I have not seen you dressed in such Viking finery before. The outfit does become you."

Thorgunn suddenly realized the great wealth of jewelry she wore. And, when she had slammed into him, her pockets had jangled. At once he understood what she meant to do.

"My lady is bedecked much as the wealthy jarl's daughter. Or perhaps it is portable fare intended for the Frisians?"

"I've no need to explain myself to you!" she sputtered, unsettled both by Thorgunn's swift logic and by the sight of the drekar's red sail slowly unfurling in the fjord harbor.

Grabbing Bronwyn's thick elbow with one hand, Braetana attempted to dart sideways around Thorgunn's imposing form, but he was faster and served as a barrier between her and the sea. This time they collided face-to-face, each pressing hard upon the other with the force of their impact.

"This is madness. Whatever Vagn told you, there will be no safe passage anywhere once you're within that dangerous hull."

Braetana again tried to move around his body. This time his hands caught her, but not before she saw the Frisian vessel part from its moorings.

"Look what you have done—they sail without us! I had but one more chance to see Glendonwyck, and now you have stolen it from me. How much more do you want?"

Thorgunn's grip on Braetana's wrists was nearly tight enough to cause pain, but he guessed the tears filling her eyes were due less to his rough handling than to her desperation.

"What did he tell you?" Thorgunn let Braetana go, sensing that she would no longer try to flee.

Because the Frisians were now rowing speedily away from her, Braetana realized there was little reason anymore to conceal her plan. "Vagn assured us that my silver was enough to buy passage. He would take us to a place called Dorstad, where he said there would be Frisian ships setting sail for trade with East Anglia. It would not quite be home, but it would be England. At least it would not be here."

"You little fool!" Thorgunn was furious with her for

the mindless risk she had nearly taken. "Think you to leave that drekar with your honor intact? Once aboard, he and his men would have had what they wanted from you, and then you'd be sold on the slave block in Hedeby."

"Well better that than my fate here. And, as I recall, my honor has already suffered much already." On reflection, Braetana knew Thorgunn was probably right about her hastily made choice to trust the Frisians. Still, it was the only trade ship she'd seen in the three weeks since her decision to flee.

"Does it matter so very much that you go home?"

Braetana's pained look answered him more eloquently than words could have. Thorgunn sighed. He had not realized, until now, how very much agony he had brought to her.

"Then I will take you."

"What?" Braetana thought, in her teary confusion, that she had somehow misheard him.

"If the white walls of your Glendonwyck are so very important, I will take you back to them. We can manage your escape. Magnus will not know."

Braetana's lips parted in speechless astonishment. What twist was his scheme now taking? Was it possible that his offer was sincere? Though she wished it were, she doubted him, for he had not made this proposition until he thought her committed to see her own plan succeed. Of course! He feared that her flight would cost him Magnus's silver. The realization set her eyes squinting in unchecked anger.

"Whatever would make you think that I should wish to share a ship with you?"

"Your desire to sail home, I imagine. I doubt from your demeanor it is from any desire for my company."

She could hardly fathom his nerve. The man was relentless and without conscience. If he thought he could betray and desert her, and then sail back into her heart with some scheme to dress up his lies, he was more foolish than she had been to trust the Frisians.

"Your coarse company is the very last thing I should wish to endure."

Thorgunn had not anticipated such undisguised hatred. "Truly? Worse than my brother's marriage bed?"

"That is nothing compared to a future with you." Braetana had not meant to say it, yet her response had given Thorgunn the clear impression that she might well wed the Viking king. He had heard her words, not her heart.

"Well, lady, if that is your choice, it is not my place to judge it." Thorgunn stepped aside, allowing Braetana to proceed on her earlier path toward the dock. But as she took a tentative step in that direction, she realized that the ship was now cutting its way well down the fjord's waters. There was no reason to go anywhere but back to Magnus's.

Confused, Braetana turned quickly in the opposite direction, motioning for Bronwyn to follow. There would be other ships.

It was worse than being on a storm-tossed drekar. Braetana rolled onto her back, hoping the change in position would help combat the wave of nausea sweeping over her, but nothing could counter the fear that she now knew to be true: She was with child.

Even at the time of her attempt to flee with the Frisians, she had begun to suspect it. Now she knew with certainty that she was carrying Thorgunn's child. And, as if matters could worsen, the *oettleithing*, her formal induction into Magnus's family, was scheduled for tomorrow. After that, she was to marry the despised Haakon. She had never thought to see either come to pass.

Braetana ached for her life to be as it had been a month ago. When her heart had been full of dreams for her life with Thorgunn. Then, to know she would bear his child would have filled her with immense joy. Now the thought only served to remind her of what they had lost.

Yet, even amid this feeling of despair, a voice within Braetana cried out for Thorgunn's touch and protection. *What madness*, she thought, *to love a man who cares nothing for me*. Thinking about him brought a tide of warm tears, and though she closed her eyes tightly to abate the deluge, salty rivulets still escaped, spilling down either side of her face.

Suddenly a huge swell of nausea overcame her. Though she thought it impossible to fight this attack off, Braetana managed to do so. She covered her mouth with her hand and pitched sideways with a low moan.

"Lady?" Bronwyn, who had already risen and dressed, heard the sound and hurried from the adjacent room to see what was the matter.

Braetana tried to rise, but the combination of queasiness and despair proved too much. Instead she collapsed into the older woman's outstretched arms.

"Child," Bronwyn consoled her, "it cannot be as terrible as all that."

"Yes," sobbed Braetana, "oh yes it is. We have managed no means for escape, and tomorrow I am to marry that odious man."

"There is still time . . . perhaps a ship will come."

Braetana sighed, tears streaming down her cheeks as she struggled to see out of her watery eyes. "It matters not. There is no more time. I carry Thorgunn's child."

Bronwyn had suspected this as Braetana's trim figure had grown fuller in recent weeks. Of all the ills that had befallen them since their abduction from Northumbria, this, more than any other, seemed the cruelest blow, for, though Braetana had worked hard to disclaim it, Bronwyn knew she still loved Thorgunn. Now, to have the child but not the father seemed a mockery of all that was just.

Bronwyn too began to cry. For several long moments, the two women held each other, their arms intertwined and their bodies softly swaying to and fro.

Bronwyn finally broke their long silence. "What are we to do about Haakon?"

Braetana's tears were by now nearly spent and she suddenly grew calm. Bronwyn's question had brought about a depressing clarity that the morning's realization of her pregnancy had disallowed.

"I must marry him," she pronounced.

"No," Bronwyn breathed fearfully, verbalizing Braetana's own horror at the thought.

"What choice have I?" Braetana cast her eyes to the side as though she could see her bleak option in the very far distance. "It is too late to flee, and were I even able to avoid the wedding, what good would that do? Haakon would see only my betrayal and another heir to challenge his throne. Surely he would have me killed. I must have a father for my unborn babe."

"Thorgunn?" Bronwyn offered hopefully, praying Braetana would at least consider the possibility.

The name barely escaped the older woman's lips before Braetana pounced on it. "Never!" she cried pointedly, shaking her head. "I do not know what he hoped for from me before, but if he wanted me now, he would have stopped this wedding. I will not use the child inside me as bait to trap him."

"You needn't tell him. He has offered us safe passage home. Could we not use his help?" Bronwyn arched her brows in a plea for Braetana to consider the option.

Braetana's eyes lowered, then closed. "No, I could only be with him again if he loved me. And he does not. I could not bear to be next to him in any other way."

"But if you stay, lady, will Haakon not know?"

The thought had already crossed Braetana's mind. "I will find a way to assure him that it is his own," she answered slowly. "If he believes the child comes early, we will both be safe—providing I go to him willingly."

"Oh, my lady." Tears again welled in Bronwyn's soft eyes. She felt as though Braetana's heart were her own and it was being broken by this painful decision.

"We have no time for tears now," Braetana cautioned, choking back her own. The thought of what she was about to do with that dreaded man nearly pushed her to illness again. She forced herself to stand, trying hard not to think of the perverse destiny tomorrow night would bring.

As she struggled to block out her thoughts of Haakon, Magnus's voice on the far side of the thick curtain drew her attention.

"Braetana? May I enter?"

"A moment, please." Braetana quickly covered her

chemise with a thick marten fur robe. "Yes, I am dressed."

Magnus had the look about him of a man expecting an argument. "The preparations for your legitimizing ceremony are in order. It will take place late day, with your wedding to Haakon to follow. The king's servants prepare even now for a great feast in his longhouse hall. It will be a celebration the likes of which few here have ever seen, for it is not often that a king takes a queen. Though I doubt to receive it, I have come to ask your cooperation."

Magnus stopped, expecting the antagonistic response Braetana had become much skilled at offering during the past month. He knew his insistence on the match had infuriated Braetana, and that her misery pained him. But, as her father and protector, he knew he must decide wisely, even if she herself had not yet come to appreciate his wisdom.

"Braetana?"

"Yes, Father," she replied coldly, "you can expect my full cooperation."

Magnus cocked his head sideways at the response, not quite sure he had heard it correctly. "Your heart has changed?" he asked, disbelieving.

"Yes." She nodded. "I know my actions thus far have done little to recommend me as a worthy daughter. I have been disobedient and have no right to dare ask your forgiveness on such counts. But now I see that my best interests are foremost in your mind, and I am sorry for the grief my resistance has brought you. I look forward to becoming Haakon's wife."

They were the words Magnus wished so desperately to hear, yet he found himself unable to place his faith in them. After all of Braetana's anger and resistance, her sudden acquiescence seemed odd. Still, even if she were up to something, he would gain little by confessing his distrust to her. Better to hold his peace and watch her closely. He managed a smile. "I am pleased you have come to this wisdom. To be a Viking queen is a special fate. I know you have much to prepare for tomorrow— Brigitta will be here soon to complete your bridal dress. I have matters of my own to attend to. But I shall make sure my future son-in-law knows how eager you are to wed him."

"Yes, Father," Braetana answered, bowing her head slightly in accession. "Thank you." Braetana didn't know how the last words got past her lips. Though her current predicament was partially of her own making, she couldn't help hating Magnus for the fate he'd brought her.

Brigitta would be here soon, eager to fit and finish the elaborate dress Braetana was expected to wear when she delivered herself to Haakon. The thought of her future husband made her want to sleep again, to forget the disaster that would soon befall her. But she knew that she needed this time to think instead.

Finding a device to trick Haakon into believing that he was the first was not the problem—she had heard enough other women's tales to already have some knowledge of that artifice. What she needed was a way to endure his unchecked lust. How could she allow this terrible man to take her?

"What will I do now?" she said out loud, sighing heavily as she sat back down on the fur-covered bed. She buried her face in her hands.

* * *

Across the village, the fire in Haakon's central hearth burned hot, warming the Viking's limbs and blood almost as much as his thoughts of Braetana. Magnus had been quick to deliver his news of her change in mood.

Haakon smiled in anticipation at the thought of having Braetana willingly in his arms. True, he had relished the prospect of a little resistance, but he still expected to find that beneath her veneer of agreement. It would all work perfectly, she the apparently willing bride, he still able to savor the wildcat in her as she bucked beneath him.

He had seen little of her this past month, wisely judging that her mood toward him was only likely to worsen with increased contact. The arrangement had been just as well, for though he by no means intended to forego his taste for other women once they wed, he would not be able to do so openly. The past weeks had given him wonderfully free reign to sate his desires without having to account for his whereabouts to a shrewish bedmate.

In fact, now that he was free from Gudrun's hawklike surveillance, he had suffered some misgivings about the advisability of marriage altogether. Magnus had eased his fears at the formal betrothal, however, offering Haakon a dowry for Braetana more heavy with silver than any in Trondbergen's living memory. Once Magnus died, not even Thorgunn, arriving with a fleet of angry drekars, would dare challenge Haakon's throne.

Haakon wondered about his brother's current disposition. Perhaps he had given up on Braetana. He considered what a disappointment that would be, particularly in light of Magnus's news that she would now willingly embrace her new position as queen. Haakon had hoped to turn the knife a little more, and, now that no love was lost between Braetana and Thorgunn, that pleasure would be greatly diminished.

But he guessed that Thorgunn must still hold some affection for the Saxon wench. Haakon suspected that his brother's current feigned disinterest was but a result of his pride.

The vision of Braetana's resistance to his own advances caused Haakon to issue a sinister laugh. Immensely pleased with the image, he rocked back hard in his chair and nearly lost balance. A loud rap at the door quickly righted him.

"Yes, enter." Haakon's response produced a silhouette of Thorgunn in the wide doorway.

"Brother!" Haakon smiled broadly. "You have no doubt come to offer your congratulations?"

Thorgunn made no answer as he walked into the cavernous hall, slamming the door angrily behind him. It was an entrance he was oft prone to with Haakon.

"Do you plan to bore me with the tedious details of these imaginary nuptials?"

"Brother, this is no dream," Haakon clucked, rising to pour both himself and Thorgunn a goblet of wine. "Look about you. The tables are being set for tomorrow's wedding feast. There is a second throne, smaller of course, adjacent to mine.

"Look to the back wall—I have commissioned a special tapestry woven in honor of the occasion. It depicts both a konungr and his queen. You know my affection for silver. Think you I'd part with so much for a wedding not likely to occur?"

Thorgunn looked slowly about the transformed room, finally settling his gaze back on his sneering brother. He had never expected the preparations to proceed this far.

His confidence that Braetana could dissuade Magnus from the match was apparently misplaced. Still, he could only believe that she would find a way to refuse him at the altar. The marriage would not come to pass.

"Surely Braetana has not agreed to this."

Haakon laughed openly, sending a dagger of fury up Thorgunn's spine as he fought to keep his rage in check.

"The Saxon bitch welcomes it! I imagine she can't wait to get her hands on me!" Haakon offered the goblet to Thorgunn, who knocked it nearly across the room. First with his fist, then with the heel of his foot, Thorgunn shoved Haakon to the floor. He towered over his frightened half brother, only a fragile self-restraint preventing him from killing this animal that passed for a man.

"You will die if you dare again speak of Braetana in such a manner. Tell me where this delusion of yours came from."

Haakon breathed hard, his throat painfully compressed by Thorgunn's muddy boot and his bravado considerably curtailed by his brother's uncontrolled aggression.

"It is no delusion," he gasped. "Ask Magnus."

"I shall." Though still furious, Thorgunn somehow managed to release Haakon from beneath his weight. But before his half brother stormed from the hall, Haakon called to him again. "I will look for you at the ceremony. The lady, I'm sure, would wish it—to ensure her continued good health."

The force of Thorgunn's departure shook the longhouse's thick walls. Haakon, who was slowly recovering from his brother's assault, poured himself a second chalice of wine.

Better today than tomorrow, he thought, downing the entire cup in one large gulp. *Tomorrow I will need no liquid to quench my thirst.*

XVII

Thorgunn's jaw clenched in fury as he surveyed the bustling activity within Haakon's longhouse. The central chamber was filled with a swarm of scurrying huskarlars and maidservants. Their ever-changing numbers rushed about him in frantic circles as they carried weighty trays of food and drink in preparation for the afternoon's festivities.

The numerous guests had already begun arriving. Common folk, the yeomen and drengrs, were ushered to the wide tables set farthest from the raised dais constructed against the hall's back wall. Nobility, including jarls, were guided to their more privileged seats just outside the silk-covered sanctuary ropes surrounding the draped platform where the wedding would take place.

Trestle tables placed around the hall's perimeter were hung with yards of heavy red linen that spilled over their edges. Their arrangement allowed each guest an unobstructed view of the room's center with its huge sunken firepit.

Thorgunn had seen the chamber similarly organized once before. That was seven years ago, when Haakon reached his majority and was formally made konungr.

How bitter was the cup Thorgunn had emptied at that occasion. But it was nothing compared to what his half brother had promised him today.

Magnus is lying, Thorgunn thought. Braetana will never consent to such a detestable match, no matter what he says. In denial of the surrounding wedding's preparations, Thorgunn struggled to believe that Haakon's confidence was misguided. Braetana was bright and willful, and Thorgunn was sure that she would find a way to refuse him.

Yes, Thorgunn assured himself, what he had come for today was to witness the embarrassing failure of Haakon's plan. And if, by some unthinkable miscarriage of fate, Braetana did agree to the marriage with Haakon, then he had come to see her, for her eyes would reveal whether or not Haakon was truly the choice of her heart.

In the seemingly unending weeks since he had last spoken with her, Thorgunn's need for Braetana had only grown. His foolish decision to allow greed more than love to guide his actions now seemed unbelievable to him.

To have been so blind to not see his need for her love and devotion was an error that had cost him terribly. Knowing this, he lay awake on his pallet each night with the painful hindsight of a man who wished he had acted differently while the chance still presented itself.

Perhaps if he had been honest in the beginning about his own destitution and about her wealth, Magnus's arguments against him would have had little sway with her. Maybe he could still prove his love if she would only give him the chance to rescue her.

But she seemed filled only with distrust for him. Braetana had denied him twice, once when she discovered his duplicity and again when he had interrupted her intended flight back to England, but there was still time. Today he would see for himself if she still wanted him. One look at her and he would know the truth.

He had made arrangements for their escape. His huskarlar Rollo waited nearby with fresh horses to carry them over the back mountains to the fjord below. There a partially crewed drekar awaited to speed them far from Magnus's and Haakon's grasp.

Sailing down the easily visible Trondbergen fjord would be impossible, but the adjacent inlet was unguarded, and he and Braetana would be able to elude any pursuit quickly. Once free of the coastline, their tomorrows would belong only to each other. It did not matter where they went, as long as they were together.

Across the village, Braetana had her own thoughts of escape, but she forced them out of her head, reminding herself that she had no choice now.

Brigitta and Bronwyn put the final touches on the arrangements of her hair and gown, and Braetana thought of Haakon waiting for her. An involuntary shudder shook her at the thought of his hands caressing her body.

"My lady?"

"It is nothing," Braetana replied. "Only a chill," she added.

I will learn to tolerate him, she vowed silently. The success of her plan to conceal her pregnancy, and perhaps save her life, depended entirely on bedding Haakon quickly and often enough for him to believe that the child might be his. Furthermore, she must convince him that her affections belonged to him alone. Braetana had little doubt that, if he suspected she still harbored some allegiance to Thorgunn, Haakon would make sure his brother's fate worsened.

It seemed so long since Thorgunn had offered to save her, and she had not seen him since. His silence could only be construed as abandonment, yet, even the knowledge that he no longer wanted her did little to lessen her feelings for him.

As painful as it was to admit, Braetana still loved Thorgunn. She would gladly take his offer of escape now, but he had not repeated it.

"At least you are a beautiful, if not a joyful, bride." Bronwyn sighed, sentimental tears welling up in her eyes. Braetana looked at the reflection in the long mirror before her. Even she was surprised at the magical transformation Brigitta's skilled handiwork had wrought. The seamstress had done her best to approximate the sort of gown to which Braetana was most accustomed, and the resulting combination of Norse and Saxon style succeeded on all counts.

Woven of snow white silk brocade with a delicate leaf pattern, the dress's low scoop neckline and form-fitting waist showed Braetana's beauty off to breathtaking advantage. A brocaded belt, sewn from the same fabric, but heavily encrusted with glistening crystals, hung about her trim hips. In front, a knot and a fringe of similar stones cascaded down.

The gown's neckline was trimmed in softest ermine, as were its sleeves and hem. Beneath the fur hung a heavy necklace of many finely wrought silver rectangles, each of a different design, but all depicting intertwined mythical animals.

The front of Braetana's fine blond hair had been pulled to the crown of her head and twisted securely, then anchored with a filigreed silver comb. The rest cascaded down her back, its movement restrained only by a silver hlao, also heavy with cut crystals, which encircled her brow.

"You are an angel's vision, child." Bronwyn admired her approvingly.

"It is not heaven I'll see tonight," Braetana answered dourly, her mind less on her appearance than her impending fate.

Hearing the despair in her voice, Bronwyn reached out her arms. She brought Braetana to her, hugging her tightly as she attempted to console her charge.

"It will be bearable," she whispered as cheerfully as she could. But her best efforts were undermined by what she knew to be the truth.

"Yes, I know," answered Braetana, trying to lift her own spirits as well as Bronwyn's.

It was an attitude she struggled valiantly to maintain on the short walk that she, Magnus, and their entourage took to Haakon's. With every ounce of strength within her, Braetana fought off thoughts of what might have been. In her mind's eye, she saw the marriage as a visible fate awaiting her at the end of a long, dark tunnel.

Haakon's dining hall was a tightly packed assemblage of all the village's men, women, and children, each family seated according to their ranking within the community. Smoke from the oil lamps and the central pit's blazing fire filled the makeshift arena. As its thick haze caught the slanted beams of light piercing down from the roof's chimney, Braetana's attention was drawn forward to the raised dais on which she would first be legitimized, then married.

As she had approached the huge hall, the sound of a

pipe and a harp filled the late afternoon air. But now that she was inside, a sudden silence fell all around her. As Braetana struggled to adjust to her strange surroundings, she slowly realized that it was her entrance that had temporarily quieted the group's merriment.

"Jarl Magnus!" a familiar voice from the room's far end bellowed. Braetana's eyes followed the sound to its source, and she saw Haakon rise from his huge wooden throne, now positioned on the back of the raised platform. "We welcome you and your daughter on this most joyous of all occasions. Shall we begin?"

"Yes," Magnus answered with sturdy conviction, taking Braetana by the arm and whooshing her purposefully forward. She had no option but to approach the dais.

Haakon, for all the evil that festered within him, had done his best to look good for the occasion. He wore a brilliant red silk brocaded jacket, with a pattern of flying beasts with interlocking feetlike talons. In contrast to her own neckline, Haakon's collar was high, fastened at the throat with a huge silver brooch inlaid with many garnets. A voluminous red cape draped from his shoulders, its edges matching Braetana's in their ermine trim.

Beneath the cloak, Braetana could see a partially exposed scabbard and sword, an addition she suspected was more for ceremonial than practical use. Still, the weapon did little to calm her growing terror.

"Lady." Haakon's eyes stared at the incredible vision before him. Braetana nearly froze in response to the unchecked lust she saw there.

"Braetana," Magnus snapped, hoping to propel his daughter forward by speaking her name. Slowly, Braetana took the hand Haakon offered and stepped tentatively onto the tapestry-covered platform. As she stood next to him, Haakon placed one hand on her left elbow and turned her to face the room before them. There were so many people, all staring at her in such a strange way. Oddly, she felt that she was dreaming all this madness.

"Jarl Magnus seeks to make this child legally his," Haakon began, suddenly drawing her attention back from the crowd. "As konungr of Trondbergen, I declare it is his right to do so. Jarl Magnus, have you ale from three measures?"

"I have," replied Magnus, dipping an onyx-studded chalice into a deep silver bowl at the dais's side.

Magnus stepped onto the platform to join Haakon and Braetana, then placed his daughter's fingers around the goblet's vine-carved stem. This was merely her legitimization, but once she had been formally acknowledged as Magnus's child, nothing would prevent her from marrying Haakon.

"Drink, Braetana!" Magnus reissued the command, this time with a noticeable edge in his voice. His daughter, half motivated by a desire for numbness and half by sheer terror, upended the chalice, fully downing its contents.

"Is the ox slaughtered?" Haakon was rushing the ceremony, eager to complete this prelude to the nuptials.

"Yes," Magnus answered. "A three-year-old ox has been sacrificed. Its hide was flayed and sewn as a shoe. I offer it here for my daughter's assumption of her rightful role as heir to all I own. Child," he continued, setting the slipper at Braetana's own feet, "step into my footsteps, and claim that which is yours."

Braetana, still somewhat dazed by the whole procedure, stood immobile. Suddenly a pair of Haakon's maidservants scurried onto the dais, removed Braetana's right shoe, then half pulled her forward into the soft, ceremonial footwear. As she stepped forward, a loud cheer acknowledging her new status as rightful daughter rose up from the hall. It was only Haakon's raised hand that brought the hurrah to an end, restoring silence.

"We must bear formal witness to Jarl Magnus's new daughter in the manner provided for by our law. She will sit with a Viking who will attest to her new position. Lady Braetana," Haakon continued, smiling, "my brother Thorgunn will be pleased to serve us." Haakon stepped back, gesturing to the dais's side. His movement revealed Thorgunn seated amid a small group of older jarls at the platform's edge.

Thorgunn! The name raced through Braetana's mind, lifting her from the thick fog of confusion that swirled about her. She had never dreamed he would agree to come here, watching her as she became his brother's bride. But there he sat, his face just as she had remembered it. His deep gray-blue eyes were a painful reminder of what they had so recently shared.

As her lips parted in indecision, she cast a quick glance toward Haakon, though she knew not what she sought there. What she did find was a smile, that sardonic, malicious smile she had seen on him so often before.

Then she knew why Thorgunn had come. His presence was designed to humiliate her by showing the entire village that Haakon had not bested him by taking her as wife.

But she would triumph over both him and his brother with her own disdain. For the first time since she had entered the longhouse hall, Braetana spoke. "Am I to sit with him then?"

"Yes," Haakon answered, still smiling. "On his lap, as the law requires. He must see the shoe for himself."

Thorgunn sat, silently disbelieving the fine torture Haakon had devised and at the same time stunned by the incredibly beautiful image of Braetana before him. Slowly, almost hypnotically, she stepped down from the dais and walked the few steps toward him.

Even in his memory, he had never seen her like this; her body was as full and ripe as it had ever been. The soft swell of her breasts beneath the silk and ermine presented an almost overwhelming temptation, as did her angel's face, its full cerise-colored lips and deep lavender eyes more exquisite than anything his imagination could have conjured.

His desire for her was not just physical, for he wanted her whole being to mesh with his own, so that they could just once more become the single perfectly fused entity their intimacy had before allowed them. Now was the time—he could take her out of here, speed her to his waiting stallion and the nearby drekar before Haakon could even begin to stop him.

Haakon's entourage had already had too much to drink and their slow response would little challenge their escape. And yet there was something more formidable that stopped him—something distant in Braetana's look, a kind of inaccessibility he had never before seen there. Why didn't she speak to him? Why was there no question for him in those amethyst eyes?

Thorgunn thought his heart would rip from his soul as understanding dawned on him. Magnus had told him the truth—Braetana no longer wanted him. He could take her against Haakon's will, but not against her own.

"My lord," Braetana said emotionlessly.

Thorgunn searched her eyes for some sign of resistance, some signal that this was all a cruel charade and that her marriage to Haakon was not of her choosing.

"You will wed my brother then?" he asked, his voice low enough that Haakon could not hear. As he spoke, his brow furrowed deeply and pain etched its way across his face, an expression that in calmer surroundings Braetana might have accurately assessed. But, influenced by her own feelings of shame at his abandonment, she saw instead only that his pride was injured.

"I am to be queen," she answered, hoping to deliver a painful blow. But instead of the intended injury, her words seemed to bring only anger. Thorgunn clenched his teeth hard, speaking through them as he extended his arms to her.

"Then let us make you Magnus's daughter first!"

Suddenly, Thorgunn took hold of her hips and spun her partially around, landing her squarely on his broad lap. As he slapped the ceremonial shoe with one hand, his face turned toward Haakon, who stood smirking on the dais.

"Konungr. I bear witness—this woman is indeed Magnus's child." Then, as abruptly as he had pulled her to him, Thorgunn again righted her, setting her roughly back on both feet and pushing her in front of him. Haakon immediately reached down from the dais, grabbed her wrist and pulled Braetana back under the sanctuary ropes to join him on the platform.

"The act is done," he proclaimed loudly to the assembly. "Now to the wedding!"

A tremendous cheer rose up from the tables below, but Braetana hardly heard.

Haakon and Magnus led her through the ensuing ritual, seating her in a chair next to Haakon's on the dais's edge while the oracle cast the sacred wooden pieces, which Haakon called *blotspann*, before them. Each stick had been marked with ox's blood and awaited the throw of the soothsayer, who was a frightening specter draped in many faded layers of tattered gray cloth.

The old woman moved her gnarled hands in a circular pass over the dais's floor, clutching the blotspann tightly. Then, chanting an incantation, she rocked rhythmically from side to side. Though Braetana still spoke little Norse, she sensed that the old woman's words were some magical charm beyond even the Vikings' understanding.

Abruptly, the soothsayer dropped the bundle of red-stained wood to the floor, hissing as her hands released it. Leaning forward, she seemed to study the configuration as if it had great import. After a long silence, she rose and gathered her strange tools into a small leather satchel that hung from her hemp belt. Her face was emotionless as she approached Haakon. In a hushed tone, she spoke briefly with him. He smiled in response, then leaned sideways to translate for Braetana.

"She has cast lots as to the auspiciousness of our match. She tells me you were destined to be a Viking queen. And that you will soon bear a child." Haakon's hand came to rest on Braetana's knee with the pronouncement, filling her with disgust.

She turned her face away from him, hoping to avoid his leer, but found herself instead looking into the piercing gaze of the hag, who now crouched on the floor at

Braetana's side. The woman's face spoke eloquently to Braetana, making her wonder if the oracle's accurate prediction had been less a chance guess designed to please Haakon than some strange omniscience about Braetana's forthcoming motherhood.

Quickly Braetana forced her thoughts elsewhere. She averted her eyes, turning back to face Haakon.

"And what happens now?"

The old woman rose and stood in the dais's center, then began to spin slowly, her arms raised overhead and her voice rising into a shrill recitation.

"She invokes the aid of Frey, god of fertility, that we may fulfill the prophecy. She asks too for Odin's anger or blessing, depending on the truth of the statements we will now swear on the sacred arm ring. Rise."

Haakon caught Braetana beneath the elbow, lifted her to her feet and moved her forward to the center of the platform where the oracle had stood. In front of them, the woman held out a huge silver arm band, thicker and more ornately fashioned than any Braetana had seen.

"It was my father's," Haakon said, "and his father's before and his before that, back 'til a time when Thor fashioned it himself with his hammer and anvil. Since that day mortals have held it in safekeeping, that we might have some symbol of the Vanir's presence. Put out your hand."

Braetana reached out tentatively, her fingers shaking visibly as they approached the huge silver coil. Haakon laid his own hand atop hers, then spoke in Norse.

"I, Haakon, konungr of Trondbergen and descendant of Odin himself, declare my intention to make this woman, Braetana, daughter of Magnus, my drottning, that I may take her to my bed as wife and protect her and our issue. As Jarl Magnus will attest, the bride price has been set, I have paid my required portion, and taken possession of the dowry. The bride veil fee shall be delivered tomorrow morning—after we are truly man and wife. Lady Braetana, you do agree to this?" Haakon turned his frightening gaze straight onto a shaking Braetana.

Magnus had advised his daughter that a simple yes would suffice since she spoke little Norse. But the one word she was expected to utter might as well have been a full Viking treatise. Try as she might, Braetana could not seem to produce any sound at all.

"Braetana." She heard her name from behind, the anger in Magnus's voice clearly audible. She was expected to agree. But, even knowing that Thorgunn had abandoned her, had literally pushed her toward his half brother, she still did not think she was capable of this most terrible bargain.

But the child . . . suddenly Braetana thought of the child within her. Her only hope to protect both it and herself rested on this devil's deal she had made. All at once, like a diver from a high cliff, Braetana hurled herself forward, afraid that if she hesitated a moment more, she would never speak.

"Yes!" she exclaimed loudly, the word sounding much as if she had taken a painful blow.

Haakon removed Braetana's hand from the sacred arm band, then encircled her wrist with a smaller silver cuff.

Instantly, the occasion's solemnity dissolved into wild revelry, a thunderous cheer rising from the crowd behind them. Too eager to possess her, Haakon crushed

Braetana tightly against his body, his mouth imposing on her lips in a press of passion.

Dear God in heaven, she thought, *I cannot even bear his kiss—how will I bear tonight?*

Finally, to Braetana's great relief, Haakon freed her mouth. He continued to embrace her, however, forcing her so tightly against him that she could see over his left shoulder to the crowd seated beyond. There, where he had been when he'd thrown her from his lap into Haakon's waiting arms, was Thorgunn. He stood still amid the surrounding merriment, his face a mask of hate and resentment.

The sight of him brought hot, stinging tears to Braetana's eyes, and though those around her might well have attributed them to joy at her new marriage, Braetana knew better. They were tears of loss. Facing Thorgunn now, she knew, despite whatever hatred his heart held for her, that she had never wanted him more. And she had never been farther from having him. Now she belonged to someone else.

As Braetana remained a prisoner of Haakon's greedy grasp, Thorgunn walked toward the door. But before he left Braetana's sight, he turned once more, hoping against all he knew that he had misunderstood her intent.

Braetana was now Haakon's wife. He had never believed that such a fate could come to pass. And yet it had, apparently of her own choosing. She alone had spoken the words of choice to both him and his brother. He had thought her different from women who married for greed. Yet why else would she have taken Haakon over him? What irony, he considered, that it was his own greed that undid them first, but hers that completed the task.

Thorgunn had suffered pain before, some in battle, some at Haakon's hands. But until today, he had felt no blade as sharp as the look on Braetana's face. Her tears of joy were an agonizing testament to his foolishness in loving her. Able to bear the sight no longer, Thorgunn turned his face away from the horrible image of Braetana and Haakon in each other's arms.

As the boisterous celebration faded into an echo behind him, so too did Thorgunn's hopes. He had sunk into his own personal hell, completely unaware that Braetana joined him there.

XVIII

Braetana looked despairingly at the face reflected in the huge silver-trimmed mirror. It was an imposter costumed like a jubilant bride, a woman whose heart no longer beat within her, but whose outward appearance bore the trappings of a celebrant.

Dejectedly, she collapsed into the cushioned chair in Haakon's bedchamber. She was exhausted; the wedding festivities had gone on for hours after the ceremony itself, the hard-drinking Vikings taking seemingly endless amusement in the jugglers, verse-makers, and dice games that noisily competed for the revelers' attention.

The meal was an impressive display of all the Norse kitchens could produce. Guests chose from a spit-roasted side of garlic-scented horse meat, juniper-roasted pork, great amounts of dried cod, and gigantic baskets of fresh elderberries, strawberries, and apples. All were served generously from huge silver-trimmed wooden platters borne by an army of servants. If the festivities were characterized by anything at all, it was by excess, a theme carried over to the constantly refilled tubs of mead and wine Haakon had ordered for the occasion.

Throughout, Braetana was obliged to sit dutifully alongside Haakon. Flanked on either side by thickly carved pillars, he held court like the tyrant she knew him to be. To Braetana's relief, he paid her minimal attention, insisting only that she play the role of obedient wife by staying at his side.

She had been spared the dubious pleasure of dancing with him, his tastes apparently running more to the willing local maids than to his new wife. In fact, having married her, he seemed almost to ignore her, a fact that filled Braetana with optimism about the forthcoming night. Perhaps he would exhibit a similar disinterest in her later.

Braetana stopped her indulgent thinking. Even if Haakon had no inclination to bed her, she had to kindle his desire. She remembered painfully that, without the consummation of their marriage, Thorgunn's unborn child would be unprotected.

With resignation, Braetana began to remove her wedding gown. Easing its soft ermine off her shoulders, she soon stood naked, except for the crystal-studded hlao encircling her head.

Bronwyn would normally have been there to help her prepare for the wedding night, but she had been refused a position in Haakon's household. To Braetana's great dismay, Haakon apparently thought that all ties with her past were better severed. He had assigned her new maidservants, but Braetana wanted no one, particularly a pair of tongue-clacking Vikings, intruding on this most difficult moment.

As she stared at her reflection, thoughts of what might have been forced their way into her mind. She dutifully quashed them, recalling the duty at hand. *I must bed him,* she reminded herself, then aloud, she said, "I must."

"I think not," a voice from behind admonished, causing Braetana to turn toward its source.

"Gudrun!" Realizing that she was completely unclothed, Braetana did her best to don the yellow sendal robe she had lain nearby across Haakon's wide bed. "I . . ." She was not entirely sure what she wished to say.

"Yes." Gudrun nodded in mock sympathy as she approached the chair Braetana had just vacated. "I can understand your loss for words. Having stolen the throne from me."

Gudrun's tone made Braetana suspect that she was on the verge of another physical assault, and she braced herself for it, her pulse quickening in preparation. "I stole nothing. As I imagine you know, this marriage was not of my choosing."

"Good!" Gudrun issued a quick angry laugh as she rose. "Then you won't shed any tears when it ends."

"Ends?"

"You will leave Haakon. Tonight. I am here to arrange it."

Braetana now understood Gudrun's purpose, but doubted that the other woman would propose such a scheme if she understood Braetana's commitment to her own plan.

"It is punishable by death to deny a Viking king. And I have no intention of losing my life to aid your plans," Braetana answered.

"That would all have meaning," agreed Gudrun smugly, "were you not carrying Thorgunn's child."

If Gudrun had only been guessing, Braetana's sharp

gasp at her words confirmed what she had only suspected.

"It is a lie!" Braetana struggled to maintain her composure. "I no longer have feelings for Thorgunn. And how would I dare marry Haakon, were my virtue sullied?"

"Nice Saxon logic," Gudrun replied coldly, her playful attitude suddenly turned somber. "Now let us dispense with this pretense. You are with Thorgunn's child. The old oracle told me so after the ceremony; she saw it in the throw of the sacred blotspann. I would she had cast them earlier, for then your little escape would not be necessary. But as it is, you will follow my instructions."

Braetana opened her mouth to protest the oracle's pronouncement. But before she could, Gudrun interrupted.

"Yes, I know you could well dispute it. But time will bear my accusation out, will it not? Assuming this all came about on Einar's island, I should think you're nigh two months with child. A birth can come early, but Haakon is no fool. The babe will look fully grown. Unless you leave him, I will make sure Haakon knows. And I promise you, his angry sword will send both you and your beloved Thorgunn looking for your heads."

Braetana steadied herself against the nearby bedpost, attempting to gather her wits. At this moment she felt like a trapped animal, confused and frantic. Still, she had not lost all grasp of reason. Before the soothsayer's tale-telling, she might have been able to pass the child off as Haakon's, but with Gudrun's loud suspicions, no such device would work. She must strike a deal.

"You want me to leave him?" Braetana questioned. "Why? He has scorned you. Where is your pride?"

"There is no room for pride when the throne is at stake. Haakon may not love me, but he will at least see how valuable I am to him and once more make me drottning, provided that he no longer has you to turn to. Now, enough of this. I trust you accept the wisdom of my plan."

"Yes." Braetana answered with all the resignation of a woman who knew she had no other choice. "You would have me go now?"

"No, there is no time. Haakon still celebrates in the main hall, but he will soon be here. We must do this later."

"But—" interjected Braetana, now resigned to Gudrun's scheme, but horrified at the idea of being subjected to Haakon's base desires before her departure.

Gudrun followed Braetana's fears and dispelled them. "You will go before that. I would not like to find you in his bed any more than you would choose to be there. In fact, if such an unfortunate turn of events should come about, I'd have little incentive to help you, would I?" Braetana nodded in agreement.

"Here," Gudrun instructed, pressing a small leather pouch into Braetana's hand. "Put this in the wine carafe by the bed stand."

Gudrun gestured toward a silver pitcher alongside the four-posted bed. "It is Haakon's habit to inspire his seductions with wine. Offer him a goblet of this and he'll sleep 'til you're halfway to Northumbria."

"You'll send me home?" asked Braetana, incredulous. Although she knew Gudrun wished her clear of Haakon's reach, she had not dreamed she would arrange her return all the way to England.

"Not immediately," snapped an irritated Gudrun. "Tonight we'll do well to make the cabin on the far side of the mountain ridge. Tomorrow we shall launch you on water."

The idea of actually seeing Glendonwyck again filled Braetana with hope. It was a feeling she had experienced precious little of since Thorgunn left her.

"Bronwyn!" The thought shot through Braetana's mind as she spoke it out loud. She could not leave without Bronwyn. "I will not go without my maid! Even if you tell Haakon, I shall stay. And, if I do, you know he'll take me before he kills me. After that, he won't really be yours, will he?" Braetana silently prayed the argument would work. "I will not go without her," she repeated.

Gudrun stood silently considering the risk. "Well enough," she finally pronounced, "I'll arrange for her tomorrow. You are the only one I can take away tonight. Use the wine. And if you ever want to see your beloved England again, keep those long Saxon legs of yours close together!"

Gudrun left as suddenly as she had appeared, slipping out a back door Braetana had not noticed before for its concealment behind a thick tapestry. Alone again in the spacious room, Braetana struggled to sort through all that had just happened. The more she considered it, the higher her spirits rose. What might have been a disaster had proved instead a salvation. She would be free of Haakon's grasp, her child would be safe, and, along with her beloved Bronwyn, they would be on their way back to Glendonwyck.

Yet the notion that England was still her home felt strange now. Though Trondbergen had shown her great inhospitality, one painful realization came flooding in on her—Thorgunn was not at Glendonwyck. Once back in England, she would never see him again, never rest in the warmth of his arms, never be able to show him the child their love had borne.

Fool! she realized suddenly, impatient with her wishful thinking. *I would not have those things here either!*

The sound of footsteps in the hallway outside Haakon's bedchamber moved Braetana to swift action. She scurried silently to the bedside stand and emptied the leather pouch's contents into the heavy pitcher. The thud of the door as Haakon threw it open caused her to drop the small sack on the floor at the stand's base.

"Shall I make you a true Viking queen?" Haakon roared, his words slightly slurred from drink.

Braetana's heart raced so hard she thought it would explode, but she made every effort to force herself back to an appearance of calm. She must play her part well, and let Haakon suspect nothing. And all the while, for her own and Gudrun's purposes, she must evade his hungry, groping hands.

"I have been waiting, my lord," she answered softly.

"I see," leered a rapidly approaching Haakon, surveying her state of undress, the sendal robe alone covering her nakedness. As he narrowed the distance between them, she caught the strong smell of wine on his hot breath, and it reminded her of the task at hand.

"A drink perhaps . . . before . . ." she suggested, pouring a goblet full of the powder-laden wine and offering it straight-armed to stop Haakon's progress toward her.

"I have drunk enough wine," Haakon answered, all too correctly. Taking the silver chalice from her, he placed it back next to the pitcher on the wooden nightstand. "No, I prefer to be heady with the taste of you."

He pressed Braetana back against the oak-paneled wall and reached up, removing the silver and crystal hlao from her head. With one hand, he easily undid the twisted topknot of flaxen hair, allowing it to fall unencumbered about Braetana's rising shoulders.

Haakon was so close to her face she could feel the heat of his breath on her. He looked intently into her frightened eyes, tracing a light path down her cheekbone with one finger.

"I saw you and Thorgunn today. It gives me great pleasure to take you from him. But I should hope your affection for him wanes, for the idea of you as wife grows on me, and I would not like to have to force you always."

Braetana sensed that, in his own perverse way, Haakon was making some effort at civility. But she could think only of how to turn his sympathy to her immediate advantage.

"I would like to be yours willingly, lord. But I am frightened," she replied. "I have never known a man before, and there was so much excitement at the feast, I could neither eat nor drink. But now, perhaps some wine would make me a partner more suited to your taste."

Haakon smiled in boyish anticipation. Against all odds, the little wench was actually willing to let him take her! The time for a sip of wine was a small enough concession for the ride to follow.

He retrieved the full goblet from the nightstand, then lifted it slowly to Braetana's lips. He tipped it toward her, ready to spill its contents down Braetana's throat, when she raised a finger to the rim, canting it back toward him.

"Sire," she whispered breathlessly, "I would drink

after you, that my lips would go only where yours have gone."

Her responsiveness stunned Haakon. True enough, at the start he had thought to enjoy her resistance to him. But this sweet acquiescence exceeded any pleasure her defiance might have brought. He could understand Thorgunn's obsession with the little minx, though he was about to taste a pleasure his brother knew naught of.

"Very well." Tilting the goblet's base up, he downed its entire contents. "Now one for my wife." Haakon reached to pour again from the pitcher, but as the stem clanked against the wooden stand, Braetana placed her hand on his, stopping him.

"Perhaps no. I just need a moment more to prepare." As she began to cross the floor, hoping to stay Haakon with more preening, she felt herself jerked violently back by her long hair. Like the beast she sensed he was, Haakon threw her on the back wall. Without further warning, he pressed his body hard against her.

"No more delays," he breathed, then forced a bruising kiss on Braetana's unwilling lips.

She struggled to twist free of him, tossing her head from side to side as best she could, but the strength of his press on her mouth pinned her against the cold oak wall. When she thought she would suffocate for lack of breath, he unexpectedly backed off her, the two of them standing in a close face-off.

"Yes," Haakon said with a malevolent laugh, "I am going to enjoy this ride." He raised both hands, gripping the inside collar of Braetana's robe. Though the garment could have been easily undone by freeing its loose belt, Haakon wasted no time. He ripped it off Braetana with one swift, violent snap. She stood completely naked before him.

Braetana gasped sharply, terrified that he would be able to proceed with his assault on her before the drug took hold.

"Oh yes," breathed Haakon approvingly as his eyes took in her nakedness, "Thorgunn's loss is indeed my gain."

Braetana crossed her arms over her breasts, attempting to cover herself. Haakon was in no mood for her modesty. No sooner did she attempt to hide herself than he grabbed both her wrists, snapped them down, and pulled her against him, one powerful arm clutched painfully tight around her waist.

Braetana struggled to loosen his hold, pushing both her fists against Haakon's partially exposed chest, but her strength was no match for his. Her frantic efforts to escape his vile embrace grew more difficult and useless with each passing moment.

Suddenly Braetana felt herself losing balance. Without warning, she fell back as Haakon forced her down on the large bed, his weight like a massive millstone on top of her.

The wine had not worked, and, despite her earlier plan to bed Haakon, Braetana's only thought at this moment was to somehow free herself from his attack.

"No!" she screamed furiously, her fists beating on the tops of his shoulders and her naked torso twisting wildly to throw him off her. Haakon gasped as he felt the sting of her fingernails raking angry tracks down his now exposed back. Yet quickly he recovered his intent, and the pain seemed only to excite him more.

His legs forced Braetana's own apart, and, even

through the thick brocade of his trousers, she could feel him hard and ready to take her.

"Dear God . . ." Braetana pleaded, suddenly awash in the realization that nothing she could do now would stop him. But just as she all but abandoned hope, Haakon loosened his grip and rolled sideways, one hand holding his forehead and the other attempting futilely to prop himself up onto his elbow.

"I must have drunk too much wine . . ." he slurred, unable to say any more as he collapsed back onto the fur bed cover. For an instant, Braetana was almost too stunned to move, her terror momentarily overcoming the need for quick escape. But almost immediately, she recovered her wits.

With her robe now torn badly by Haakon's hungry hands, Braetana redonned the white silk wedding dress. As she finished the back's last button, the tapestry covering the bedchamber's backdoor again parted, revealing a satisfied Gudrun.

"Nicely done." Gudrun clapped her hands in mock applause. "I see I have underestimated you."

"You heard?" asked an enraged Braetana, unable to understand why Gudrun had not come to her aid.

"I trusted your commitment to avoid him. But I do not trust Haakon to waste any time in searching for you once the wine wears off. Here," she added, hurling a heavy red woolen cape at Braetana. "This will do for tonight's journey."

"What of the other provisions we'll need?" Braetana asked.

"The cabin is well stocked. It is a hunting lodge for the mountains just beyond. We shall be safe there to-

304 / BLAINE ANDERSON

night, and tomorrow we will travel to the ship I've arranged for you."

"And Bronwyn?"

"I told you, she will come," snapped Gudrun impatiently. "One of my huskarlars will bring her tomorrow. But if we do not now make haste, your cherished nursemaid will find herself lacking a charge."

Gudrun jerked back the tapestry, pushed the door open, and allowed a rush of cool night air to enter the cabin. As Braetana scurried out, quickly lifting her skirts and mounting the large palfrey tethered just outside, Gudrun turned back to look at the sleeping Haakon.

He is a child, she thought, *a man undone by his own appetites.* But at least he would have her back to watch over and guide him, providing she dispensed with Braetana.

Gudrun's animal, a massive dappled gray gelding, was tied alongside the chestnut mare she'd brought for Braetana. Seeing her companion already mounted, Gudrun wasted no time in using the square-looped stirrup to boost her onto her own horse.

Braetana felt somewhat awkward on her animal, the riding apparatus itself being much different from that to which she was accustomed at Glendonwyck. But this was no time to take issue with such small discomforts. Adjusting quickly to the odd seat, she spurred the prancing mare forward into the darkness, following Gudrun's swift lead.

Nighttime travel was precarious at best. Certainly it was made all the more difficult by the fact that the trail they followed was narrow and winding, leading them into steeper and more rocky terrain with each passing mile. Still, fear was a great motivator. Despite the disadvantage of darkness, the two women made good progress, reaching the small shack in less than two hours.

They had spoken little on the trip, their minds more bent on quick escape than conversation. Even if they had not been preoccupied with their flight, there was little to say. Braetana was thus quite surprised when they finally reached the cabin, Gudrun having given her little warning they were even close to their destination.

Once they arrived, Gudrun hurriedly dismounted and entered the dark, dank-smelling structure. In the moonlight, it appeared only about half the size of Einar's modest longhouse. Braetana knew it was only a hunting cabin and that the house was unlikely to have any occupants, but something about the place unnerved her. Though Gudrun had long since dismounted, Braetana remained atop her palfrey, the discomfort of the saddle competing with her reluctance to spend a night inside the small longhouse with only the sour Gudrun for company.

"You won't do yourself much good out here," Gudrun announced brusquely, appearing at the door holding a soapstone dish lit with burning oil. "Unless you plan to freeze to death," she added, thinking that such a development would certainly ease the unpleasant task before her.

Braetana responded to Gudrun's admonishment, shaking off her apprehension and dismounting. No harm could come to her now that she was safely out of Haakon's reach. Or was she? The thought still troubled her.

"Haakon will not find us here?" As she entered the cabin, Braetana surveyed the hanging dried fish and casks of mead that framed the building's walls.

"Not tonight," answered Gudrun curtly, closing the door behind them. "The wine should keep his sweet head on the pillow 'til tomorrow. But by then, you'll be en route back to that precious home of yours."

Braetana did not miss the ever-present irritation in Gudrun's shrill voice. "I should think that would please you," she fired back. "Is that not what you wanted all along?" Braetana stood facing Gudrun and, for the first time, she became truly aware of how much she towered over Haakon's shorter and stockier consort.

"What I wanted was to remain as queen," Gudrun answered candidly. "Without intervention from some half-Saxon . . ." Gudrun caught her tongue. Antagonizing Braetana now would only cause more distrust.

"You know well none of this was of my choosing," answered Braetana angrily.

"And what would you have chosen? Haakon's brother?" They both knew it to be true, but Braetana was disinclined to reveal her heart to a woman who clearly wished her ill.

"It matters little now," Braetana answered as she turned away, her tone dismissing Gudrun's prying. "Now I choose to return home as you have so conveniently arranged for me. How is it you came by a long-ship? I thought all of Trondbergen drank to my wedding night."

"I may no longer be drottning," Gudrun answered, "but I still have silver and power of my own. I bought you a crewed ship and a pilot who knows your course home. It was not that difficult. It is not that big a ship." Gudrun smiled at Braetana, who, for want of a fire, clutched her woolen cloak about herself to stay warm.

"I trust it's sufficient to weather the North Sea?"

Braetana questioned. "As you may recall, I have already had my swim there. I should not wish to repeat it."

"No," agreed Gudrun, "we would not want that. It would be in no one's best interest were you to wash up in the fjord's channel."

Something odd underscored Gudrun's comments to her. Though Braetana could not exactly pinpoint it, she sensed there was some element of danger in further conversation between them. She gestured as if to take Gudrun's lamp.

"Going outside?" Gudrun asked tartly.

"Building a fire. I trust you can show me wood and kindling."

Gudrun smiled sardonically. "You are quite useful, aren't you? I would not have credited a Saxon noblewoman with such practical skills."

Braetana could have slapped her insolent face right then and there, but resisted the urge in the interest of her own and Bronwyn's eventual safety. "A little trick I learned while shipwrecked."

"Among others," muttered Gudrun, speaking low, but still loud enough for Braetana to hear.

Braetana spun angrily toward her. "Gudrun, I like your company about as much as you like mine. Since I have known you, you have assaulted me, insulted me, and forced me into treason, which, although it did ultimately serve my own interests, is certainly designed for yours. If we parted now, it would suit me well. But, as it is, we appear slated to keep company for one more night, after which I'll be denied the pleasure of your sweet face forever. I suggest in the meantime that we make the best of it."

Gudrun could see the attraction this woman held, the

wiles she worked on both Thorgunn and Haakon. She was not only beautiful, but she was also bright and quick. Gudrun had a good head too, yet Braetana's wit seemed suffused with a gentleness, a sort of decency that Gudrun knew would escape her no matter how she tried to make it her own.

Men were such fools, to be duped by this artifice passing as gentility. But after tomorrow, Haakon's stupidity, and Braetana, would no longer pose any problems.

She had the knife. She had only to muster the nerve to use it. It was an act of courage that seemed simple enough as she faced the woman who had brought her so much misery.

The trick had been pitifully easy, convincing Braetana that she would help her escape. But ever since the oracle had come to her after the wedding, knowing Gudrun would pay much for news of what the blotspann really spoke, she had sensed her bad fortune about to turn.

Amazing as it was, Braetana did not seem to even want Haakon. It was a sentiment incomprehensible to Gudrun, but one that she attributed to the Saxon's enduring affection for Thorgunn. Even without the knowledge of her pregnancy, Gudrun might have convinced Braetana to leave. With the leverage of the oracle's knowledge, it had all been too simple.

It would be easier now if Braetana didn't have to die. But Gudrun knew there was no choice. She understood Haakon better than anyone. Assuredly, he would never let Braetana escape her vows, and no drekar was fast enough or sea so wide that she could flee his wrath. Even were Haakon not to capture her, Magnus certainly would.

Once found, Braetana would certainly betray Gudrun as accomplice in the matter. That would spell nothing if not her own end. No, this was the only way.

Tomorrow, Gudrun would lead her from the cabin under the pretense that they were to meet Bronwyn at the adjacent fjord's mouth. But Braetana would never see the fjord or the imaginary longship she counted on. Instead, the Saxon would meet her end at the tip of Gudrun's sharp dagger.

Haakon would search for her at first, but, finding no trace, he would soon conclude she had fled on her own. Eventually, he would abandon his efforts, and in time, his affections would return to Gudrun. She would again rule as drottning. Only this wench across the room now stood between Haakon and her destiny with him.

By now Braetana had stoked a roaring fire. Surveying the room, she noted two simple pallets well suited to their sleeping needs.

"If you do not mind," she addressed Gudrun, "I shall sleep here." She gestured toward the bed closest to where she stood. Receiving no objection from Gudrun, Braetana lay down on the fur cover and pulled her long cape about her for warmth.

"Sleep well," admonished Gudrun. "Tomorrow will be a most special day."

XIX

"How do you know she's gone?" Thorgunn shook his frightened young huskarlar Rollo by the shoulders. It was as if in jostling him he thought he could release the information he so urgently wanted.

"I heard from a servant at Haakon's. When the konungr awoke this morning, she had fled. No one knows where. But I pity her fate when Haakon finds her. By all accounts, he's in a wolf's rage and even now mounts a party to search for her."

Thorgunn could hardly believe his ears. Just yesterday he had seen Braetana willingly wed to that miserable brother of his, yet today she had fled him. Why? What had he done to her to so quickly change her feelings?

Thorgunn banished the possibilities, all of them grim, from his mind. What mattered now was that Braetana had left Haakon. He must construe that to mean she regretted the choice she had made.

However little or much she felt for him, he could not allow her to be held prisoner in a marriage she would flee. Despite having witnessed her choosing another as husband, he could not stop loving her. Perhaps he could try again to persuade her of his changed intent. She might refuse—but whatever would or would not happen between them, he could not let Haakon get to her first.

"Get Loki! Bridle him only, there is no time for a full mount. Quickly!" His sharp command sent Rollo scrambling out the door to the side stable where the animal was tethered. As Thorgunn hurriedly donned his trousers and tunic, throwing a heavy traveling cape over the sword and scabbard he'd cinched on, he considered how best to reach Braetana before Haakon did.

The immediate problem was that he didn't know where she'd gone. Thorgunn's mind clicked through the possibilities. Rollo said it was suspected that she had gone alone. If this were true, she certainly would not have taken to the sea. She was not enough of a sailor to manage even a small boat by herself, and she was far too bright to try to do so.

Barring the fjord, Thorgunn guessed Braetana would have fled through the mountains ringing Trondbergen, going by foot if necessary, by horse, if possible. The place to begin was at Haakon's bedchamber; at least he knew she had started there.

It occurred to Thorgunn that Haakon had followed a similar train of thought and might well have already begun pursuit of his new wife. But he probably would not track her alone, instead marshaling a search party of jarls, maybe even including the slow-moving Magnus. This would buy Thorgunn time. Even if it didn't, he could little afford not to try when Braetana's very life hung in the balance. If Haakon found her first, he would surely kill her; that much Thorgunn was certain of.

Loki's whinny outside Thorgunn's door called to him. Almost instantly, he had mounted bareback. Sure-handedly, Thorgunn guided the horse toward his brother's, going slowly so as to avoid unnecessary attention.

If Braetana left from Haakon's, Thorgunn doubted she'd used the front entrance. The wedding festivities had gone on even into the early morning hours, and she surely could not have fled through that door unobserved. He would try the back instead.

As he rounded the huge longhouse's perimeter, Thorgunn saw what he sought. There, marked clearly in the soft mud outside Haakon's door, were fresh hoof prints. But instead of the one set Thorgunn had expected to find, there were two.

Quickly dismounting, Thorgunn crouched in study over the deep imprints. Suddenly his eyes grew wide at what he saw. It was Gudrun's horse, the right front hoof mark misshapen as only he, who had sold her the animal, could know it to be. For a brief moment, Thorgunn thought that the trail might not be Braetana's.

But the tracks were so fresh, and beside Gudrun's horse, there was a second set. Of course! It was Gudrun who had taken Braetana away. He knew Gudrun's fury at his brother's plan to marry the Saxon, and who better to relieve Haakon of the temptation?

Quickly, Thorgunn reached a frightening conclusion. Knowing Gudrun as he did, he knew that her plans must involve great danger to the woman he loved.

Now he must find Braetana more quickly than ever. Thorgunn hastily swung himself atop his anxious destrier, digging his heels sharply into Loki's side. With the loud pounding of the animal's heavy hooves, the two of them sped up the hill, leaving the longhouse to grow smaller in the distance.

* * *

"So." Haakon hissed angrily as he watched them depart, "this *was* my brother's doing after all, and he shall pay." *As shall that half-Saxon bitch,* Haakon thought, struggling to give Magnus no indication of his rising fury.

Haakon's discovery of Braetana's escape had given him cause enough for rage, and his anger had grown greater after finding the empty leather pouch at the nightstand's base. But once word of Braetana's flight was out, and Magnus agreed that it must have been Thorgunn who had caused such disaster, Haakon's fury rose to even greater heights. It was bad enough to be cuckolded—but by his own despicable brother!

Haakon had been careful not to alarm Magnus with any talk of retribution against Braetana, even though both suspected that she was a willing participant in abandoning her new husband. Haakon, especially, was certain that Thorgunn and Braetana had planned their flight all along, and that they were enjoying it all the more for the insult of its timing.

Thorgunn had surely arranged for Braetana to leave him. Now, riding just as if he knew where to find her, his half brother was off to meet his beloved, hoping that by delaying their rendezvous he would avoid discovery. *I will give him no such pleasure,* thought Haakon as he steadied his prancing stallion.

"Jarl Magnus, the traitor Thorgunn leaves, no doubt to meet your daughter. If we are careful, we can follow undetected. Mark my words, Loki and that kidnapper astride him will lead us straight to Braetana."

"I will follow you," Magnus answered. Haakon dug his heels into his large destrier's sides, propelling him forward. His entourage followed suit.

The narrow trail to the cabin wound steeply upward, its rapid assent marked by the disappearance of the spring flowers that had surrounded the town's open fields and the advent of a thick, flowerless forest still much in the wintry grip of the higher altitude.

The trail had been carved through the fir forest to allow access to a small cabin used as a hunting base during late spring and summer. Thorgunn knew that it had been recently occupied and likely had a well-stocked larder.

This was a fact Gudrun surely had counted on. As he worked through the logic of Braetana's abduction, it grew clearer to Thorgunn that this was most certainly where she had gone. Even without Gudrun's aid, Braetana might have been able to follow the well-marked trail. But the two sets of hoof prints in front of him gave evidence that someone had guided her. He could imagine no one save Gudrun who would have sufficient motive or gall to cross Haakon so gravely.

Thorgunn guessed that his brother would soon follow him. Whatever Haakon's intent, though, it was unimportant, providing that Thorgunn reached Braetana first. He rode as swiftly as the steeply pitched terrain would allow. Thorgunn and the animal made good time, and he was confident that they would find Braetana before Haakon did.

Once at the cabin, he would relieve Gudrun of her captive. Odin willing, he and Braetana would then seek refuge in the forested mountains beyond until they could safely escape by fjord.

One mountain range over from the Trondbergen fjord, another deeply carved inlet worked its way westward, it too eventually spilling into the sea. It was here that

Thorgunn had yesterday sent a crew and drekar in the hopes that Braetana would accept his offer of rescue. She had refused him at the wedding ceremony, but his plans still might serve them well.

He issued a silent prayer to Frey that Braetana would reconsider his suit. At the very least, he hoped she would allow him to free her from the punishment that he was sure Haakon would mete out once he found her.

Thorgunn still ached with longing at the thought of her. It had been a month and a half since he'd made love to her, yet it seemed a lifetime ago. He considered that, had he been truthful, he might have had both Braetana and her inheritance. Now, as a result of his duplicity, he had lost both.

Strangely enough, the silver seemed of little import now. No fortune could buy back his heart's most precious desire—Braetana's love. He thought sadly that she had every right to refuse him. All he knew with certainty was that he must free her, even to return her to England. Though Loki was making good time up the terraced trail, Thorgunn urged him on as best he could with a hard heel tap on his full sides.

A short distance away from Thorgunn's fast moving destrier, the chill of the morning air nudged Braetana to unwilling wakefulness. The woolen cloak she had wrapped herself in the preceding night had proved scant protection against the cold's sharp snap. For a moment, Braetana remained absolutely still, disinclined to disturb the small amount of heat her huddled form had managed to capture.

She was at first unable to recall where she was. Then, turning her hood-covered head sideways on the pallet, a glimpse of Gudrun across the room brought last night's agonizing chain of events quickly to mind.

How narrowly she had escaped what certainly could have been her worst fate since her kidnap from Glendonwyck. She desperately wished that she were back home now, safe within the beloved walls that had sheltered her for so many years. Even Edward's forced attentions would do little to rival Haakon's crude assault. With all she had thus far been forced to bear, her travails in England, which once seemed so terrible, now paled dramatically in comparison.

How different, she thought, from her feelings a short while ago. The bliss of her time on Einar's island flooded her mind and heart, bringing a wash of warm tears to her eyes. She remembered the gentle caress of Thorgunn's touch. She wondered if he turned his thoughts to her at all now, if he questioned why she had fled his brother's bed.

It was presumptuous to assume he had any reaction, given his behavior at the wedding ceremony. Never had she thought to see such contempt for her in his eyes. Could those truly have been the same eyes that had adored her such a short time ago? Was it only her fortune he sought? How could he relinquish her so easily to Haakon's bed? The questions tormented her and she forced herself to dismiss them before she began crying again.

"It does not matter now," she whispered to herself. "It matters only that I escape safely with my baby and Bronwyn."

The words, though quietly spoken, nudged Gudrun from her own sleep.

"It is daylight!" Gudrun screamed with alarm, sitting

quickly upright. She glanced nervously around the room, looking agitated and disoriented.

"It has been for some time, I think. I have listened for your huskarlar and Bronwyn, but I heard nothing. Should they not come soon?"

Gudrun hated this ridiculous charade, and her irritation registered easily in her voice.

"I told you to stop badgering me with your incessant questions. We will meet the old woman soon enough!" Gudrun was less annoyed with Braetana's inquiry than with herself for sleeping so late. The stress of the preceding night's flight had apparently taken its toll on her. She had planned to rise early, sweeping all traces of Braetana from the cabin before a search party could locate them. Already, she had lost valuable time.

The small longhouse was an easy choice as their likely refuge. Gudrun knew that it would not be long before Haakon and a party of his men arrived, angry and ready to exact vengeance for the insult he'd suffered. That was why it was important to get Braetana outside and lure her off some distance into the woods. There, Gudrun's small but lethal dagger could do its devilish work.

As she rehearsed Braetana's death in her mind, her hand instinctively flew to the sheathed knife that hung from a hip belt atop her chemise. The blade itself was not suspicious. Many Viking women carried similar knives, but for household use, not for defensive purposes. It was remarkable for a woman of Gudrun's wealth and station to adopt such a practical accoutrement, but Braetana was ignorant enough of local custom to find anything improper about the leather-encased blade. As Gudrun's fingers worked the contours of the small iron weapon, she looked up in horror to see that Braetana had successfully managed a small fire in the corner hearth.

"Are you mad?" Gudrun screamed, rushing to intervene. "Do you want Haakon here this moment? What could you be thinking of, to build a fire?"

"I was thinking that I was cold," Braetana answered calmly. She stepped in front of the growing flames, effectively stopping Gudrun's intent to douse them. "You said it would be some time before he followed us. In any event, we cannot leave until Bronwyn arrives. Fire or no, we must wait for your huskarlar, and I saw no need to freeze in the process."

"I told you that we would meet the old woman at the fjord," Gudrun snapped, annoyed.

"But if this is the only path," Braetana reasoned, "does it not make sense to wait for her? Surely we will have a greater chance of finding Bronwyn here than in the woods."

Damn this intractable bitch! Gudrun cursed silently. Based on what she had told Braetana, her captive's conclusions were not altogether unreasonable. But they were based on two fallacies—one, that Bronwyn was indeed coming, and two, that Gudrun had no reason to want to leave the longhouse.

It was unlikely that a short additional stay there would risk Haakon's discovery of them. Gudrun knew him to be a rather inept and slow rider. Still, it was important to dispense with Braetana quickly, both for safety's sake and also because Gudrun wanted to get the dreaded deed over with.

She had never killed anyone before. Though she had few doubts about her ability to do it successfully, it was hardly a task she relished. Now, just when she was ready to move Braetana out and finish her plan, the contentious little wench decided she was cold.

"Braetana, we should go. We can meet Bronwyn on the trail to the fjord."

"I am afraid she will not find us," Braetana snapped back. "And as I've told you before, I go nowhere without Bronwyn. Perhaps you could see back down the trail?" Braetana scrutinized Gudrun, now not quite sure that her plan was what she'd promised.

It occurred to Braetana that the Viking woman didn't intend to bring Bronwyn at all. She tried to dismiss the thought, knowing that, because she refused to travel without her companion, Gudrun would gain little by lying. Still, just as she'd felt a strange uneasiness about the cabin itself, there was something about Gudrun's present manner that set Braetana on her guard.

The expression on her captive's face did not go unnoticed by Gudrun. Once Braetana's suspicions were aroused, she stood to lose all. It was critical that she assure her reluctant companion that the original plan still held.

"You are right, of course. Bronwyn is probably nearly here by now. There is a vantage point atop a rock face just above us. I could watch from there." Gudrun felt she had recovered her composure.

"Yes," replied Braetana cautiously as she stoked the nearly roaring fire. "It would be helpful to know."

Gudrun opened the door to the small, smoky cabin, wrapping her own woolen cloak tightly about herself. Of course Bronwyn wasn't en route, but Gudrun needed to escape from what she perceived to be Braetana's scrutiny. She must rethink her plans. As her mind spun in search of new options, she strolled absentmindedly toward the vantage point she had mentioned to Braetana. She might as well survey the trail for followers, though she expected none so early in the day.

Braetana was obstinate about not leaving the cabin. To kill her there would be untidy at best and would certainly make it clear that her flight from Haakon was more abduction than escape. As Gudrun reached the rock table above the cabin, great swirls of white smoke caught her eye as they curled skyward from the small chimney opening.

This was the answer! Longhouse fires were not uncommon because the oak walls and dried grass roof of a Viking building provided ready tinder. If an accident were to occur here, and Braetana were to be somehow trapped inside, it would not matter who found her. It would be assumed she had fled on her own, found the cabin, and met an untoward fate in some fiery accident.

Gudrun smiled at the efficient scenario. Down below her the hearth blazed; Braetana was inside. Gudrun's only task was to spread the flames and make sure Braetana stayed inside long enough to meet her death.

The hemp rope from Gudrun's saddle, lashed to a thick beam that bisected the structure, would ensure that Braetana remain inside. Once Braetana was tied securely to it, Gudrun would only need to return to the village and secure her alibi. Then she would set about reclaiming her rightful position as drottning. Her goals were about to be realized, and the thought caused her to smile broadly.

As Gudrun looked down the trail and saw a man on horseback a short distance away, she squinted, trying to bring the stranger into better focus.

He was too far away for her to see his face, but she could make out a large black marking on the animal's front flank. Damn him to hell—it was Thorgunn! Come to rescue that half-breed Saxon, no doubt!

With the purpose of a woman better experienced in such unsavory matters, Gudrun rushed back to the house, her voluminous skirts nearly tripping her in her speed. She knew what she must do, and she must do it now, before Braetana's would-be deliverer arrived.

Gudrun grabbed the saddle's rope and burst so quickly through the door that Braetana barely had time to look back over her shoulder before she was encircled with a tight ring of hemp. Before Braetana could speak, Gudrun violently jerked her straight back, running the rope so tightly around the oak pillar that it caused her to cry out sharply in pain.

"What are you doing?" Braetana screamed, struggling hard against her restraints. She grew more powerless each moment as Gudrun wound turn after turn of hemp around Braetana and the post.

"We are having a small accident with the fire," Gudrun answered acidly. Dexterously, she tied off the last bit of loose rope, then rushed to the hearth as she searched for tools with which to set the blaze.

"Gudrun . . ." Braetana abruptly stopped speaking as she realized that this madwoman meant to burn her alive. "Do not do this," she pleaded. "I will go alone, I'll not see Haakon again. He shall be yours."

"He shall be mine anyway," fired Gudrun, smiling sardonically. "Did you really think I would let you go? Risk Haakon finding you and forgiving your transgressions? I need more assurance than that." Gudrun pulled a large log from the hearth, holding it by its unlit end while its opposing fiery tip flared angrily. Within seconds she had run the perimeter of the small room, lighting the thick curtains hung to keep drafts from seeping through the wall.

The weight of the fabric at first made each tapestry merely smoke, but as the fire caught the woven panels burst one at a time into flames, drawing Braetana's attention first in one direction, then another. Filled with horror, she turned her head in frantic awareness of the inferno building around her.

Braetana felt that dread she had sensed when they first arrived here, the uneasiness she'd seen in Gudrun this morning. She struggled with all her will against the hemp rope, but her bonds seemed only to grow tighter with each useless twist.

Pitching her makeshift torch as close as she could to Braetana, Gudrun hurriedly pushed open the huge door. She herself was now nearly overcome with the intense smoke that filled the room.

"Please," begged Braetana, hoping desperately to appeal to some shred of decency in Gudrun. Her captor only smiled at Braetana's terror, stepping outside and leaning slightly back in before she finally departed.

"I am glad you built the fire," she cooed sickeningly, then slammed the door hard, leaving Braetana alone with the choking fumes and rapidly advancing flames.

The blaze grew in wild, unpredictably loud bursts. With horrifying ease, the walls began to catch and the floor sent swirling curls of smoke rising up from its dry planks.

Braetana fought valiantly against the hemp bonds, but both her heart and her body quickly learned the hopelessness of protest. She coughed in more and more of the stifling smoke, and breathing now seemed to require every ounce of her energy. Soon the air in the room thickened until it was little more than a gray fog. As Braetana gasped for even the tiniest bit of breathable air, she felt herself slipping from consciousness.

Suddenly a rush of smoke escaped the cabin's open front door. The haze was so thick that had Braetana been conscious, it still would have taken her a moment to recognize the form outlined against the blue sky beyond.

Thorgunn raised his hand to shield himself against the incredible heat, all the while squinting against the strong fumes that stung his eyes. Despite the extreme conditions, he forced himself inside, sensing that he would find Braetana there. When he saw her, Thorgunn was so relieved he became almost unaware of the danger surrounding them.

His dagger cut swiftly through the layers of rope that held Braetana's limp form upright. Sweeping her easily into his huge arms, he took several steps back toward the entry. Yet even with the door ajar, the flames formed a virtually seamless wall between the two of them and the fresh air beyond.

He spun to quickly survey the blazing room. His attention was caught by a strange smoke pattern on the back wall. There, exposed by the burned-off tapestry, was another door, this one still closed but less engulfed than the front portal by the lapping waves of fire that washed all around them.

In three long strides he reached the opening. With a powerful kick, Thorgunn freed the door from its stuck position. Almost instantly, he and Braetana burst outside. Suddenly, they were clear of the inferno that threatened to swallow them alive, safe in the clarity of the crisp spring air.

With Thorgunn's haste, the two of them quickly made their way a safe distance from the fiery longhouse. It was only as Thorgunn laid Braetana's motionless form down atop a moist blanket of moss and grass that he became aware that she was unconscious, and he feared that his rescue had come too late.

She lay completely still, her beautiful face lifeless and unmoving, her long loose hair saturated with the smell of burned wood. She was dead. The realization felt as though some flame within Thorgunn that had burned as white-hot as the cabin they'd fled had abruptly gone cold, extinguished in one horrible moment.

He knelt over her unmoving form, wanting to disbelieve what had happened. His hands, then his face, nuzzled into the soft fall of silvery blond hair that spilled across her reddened cheek and down onto the wedding dress she still wore.

"Braetana," Thorgunn spoke softly, his voice a blend of pain and rage. "I love you, my darling, I love you. . . ." As Thorgunn spoke, tears filled his closed eyes and agony engulfed him like a great drowning wave.

Holding her lifeless body gently in his arms, Thorgunn softly rocked Braetana as if she were a child. Time seemed to slow, then stop. They had known each other so briefly, and yet he could not grieve more had they spent a lifetime together.

Without warning, Braetana gasped. Then, as Thorgunn pulled back in disbelief, she coughed weakly and opened her deep amethyst eyes.

"Braetana! I thought. . . ." Thorgunn felt his heart

would burst at the sight of her. She was soot-stained and exhausted, but obviously very much alive. He pressed his lips against hers, meeting her yielding mouth with a long, deeply passionate kiss. Finally, Thorgunn pulled slightly away, then he clutched her to him again, this time whispering what she had come to know as his own special Norse endearments in her ear.

Braetana could hardly believe this was happening. Only moments ago, she had thought that her life was ended, the cabin destined to be her fiery grave. Miraculously, she was now not only alive, but also held tightly in the arms of the love she'd thought lost.

"Thorgunn," she breathed incredulously, "why are you here?"

"Oh, my love," answered Thorgunn quietly. Still pressing her close against him, Thorgunn covered her head and neck with a torrent of small kisses, lifting her up slightly off the grass in the process.

"Thorgunn!" Braetana cried in sudden horror. "Look there!"

The change in position caused by his embrace had afforded Braetana a view toward the burning cabin. What she saw rivaled all that had thus far happened in its madness. Dismounting his sweating, panting steed and rushing headlong into the wild inferno of the long-house was Haakon.

At Braetana's cry, Thorgunn turned. As he too watched the unbelievable sight, Thorgunn heard him shout, "Braetana!"

Thorgunn's mouth opened in shock at the scene unfolding before him. Haakon, thinking Braetana still in the longhouse, had gone in after her. Suddenly something Thorgunn had never before felt welled up in him, some undeniable allegiance that even all of Haakon's well-designed torments could not crush. It was his brother in the midst of that fire, and Thorgunn knew, despite all that had passed between them, that he must not let him die.

Rising so suddenly he virtually dropped Braetana in the process, Thorgunn took off at a run toward what was now little more than a huge uncontrollable blaze. The cabin was a considerable distance from the meadow Thorgunn had carried Braetana to, and, though he was a fast runner, he knew that the time he spent trying to reach the longhouse could well mean Haakon's death.

His feet kicked up great clumps of moss from the moist turf below. Then, still running, he saw an even more incredible sight come before him. There, seemingly appearing from nowhere, was Gudrun. With raised palms, she braced herself against the fire's intense heat and followed Haakon's path into the hellish flames.

But just as Gudrun fought her way into the fiery longhouse, Thorgunn stopped at the sound of a deafening crack. Its echo was followed by a wild, flaming explosion.

The cabin's support had been charred and weakened, and its roof collapsed with a reverberating crash, flattening almost all that had been beneath it. Only the house's center post rose like a fiery spire above the angry red blaze.

Thorgunn stood aghast at the sight before him. He could do nothing—Haakon and Gudrun were already dead.

XX

Thorgunn hoisted Braetana gently atop Loki. The animal stood unmoving, as if in acknowledgment of the precious cargo he bore.

Few words had passed between them since the horrible sight of the longhouse's fiery collapse. The specter of Haakon and Gudrun trapped helplessly inside cast a pall over what, under other circumstances, might well have been a rapid exchange of questions and answers.

Thorgunn could see the deep fatigue in Braetana's eyes. Well aware of the agony she'd suffered at Gudrun's hands, he thought it best to remove her from the sight of the cabin's smoking remains. With a quick jump, he mounted the destrier behind her, tapping Loki's sides with his soot-marked boots. Slowly, the three of them moved up the trail.

"Where do we ride?" Braetana asked quietly, her voice full of anguish.

"Haakon's summer house is but a few miles further," Thorgunn answered, urging Loki up the rocky path. "You can rest there." Unable to see Braetana's face, Thorgunn listened carefully to her response, half expecting a protest. But instead he received only the wonderful feel of her body as she leaned against him, her head tipped forward in much-needed sleep.

The ride was brief, but not sufficiently so as to allow Thorgunn to dismiss his doubts about Braetana's feelings for him. She had seemed happy enough at their meeting a few moments ago. But he was disinclined to put too much trust in that. Perhaps what he'd seen had been relief at her rescue from the advancing flames. He lacked any assurance that she had fled Haakon willingly.

In fact, it was Braetana who had alerted him to his brother's entry into the cabin's inferno. And Haakon had gone in after her—hardly a likely move for a scorned husband. There was no reason to believe her heart had changed. All he could do was hope. Once they were safe at Haakon's country lodge, he would press his suit once more and pray to Frey that she would be willing to hear.

Like the now destroyed cabin, Haakon's longhouse was well stocked with supplies recently stored in anticipation of the king's use. The structure was uncommonly spacious, designed to accommodate Haakon's large entourage, and was as luxuriously appointed as his Trondbergen residence. Past the front door was a central hall that was used for dining. A generous kitchen flanked one side of it, and the layout was matched on the other side by several chambers partitioned by curtains.

Thorgunn dismounted and carried the still-sleeping Braetana inside. Gently, he laid her atop the bearskin cover on Haakon's huge bed, nestling her amid several other luxurious skins.

"Thorgunn!" Braetana's cry filled him with alarm. Racing to her side, he breathed a sigh of relief when he saw that she was sitting up and was apparently fine.

"I was frightened," she explained timidly, leaning back on the elbows of her fire-blackened wedding dress. "Where are we? Is this Haakon's?"

"Yes." Thorgunn sat cautiously on the pallet, careful not to touch her. "I thought you in need of rest. I can see that I was right."

Braetana raised a hand to her brow, turning the silver bracelet Haakon had placed on her wrist toward Thorgunn. The memory of all that had occurred that day suddenly flooded in on her.

"Haakon! Oh, dear God. And Gudrun too! They are...?"

Thorgunn interrupted before she spoke of their terrible fate. "Haakon thought you inside. He tried to save you, but the fire was too great. There was no hope for him or Gudrun."

Braetana let go a deep, exhausted sigh and covered her face with her hands. Thorgunn struggled to interpret her distress. Was this sorrow for a lost husband? Perhaps his own worst fears were true.

After a long moment, Braetana dropped her hands into her soot-stained lap as her anguished eyes turned to Thorgunn. "It was horrible. Gudrun bound me to the post. She laughed. She thought I wanted that vile man."

"What?" Thorgunn pressed.

"Haakon!" Braetana spoke the name strangely, almost as if a question. "She thought I wanted Haakon. It was all a ghastly mistake. How could I want him, when I truly loved you?" The words escaped uncensored, no longer within the realm of her control. Braetana suddenly raised her hands, extending them to Thorgunn. "Please, I don't care about the silver. You can have it all."

Thorgunn could hardly believe her. She still wanted him! He lunged forward, sweeping Braetana quickly into a tight, unyielding embrace and pressing his head close against hers.

"I had thought that you would never again want me because of my foolish greed. I was stupid in the beginning, and blind to my real love for you. Then, once I could see, I feared you would never again let me into your heart. Magnus said you had chosen Haakon. . . ."

Braetana knew well the reason for her terrible choice. Now was not the time to share it with Thorgunn.

"Yes, I did go to him willingly, but only because I thought you lost to me. Such a mistake would not have come to pass had you still wanted me."

Thorgunn could not believe she had so misunderstood his intentions. "Of course I wanted you. Did I not offer to take you home?"

"I thought you feared the loss of Magnus's silver if I fled."

"It had already gone."

"What do you mean?" A look of confusion swept over Braetana's face.

"There is no silver." Thorgunn could not imagine she thought him still in possession of it. Had she not heard him return it?

"But you took it . . ."

"Dropped back into your father's coffer the day you denied me. Did you not . . ." Thorgunn at once realized that she had not faced him when he replaced the satchel, and she had been crying loudly. Braetana apparently did not know he had refused the payment. "I gave the fee back to your father."

"You renounced it? Why?"

"I hoped only to prove the truth of my assertions to you. It came to have no meaning without your love."

Braetana's face and heart softened at his words. He had not made greed his god, as she had thought. But why had he not continued to press his suit for her? Why had he let her marry his brother?

"Still, you left for Einar's . . ."

"I sought to free my heart from yours. But it was too closely bound. It still is."

"How then could you see me Haakon's bride? You came to witness it."

"I believed it was your wish to wed him. I came to see your denial. And to see you safe. Haakon promised you harm in my absence."

Braetana suddenly realized the great painful cost of her lack of faith. "I have undone us with my weak trust." She leaned her face into her hands as hot tears began to fill her lilac eyes.

"Shhh . . ." Thorgunn wrapped his arms around her slender, shaking form and held her close against him. "Nothing is undone if our love survives." He tilted her face to him. Brushing aside her tears, he pressed his hungry mouth against hers with a deep, passionate kiss. Suddenly he pulled back. The closeness reminded him that Haakon's lips had but recently traveled the same path.

"With Haakon—was it terrible?"

"Yes," answered Braetana, lowering her eyes. "He was cruel. He tore at my clothes." Thorgunn closed his own eyes, unsure he could bear for Braetana to continue her story. Yet he knew he must hear what she would tell.

"He would have taken me had Gudrun's drugged wine not worked its wiles."

Thorgunn's eyes flew open. "Then you and Haakon did not. . . ." His voice trailed off, hopeful and incredulous.

Braetana suddenly understood his logic. Of course! He could not have known that she had been spared Haakon's final insult.

"No, my love. Haakon did not have me. You are the only one." As Braetana answered, she leaned into him, covering his shocked face with a flurry of feather-light kisses.

The answer stirred Thorgunn's passion even more, reminding him of the sweet union they once shared. Cupping her head in his huge hands, he again pressed his lips hard against her own.

Sensing no resistance there, Thorgunn pushed Braetana back onto the fur pallet, whispering soft endearments in her ear. Silently they began a dance of building tension. She lay breathless as he commandingly removed the soft folds of her wedding gown. He registered delightful surprise at her dexterous undoing of the leather buttons on his woolen tunic.

In an instant they were both naked, side by side on the soft bearskin. Their eyes locked in longing and their bodies were poised to savor the sweet pleasure they both knew was to soon follow.

Slowly, as he had done that first time, Thorgunn's hands stroked a feather-light path around Braetana's erect nipples. Then, with maddening quickness, his fingertips brushed over their tops. He lowered his mouth, retracing the wildly pleasurable course with his moist tongue.

Braetana recalled with eager anticipation where this wonderful torture would end. When she thought she could bear no more, she cried out in a small pleading moan. In answer, Thorgunn swung himself astride her, allowing her to feel the urgency of his hard, throbbing manhood. With one powerful, bracing stroke, he entered her, leaving her breathless with the explosion she could feel already building within her.

Again and again, Thorgunn filled her; it was less a physical act than a quicksilver bonding of their souls. As he rode her, he was surer with every successive stroke that the next one would bring a complete loss of control.

Braetana clung to him, her hands moving across his broad back and through his thick blond mane. How she had longed for this. The granting of her desire to have him was a gift she could hardly believe.

Suddenly, Braetana felt as if a great wave had caught her atop its crest. With delicious, unthinking abandon, she allowed herself to spill down over it, the descent triggering a thousand small explosions everywhere on her body.

Thorgunn's passion rode a similar swell. He locked himself inside her with one final great thrust, collapsing atop her as he said, "My sweet darling. How close I came to losing you. . . ."

"Never again," Braetana replied softly. As she uttered the words, she began to wonder if such a promise could be undone. "Magnus will come after me, will he not?"

Thorgunn rolled to Braetana's side, resting on one elbow as he smoothed back an errant strand of hair. "He may. Providing he knows that you escaped the flames. I suspect he knew that I rode after you, but I doubt he saw us escape. He may well think you lost with Haakon and Gudrun."

334 / BLAINE ANDERSON

"He has been unkind in many ways," Braetana said sadly, "but I would not wish him to think me dead. He has suffered much pain already with the loss of my mother. Can we at least send word I am safe?"

Thorgunn wanted only to make love to Braetana again, not to think of practical matters. But he knew she needed an answer. "If we return, Magnus may still intervene to separate us. You are, after all, still queen. The nobles will meet to choose a new konungr. Once that is done, they may wish to wed you to Haakon's successor."

Braetana's eyes grew wide with horror at the prospect of yet another loveless marriage. "Never!" she cried. "It is *you* I love, Thorgunn!"

"And I you," Thorgunn answered, gently kissing Braetana's soft cheek. "But such matters will not concern them. If we are to be sure, we must leave."

"Where shall we go?"

"Wherever you choose, my love. My choices thus far have only caused you pain. We can still reach the next fjord and sail. After that, there are a thousand inlets to hide us. It could be difficult, but I know enough of survival to ensure our own. Or we could return to Northumbria."

Braetana rolled quickly toward Thorgunn, her face etched with shock at his words. "You would take me home and stay with me?"

"I would take you, love, wherever your heart would go, as long as mine goes with it." Thorgunn kissed her lightly on the mouth.

"No." Braetana's response was slow and measured. "There would be no place for us there now. I am less Saxon than I am yours." She smiled, then sobered as she again considered the import of what Thorgunn had just said. "To live outside your people would mean a life very different from what you've known, and one without silver."

"Little bird," Thorgunn answered playfully. "Don't you know that does not matter now?"

"Would it matter if you were king?" Braetana questioned, the idea only now coming to her. "You are Haakon's half brother. Will they not make you his successor?"

She could see by the expression on his face that Thorgunn had already considered the possibility.

"It is not likely," he answered. "Konungr is chosen at mun banda, by the will of the gods, not by happenstance of birth. The nobles may choose whomever they wish. If my father had not passed me over, perhaps, but it is not likely."

As if her memory had been clouded by the fire, Braetana only now recalled that Thorgunn had run toward Haakon when he entered the blazing longhouse.

"You went after Haakon."

"Yes. My feet had no logic."

"After all he has done, you would still save him?"

"It is true I have had reason to hate him. Still, something stronger than the anger between us drew me toward him. It is a feeling new to my heart."

"I am sorry that you need suffer such loss to bring you back to me."

"All I could not bear to lose," countered Thorgunn, "is you."

Again their lips met in a deep kiss, Thorgunn's tongue taking full command of Braetana's willing mouth. With a fervor that bespoke their long and painful separation, they again joined in the communion of body and spirit that left them as one.

A loud rap at the longhouse's front door snapped Thorgunn to attention. Before Braetana could clothe herself, he quickly rose, ready to defend her.

Thorgunn pulled back the heavy oak door. Its opening revealed Magnus. "Is my daughter within?"

Thorgunn would have lied had he thought it would help, but he could see that Magnus was already convinced of Braetana's presence. An honest defense would now serve them better than deception.

"She is here. But you no longer have the right to see her." He spoke commandingly, his expression strong and emotionless.

"She is with you of her own choice?" Magnus's eyes narrowed slightly.

"I am." Braetana's voice echoed from the back of the longhouse's great hall. "Father, hear me. My marriage to Haakon was a grievous mistake. It is Thorgunn I love, and I will not leave him. Strike me down here and now if you wish otherwise, for I am bound to him more than to life itself."

Thorgunn's heart swelled at her courage. She did indeed still love him.

Whether or not Magnus heard her plea, Thorgunn was not prepared to give her up without a fight. He fiercely hoped the old man had taken her words to heart. He had just again found Braetana, and he would not choose to lose her now over the death of her father. Still, his eyes drifted instinctively to the place by the door where his sword rested.

"I have caused you enough suffering," said Magnus

quietly, his voice and eyes softening. "I do not come to offer you more."

"Did you not ride with Haakon to the cabin to return me to his bed?" Braetana's eyes, though reddened and tired, suddenly grew accusing.

Magnus lowered his head as if some great weight drew it down. "Yes, it is sadly true. But then I thought you had fled to meet Thorgunn. It was only when Haakon found Gudrun near the the cabin and shook the truth from her that I realized that you had been forced into actions not of your choosing. And Haakon..." Magnus's voice trailed off, his eyes withdrawing in troubled thought.

"What of him?" Braetana sensed Magnus knew something he chose not to tell. "Animal though he was, at least he would not see me burn."

"It pains me to tell you the truth, but it is your right to know. Haakon would not have gone after you had not the nobles forced him. When Gudrun told him she had left you within, Haakon hesitated, then began back toward his destrier. The others, all farther away, could not reach you in time. We called to Haakon, and made it clear that his cowardice would not be allowed in a Viking king. He ran back toward the flames, thinking only to save his throne, and Gudrun followed. It was not love, but greed, that brought them to their deaths."

Braetana's narrowed eyes registered comprehension. Though she had seen it, Haakon's attempted rescue had left her baffled. Now she understood. Although her father was nearly a room's breadth away, Braetana could see his eyes begin to fill with tears. After a long silence, he again spoke.

"As I was with your mother, I have once more been

misguided. No doubt my foolishness has cost me any chance of earning your love. Even so, if you choose this man as husband, I will not stand in your way."

Braetana stepped toward him, her anger suddenly lessened by his generous words. Slowly, she extended her hand in silent forgiveness. As she reached out, however, her eyes caught the sudden appearance of a large group of Vikings, armed and standing in the longhouse doorway. Instinctively, she withdrew, backing into Thorgunn's protective embrace.

"Jarl Magnus." It was Knut, Magnus's huskarlar. He stepped from the group and bowed slightly. "The nobles have met. I come bearing their decision—one which all within should hear. Have I your leave to speak?"

"Tell us," Magnus commanded.

"I am charged by our warriors to offer Thorgunn his rightful place as konungr."

Thorgunn's face tightened in befuddlement at the messenger's strange words. After all that had passed between them, how could it be that they now offered him a crown?

"All knew that Haakon was a poor ruler, a man spun by Odin's folly into dishonorable ways. Had Harald not anointed him, he would not have been konungr. And now, to all the anguish suffered, there is a further shame. Ingrid has come forward and confessed her lies.

"When Harald died, it was not Haakon that Harald chose—it was his older brother Thorgunn. The jarls could not have known. Ingrid's heart was full of greed and selfishness. When she was alone with Haakon at Harald's death, she paid her huskarlar to repeat the shameful lie. But now, with Haakon gone, she has spoken the truth. The fighting men of Trondbergen have decided that you,

Thorgunn, are our rightful konungr. The dishonor of our past mistakes weighs heavily, but fate, in taking Haakon and delivering you, offers one more chance. The decision is now yours."

Thorgunn stood silently in disbelief. The years of suffering under Haakon's heavy yoke, and the refusal of his father, were all a cruel mistake? Merely a second wife's ugly lie? Now, to be allowed to reclaim his heritage and destiny was a gift he had never thought to receive; but not one worth having if it meant losing Braetana. He would not gamble again with her love. He had promised to follow her heart's wishes. He would fulfill that vow.

Slowly, he walked to where she stood at the back of the hall. "Do not fear, little bird, this crown is a pittance compared to the wealth bestowed by your love. We will leave as we have planned." Thorgunn planted a light kiss on Braetana's forehead.

"You would forfeit all for me?" she asked, incredulous.

"I forfeit nothing if I have you."

Tears of gratitude filled Braetana's violet eyes as she beheld him. In his willingness to abandon all he had ever sought, Thorgunn had just made relinquishing it unnecessary.

"I would ask of you . . ."

He already knew her heart's desire. Despite her claims otherwise, surely she wanted Glendonwyck. "Yes, we shall go," said Thorgunn.

"I would ask you to take that which is rightfully yours. You are king—your nobles have decreed it," she replied, smiling.

"It matters only to me what *you* have decreed. I would have nothing without you. Are you sure of this?"

Braetana nodded quickly, then embraced him, pressing her cheek against his still-naked chest. "I am already queen," she answered flirtatiously.

"Then I shall make you that twice over," Thorgunn replied, pulling her even tighter against him.

"And more," answered Braetana, dreaming of the soon-to-come night when she would tell Thorgunn that he was to be a father as well as a king.

GET
LOVESTRUCK!

AND GET STRIKING ROMANCES FROM POPULAR LIBRARY'S BELOVED AUTHORS

Watch for these exciting
LOVESTRUCK
romances in the months to come:

 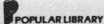

375